# THE BROUGHT FAMILY SECRETS

## Defenders of The Light

# THE BROUGHT FAMILY SECRETS

## Defenders of The Light

A CHRISTIAN SCI-FI / SUSPENSE NOVEL

By Tami Stevenson

Iosco - Arenac District Library
East Tawas, Michigan
Published by
Suwannee Valley Times
Live Oak, Florida

CHRISTIAN SCI-FI / SUSPENSE
THE BROUGHT FAMILY SECRETS: DEFENDERS OF THE LIGHT

Copyright © 2022 by Tami Stevenson
First Edition - Revised

Published by Suwannee Valley Times
PO Box 1475
Live Oak, Florida 32064
www.tamistevenson.com

All rights reserved under International Copyright Law. No part of this publication may be reproduced or transmitted in any form or by any means, electronic or mechanical, including photocopying, recording, or by any information storage and retrieval system, without written permission from the publisher. The only exception is brief quotations in printed reviews.

Unless otherwise noted, all scripture quoted is taken from the 21st Century King James Version®, copyright © 1994. Used by permission of Deuel Enterprises, Inc., Gary, SD 57237. All rights reserved.

ISBN 979-8-9867301-0-3
Library of Congress Cataloging-in-Publication Data available upon request.

Although certain actual facts, names and locales are mentioned or referenced in this book, it is a fictional story. Characters, places and incidents are the product of the author's imagination or are used fictitiously.

Printed in the United States of America

Edited by April K. Remy
Cover design by Tami Stevenson

To my daughter, Gabrielle and my grandson, Wyatt.
May you both ever grow in the knowledge of Jesus
Christ and His great love for you.

Also in memory of my husband, Mark, for his
encouragement and support of this book.

Special thanks to April K. Remy for your
encouragement and expertise, not only as my editor
but in your knowledge of God's Word and the Hebrew
language. It has been invaluable. Thank you so much
for sharing your time with me and the many hours
you spent editing this book. You have encouraged me
through it all and I can't thank you enough!

# CONTENTS

Chapter 1: Eliel ......................................................................... 1
Chapter 2: The Starling ............................................................ 9
Chapter 3: Secrets ................................................................... 18
Chapter 4: Forgotten ............................................................... 25
Chapter 5: The Ancient Ones ................................................. 35
Chapter 6: The Grigori ........................................................... 41
Chapter 7: The Willows .......................................................... 48
Chapter 8: Progeny ................................................................. 57
Chapter 9: Engaged ................................................................ 66
Chapter 10: Scare Tactics ....................................................... 73
Chapter 11: Wedding Plans .................................................... 81
Chapter 12: Discovery ............................................................ 88
Chapter 13: Lessons Learned ................................................. 97
Chapter 14: The Great Rock ................................................ 113
Chapter 15: The Reptilians .................................................. 122
Chapter 16: Commiseration ................................................. 134
Chapter 17: Commitment ..................................................... 145
Chapter 18: Animals in Heaven ........................................... 156
Chapter 19: For I Know the Plans I Have for You ............. 160
Chapter 20: Rose Petals and God Bubbles ......................... 177
Chapter 21: The Wedding .................................................... 185
Chapter 22: Finally Alone! ................................................... 196
Chapter 23: The Dig ............................................................. 210
Chapter 24: My Yoke is Easy ............................................... 222
Chapter 25: Voices ............................................................... 232
Chapter 26: Reptilian Watchers ........................................... 241
Chapter 27: Hostages ........................................................... 249
Chapter 28: Removing the Seal ........................................... 260
Chapter 29: Cat and Mouse ................................................. 273
Chapter 30: Dome of Darkness ............................................ 290

# Chapter 1 – Eliel

He could feel his heart beating faster in his chest as he looked out of his second story bedroom window. *Who are they?* He wondered, clutching his new John Deere Model "L" tractor with mud lug wheels his father just bought for him yesterday at the hardware store in town.

Although Joey was an only child, he didn't get new toys very often but this year his parents said they could perhaps afford a new toy for his eighth birthday. This was the third year into WWII and the Great Depression was over. The shiny green and yellow metal toy that looked just like the real tractors he'd seen in town seemed to give him comfort as he held it close to his chest while his mind tried to catch up with what his eyes were seeing.

As he looked out over the apple orchard, Joey saw five very tall men dressed in shiny, white clothes. They all had light colored hair and bright faces. They were walking around this long, oval submarine-looking thing that was the color of gun metal. He couldn't see any tires, *but how did they get it out there? There's no sound.* It was sitting on the ground at the edge of the tree line and had ten windows on the side he could see. He had seen his parents walking under those trees many times, from this very same window, but they didn't have to duck under the branches, their heads were far below them. *These men were really tall because they had to duck! What are they doing?* It looked like the thing was broken down and they were trying to fix it.

As he watched in amazement, trying to figure the whole thing out, all of a sudden, he felt as if they were watching him watch them. Then one of them looked up and stared straight at him through his bedroom window.

He felt a sense of peace come over him and his fear was gone.

The next thing he remembered was his mother calling out from the bottom of the stairway, "Joey, dinner time." He turned away from the window and suddenly forgot everything he just saw. He ran downstairs, sat down at the table and ate dinner as if nothing happened. But something was different, his mother and father seemed – distracted during dinner.

It wasn't until the next morning his memory began to trickle in with images of what he had seen at dusk the evening before. *Was it a dream?* He jumped out of bed and ran to the window - nothing there but the early morning fog rising out of the orchard. He wondered if there may be tracks around where they had been. His mother and father were avid hunters and his father was teaching him about tracking.

With excitement Joey ran downstairs and out the back door, he realized he left his jacket behind as the brisk morning air hit him. He didn't mind, he just wanted to get to the orchard. As he approached the area he could see patches of black, burnt grass where the thing sat. There was a funny smell, like the smell of a match being lit. He could see where they had walked around it as the foot tall grass was all trampled.

"Joey! What are you doing out there?" His mother, Helen, called from the back door. "Get back in the house," she exclaimed with a hurried tone.

*Why would Ma care if I'm in the apple orchard? I play here all the time. Unless ... they knew they were here too ....* He headed back toward the two-story farm house, built by his grandfather and namesake, Joseph Brought.

His small-framed mother with her long, brown hair hastily put into a bun on the top of her head was at the stove getting breakfast ready as he came through the door.

"What were you doing out there?" She didn't look up as she flipped the hotcakes that smelled like heaven.

"Nothing, I was just playing," Joey answered.

"It's pretty early to be playing, the sun's barely up," she said, pulling the hotcakes out and pouring more batter into the huge cast-iron skillet.

"Anyway, I don't want you playing out there for awhile, stay away from the orchard."

"Why not, Ma? ... Who were they?"

She quickly looked up at him, surprised he remembered so soon, then quickly looked back down at the hotcakes. It took her a minute to answer, dragging it out, as she flipped the cakes from the pan to the top of the 'done' stack.

"Just some old friends of the family," she said as she poured the last bit of batter into the pan. She felt her son should be a little older before he was introduced to certain family friends, *perhaps the next time they come,* she thought. "But don't be playing around the orchard for awhile, you hear? Now go to the barn and help your father finish milking." Glancing up at him only for a moment to make sure their eyes met.

He knew better than to argue with her, and could tell she didn't want to discuss details with him. His mother may have been only a few inches taller than he was, but she was a spit-fire if you got her angry. Without saying anything further, he headed off to the barn to help his father.

As Joey approached the barn he heard his father's voice.

"Like the morning dew that drips from the leaves of the trees to the ground, Father, may this day be filled with Your goodness and blessing. May we receive everything you have ordained for us, as honey drips from the comb, may Your goodness drip down from heaven fresh and new to us this day, in Jesus' Name. Amen." His father prayed that prayer often. So much that Joey remembered it and taught it to his children and they taught it to their children.

## CHAPTER 1 - ELIEL

**Present Day –**

"Ben! Benjamin, did you hear anything I just said?"

"Aghhhh!" Ben squirmed to catch her as Elizabeth playfully plopped sideways in his lap, giggling, with her waist-long red hair flying through the air. She was excited about their plans to drive to the river today.

"Were you deep in thought again, off in La La Land?" She kissed his cheek.

Ben looked at her and smiled with that handsome, confident smile she so admired, as he wrapped her in his arms.

"Yes," he said, then his serious look returned as he fixed his eye on a bird sitting on the branch of a tree outside the living room window. She loved the way the golden-brown specks in his hazel-green eyes seemed to dance around when he was concentrating on something.

"I was just thinking about my great-granddad again." But they were more than just thoughts to him, they seemed almost like memories playing in his mind.

"Yeah, your great-granddad was pretty cool! But back to the present, were you able to fix my pole?" Elizabeth asked, looking up at him with her huge, blue-green eyes, bringing him back to the day ahead.

After a long battle with a log in the river last week, the drag was too tight and couldn't be adjusted, she couldn't cast – then the line got all messed up.

"Yes," Ben said, letting out a big sigh of relief, remembering what a bear it was to fix, as she climbed off his lap. "It was pretty messed up, but it's working now." He looked at her bright face adorned with freckles he thought were all in just the right places. "But be more careful where you cast your line from now on." He warned her with a smile.

"I will." She smiled back and went to pack the cooler for the day on the river.

Just then his phone dinged, a text from Mom.

"I'm stopping to the store on my way home, need anything?"

"Lizzy, do we need any food to take with us today? Mom's stopping to the store on her way home," Ben called to her from the living room.

Elizabeth was in the kitchen and had her head bent down in the cooler as she arranged the ice around the drinks and bait.

"I got chips, drinks and worms – think we're good," she exclaimed as she pushed on the ice to get the lid closed.

"What? No sandwiches?" He quickly texted his mother back and asked her to get his favorite – ham, and some bread. She was on her way home from working the night shift at the local manufacturing plant in Elm Creek.

"What's that?" Ben smiled as he looked up from the chair, shoving his phone back in his pocket.

Elizabeth was standing in front of him brandishing a big, floppy, purple, fishing hat on the top of her head with various lures attached for authenticity, a taupe sweater, purple tank top and jeans. The hat was really a sun hat, but with her shiny red hair flowing out of it – attached to her perfectly proportioned 5' 6" frame – she could wear a gunnysack and he would still think she was beautiful.

"What do you think? I made it myself," Tilting her head just a bit and curling her nose, "To keep my freckles at bay." A huge smile rose from beneath the hat hoping to get his approval.

As Ben stood up, his 6' 3" frame towered over her. A few strands of brown hair hung haphazardly just below his eyes above his short, well-kept beard. His hair was short too, all but the top. He wrapped his arms around her and held her close. "I think it's ... you, I love it, and I love your freckles too." He bumped the hat off her head with his nose as he bent down to kiss her. Neither of them seemed to care as it rolled to the floor.

Then, without a sound, the slightest twinkling of tiny orbs of light began to dance above their heads as they kissed. First three or four, then growing into hundreds of twinkling tiny orbs falling all around them like dew, sparkling as they danced around them. Ollie, the family dog, didn't bark but began to whine and yipe excitedly as the tiny lights grew in number. They joined into one glowing orb about the size of a basketball. The white light filled the house to every room. It hovered above their heads, then floated about six feet away. Ben and Elizabeth held their hands in front of their faces to shield their eyes from the glow. It began to change into the shape of an oval with points on the top and bottom, growing thinner and taller until it touched the floor and the ceiling. The center began to bulge slightly as if it were an elastic zipper being unzipped from the center out. As it opened, more bright white light escaped through the opening. Through the light, the figure of a huge man began to take shape. As the man became more visible, the light drew back inside of him until it was gone.

A tall, warrior-like figure stood before them with golden-blonde hair that hung almost to his waist. He was dressed in white and what looked like the golden armor of a king from a medieval kingdom. He wore an intricately carved golden breastplate, gold armbands and a belt around his waist that was inset with jewels of all colors. A long, golden sword hung from his belt with matching jewels in the handle and down the scabbard. A few long strands of thin braids hung down from his thick hair with the sides pulled up to the crown of his head. It was held in place by a golden hair piece, also inset with jewels. And ... he had the most beautiful wings with long, white feathers that seemed to glow with all the colors of the rainbow! His face was overwhelming. His eyes were like white light. He was glowing, but the strong, chiseled features of his face beneath the glow were still visible.

A warmth filled the room, a peace ….

"Greetings in the Name of the Lord, young Benjamin and Elizabeth!" A resounding, deep voice came from the tall being that now stood before them. The top of his head touched the eight foot living room ceiling.

"You know, someday when we have kids, you won't be able to enter the room like that." Ben smiled and reached up to shake his hand. "How are you Eliel (El-ee-el)?"

As Eliel's glow began to fade, so did his golden armor. Right before their eyes his wings, his armor and sword faded into jeans, boots and a t-shirt, similar to what Ben was wearing. He now looked the same height as Ben. A handsome, muscular, young man with the sides of his hair pulled up to the crown of his head with a simple rubber band as the rest hung freely down his back. He looked to be in his mid twenties.

"I am well," Eliel shook his hand then pulled them in for a hug.

Ollie, a blonde and white four year old Border Collie/Golden Retriever mix, that Ben and his mother had rescued from the pound when he was a pup, was beside himself. His huge tail wagged as loudly as his whines, waiting for Eliel to greet him too.

"And hello Ollie, Eliel bent down and gave Ollie a friendly hello.

"So, did you come to go fishing with us today?" Ben asked, knowing he would already know all about their plans for the day and how fishing was somehow not on his agenda.

"Actually, yes," he hesitated, "In a way."

Just then Ben's mother, Rachel, pulled in the yard. She bought extra groceries knowing how her son's appetite, which was huge to begin with, had grown ever since he came into another one of his gifts last month. A closely guarded family secret passed down from generation to generation, only known now to Benjamin, Elizabeth, Rachel's mother, Sarah, and

# CHAPTER 1 - ELIEL

Rachel.

She turned the key off in the ignition as the three entered the garage to help with groceries. She already knew Eliel was there and was excited to see him. It had been six months or so since Eliel's last visit. Ben, Sarah and Rachel all had gifts in varying degrees, but Ben's were the strongest and most diverse.

Rachel had recently turned forty and had been a widow since Ben was three years old. Although some neighbors thought it was odd that she never remarried, it certainly wasn't because of the lack of suiters through the years. She was a beautiful 5' 4" brunette with intense hazel green eyes, like her son's, that seemed to pierce through to your soul; but she was content with her life. It was complicated enough. Now, they were the only ones left that knew about the gifts. Rachel was glad the Lord chose to include Elizabeth, although she wasn't technically family. *They're not married ... not yet .... But I think she has an emerging gift as well ... so ....*

# Chapter 2 - The Starling

The water was a little higher than normal because of all the recent rain. The current was strong today, as the three of them approached the banks of the Au Sable River in Ben's truck. *I love this river*, Elizabeth thought as she admired the breathtaking view from the winding, narrow trail. The river ran from west to east through the Huron National Forest and into Lake Huron. Its highbanks jutted out in places, some with different colored layers of sand. It looked like someone took a giant knife and sliced the hills in half leaving the various layers of earth forever exposed looking down on the river below. Rich hues of green leaves hung from the bright white bark of the many birch trees. Their bark stood out from among the other trees of maple, oak, elm and poplar that all grew right up to the river's edge reaching into the nearly cloudless blue sky. The pristine deciduous forest looked much like it would have in the days when the Indians lived here, she thought. She adjusted her new fishing hat to accommodate for all the bouncing around as the truck wound its way along the one-lane trail to their favorite spot.

It was the first part of August and fall would be here soon. Some of the trees along the highbanks were already beginning to turn, which was earlier than normal. Hints of red and orange began to form small patches in the forest. The number of tourists in canoes, armed with cameras would increase, coming from far and wide for the spectacular changing of the trees into rich reds, oranges, yellows and browns along the banks of the river each fall. Not to mention the trout and salmon fishermen armed with all manner of fishing gear.

Elizabeth was born and raised in northern Florida and loved Michigan summers most. It took a couple of years, but she learned to adjust to the cold, wintery months and discovered snowmobiling, ice skating and ice fishing were actually fun.

When she was twelve, her father was offered a good paying management position at a factory that made car parts for Ford up north. She and her parents, John and Samantha Shiels, moved to the tiny town of Elm Creek, Michigan, which is in the northeastern lower peninsula, where the factory was located. That is where she met Benjamin Adan in the seventh grade and they seemed to connect almost immediately.

After applying what she thought was a good amount of sunscreen to protect herself against more freckles, she jumped out of the truck and hurried to catch up with Eliel and Ben who had already reached their favorite spot on the riverbank. She looked up and saw them talking with a small-framed old man standing on the river's edge. His brown fedora hat and plain clothes looked as worn as his face. He looked up in the sky and pointed with a long, boney finger, then pointed at the river and the highbanks. She was only about twenty feet away now, but couldn't hear them talking, *because they weren't talking.* As the head nodding and other bodily gestures continued, she felt an urgency in the man, like something was about to end, and something new was about to begin.

Then, the old man reached out with two of his boney fingers and touched Ben's face ever so tenderly, looking deeply into his eyes ... then he smiled wide with what seemed to be satisfaction. As he looked into Ben's eyes, the man slowly became transparent, then vanished completely into the air. She saw a small flash of light, just for an instant on Ben's cheek where the man's fingertips touched him as he disappeared. Ben and Eliel then lifted their hands into the air, bowed their heads and worshipped, for the Spirit of the Living God was strong in the air. Elizabeth felt it too and worshipped.

"What was that all about?" She asked as Ben and Eliel came and sat next to her on their favorite log.

"A temple is going to be discovered here," Eliel said. "Soon."

"It's right beneath us and runs from over there," Ben said, pointing east to one of the hills on the riverbank in front of them, "All the way to that hill over there." He turned, and pointed west to one of the tallest hills about half a mile upstream. "The entire complex goes on under the forest and covers about one square mile."

"Well that's gonna change things ... wow," Elizabeth said. "What did that man give you?" Elizabeth looked at Ben, "When he touched your face?" Searching his eyes to see if he was any different.

"He gave me a memory of the past," Ben said with a solemn face. Then looking up, he said, "And a memory of the future."

Eliel was silent, he knew it would take some time for Ben to process everything. He motioned for Elizabeth to take a walk with him. They headed west along the riverbank towards the other hill Ben pointed to.

"Elizabeth, you know some people are born with certain gifts. Some are more pronounced than others ... but they only mature with use." Eliel was smiling as he looked down at her, their eyes meeting as he added, "As Ben's gifts develop and mature, yours will also."

Her face lit up! She stopped in her tracks. "I knew something was going on with me, I knew it!" She did a little dance of delight. "I can feel things. And sometimes I see things in my mind, but I thought it was just my imagination." Then her face became serious, "But it's not my imagination ...." She looked up at Eliel, "Is it?"

She remembered that everything she felt and saw was not always ... pleasant. Sometimes it was so horrific, she struggled to get the visions out of her mind. Other times they were so beautiful and so full of love and wonder, she wanted to capture those moments and live forever in them.

"It's all part of your gift," Eliel said, knowing she was thinking of the good and the bad, as they continued walking. He smiled at her as if a long awaited day had arrived, and it had.

She was the first in her family to receive a gift, but Ben's family went back generations on his mother's side.

"Your gifts will unfold and mature, just like Benjamin's. You'll learn how to control them."

Elizabeth didn't ask him anymore questions right then. They just walked along the riverbank in silence, as she leaned on his arm.

Ben stood looking east down the river trying to imagine the days when others lived here. From the memory of the old man, the Starling ..... Ben saw them. *That temple complex below us is enormous! And everyone is gonna think the Indians built it.* He let out a sigh as he looked around – remembering the intricately carved huge granite walls that he saw in the old man's memory. *Copper and stone chisels didn't build that ....* Then he laughed out loud.

He looked down into the riverbed and reached out his hand for a rock he saw just beyond the water's edge that looked like it was glowing. The rock obeyed and leapt into his hand. It had an orange glow, like a hot ember, but it wasn't hot. *This is one of those fluorescent rocks, or whatever they call them ... a syenite rock.* They are normally not found this far down in Michigan. He had only read about them being in the Upper Peninsula (UP) on Lake Superior. To most, with the naked eye, the rocks are a common gray color and don't look like anything special. Only under a UV light can most people see the orange glow, but Ben could see its energy. He was born being able to see the energies of all living things.

That is what drew him to Elizabeth. He was in the seventh grade hurrying down the hall, trying not to be late for class when he saw the most beautiful energy coming from someone in the crowd that stood out from the other students. Distinct blues, reds, purples, greens and yellows, all sparkling around someone walking through the doorway of his homeroom class. He caught a glimpse, it was a girl, *she must be new*. When he saw her, he thought she had the most beautiful red hair. It flowed down to her waist. He had to learn more about this girl with such intense, positive energy. None of the other students shined like her. She had a beautiful spirit. He knew as soon as he saw her bright, freckled face and heard the sound of her voice saying hello to him for the first time – then and there – she was the only girl he would ever love. He said to himself, *"I'm gonna marry her someday!"* Ben may have only been 12 years old, but he never changed his mind.

Until he was three and a half years old, Ben thought everyone could see energy like him .... But he was wrong.

He was with his father and mother, Mike and Rachel Adan, in their four-door sedan, on their way back home from a shopping trip in Ann Arbor. They stopped at a gas station on Jackson Avenue to fill up. Ben was in the back in his car seat looking around at the people coming in and out of the station while his dad filled up the car. Mom was sitting in the front pressing buttons on the radio trying to find a station.

Ben enjoyed watching the different energies coming from people, some had blue, purple, yellow and red - smooth and sparkly hues, they all varied and no two were exactly alike. He liked watching the bright colored people most, but there were not very many of them.

When Mike had finished pumping the gas, he went inside to pick up some munchies for the nearly three hour ride home.

As young Ben continued watching the people from his car seat, he saw an energy he'd never seen before. Ben's little heart began to beat fast inside his chest, something was bad about this man, real bad ... he was black. The man was just standing at the corner of the building. Ben had an overwhelming feeling of doom.

"Mommy, that man is bad," Ben was almost in tears.

Rachel turned to see who he was looking at. "What do you mean, honey? Who's bad?"

"That man," he pointed. "He's black!"

The man headed towards the door of the station and looked around the lot as he went inside. Rachel knew instinctively what Ben meant. *Mike is in there!* She reached for her cell phone, it seemed like forever before the phone rang.

"Pick up, pick up," the panic in her voice was growing as Mike finally picked up the phone. The last word she heard him say was, "Hello."

Four shots rang out through the phone .... Then a fifth....

Three people were killed by the gunman in the store that day. The clerk, Ben's father and the gunman, an ex-employee who turned the gun on himself afterward, then stumbled out of the door just before he fell to the ground.

Ben remembers the pain mostly. His mind mercifully blocked a lot from that day. The lights and sirens, the men dressed in uniforms asking his mother questions, everything was like a bad nightmare – one big, dark blur. He thought his mother could see the black, smokey looking man too, but she couldn't.

"What is your son talking about? A black man?" The officer asked Rachel. "Was there someone else with the gunman?"

Ben kept wailing through his tears, "The black man ... the black man is a bad man!" At that point he only knew the black man made Mommy cry and Daddy was still inside the store. *Why wasn't he coming out? And why was Mommy crying so hard?* "Did he do something to my Daddy?" He shrieked, "Where's my Daddy?"

The gunman was a white man with short brown hair. He was also wearing a black coat, so Rachel told the officer Ben was talking about the man's coat.

"You know kids," Rachel choked out the words, wiping her son's tears as the blue and red lights flashed over and over from the police cars. "He's just upset and confused," she added as she held Ben close on her lap, rocking him back and forth on the seat of the car.

Later, Ben found the only other person he knew that could see like he could, was his grandmother. Mike was the last in the Adan line until they had Ben. It was up to him now, to carry on the family name.

Ben still had the rock in his hand when Elizabeth and Eliel walked up. He tossed the rock to Elizabeth.

"What's this?" She asked, looking down at the plain, gray rock.

"That's one of those glowing rocks. I think they call them syenite. They glow orange if you hold it under a UV light," Ben said.

"Oh wow, can you see it glowing now?" She asked.

"Yup ... they're pretty cool looking," Ben added.

"Where did you find it?" Eliel asked.

"Right over there," Ben said, pointing to a shallow spot in the river. "I saw it glowing under the water."

Eliel walked over to the river's edge where Ben said he found the rock and looked closely at the riverbed there.

"Is it important?" Ben asked.

"It could be." Eliel answered, still looking at the riverbed. "When this site was covered over, these rocks were used as markers. This part of the river was a little north of where we are now, and this was dry ground."

"Okay, but maybe the current carried it downstream or something. These rocks are usually only found in the U.P., from what I've heard. Anything could have moved it after all these thousands of years." Ben said.

"Not likely." Eliel, now satisfied nothing unusual was poking up through the riverbed, stepped back from the bank. "The rocks that were put down are markers and will not leave their place."

"Well then, how did *I* move it?" Ben asked.

"Elizabeth," Eliel called, "set the rock on the ground and look away, Benjamin, you too." Even Eliel looked away, just for a moment .... "Okay now look." Elizabeth looked down where she set the rock and it was gone. Ben searched the riverbed where he had called it from ... there it was, back in its place, glowing like before.

"That's so cool!" Ben said.

"So it *is* one of the true markers," Eliel said, walking back to the riverbed to take a closer look at the area around where the stone lay. "Most people would never be able to find it again."

Ben took Elizabeth over to where the rock lay and pointed. "It's right there about twelve feet from the water's edge."

"What if someone picked it up and held it until they got home and put it in a box or something?" Elizabeth asked. "Would it still find its way back when no one was looking or holding it?"

"Yes," said Eliel. "No matter where they are, the markers will always find their way back."

"Okay, so ... " Elizabeth smiled and looked at them both, as if it was time to 'fess up. "Who was that old man and what kind of temple is this we're standing on?"

Ben looked at Eliel …. Eliel nodded.

"Lizzy, the old man is a Starling … from a planet called Nibiru. The original temple was built before we were even here."

"So … the guy's not … dead?" She asked.

"No." They shook their heads, smiling.

"Okay, that's good …. " She let out a sigh of relief already thinking about her next question. "So … what's a Starling?"

Eliel smiled, "The next time you visit Sarah ask her about them."

Eliel looked around at the river and the woods as if assessing everything once more. "It's time for me to go now, but pay your grandmother a visit. You will learn a lot about their history."

He had a way of coming and going without warning. He began to glow white. As the light grew brighter, he said with a loud voice, "Praise be to the Living God, my God and yours." He smiled as the sparkling light engulfed him and shrank back to basketball size. Suddenly, as it hovered, it exploded in an instant, spreading thousands of tiny lights out into the atmosphere ... and he was gone.

"Show off!" Ben smiled as Eliel disappeared.

Ben and Elizabeth sat for awhile on their favorite log, no longer interested in fishing. Ben didn't want to talk right now about the memories the Starling showed him, especially the memories about the future. They realized everything about their favorite spot on their beloved riverbank was going to change once the digging began, but when would that be? Ben sat with Elizabeth as he skipped rocks across the water. He called various ones back and threw them over and over, never having to leave the log. Elizabeth felt safe in his arms. They just enjoyed being together on the river for the rest of the afternoon.

# Chapter 3 - Secrets

Elizabeth became accustomed to seeing strange things only two weeks after she met Ben so now there wasn't much that shocked her anymore.

Her parents, shortly after moving to Elm Creek, through Ben and Elizabeth's immediate friendship, became friends with Ben's family, his mother and grandmother. One Friday night in mid November, they made arrangements with Rachel for Elizabeth to stay at their place for awhile so they could go Christmas shopping. They didn't want her staying home alone yet in their new house with unfamiliar surroundings, she was only twelve.

Elizabeth surprised Ben in the back yard that day. He was jumping … and jumping … higher and higher … higher than the trees …?

She just stood and watched for a few moments in disbelief. It was the strangest looking thing to see her friend vaulting 50 feet in the air, over and over again… *Am I dreaming? Is this for real?* Until Ben saw her.

He had jumped just about to the top of the tall pine in the back yard, which was about 75 feet in height, when he saw her standing there, looking up at him from below.

*Great … how am I gonna explain this* … He actually froze in mid-air for a moment and looked down at her. His mind raced for a legitimate excuse … but there wasn't one ….

As he landed back on the ground and moved toward her, she turned and ran. She ran through the front yard, then down the driveway and down the road without looking back.

Ben just stood there, not quite knowing what to do, "Lizzy." He cupped his hands around his mouth, "It's not what you think … Lizzy please come back."

Suddenly, he was walking next to her on the road as she headed in the direction of her house. "Lizzy, please, let me explain …"

She jumped at the sight of him suddenly … there … and pulled away as he reached for her arm.

"Stay away from me! What are you, some kind of freak?" She looked him straight in the eye with the best angry face she could muster, although it was really fear. *What kind of freaks live in Michigan? Are they all freaks?* She just wanted to go back home to Florida.

Ben knew it was fear and not anger. Her aura was a muddy pink and dark blue.

"Lizzy, I'm not going to hurt you. Please let me explain."

She kept walking, "Freak!" She said, fighting back her tears. *How am I going to get away from him?*

They walked in silence for a few hundred feet.

"I was born this way." He struggled to put it into words. "It's a gift from God, Lizzy, I didn't ask for it."

She turned and looked at him with the mention of God. She believed in God, but had never heard of anything like this. She turned back toward the road ahead and just kept walking.

"Lizzy, please don't tell anyone." Now Ben's aura was turning a little muddy. "It's … a secret."

Just then Rachel pulled up in the car and rolled down the window. "Hey there, you two okay?" She sensed what was going on.

Elizabeth kept walking with Ben following along behind her as Rachel kept pace in the car. It was a dead-end country road and not prone to much traffic since they were the only family living off it. Finally, Rachel convinced them to get into the car and drove them back to the house.

Elizabeth, hoping her parents would be there soon to pick her up, sat in the living room watching TV, not talking. Rachel didn't pry, she kept busy making dinner and Ben went to his room. Finally he came out and asked her if she wanted something to drink. She was dying for a Coke but just turned away from his stare. Ben brought her one anyway and sat it on the coffee table, then went back to his room without saying anything more.

Dinner was strained. Rachel and Elizabeth made small talk about Christmas traditions and how beautiful the first snow always is, since Elizabeth had never seen snow.

Her parents arrived just after 8 o'clock and she ran out the door as they pulled in the yard, barely saying goodbye to Rachel, let alone Ben.

Saturday went by – Sunday came and went – She wouldn't return his phone calls.

Rachel told Ben she felt it was best to just let it be and see what happened. One of her gifts was reading people and she thought Elizabeth would keep it to herself, even if she didn't want anything else to do with them.

"Elizabeth is a very sound person for a young girl of twelve, very level-headed. It sounds so far fetched. She'll figure out that no one would believe her anyway."

It was Monday morning, Ben didn't know what Elizabeth was going to do. Was she going to tell everyone at school what she saw? He hated the very thought of going that day.

Her parents seemed fine. Rachel spoke with them Sunday evening over the phone. Ben listened intently but their conversation was normal. *She didn't tell them* .... That gave him some hope.

Ben stood at his locker just before first bell, getting his books. He heard Elizabeth's voice behind him.

"So …" she paused.

His heart leaped. He loved the sound of her voice. But was she going to hate him forever? The girl he wanted to marry someday. Had he lost her already? Was she going to become his enemy? The next words out of her mouth would give him his answer. He almost didn't want her to speak. He wanted to just stay frozen in that moment till the end of time ….

"Are you going to walk me to class?" She smiled up at him as he turned to face her. She was glowing and sparkling with all the colors of the rainbow again. He could see her fear was gone and she had forgiven him.

Ben grabbed her up in his arms and spun around. He had never done that before and hoped he didn't scare her again. As he realized that, he set her on the ground ever so carefully.

"I figure there are worse things in the world. Actually, once I got over the shock, I think it's kind of cool." Elizabeth confessed.

She decided he wasn't going to hurt her or he would have done it by now. He just let her go, knowing his secret. That – and the fact that he mentioned God in the mix made her even more interested in him.

Ben and his family found Elizabeth was incredibly resilient. She accepted the whole gifting thing and took it all in stride, as if it was a part of her for her entire life. She kept their secrets, not telling a soul, not even her parents.

The next day, after their visit to the river, Ben was looking forward

## CHAPTER 3 - SECRETS

to spending time with Grandma as he climbed into his truck to pick up Elizabeth. Even though Grandma lived next door on the same property, Elizabeth lived five miles away. Rachel and her late husband, Mike, had added a double-wide trailer on the property shortly after her father passed away, as Rachel refused to let her mother live alone on the family homestead.

The truck was a gift from Grandma when Ben turned sixteen. It was Grandpa Jerry's truck, who passed away a few months before Ben was born. Grandma had kept the old faded red truck in the garage all these years to give him a project to work on when he was old enough, and project it was, but it was a treasure to him. It was a 1995 Ford F-150 Flareside 4x4, with a 4.9 inline 6 engine.

Ben loved his truck even though it was nearly thirty years old, mostly because it was his grandfather's, but also because of the countless hours he spent working on it. The right rear fender had some rust so he learned how to sand and work with body filler. The original Vermillion Red paint, which he was insistent on getting, was at the house. He still hadn't made the time to paint it.

With the help of his mechanic friend, James Selvy, they replaced the fender, the fuel pump, the water pump, some hoses and other things, gave it a tune-up and got it running. He had been working part time at Selvy's Garage since he turned sixteen, and, with James' help, working on his truck.

Ben took after his Grandma Sarah Brought-Imswirth, his mother's mother. She was a little rough around the edges but underneath her slightly plump, 5'7" exterior and mousy gray hair, was a sweetheart of a grandmother who thoroughly loved spending time with her grandson and Elizabeth.

Sarah accepted Elizabeth and treated her as another grandchild from the start. Elizabeth's beautiful aura and spirit captured Sarah's heart as well. She even allowed Elizabeth to call her grandma. She loved their inquisitive minds and how they liked listening to her talk about the past, and the gifts that had been in their family for generations.

"Don't tell anybody!" Sarah could remember her grandmother and her father warning her as they shared their experiences when she was young. "People will think you're nuts!" Although she never told anyone, she sometimes laughed to herself at their paranoia.

She began to take them a little more seriously when one day they said, "If the government ever knew, they would take us away." Sarah remembered how people with unusual abilities would disappear. She recalled one of the stories about a young girl in the 1980's that could wave her hand over flowers and they would bloom right before their eyes. There were other stories as well, of people with "gifts," but that one stuck in her mind. Not long after their stories got out, they seemed to vanish. Whatever happened to them? No one seems to know .... So, yes, don't tell anybody .... Especially about their friends from Dubhe.

They were the tall, blonde people in shiny clothes that came to visit two or three times a year. The people Grandpa Brought saw from his second-story bedroom window when he was eight. Growing up with them seemed natural to Sarah. They were like family, especially since they had been visiting them for generations. *Why didn't everyone have people from another planet visit them?* It seemed normal to her, like people visiting from another country.

Sarah remembered her six-year-old, inquisitive mind trying to comprehend why she couldn't talk about Shemariah, Noam, Uri and the others. They were called the Dubheians, because they come from the

North, a planetary system from the pointer star of the big dipper. Their names were all Hebrew names because, according to them, it was the first and only universal language. Although all of the Dubheians didn't have Hebrew names, many of them did. She thought they were nicer, and felt more love and peace from them than other people she'd met, even at church. The only difference, to her, was they were shiny. Their faces glowed and they were tall, but she was obedient and was careful not to mention them to anyone outside of the family.

# Chapter 4 – Forgotten

Now that Sarah sold her gift shop uptown and finally retired, she purchased a kiln and pursued a hobby working with clay, making coffee mugs and other creations. She was still involved pretty heavily with her church. With her inherited gifts, she felt God's calling on her life since she was a little girl. She was sometimes asked to teach on Wednesday nights and even speak on Sunday mornings, from time to time.

"Hello!" A wide smile lit up her kind, slightly weathered face as she greeted Ben and Elizabeth in the shed next to the apple orchard where she was working on some new coffee mug designs.

Cookie, Sarah's white and brown, twelve-year-old, half Poodle/Shih Tzu mix, was happily barking, standing on her back legs waiving her front feet in the air and dancing around. She was happy to see Ben come home, but ecstatic to see Elizabeth! She absolutely adored her, and Elizabeth adored her right back!

"House of Worship" by Brandon Lake was playing on her phone app as she reached to turn it down.

"So ... you two want to know more about the Starlings? Let's go in the house where we can talk." She said, removing her spattered apron, revealing her lavender cotton blouse and blue-jeans while wiping the wet clay off her hands before they headed inside the old two story farm house built by her great, great grandfather, Joseph Brought in 1925. As she made her way to the old porcelain sink in the kitchen to give her hands a good scrubbing, Elizabeth got them all a glass of iced tea from the fridge.

Elizabeth loved the old sixth generation family home with its birdseye maple floors and woodwork. She was as comfortable there as she was in her own home. She liked to think about all the memories created within these spacious walls, and listening to Grandma and Rachel talk about their childhoods and the family history.

"Eliel told me, yesterday, that I have gifts!" Elizabeth could hardly contain her excitement.

"Lizzy, that's awesome!" Sarah shared her enthusiasm. "What did he tell you about them?"

"Well, he said I would discover them as time went on and they would mature with use. And just as Ben's emerge and mature, mine will too. I knew I could sense things and have always felt like I know what animals and plants are feeling, but I always thought it was just my imagination!" Elizabeth elaborated as Cookie jumped into her lap. "Sometimes I thought it was just wishful thinking when I would sense the same things as you and Rachel, you know? Or just from hanging around you both so much, but it's not! I have real gifts! All I need to do is work on them. Kind of like learning to play an instrument … practice." Elizabeth beamed, "I can't wait to tell Rachel."

"What's Rachel doing today?" Sarah asked Ben. It was Saturday and although they lived just fifty yards from each other, she hadn't poked her head out of the house yet.

"She's enjoying her day off. Said she was gonna do some house work, then morph into a couch potato the rest of the day," Ben answered. "We'll go see her later and catch her up on everything."

"So, Cookie, how are you feeling today?" Elizabeth asked as Cookie readjusted herself on her lap. She didn't feel anything except happiness from her. "How does this work, Grandma? Do they answer you?"

"Not in words … it's telepathic … so it's more like impressions and sometimes visions of things they've seen," Sarah explained. "Give it time. Keep trying, and you'll get it, I have no doubt."

As they sat around the kitchen table, Sarah began.
"So as we all know, much truth has been erased and hidden from mankind, and we can't just tell everyone what we believe to be true. They really would think we were nuts, like my dad used to say." She chuckled. "But some of this knowledge is coming to light and it's given us the opportunity to shed more light using these things to witness to people. There are ancient books called 'The Books of Enoch.' Some of them were said to have been part of the Bible before they burned them all in the middle-ages. They removed a number of books from the Bible in that time period, and people are finally beginning to realize that statement might be true."

"Why would they do that?" Asked Elizabeth. "Isn't there some kind of curse on anyone that adds to – or takes away from – the Bible?"

"Yes, but they were committing so many atrocities at the time, I guess they weren't worried about the Lord's threat of a little curse." Sarah admitted, helplessly. "People are starting to dig into this more now and they believe the dissecting of the Bible began with the Council of Nicea in 325 A.D., during the reign of Emperor Constantine forward. There was a lot of theological debate over the next couple hundred years. The winners got to decide which books would stay and which had to go, according to some research I've done."

Sarah sat down between them with the book. "There are two books we have today from Enoch, and other ancient books, like the books of Adam and Eve and others that mention the Watchers. Even the Bible mentions them. That's who your Starling is, Ben. He's a Watcher."

"Watcher?" Elizabeth exclaimed. She was startled. "Weren't they some of the ones that led the people astray? I felt the Lord, while he was there, you did too," she looked at Ben. "I saw you and Eliel worshipping after you saw him ... I was worshipping the Lord too, how can that be?"

"Not all of them are bad," Sarah added, with her kind, wide smile and understanding, hazel-green eyes. Yes, the Brought family genes always seemed to pass down the eyes. "Remember, they had good intentions in the beginning. A Starling is an overseer that did not leave his post. His mission - still - is to watch over mankind. He didn't join the others in their debauchery."

"And he paid a heavy price," Ben added. "They locked him away underground, where he stayed for a long time until Michael and Gabriel came just before the flood. When they came to confuse the giants, to make them turn on each other. That's when they freed the Starling."

They both looked at him, "Wow, really?"

"That's what I saw, he was in darkness." Ben admitted. "But he's okay, that form he took at the river isn't really what he looks like."

"What does he really look like?" Elizabeth asked.

"I couldn't actually see him, I just had a sense he was big ... and strong. He said he comes from Nibiru. That's in our northern sky, isn't it?" He looked at his grandmother, remembering where the Starling pointed in the northern sky.

"Yes, it's actually one of the three polar or north stars, called Thuban today," Sarah said. "Enoch called them the Grigori, a race of giants. Some of them were sent here to watch over mankind."

She continued, "Even in the New Testament, some of Enoch is quoted in Jude, almost word for word. Fragments of Enoch were found among the dead sea scrolls in the 1940's. So it's believed that Jesus and the other early Christians all knew about it and accepted Enoch as part of the Bible because it was part of their teachings from the beginning. And the books are really

... 'out there,'".... She continued, "They talk about angels, giants, spirits, demons, and all that, in great detail. Some believe they removed the books because they were considered too far fetched to be real and the powers at the time didn't want people imagining those sorts of things."

Sarah smiled and looked up at Ben, "But we're pretty ... 'out there' ... too, aren't we?"

Ben returned her gaze, "And we're real ...." They all laughed shaking their heads.

"So are you saying all these myths from ancient times are real?" Elizabeth asked.

"Well, yes, some of them are. People are uncovering all these ancient temples and ruins they thought were myths with that new underground mapping technology or whatever it is. They're finding skeletons from other species of humanoids that walked the earth – at the same time as humans – but not related to humans, according to their DNA ... giants ... dinosaurs. The city of Ur, and Nineveh, for example, were thought to be a myth from the Bible until someone discovered them. I believe these books may have been inconspicuously hidden in a conspicuous place until such a time as this," Sarah mused. "Because the Ethiopians have always had the book of Enoch and others, as part of their Bible to this day."

"They describe, pretty well, about how beings from other worlds were commonplace and everyone knew about it. They coexisted. And they *all* had the same Creator."

Sarah continued, "Many people think God created the entire universe, this world and every living thing in just seven days. We all know He could have, He's God, and can do whatever He wants. But there is a scripture that should make people wonder - those 'days' mentioned in Genesis may have been eons or eras. The Bible says in Genesis 2:4, "These are the generations of the heavens and of the earth when they were created, in the day that the

Lord God made the earth and the heavens." But strangely enough, the word 'generations' was only in a few of the versions, that I could find."

"I wonder why? More cover up?" Ben asked.

"Maybe, I don't know, it's weird. I looked at five or six different popular translations and they all say something that changes the meaning entirely. Things like 'these were the *accounts* of the heavens and the earth. Some use the word *history or origin of,* or the word *record,* in place of the word generations. It really changes the meaning, to me, because Satan's 'fall' was believed to be on the second day, according to some mythologies and Enoch scholars. A whole lot of things went on during his fall, and it should make more sense to people when they realize these 'days' may have been longer than an earth day. A thousand years are as a day and a day is as a thousand years to God." As Sarah took a sip of tea, she regrouped her thoughts.

"Also ... the creationists say the plants couldn't have survived because the sun wasn't created until after the plants. Apparently they are forgetting in the very beginning, the first thing God said was, 'Let there be light.' And in Revelation it talks about a time when we will have no need for the sun or moon because God Himself is going to be our source of light. It should beg the question for people that it may have been a similar situation in the beginning. God was the source of light for the world."

"That's awesome," Ben said as he stroked his beard, thinking.

"I'm not encouraging anyone to make up their mind on either of those points. I'm just trying to get people to look at the scriptures with an open mind and let them decide." Sarah admitted. "We know what we believe, but trying to show people through the scriptures is getting easier in these last days. God can do whatever He wants, He's God. And the Bible has never been proven wrong, and it won't be, because God can't lie! Man has misinterpreted it."

Just then Sarah's phone rang. It was her friend, Sophie Gimond. She was a widow as well, and a good friend to Sarah. They were also church buddies and usually rode to town together every Sunday. She lived a couple miles away on a little farm where she raised chickens and sheep. She had one horse, a white, 4 year old, half Percheron and half Quarter horse mare that was her baby.

"She must have gotten out during the night," Ben and Elizabeth overheard Sophie say, "The vet said she was with foal ..." They couldn't make out the rest as Ben grabbed his keys from his pocket.

"Tell her we'll be right there," he said, as he and Elizabeth headed for the door.

"Wait, I want to go with you." Sarah hurried as she said goodbye to Sophie. "I don't think Tilly has ever gotten out before and I'm a little concerned."

"Ben, I'm gonna take my car too. Lizzy, will you ride with me?" Sarah went to find her purse, making sure she had her cell phone and keys. "We can go look for her while Ben looks over the fence to see where she got out."

Sarah didn't go to Sophie's house, instead she drove behind her house on a side road. She stopped the car when they were directly behind Sophie's farm, which was obscured by trees.

"Do you see her?" Elizabeth looked around, wondering why Grandma had stopped.

"No," Sarah cleverly smiled and turned in her seat to face Elizabeth, "But how would you like to use your gifts to see if you can find Tilly."

It took her a moment to process. "Sure! ... I'm up for that!" A wide adventurous smile beamed over her face thinking about the possibilities this gift would create, "How do I do it?"

"You know Tilly, right?"

"Yes."

"Okay, close your eyes and concentrate on her. Relax and try to feel her." Sarah had the same ability, but she refrained from allowing herself to use it in case it might unwittingly influence Elizabeth.

"Remember her beautiful thick white mane? Her soft muzzle? Ask the Holy Spirit to help you."

Elizabeth closed her eyes and prayed. She pictured the graceful, white beauty with her long, flowing mane and tail. She remembered how much she enjoyed helping Ben feed and water Sophie's animals a couple of months ago while she was away. They brushed and loved on Tilly while she stood in her stall happily eating her sweet-feed freshly poured into her feed bin. Although she was sixteen hands, Tilly had a gentle and loving spirit.

"I see her!" Elizabeth called out. "Go left, around that corner." Pointing to the dirt road up ahead.

"Well done!" Exclaimed Sarah as she put the car in gear. Just as they turned the corner, there she was, on the side of the road in a patch of Queen Anne's Lace, eating as much of it as she could.

"Oh, baby, that's not good for you!" Sarah and Elizabeth quickly got out of the car. Tilly raised her head to greet them only for a moment as she reached down to pull off another bunch of the huge white flowers sticking out from both sides of her mouth as she happily chewed.

"Are you craving odd stuff that's not necessarily good for you just like we do when we're pregnant?" Sarah's hand disappeared beneath Tilly's thick, white mane as she stroked her long neck. Tilly nuzzled her nose in Sarah's other hand looking for something tasty, still chewing on the flowers in her mouth. She usually brought her a treat when she greeted her.

Elizabeth reached in her pocket and found a little pack of crackers to give her.

"Lizzy, will you walk with her towards home?" They were about half a mile from the house. "She'll go with you, but I'm going to get a halter so Sophie won't get suspicious. Animals normally won't walk along with people without a rope or something ...."

As Sarah drove off, Elizabeth said, "C'mon Tilly, let's go home." As they walked, Elizabeth stroked her belly. *It's a girl! ... I can feel her!* "Hello there, how are you?" She said out loud as she stroked Tilly's belly. Tilly gave out a soft whinny, approving of Elizabeth's inspection. Animals always seemed to be drawn to her as if they could tell she loved them and meant them good, not harm. And Elizabeth always seemed to know what they were feeling. She would usually second guess her assessment and shrug it off, but not anymore.

Ben found the place where she escaped her fifteen acre pasture. The fence was loose and bent almost to the ground between two posts where Tilly had been reaching over. *The grass is always greener,* he chuckled to himself. He had remembered to get some staples from the barn but forgot the hammer. *I don't think Sophie would know whether I used a hammer or not anyway.* The nearest neighbor was a quarter mile down the road, so Ben stretched the fence with one hand and effortlessly pushed the staples in the post with his other, tightening up the slack and straightening out the crooked parts of the wire as if they were butter. "Good as new." He said out loud, then walked the rest of the fence to make sure there were no other weak spots, which took him about three seconds.

"Thank you," Sophie exclaimed to Sarah and Elizabeth, with a huge sigh of relief as she met them in the driveway. She was a tall, slender woman with long, white hair she kept tied in a bun on top of her head. She wore a blue plaid shirt tucked into her jeans with cowboy boots that hit the ground with a thud as she hopped down out of her black 4-wheel drive chevy pickup. She had been searching north of the house when Sara called to tell her they found Tilly.

"Thank you, Jesus," Sophie ran her hands all over her horse, looking to see if she had any marks or was hurt anywhere. She was not. "Where'd you find her?"

"Right behind the house on that side road back there." Elizabeth smiled proudly, as she pointed south of the house.

"She was eating Queen Anne's Lace. I think she might be craving it now that she's with foal," Sarah added.

"Really? Well, I know they're mildly toxic to horses, but I'll find out from the vet if she can have a little."

Sarah knew if the vet said she could have them – Sophie loved that horse so much – she would go out and pick them especially for her.

Just then Ben walked from behind the house, "All fixed."

"Thank you, Ben. Where'd she get out at?" Sophie scanned the fifteen acre, partially wooded pasture, but it went too far back to see it all from where they were standing. He pointed to the area and told her about how Tilly was apparently reaching over to eat grass, or whatever was on the other side – and weakened it, "... she finally must've just hopped over it."

# Chapter 5 – The Ancient Ones

It was late afternoon by the time they got back to Sarah's.

"Are you two on a time frame, or do you want to come have dinner with me?"

They both had the rest of the day and most of the night to spend with her and were eager to talk more.

They had both graduated this year and were enjoying the summer. Ben kept his part time job at Selvy's Garage, but tomorrow was Sunday. Elizabeth was taking the entire year off. They both planned to start college the following year.

They each had birthdays coming up, Ben's was August 12th and Elizabeth's was August 19th, exactly a week apart.

After telling Ben how she found Tilly, Elizabeth called her parents to let them know she'd be later than planned. Her parents didn't mind her staying, they were great friends with Sarah and Rachel and loved and trusted Ben.

Sarah looked through her refrigerator. "I've got everything to make spaghetti. How's that sound?"

The two agreed. Ben loved his grandmother's spaghetti. It had more ground beef in it than sauce, with just the right amount of spices.

While Sarah and Elizabeth were making dinner, Ben thought more about the memories the Starling gave him. He couldn't help but wonder when they were going to discover the temple at the Au Sable. In the memory from the Starling, Ben saw the great granite blocks being levitated into place, the intricate statues and hieroglyphics .... *They're probably gonna turn it into some kind of theme park or museum site, and of course, sell tickets. The county's gonna manage this really close to make sure they get as much money as they can off this. They'll probably clear out half of Huron Forest for a parking lot ....* He knew he was exaggerating a little, the forest was huge, but still. *They're gonna have a hard time relocating the river in that spot where the complex goes under it....if they'll even go that far...*

"Grandma, do you have any idea when they're gonna find the temple? I mean, is it gonna be weeks, months ... years?" Ben finally asked.

"Well, Eliel just said, 'soon.' So I don't know."

"Yeah, soon to Eliel could be a hundred years!" He smirked.

"Yes," she laughed as she stirred the spaghetti sauce, adding more oregano and basil. "But it'll be in our lifetime, or he wouldn't have showed you that. And the Starling wouldn't have told you about it either ... so ...." She held a spoonful of sauce to her lips, blowing on the hot tomato and hamburger mixture before tasting it. "That'll do! Dinner's ready!" She declared.

"So, Grandma ..." Elizabeth asked, "Did Eliel look like he does now, even when *you* were our age, or was he younger?"

Sarah laughed, "Lizzy, Eliel looked like he does now when *my* grandmother was your age!"

Elizabeth looked at Ben as both their eyes widened; neither of them really thought about it before. Never growing old was cool!

"How long has he been guarding our family, anyway?" Asked Ben.

"You know, I never asked him. It's funny because I've wanted to ask him that very question – there are so many questions I've wanted to ask him through the years and for some reason, every time he comes, there's always something going on. You know how that is – and I forget all about asking him, and then he's gone again." She laughed, "He might be doing that on purpose! Maybe we'll have to try and corner him on some of that stuff one of these days."

Over dinner Ben and Elizabeth listened as Grandma explained more about the ancient ones.

"The books of Adam and Eve really get into the 'others'. Those books were never part of the Bible, as far as I know, but were passed down by word of mouth, from generation to generation. Kind of like the American Indians, how they pass their heritage down through word of mouth. Some of it may not be true, but it's a good read either way." She added that an unknown author compiled and penned the Adam and Eve stories into two books, much later, of course, and it has been re-written a few times with each author seemingly adding their two-cents worth.

"But have you ever wondered what happened to Adam and Eve? Were they sorry? Were they saved? Were they reprobates? Those unanswered questions always bothered me, but I've never asked anyone about it."

"I *have* wondered about that," Ben commented as he reached for more spaghetti. "Nobody talks about it and it doesn't really say in the Bible," as he piled more garlic bread on top of the spaghetti on his plate.

"I should ask the Dubheians about Adam and Eve. Shemariah would certainly know. He's really into the history of mankind."

"Why couldn't we ask Eliel?" Elizabeth wondered.

Sarah answered, "Because Eliel is an angel, he's God's messenger. He's only here to do God's will, not our will or even his will. Because angels are so beautiful and ominous, a likeness of God way higher than our likeness of God, it's easy for man to want to worship angels. That's how we got into this 'worshiping other gods' thing in the first place. So we try not to ask him too many questions."

"I never thought of it that way, but yes, you're right, Grandma," she answered. "So what does the book say? Were they saved? Were they sorry?"

"Yes, they were *really* sorry – and yes, they *were* saved, God forgave them. And these books back that up. That's why Satan, or the 'Satans,' hate mankind so much, they know we'll be forgiven and they won't. Actually, Adam and Eve's story in the book broke my heart, I couldn't read it without a box of tissues next to me. It gets me all choked up just talking about it ...."

"But we need to use wisdom and caution when telling others about this. Always remember these books have been compromised, and to what extent, I'm not sure. We need to remind people that whether any of this is true or not, it doesn't matter when it comes to their salvation. They need to back everything up with scripture, if it goes against something in the Bible, then don't follow that. People can get off so easily and create a new cult if they don't study the scriptures. Just as long as they know Jesus is the Son of God and they follow Him, their salvation is secure." She was very adamant about that. Then added, "But *not* knowing these things has caused many to think the Bible is wrong and abandon their faith, even pastors. All three of us in this room *know* there are more things to this world than what meets the eye ... physical and spiritual."

They both agreed.

She went on, "According to science and carbon dating, which has many flaws and is way off base on many things, say the earth could be millions, if not billions of years old. Some scientists believe our DNA may even be billions of years old as well. And – think about this – it's far fetched, yes, but it could be, if we have God's DNA ... being created in His image, anything is possible with God."

Sarah added, "God told Jeremiah, 'I knew you *before* you were in the womb.' In Isaiah 49, when he's prophesying about Jesus, he said the

Lord called him from the womb and made mention of his name from his mother's belly. And Paul talked about it in Galatians, that God had set him apart from his mother's womb and called him by His grace." She added that in Romans it says, for those 'He foreknew, he also predestined to be conformed to the image of his Son, that He might be the firstborn among many brethren.'"

"Wow," Elizabeth exclaimed. "I'm getting goose bumps!"

Ben reached across the table and took her hands in his. He knew what she was thinking.

"That's just so cool," she looked up into his eyes as she imagined the children they hoped to have someday. They both shared the thought – that God already knows them and has plans for them – so awesome.

Ben saw her aura. It was beautiful. Sarah saw it too. All of their sparkly auras were so sharp and clearly defined at that moment. They gracefully moved and intertwined with one another. It was exquisitely magnificent to watch. Ben wished Elizabeth could see them too.

"Praise the Lord," Sarah whispered almost under her breath, "Praise the Lord."

No one spoke for a few minutes, they just sat there thinking about how awesome the Lord is, and enjoying His presence.

Then Elizabeth asked, "Are you ready to talk about the future memory the Starling gave you?"

"No, not yet." Ben tensed up a little.

"Okay." She said. She was willing to be patient about that. But then asked, "So, about the past memory ..." She pressed with a smile, "Did he give you emotions along with the memory? Or was it more like a movie playing in your head where you had to figure out what's going on?"

Ben thought about that as Sarah and Elizabeth cleared the table, "That's a good question ... I guess I'd describe it as a mixture of both. Like I was there watching, but there was a … great sorrow … that I know didn't come from me. It was the Starling's sorrow I felt."

He thought some more, "I sensed the tribe's way of life to a small degree. It was horrible, and filled with fear, wondering who would be chosen to be sacrificed next, you, your wife, your child or someone else or their child. And … there was a pride in being sacrificed. So they felt bad and proud all at the same time. They were messed up, man …." He shook his head.

As Sarah and Elizabeth washed the dishes, Ben continued.

"It all poured into me so fast, I'm actually still processing it. They didn't love each other like we do. They were pretty barbaric because that's what their gods taught them. Everything about their religion was horrific, human blood everywhere." Ben looked up at his grandmother … "And we just ate, I'm sorry." They all laughed. He knew Grandma didn't have a weak stomach, she used to help butcher cows, chickens, deer … and who knows what else. Elizabeth never showed signs of being squeamish either.

"But the thing was … I believe this was from the Starling … that the Watchers, the fallen angels/demons, whatever ... knew they were going to be punished. So they decided to go all the way and tell the people they were their gods. They were their creators because they wanted to be worshipped. They built huge temples and taught men to build temples that pointed to their home stars and planets, like the Pleiades and Orion's belt. They told the people that was where they were from as well, that was really their home too. Then they set up rules that defied God, their Father. Anything to mock Him, basically – like human sacrifice. They knew He would hate that. The people were evil because their so-called gods were evil." He added, "The people, by that time, really didn't know any better. I believe that knowledge came from the Starling because he felt betrayed by them."

"Now that is a revelation we can tell people about, that's Enoch, right there, and the Bible." exclaimed Sarah.

# Chapter 6 – The Grigori

They had finished the dishes and sat back down at the table as Sarah began again.

"So, in the book of Enoch, it talks about how the Watchers, or the sons of God, saw that the daughters of men were beautiful and they lusted after them. Not only did they want to experience sex, they wanted to know what it was like to have children. They were all created at one time and this was a new thing to them. Their leader, Semjaza, or another spelling may be Samlazaz, said he feared they would not all agree to do this thing and he alone would have to pay the penalty for this great sin. So they swore an oath and bound themselves together with mutual curses. There were two hundred of them that agreed and descended on Mount Hermon in the days of Jared. It says they each took for themselves one wife from the daughters of men, in the beginning. The children they produced were giants. The first giants grew to three thousand cubits tall, it says. If a cubit is eighteen inches, these first giants were forty-five hundred feet tall!"

"People are going to find that hard to swallow, that's almost a mile tall!" Ben exclaimed.

"Right?" Sarah added, "They grew smaller with each generation, but the book of Enoch says they consumed all the work and toil of men. When that ran out, the giants turned on men and were devouring them. They even turned to devour one another's flesh and drink the blood. This is where, I believe, human sacrifice originated. These giants were the 'men of renown' the Bible calls them, the Nephilim and other names, because the Bible tells us some of them survived the flood."

Elizabeth added, "Remember the Greek myths about the god Cronus who ate his children? Kind of sounds familiar here …"

"Yes, it does." Ben remarked. "And the pyramids? The great temples they're uncovering today? The Tower of Babel?"

"Yes," Sara agreed. "The Watchers also gave men knowledge and technology that was forbidden. They were supposed to develop and find these things out on their own." Sarah took in a deep breath and exhaled as she reached for her iced tea.

"The first Watchers broke their mandate. This may sound odd to many, but just like in the Star Trek episodes …. Kind of makes you wonder how Gene Roddenberry came up with these ideas because part of their federation rules, their mandate, was to never interfere with a species that was not as advanced as they were, and that is a reality. That's really how the extra terrestrials operate and how God mandated it."

"So Enoch says the cries of men, from their torment, reached God's ears. It was so bad that God sent some of his archangels, Michael, Uriel, Raphael and Gabriel down to turn the giants against one another and they destroyed each other, most of them. The evil spirits that came out of the dead giants are roaming the earth today, they are the demons that torment us. They locked up all the Watchers that went rogue too. They are all under the earth awaiting the day of judgement. And after that, God brought the flood because the sins of men were so great, they were utterly spoiled."

"That must have been when they released the Starling," Ben was putting it all together.

"The word 'angel' is translated to simply mean 'messenger,'" Sarah explained, "but there is a difference between ET's and God's holy angels, his archangels, the seraphim and cherubim and so forth. They actually walk in the presence of God. They have knowledge the others do not."

"Eliel," Ben added.

"Yes, Eliel." They all felt such a warmth and peace when he was with them. Just thinking about him always brought a smile to their faces, although his visits often times turned into quite a roller-coaster ride.

"So did Enoch say anything more about the Grigori?" Elizabeth asked.

"Well," Sarah said, "there were two angels Enoch called giant men that came, in the second book of Enoch. He said their faces shined like the sun, with eyes that were like a burning light and fire came out of their lips as they sang and praised the Living God. They were dressed in purple with wings brighter than gold. Enoch said they came and took him through different levels of heaven. One of the stops was what he called the fifth heaven – so I'm thinking Nibiru is in the fifth heaven – he saw countless giant soldiers called Grigori. They were even bigger than the greatest giants on earth, of human appearance, but their faces were all withered and they were silent. Enoch asked why they were all withered looking and silent. The men that brought him said the Grigori were mourning their brethren that were a part of the Watchers that defiled themselves on earth and were being punished. So they ceased their service to the Lord because of their sadness, basically. Enoch asked the Grigori, 'Why do you stand there, brethren, and do not serve before the Lord's face? You could anger your Lord completely.' Enoch said they listened to his advice and blew four trumpets with a loud voice and the Grigori all broke into song with one voice that went up before the Lord mournfully and touchingly."

"Wow!" Exclaimed Elizabeth. "That is some kind of awesome."

"Yeah, I think it's cool that he called them brethren," Ben added.

"Exactly," Sarah agreed. She explained that in those days before the flood, mankind's sexual immorality was hideous. By the time the flood came, mankind didn't even know right from wrong, except the few that stayed on the Holy Mountain that held the Cave of Treasures described in the Adam and Eve books. Men and 'others' would come and take someone's children and force them to have sex with them right in front of them. Sons would have sex with their mothers and so forth, it was really horrible. Those Watchers really did mankind wrong... teaching them all kinds of witchcraft and other things.

"The Watchers actually thought God was going to forgive them." Sarah explained that they went to Enoch, before their demise. They called him Enoch the scribe. They asked him to pray for them and to ask the Lord to forgive them for all they had done. Enoch did as they asked, he even prayed for them, but the Lord told him in a dream their petitions would not be granted. God said man shouldn't be coming to Him on their behalf, they should be coming to Him on man's behalf. The Lord said he did not create the earth to support giants. He did not create the Watchers to have children, they were from the stars and were created for a different purpose. Since they left their first positions to be like men, along with all the atrocities they committed against mankind, God said their sins would not be forgiven.

She also said the Apostle Paul talks in Ephesians, chapter three, about making all see what is the fellowship of the mystery, through Jesus Christ. That by the church, the manifold wisdom of God might be made known to the principalities and powers in heavenly places.

"He's not talking about humans there. So we can pose the question to people that have seen unexplained craft in the sky and other things, that perhaps God is using us to witness to the extra terrestrials that are watching us? Those that have gone astray, like us? What if we're all one? What if we're all connected to each other? Could Armageddon be a battle *everyone* will fight from this universe? We already know Satan and his angels are going to be in the fight." She added, "I'm not trying to provide an answer here for people, I'm just asking these questions to get them thinking."

Sarah continued and talked about how the Scriptures say Satan's great trade, wealth and beauty was what lead him astray. In Ezekiel 28:11-19, most scholars agree that although in part, he is talking about the king of Tyrus or Tyre, it is believed he is also talking about Satan. "We know, for instance, that the king of Tyrus was not in the Garden of Eden. The human king was not a Cherubim. He was not created, he was born. He was never 'perfect' in his ways."

Sarah went on to explain the great city of Tyrus was an island. It was ultimately covered by the sea, as Ezekiel predicted, never to return. It never did. They built a sister city opposite the former city, which was also an island. They called it Tyre. It was conquered by Alexander the Great sometime around 300 BC. The remains of that city still exist today.

"But about Satan, the scripture says things like, '…by the abundance of your trading you became filled with violence.'"

"By the multitude of your trading?" Elizabeth echoed with a question.

"Okay, trading with who? Satan's fall was before man was ever created." Sarah stated.

"We just need to encourage people to pay more attention to the text and keep an open mind," Ben added.

"Precisely!" Sarah exclaimed."

She mentioned how it is documented that three modern day Russian cosmonauts on the Salyut 7 Space Station, in July of 1984, said they actually saw angels in space. They were said to have faces that were human looking with halos. According to the reports, the astronauts said they were huge, up to eighty feet tall and had wings. They also said they flew alongside them for ten minutes. The reports then stated this happened at least twice. Later that summer, three more cosmonauts joined the crew. That time, all six of them saw the angels. Of course, officials wrote it off as mass hallucination.

Members from each team, not afraid to come forth, said they felt a sense of well-being and peace. The angels spoke to them telepathically and told them everything about themselves, things no one else could know. They also told them to go back home, they were not ready for space travel.

"These were trained, highly respected, responsible people that are not easily spooked. They know what they saw." Sarah added, "They may have looked similar to the angels Enoch described."

Ben added, "They're afraid to speak up because they've been intimidated and could lose their jobs. And … governments make trades and agreements with the ET's for technology. Keeping this under wraps is to their advantage."

"Exactly how I feel. They use the excuse for hiding their presence because of the mass hysteria it could create. Some of that may be true, but I believe even more than their physical presence, the mass hysteria, anger and conflict is going to be from what they tell us. There is only one Creator, and the good ET's would make that known. Many would be saved, yes, but not everyone is going to want to believe them."

"Just like the Bible says," Ben added, "that even if angels were to come and witness to them …"

"Some still would not accept it." Elizabeth finished his sentence.


"Grandma?" Elizabeth looked at Sarah, then to Ben. Sarah had a far away look on her face. She was staring into the living room. Then, without changing her gaze, she said, "Ben, get your mother."

Ben reached for his phone.

"No, honey, go get her now." She said, calmly but firmly. "Lizzy, stay with me."

Ben didn't take the time to ask why, he was already standing before his mother in the living room as she sat on the couch with Ollie, watching television and surfing Pinterest on her phone.

"Woe, Ben!" Rachel jumped up at his appearing. "What's up?" Ben didn't answer. He just put his arms around her and suddenly they were in Sarah's kitchen. Rachel knew why as soon as she saw her mother. This was not the first time they had been visited by strangers.

## Chapter 7 - The Willows

They stood up and took each other's hand. "Don't let go," Sarah took her gaze off the living room long enough to look at each of them. "I don't know this group."

Cookie was barking, but not growling, which coincided with what Sarah was sensing. It gave her some comfort about the nature of these new visitors. Sarah asked Ben to put Cookie in the bedroom.

Rachel stood to her mother's left, Elizabeth stood between Ben and Sarah on Sarah's right. Elizabeth had never witnessed an encounter before, she had never even met the Dubheians yet. Her heart was beating so loudly in her chest, she thought everyone could hear it. Then she heard Ben, not with an audible voice, tell her everything was going to be all right. It helped …. Instead of a loud roar, her heart went to a less intense, rapid thudding as she squeezed Ben and Sarah's hand.

A white light about a foot in diameter beamed down from the center of the ceiling. Once it touched the floor it spread out like a fan and without a sound the ceiling disappeared to reveal the night sky. A huge, round craft hovered directly over the house far above the cloud cover. Only they could see the light beam coming out of the center of the bottom of the ship. The ship was undetectable to radar and hidden by the clouds to the naked eye. Three beings about twelve feet tall appeared before them through the light.

*No wonder they had to take the roof off*, Ben thought.

A sweet, earthy scent filled the room. As their features began to take shape through the light, they could see that they stood upright with two arms and legs, like humans, but were very thin. Their multi-colored, brown skin resembled tree bark, thick and layered, with scale-like bark, hard on the outside, yet soft and pliable underneath. They had four long, skinny fingers and a thumb. They seemed to be wearing long coat-like garments made up of plant shoots with hundreds of tiny green leaves. The shoots hung down like willows from their shoulders. They shimmered as they moved with the tree beings. Their coats were alive. The tops of their heads were also covered with the shimmering tiny green leaves and stems that resembled living hair, but like willow shoots or wisps hanging down from their heads.

Sarah realized they were symbiont beings.

They had large eye sockets that looked like knots in a tree and their amber and green eyes were like a burning flame inside their sockets. They had a nose and mouth that also looked like knots in a tree.

They spoke telepathically. *Greetings Brought family. You have nothing to fear from us. We have come to witness the excavation of the temple,* the being in the middle said. He looked at Ben. *You have seen the Starling. He showed it to you.*

Ben braced himself. He wasn't going to tell them anything without knowing who they were and what their agenda was.

The being sensed how he felt, how everyone felt. He told them his name was Byron, to his left was Trazier and to his right was Ombeye. *We are from a star system just beyond the star you call Mintaka, the star on Orion's belt. You haven't named our sun-star yet, but we call it Jetharne. It is approximately the same size as your sun and our blue/green planet, our home, we call Shearn. It is very much like your earth. It is also the third planet from our sun.*

As he spoke, or gave his thoughts to them, he lifted his arms and stretched out his long fingers. Between his hands an image of their solar system formed showing twelve planets orbiting a sun, much like earth's solar system. Then the image zoomed in on their home planet, showing huge mountains, rivers, waterfalls and giant trees, beautiful flowers and exotic plant life. Living trees that weren't rooted in the ground like earth's trees – they walked. There were no buildings or structures of any kind. Everything there had a self awareness. They could communicate with each other. It was beautiful.

*We were created long ago. We are the guardians of all that grows from the ground, from the great trees and forests to the grass in the fields. Our creator sent some of us to your earth, in the third day, to look after your trees, your grass and all that grows from the ground. We are all one.*

"So you were Watchers for the plants!" Exclaimed Elizabeth – out loud.

Byron fixed his gaze on her and said in an audible voice that sounded like leaves rustling when the wind blows, "Yes." The tiny willow-like leaves attached to his head and shoulders shimmered briefly. They seemed to like Elizabeth. Then he added, silently, *The Great Counsel has asked us to come watch over the river you call Au Sable and the forest you call Huron. They, like the humans, will undergo great stress during the excavation of the temple.* He took a step closer to them. "Rachel and Elizabeth," He said their names out loud, and again, it sounded like the wind brushing through the trees. "You are one with the earth. You know the forests, the rivers and the beasts – and they know you."

Elizabeth felt a chill and a confirmation all at the same time – solidifying what Eliel told her and how she felt – she *was* connected to other living things, like Rachel. She *could* sense how animals and plants, even the forests felt – and what they needed.

*We have come to ask for your help, for all of your help. The river and its forest has been at peace for thousands of years. The temple was built long ago, by others that were here before. But when man came, after the flood, they found the temple abandoned. The spirits of the fallen ones, the Watcher's offspring, that are bound to earth, devised false river gods for man to worship. Their priests required daily human sacrifice. Their intent was to eventually kill them all and steal their souls. The time came when nearly half of the people were sacrificed from the tribe. The people that were left turned on the priests and killed them. They buried them in the temple with a seal, and put an end to their treachery.*

*When the temple is unearthed and they break the burial seal, the demon spirits that attached themselves to the river priests will be unleashed. They have an unquenchable hunger to possess men and other living things, even the river and forest, causing much destruction.*

*Can we kill them?* Ben asked.

*No, they do not have a mortal body. But we can bind them,* Byron explained.

*We are spirit beings – all created at one time – and born in the Light.*

*Humans are spirit beings too, but you are different in that you were born over time from a man and a woman, in darkness. You are opposite from us.*

Byron continued, *humans that have not yet come to the knowledge of the True Light are easy prey for the temple demons. They are extraordinarily cunning and destructive. They must be bound. With your help we can accomplish our mandate.*

After listening to Byron, they all sensed these tree people would be allies. Sarah and Ben couldn't help but see their well defined yellow and blue life energies, which are good. They decided to trust them.

"So how do we do that?" Ben asked.

Audibly now, with his willow voice, Byron said, "Only those that possess the seal of Light have the power and authority to bind them on earth."

## CHAPTER 7 - THE WILLOWS

"What seal?" Ben asked.

"The seal of the Holy Spirit," Sarah exclaimed.

"Yes," Byron admitted. "In the Name of The One who overcame – The Risen One … who is three. The firstborn of many." As he spoke, long tentacle-like branches emerged from his sides. "He is the greatest warrior among all that is. He is fearless and just. He is one with the Father of Light."

The branches began to weave something in front of them – faster and faster. So fast, that whatever Byron was creating became a bright sphere of light they couldn't see through.

Byron continued, "He holds all power and authority …. Much of the peoples of earth were deceived and believe there are many gods," Byron tilted his head to the right as he worked on the creation between his long arms, and simply added, "But there is only One."

The branches were finished and withdrew back inside him. As the light faded, they saw a large, glimmering, multi green and copper colored egg shape, approximately the size of a bushel basket. It was woven so tightly; it was harder than steel.

Byron continued, "The sons and daughters of men with the seal have been given the power to use that authority." He stepped back and looked at the oval shape on the floor. "Once you bind them, this cocoon will hold them."

Trazier bent down and picked up the cocoon.

Elizabeth saw it move as Trazier held it in his branch-like arms … *it's alive!* She squeezed Ben's hand.

Byron looked at Ben, "Will you help us?"

Ben looked at each of his companions …. They gave their approval.

He looked back at Byron and answered firmly, "Yes. We will do what we can."

Byron nodded. "We will return when it is time." The beam of light reappeared and they all disappeared into it.

"So ... when will that be? Exactly...?" Ben shouted after them but it was too late. Just as suddenly as they came, they were gone. The ceiling returned and everything was as before.

They all stood in silence for a moment.

Then suddenly Elizabeth broke out, "Wow! That was so cool!"

Rachel looked at her and thought, *Most people would be in a fetal position right now, especially for their first time. This girl has no fear!* She gave her a hug. "Lizzy, I love you!"

They all sat down in the living room and collected themselves. Rachel went into the kitchen and made chamomile tea to settle everyone. Tomorrow was Sunday and they all had to get up in the morning for church.

"That was so awesome the way they talked about God, about Jesus and the Holy Spirit! He *is* the greatest warrior that ever lived, but it was so cool to hear *them* say it! The One who is three." Elizabeth could hardly contain her excitement. She added, "And did you see that cocoon? It was alive! I saw it move!"

"Yeah, that cocoon was pretty incredible," Ben admitted. He was pumped and ready to go ... tonight! "So I wonder if we're going out in teams with the tree people or what?" Ben began to pace the living room floor.

"Maybe ... but one thing I've learned," Sarah cautioned, "is not to overthink these things. Keep your mind from trying to figure it all out because it almost never happens the way you imagine."

"Well," Rachel said, as she came in with hot tea for everyone, "at least we can surmise this is going to happen very soon, or they wouldn't have come."

They all agreed.

Ben finally sat down next to Elizabeth on the couch, reached for his tea and decided to take Grandma's advice and try very hard ... not to overthink this.

The next day Elizabeth rode home from church with the Adan's. Her parents were used to her not being home much anymore. Since she graduated, she spent nearly everyday with Ben and his family and today was no different. Although today, Sarah decided to cook everyone a big roast beef dinner with all of the trimmings and had invited her parents over around 4 o'clock.

The August weather was perfect, around 78 degrees and sunny with a few big, puffy cumulus clouds in the sky and a light breeze.

Rachel took Elizabeth outside to work on her communication skills before her parents arrived. Although everyone was a little tired from last night's episode, they wanted to take advantage of every opportunity to get prepared for what was coming.

Ben went out do some tree-vaulting in the woods behind the house. It was his favorite time to talk to the Lord. He also took the opportunity to use the new gift he became aware of about a month ago. He closed his eyes and scanned the huge 500 acre deciduous forest. There was a winding, hilly trail that ran from the east to the west side of the big woods that was popular with horse enthusiasts, four-wheelers and hunters during hunting season. *Just some deer to the west and a black bear in the north corner, no other humans except Lizzy and Mom.*

Before he knew he could scan things with his mind, he had to be careful not to let anyone see him vaulting – like Elizabeth did when they were kids. Although he could stay in mid-air for a few moments and look around a little, he would use the cover of a tall tree and take his time for a more thorough view. But now, he could simply concentrate on his surroundings to know if anyone was there. He could feel what was there, but could also see everything, as if he were flying over it but much faster, like a visual knowing.

Elizabeth rarely came with him. She wasn't afraid of heights but preferred her feet on the ground. However, she loved the teleporting thing. They actually had done some discrete travel, visiting the Grand Canyon, the Eiffel Tower and other places of interest. Distance didn't matter with his gift, and so far, there was no place he was not able to go.

"Yes, I can feel it!" Elizabeth beamed as she felt the life-pulse of a raspberry bush. There was an entire patch of them on the edge of the woods that had been there since Sarah's grandmother planted them some 90 years ago. They simply kept growing with no help from anyone, year after year.

"Now concentrate on the big sugar maple over there," Rachel said, pointing in the direction of the tree about 40 feet away.

Elizabeth couldn't feel anything.

"It doesn't matter how far away you are, just clear your mind and concentrate on the tree," Rachel instructed.

Slowly, Elizabeth began to feel the wind that blew the leaves hanging on its branches. The tall, wide, majestic tree was about 200 years old and was a spectacular red in the fall. She saw people dressed in different clothing that varied according to their time period, signifying the different generations that enjoyed its shade through the years. She marveled how it even remembered the Indians – birds and animals that nested in its branches. It was a happy tree and its roots were well fed.

Once she focused on the roots of the tree, she began to feel the other plants around it. Soon she could feel all the plant-life in the entire forest.

They were all connected. They too, seemed to have a self-awareness. She remembered what the Willows said last night about them all being one.

"Oh!" She suddenly jumped. "Hi Ben!"

He was sitting in the top of a tree deep in the center of the woods talking to the Lord about his plans to propose to Elizabeth on her birthday. He saw her ... and heard her!

"Whoa!" Ben was amazed. "How are you doing that?"

"I'm talking with the big maple at the edge of the woods, the one on the hill." She explained, "I can feel the entire forest through its roots."

"That's amazing!" He grinned from ear to ear as he leaped out of the tree.

"I love you, Lizzy." Now Ben was suddenly holding her in his arms and twirling her around. "I'm so proud of you!"

"Ben," Rachel scolded, "you should give her a little warning before you do that. Geez, you're gonna scare her half to death!"

"It's okay, I'm getting used to it," Elizabeth glowed with her arms around his neck as she reached up to kiss him.

"Oh, hey ... Lizzy, your parents are on their way." Rachel saw them leaving their driveway.

As they walked toward the house Rachel said, "Lizzy that was very good. I couldn't feel the rest of the forest until my third session with the maple. And I never was able to talk to Ben. I've seen him in the woods, and other people, but I could never communicate with Ben! You're well on your way, praise God."

"It was fantastic!" Elizabeth exclaimed, "I can't wait to do it again."

Rachel smiled as she gave her a hug. *I love this kid ... she's such a pleasure to work with.*

# Chapter 8 - Progeny

A silver, Ford Expedition carrying John and Samantha Shiels pulled in the yard just as the table was being set. The savory aroma from the roast with onions and carrots fresh from the garden permeated the house and wafted out onto the porch.

"Oh, man, that smells good!" John commented as they stepped onto the porch.

"It does," Sam exclaimed. "That woman can cook!"

"Hello!" Ben greeted them at the door as they stepped into the entry way.

"Hope you're hungry." Sarah called out from the kitchen.

"Oh, we are!" Said the tall, medium built, bald man in his mid 40's, with a warm, amicable face. "I wanted to have a snack after church but Sam wouldn't let me."

"Yeah, I'm the meany." Sam spoke up. It was easy to see that Elizabeth got her hair and figure from her mother. The tall, slender woman had long, red hair that was twisted tastefully up on the top of her head with a few curls carelessly hanging down. She radiated with a wholesome, gentle beauty and looked much younger than her 42 years.

Everyone sat around in the living room after dinner trying to find room for strawberry shortcake with fresh strawberries from Sarah's garden, homemade biscuits and whipped cream. Elizabeth poured everyone a fresh cup of coffee. She set the tray of cream and sugar on the birdseye maple coffee table that sat in front of the huge, welcoming, brown leather couch.

The coffee table had thick, intricately carved legs. The top was inlayed with twelve, eight-inch tiles that were multi-colored earth tones of blues, tans and reds. Sarah believed that if you had a piece of furniture that could not be used, why have it? The coffee table with its matching end tables was built by her Grandpa Brought and had been a part of the family since before she was born.

Rachel and John chatted about work. She was head of quality control at the factory where she worked. They made molded window edging and other car parts for Chevy while John was still at the same job he moved his family to Michigan for – managing the factory that supplied Ford with similar parts. The car companies were still outsourcing, but many were outsourcing to smaller U.S. towns rather than other countries. The factories were in Elm Creek and they were both hiring. The two factories were great for the economy there, but since the coronavirus pandemic that began in 2020, workers were few. Many businesses collapsed and unemployment sky-rocketed.

Then the government began compensating the unemployed with more money than many were making while they were working, so no one wanted to go back to work, which made the economy even more unstable. Once the government stopped the extra unemployment checks, people began to return to work. Those that could, worked from home.

With the vaccines and overall immunity from people that had already had the virus, people were slowly becoming 'not so afraid' to come out of their houses again. In spite of the variant strains of the virus that were emerging, people were still becoming less afraid to go out.

" … There were people lined up all the way out the front door at 7 a.m., Friday. It was great to see the turnout for people wanting a job, but I was glad my shift was over." Rachel admitted.

"Yeah, I don't envy the H.R. department right now," John agreed. "But getting people back to work full-time is the main thing."

Elizabeth and Ben washed the dinner dishes and cleaned up the kitchen while the 'old folks' visited. Ben was his usual self, showing off for Elizabeth to make her laugh. They couldn't see them from the living room. He was tossing coffee mugs in the air and before one fell, he would put another one in the cupboard. He ran out of mugs and began using plates. He started doing two at a time, then three. Then Elizabeth flashed him one of her wide smiles and winked at him and he dropped them all! It was fun to watch him scrambling to catch them before they hit the floor, but none did.

Sarah and Sam went to the shed to look at some of Sarah's new pottery work.

"I really love your mugs, Sarah," Sam reached for one that caught her eye as she looked over the shelves that lined the walls filled with various mugs, plates, bowls and other creations. In the center of the shed was Sarah's wheel, work table, glazes and tools, along with various bags of clay. In the right corner was her prized kiln, it was tall and wide enough to accommodate larger pieces. Sarah did not like putting limitations on her creations and looked for the biggest kiln she could afford. Behind the kiln, the walls were lined with red, fire retardant brick she and Ben put up.

Sam was accumulating quite a collection of the pottery Sarah had created. She especially loved the three-quart covered baking dish Sarah was going to throw out a couple years ago. She was just learning then, and it had some flaws, but Sam insisted on keeping it and said that was why it was so special. It reminded her that just like the clay dish with the bump on its side and slightly skewed cover, we are all still useful.

After everyone had gone home that night, Ben lay in his bed thinking

## CHAPTER 8 - PROGENY

of Elizabeth. Then trying *not* to think of Elizabeth. They were both still virgins. Ben made a commitment to God when he was just 13 years old, that he would not cross that threshold until he properly married her and he meant to keep it. He remembered the talks he had with Pastor Matt over the last few years.

" … Son, just don't allow yourself to get too hot and bothered when you're alone together." The Pastor advised. He was a tall, sprightly man of medium build in his early 60's with salt and pepper hair.

"That's the best counsel I can give you. Have enough respect for her and for yourself, and the Lord, to stop *before* you get to that point … BEFORE … you get to that point." He reiterated more strongly.

"If that isn't working, don't allow yourself to be alone with her if you're feeling vulnerable, wait until you know you're not. God will bless your marriage in so many ways if you stay virgins until your wedding night, Ben."

"And I get it – I know that's not the norm in today's society, but it's not impossible, people do it everyday and God wouldn't have required it if it was impossible." His kind, wise face was always full of hope. "Actually, I believe today, there are more young Christians waiting until they're married to have sex than even in my day."

He added, "But don't go home and look at porn either. Don't go there. That'll cause more problems than you can imagine and it's the same as being unfaithful to her. Keep yourself before God in this. Keep yourself busy in other things and don't allow your mind to dwell on sex too much before you're married. If you do, it will become unbearable, be careful there."

Pastor Matt smiled and put his hand on Ben's shoulder as they walked side by side, "If you two succeed in this, and I believe you will … you'll have a happy, vibrant and blessed marriage. You'll enjoy each other and enjoy being together your entire lives. You won't have all the problems so many couples carry into their marriages today, because the trust factor will be there. It may not sound like much now, but that's huge, Ben, that's huge." He looked directly into Ben's eyes, "But that's not that there won't ever be problems. Every marriage has its problems, but they'll be more easily overcome when the marriage bed is undefiled, believe me."

Ben accepted Pastor Matt's advice and kept his commitment to God. But the days of late were getting more and more difficult. He would marry her tomorrow, if he could. He'd marry her *tonight* if he could! They'd never have to be apart again.

The ring was on layaway at the jewelers in Elm Creek. He had been paying on it for almost a year now and only had one payment left. It was actually a wedding ring and an engagement ring that fit together as a set. He pulled the receipt out of his wallet and looked at it using the light from the moon streaming through his bedroom window. It read: 1 CT. T.W. Marquise Diamond Bypass Bridal Set in 14K Gold. It was marked down from $2400 to $1999.99. The balance owed was $240. He was paying it off this payday – his birthday. He would be 19. Elizabeth's birthday was the following week, and she would be 19. Her birthday was the big day. The day he was going to properly propose and finally place the engagement ring on her finger.

Mom and Grandma helped him pick it out. They thought it was a little over his budget, but knew he would keep his commitment to pay, even if he had to get a second job to do it. He never once asked them to help pay for it either.

It had one larger marquise diamond in the center with other smaller diamonds around it and down either side of the band. He thought it was beautiful and could hardly wait to see it dangling on Elizabeth's finger and hoped she would like it as much as he did.

As he continued to stare at the ceiling, unable to sleep, he recalled his talk with her dad last year, after he turned 18. He was so nervous. *What if he says no? What if he says I'm not good enough to marry his daughter?* Ben felt he would never be able to give her the luxuries she enjoys now. John's job put them in the upper middle-class and Ben's family was lower middle-class, but that never seemed to bother them all these years while they allowed Elizabeth to be with him.

He was at Elizabeth's house in the backyard with her father helping him take the top off a large cement birdbath. The water wasn't pumping and John thought there might be a leak somewhere in the hosing. It was Sam's birdbath. She loved sitting in their kitchen nook in the mornings with a cup of coffee watching through the window as the birds splashed around in the water.

Elizabeth was off shopping with her two best friends from school, Laura and Brooke. All three wanted to look for some non-school clothes for the summer.

Ben felt so awkward and didn't quite know how to start the conversation on marrying his one and only daughter – his one and only child. Finally, while they were digging into the hosing, Ben blurted it out.

"John," he hesitated. John looked up at him from where he knelt working on a hose fitting with a wrench. "I would like to ask your permission to marry your daughter." His voice was a little shaky as he forced the words through his lips. Then he noticed the wrench in John's hand and wondered if maybe he should have waited ….

John smiled, shook his head a little, and went back to work on the clamp he was tightening. The twenty to thirty seconds of silence were deafening to Ben. His mind was racing with different outcomes of this scenario.

Finally John answered. "Well, first of all, I appreciate you asking me, Ben. Most young men today don't even bother to ask what the girl's parents think or want. But you're not like most kids your age and I like that about you. But you two are awful young to be thinking of marriage."

Ben interrupted, "I know I can't give her the material things she's ..."

"I'm aware of all that." John stopped him, "Money isn't everything. It's just a tool. Being happy and productive with your life together ... now that's important." He stood up, putting the wrench and hoses aside. "But you're pretty industrious. You never know, Ben, you might wind up a millionaire. Don't cut yourself short."

John began to walk further into the back yard as Ben kept pace. "Now I know you two say you aren't having sex, but I have to ask you this," He stopped and looked at him intently, …. "Is she pregnant?"

"No Sir!" Ben sounded like a private answering his Army sergeant. "We've never had ... sex." He added, more calmly, as he gathered himself and shifted his eyes away from John's. He didn't want to look him in the eye and utter that word, at the moment.

"Well, thank God, that's a relief." John stood there looking up at the clouds searching for his next words.

"You know, Ben, Sam and I have been praying for Lizzy's husband since the day she was born." He continued walking with Ben at his side. "Our prayer has always been that the man she marries would love God more than he loves her, and love her more than he loves himself."

Ben thought for a moment, "Well, you know, that may sound like a pretty tall order for some. But to be honest, I've felt that way about Lizzy since the day we met and that's never changed. It's grown."

John waited another few moments before asking, "Okay, but where's God in all this?" John looked intently again into Ben's face.

"God is always at the top ... He's always number one – in more ways than most people realize." *I wish I could tell him everything!* ... "He makes us more ... than who we are. There's nowhere else to go, but to God ... He's ... our Father," Ben confessed. "He loves Lizzy more than I do, so why wouldn't He be first?"

John smiled with a sigh of relief. He saw the boy was sincere. He knew from watching him grow up these past six years, he had a strong love for God and sticking up for what is right. He just wanted to hear it from his lips, in his own words. *And – he comes from a good, God-fearing family.*

"Have you thought about how you're going to support her? Where you're gonna live?"

"Yes," Ben answered, swallowing hard as he prepared himself for this next hurdle. "I was talking with Grandma about it and she wants us to live with her. She wants to will the house and property to us." He waited. "If that's all right with you and Sam."

"Well ... does Lizzy *want* to live there?"

"I haven't told her about it yet. I wanted to wait until I ... propose. But she loves that old house so much, and Grandma. I'd be surprised if she said no." Ben answered.

"Yeah, I think you're right there. What about work? Are you planning on getting a full-time job? I thought you wanted to go to college?"

"I do. I was hoping since we'd be living with Grandma, I could keep my part time job at Selvy's and go to college on my days off and at night. Lizzy could go during the day."

John put his hands in his pockets, looked at the ground and continued walking as if he were kicking an invisible pebble around. "Lizzy's college is all set." He finally said. "I don't want you," he stopped and looked at Ben directly, "Or her ... messing that up." John could be downright direct. It reminded Ben of Grandma Sarah. When she had a point to make she could be blunt too.

"I understand. We won't … and she wants to go, so … it should all work out." Ben was getting a little nervous John was going to say he felt they needed to wait until after college to get married.

John continued to meander towards the walkway behind the house with his hands still in his pockets.

Ben put his hands in his pockets too, and just stood silent – waiting.

After a few minutes, John broke the silence. "Well, Ben, to be honest, I would be proud to have you as a son-in-law." A hint of a smile crossed his face for the first time.

Hearing that, Ben wanted to jump as high as the clouds and shout from the rooftops! A wide smile broke across his handsome face. His hazel eyes glowed with joy.

"You're responsible. You're not lazy. And we know you love Lizzy. There's nothing you and your family wouldn't do for her, we know that. But how soon were you wanting to do this? You both just turned 18."

"Well, first I wanted to get your permission, then I wanted to pick out a ring. I wanted to propose as soon as I have it. I found one at the jewelers I think Lizzy will love. I figure it'll take me about a year to pay off. So I'd like to propose next year. Then get married … as soon as she'll have me."

John was relieved with the time frame Ben laid out. *At least it wasn't next month.* It was still too soon to lose his little girl, but he and Sam saw this coming. He nodded as if agreeing to something he wasn't quite ready for but knew it was going to happen. "Let me go inside and talk to her mother, you wait here."

It wasn't five minutes – Sam opened the door and called for Ben. They not only gave him permission to marry their daughter, they gave him their blessing and prayed with him.

# Chapter 9 - Engaged

The next two weeks drug on. Everyday seemed like an eternity. Ben had been working everyday since the Sunday before last, to pay off the ring, take Elizabeth out to dinner and have a little money left over.

Although he could have whisked her off to France or somewhere else for dinner to propose. He wanted it to be a place she could talk about with her friends and family. A place where she wouldn't have to keep secret. So he decided to take her somewhere local, to one of their favorite seafood restaurants on the water in Bay City. He made reservations to be outside on the second level overlooking the Saginaw River. He hoped nothing else was going to happen with the temple and no new 'visitors' were going to pop in until *after* he proposed.

James Selvy, his friend and boss, had been ribbing him at work – and offering his advice – especially for the last two weeks. He was in his early 30's and had been married for ten years. He and his wife, Shiela, had three kids, Natalie was eight, James Junior was five and their youngest, Billy was three years old.

"… and when she tells you about something that went wrong in her day … don't try to fix it, trust me … just say, that's too bad, honey." James' voice bellowed from under the hood of a car.

Last week, on his 19th birthday, he was waiting in line at the bank to cash his check as he opened the envelope. Their was another check with his paycheck for $200. A little note was attached that said, "Congratulations and happy birthday!" It was signed, 'The Selvy's.'

He wasn't expecting anything like that and frankly was not sure if he should accept the extra money. Then he recalled his grandmother's words.

"If you're always the one doing the giving and have trouble accepting gifts from others when they want to give you something, that's not right. Don't rob the giver of their blessing from the Lord, accept the gift and enjoy it."

*I love working for them! They're good people.* Ben thought as he texted to thank him, then headed for the jewelry store.

The springs were stiff. He held the box tightly as he opened it to see the ring before he paid off the balance. It was just as he remembered. He hadn't seen it since he first laid it away last year.

When he got home, Ben showed it, again, to his mother and grandmother. He could hardly wait to put it on Elizabeth's finger. *One more week to go!*

"It's more beautiful than I remember!" Rachel and Sarah were really proud of Ben, how he planned this all out. Now – seeing it all come together, they both were in tears.

His birthday was somewhat of a blur. The entire week was pretty much a blur – although it never seemed to end. Elizabeth got him a sweater and a new fishing pole he had been drooling over at the local hardware store. His mom and grandma decided that instead of a gift, this year, they would give him money.

It was *finally* here – Elizabeth's birthday – as he stepped out of his truck at Selvy's, it was 8:00 a.m.

"Ben, I'm gonna need you to work late tonight. I've got to have this car done by Saturday and there's no way I can do that without your help." James called out from underneath an older Dodge Charger.

"No, no, no … I'm not falling for that!" Ben laughed. "I'm leaving at three o'clock and that's it!"

James laughed. "Oh well, you know … after you've been married for awhile, on those mornings when the kids are all screaming, there'll be days you can't wait to come to work."

"Maybe so … but not anytime soon." The teasing was all in good fun. Ben thought about the children they wanted to have. They wanted at least three, maybe five. Although they intended to wait until after Elizabeth graduated college to begin having kids. With today's birth control, they didn't see any reason why they couldn't make that happen.

He made it! It was finally 2:55 p.m. He would be off work in five minutes!

Nothing happened at the Au Sable and no new visitors showed up. Everything seemed to be going according to plan. Ben felt his stomach flip. *It's finally here! Thank you, Father!* He'd been praying for and looking forward to this day for the last seven years, ever since they met in the seventh grade.

"There he goes, in such a hurry to throw his freedom away." James taunted as he watched Ben cleaning up to leave for the big night ahead. Ben paid no attention. He was too busy getting everything done, being careful not to move too fast … at least while anyone was looking ….

"Seriously, Ben, congratulations. You two were made for each other and I wish you the best tonight." The short, brawny man reached to shake his hand. His reddish-brown mustache moved up and down as he chewed his late lunch. "Tell Lizzy we said happy birthday too, by the way."

"Thanks, … and I will." Ben said as he barely stopped long enough to shake his hand.

"So, do you think she suspects?" Rachel asked her son as he blew through the door.

"I really don't think she does, unless someone told her …." He looked at his mother with a suspicious grin.

"Are you kidding? I certainly did not! And I know Mom wouldn't have either. But with her new gift, she might have an idea that today is special ..." She mused, "I mean, besides the fact that it's her birthday."

"Yeah, well ... that's different. Even if she suspects, as long as no one told her outright, she'll still be surprised," Ben added. "Have her parents mentioned anything about it to you today?"

"Oh, yeah. They're happy about the situation, but you know, that's their little girl. They're happy and a little apprehensive all at the same time," Rachel added. "Even though there won't be much change to the way things are now once you're married," she laughed. "She's over here almost everyday anyway."

"Right?" Ben added, beaming, as he headed for the bathroom to shower and trim his beard. He had just gotten his hair cut last week and was proud that he had become proficient at trimming his own beard.

It was almost six o'clock, Elizabeth was sitting on the couch. Ben would be there soon. Her mother had helped her put her hair up with a silver comb that was an heirloom from her grandmother. It was inset with rubies and pearls. Her hair was beautiful, the way certain strands curled down around her face and neck from the top of her head.

After trying on every feasible outfit in her closet, she decided to wear a black and white checkered jacket with a matching smaller checkered skirt and a white blouse with black polka-dots. She loved the fact that Ben was tall. She could wear literally any size heal and never have to worry about being taller than him. She decided on her black lace up sandals with a six inch stiletto heel.

She hadn't seen as much of Ben these last two weeks as he had been working, and she missed him. She knew he was taking her to Bay City for dinner and was excited about their evening, yet, something was nagging at her. A feeling of caution. She couldn't quite put her finger on it and dismissed it as birthday jitters ... and missing Ben.

Just then a red 2020 Chevy Impala pulled in the yard. It was Ben, driving his grandmother's car. Elizabeth watched from the living room window as he stepped out of the car. He was wearing his church shoes, black slacks, a button-up sea-foam green shirt with a black sports coat. She thought he was the best looking man on the planet.

Sam caught the door and greeted him. Their eyes met for a moment as she gave him a hug, knowing what tonight was going to bring. Ben was a little relieved that John was still at work. Sam's aura was a little muddy. He could tell she had been thinking about the engagement, and was worrying again. He knew a part of her felt they were too young to be getting married, but she also trusted him to do the right thing by her daughter.

"You look beautiful!" Ben reached for Elizabeth as she jumped into his arms. "Happy birthday, Lizzy!" He picked her up and gave her a twirl before setting her down with a kiss.

"If we're going to be past midnight, I'll send you a text." Ben said to Sam as they headed out the door, he turned and smiled at her with a wink.

"Okay, have a good time and drive safe," Samantha called as they practically ran out the door.

"That was nice of Grandma to let you take her car," Elizabeth said as Ben opened the car door for her.

"Yeah, Grandma's awesome," Ben climbed into the driver's side.

The restaurant was already beginning to fill up. Their reservations were for seven o'clock. They were a few minutes early, but their table on the second level was ready. As the hostess led them outside to their table, the waiter was already setting a bottle of non-alcoholic champaign in a bucket of ice on their table. Ben had ordered that when he made the reservations and told them he was proposing. The view was excellent overlooking the river. In the summer months, the outside filled up faster than the inside, when the weather was nice.

"Wow, the bubbly!" Elizabeth exclaimed. "How fancy, Ben!"

He got a little nervous thinking she was getting wise to him. "Well, it's non-alcohol, of course. And I thought it would be a nice touch for your birthday. This is our last year being teenagers. It's all downhill from here, according to the old folks." He smiled as he pulled out her chair.

They both ordered lobster and it was delicious. Over dinner they made small talk, Elizabeth talked about a recent shopping trip with Laura and Brooke. Ben talked about work.

All of the outside tables were now full and the inside looked full, from what they could see, as the evening progressed. Ben still enjoyed watching the various auras surrounding people. Everyone looked as if they were having a good time.

Their meal was over. *It's now or never!*

Elizabeth was talking about something. He didn't hear a word she said just then.

He interrupted her, "Lizzy ..." He smiled a nervous, apologetic smile for interrupting her. "I love you so much." He looked into her deep, hazel-blue eyes. She stopped in mid-sentence as Ben stood up, then got down on one knee beside her. He loved being traditional. Now – she completely forgot what she was talking about and began to cry. The guests seated outside also stopped talking as everyone turned to watch the handsome young man propose to the beautiful red-head at table number three.

Ben reached in his pocket and pulled out the box containing the ring. As he opened it before her, he said the words, looking intently into her eyes.

"Lizzy, I have loved you since – forever." He hesitated, "And I want to

## CHAPTER 9 - ENGAGED

spend the rest of my life with you. Will you marry me?"

Through her tears, Elizabeth said, yes! The thought crossed her mind before, that it would be awesome if he proposed to her on her 19th birthday, but didn't believe it would happen this easy.

"It's so beautiful!" She exclaimed as she looked at the ring still in the box. "It looks way too extravagant for me, Ben."

"Never you mind about that, nothing's too extravagant for you."

He took the ring out of the box. As she held out her shaky hand, he slipped the ring on her finger. They both just stared at her hand for a minute looking at the ring sparkle on her finger. They had both waited so long, it seemed, for this day.

Now Ben was welling up with tears too. He reached and gave her a long kiss as they embraced.

# Chapter 10 - Scare Tactics

Ben was still kneeling on the floor when the middle-aged blonde lady from the next table came over and stood on the other side of Elizabeth.

Before she could finish the word … "Congra … tu … la…" Her smile faded and her bright aura changed into a smokey black. Her physical appearance changed into this hideous creature with black, sunken eyes, wrinkled skin and jagged teeth. Elizabeth saw it too.

Ben felt a familiar chill down his spine. He remembered that was the way the 'black man' looked before he killed his father. He could feel the evil. He jumped to his feet and pushed Elizabeth out of the way.

"Benn—jja—mmin Aaa—dan," this deep, growling voice slowly said his name. The creature looked at him, then at Elizabeth as she stood to her feet. "The end is near. You will never win. You – or your children."

Ben saw the flash of another black aura in the corner of his eye, to his left. He glanced in that direction and realized all the people on the entire outside level, about twenty people, had all changed into these demon creatures! All their energies had turned black. Their eyes became sunken black holes. Their skin was all wrinkled and withered. They were hideous. He looked into the restaurant through the glass and everyone else was going about their business. *Is anyone else seeing this?*

Ben looked at the demon creature before him. With conviction and power, he said, "We are blood bought children of the Living God! You have no power over us! In fact, Jesus gave us authority over you, so all of you, come out of these people and leave!"

At those words, they all started to make a sickening, deep guttural sound and moved towards them. There was a horrible smell.

Ben didn't back down, he kept ordering them to leave, "Father, You have given us authority over these demons in the name of Jesus! And in the Name of Jesus, I command you to leave, NOW!" Then he said, "Father, I will praise *You* all the days of my life! You are the King of kings! Your Name is above all names! Jesus, You have been given all authority and power, and have shared Your power with those that have Your Holy Spirit! I have the Holy Spirit and I command you to leave!"

At that, the demons all moved to about twelve feet away from them. Their guttural sounds became high pitched screeching.

Ben looked at Elizabeth.

She chimed in. "I plead the blood of Jesus over us! Father, protect us from them! For Your mercy endures forever! We will praise You no matter what they do to us! They can't take You away from us!"

Their prayers had caused an invisible barrier the demons could not cross. They reached and clawed at them, but could not touch them.

"You will never drive us from the temple. It is ours!" The leader growled.

Ben and Elizabeth began to thank God for pushing them back.

The sound of the creatures became even higher pitched with every praise they spoke out. They turned into deafening screams. They began to wreathe in pain, falling on the deck and slithering up and down the wall of the restaurant, along the railing and up and down the windows.

The people sat inside, inches away from them on the other side of the glass, laughing and talking, completely unaware!

They no longer moved like humans. *Humans cannot contort their bodies like that.*

As Ben and Elizabeth continued to praise God, a soft breeze came through. Their screams began to fade. They sounded farther and farther away, even though they were right there in front of them. It was as if the breeze was carrying their voices away. Their black energies began to melt. One by one they were swept away like smoke, floating off into the twilight.

After the last of the screams and black smoke floated away, the people they had possessed were lying all over the floor, outside, on the second level of this restaurant ... and no one seemed to notice! All they had to do was look! But no one looked.

Elizabeth and Ben wondered if they were all dead. *How could they still be alive after their bodies were mangled like that?* Then, after a minute or so, they began to wake and move around. Ben and Elizabeth watched in amazement as they picked themselves up, wiped their faces, straightened their hair and clothes – and never once glanced in their direction. They all sat back down and continued talking, eating and drinking like nothing ever happened!

Ben and Elizabeth rushed to gather their things and get out of there. As Ben held the door for Elizabeth, the leader, the blonde lady that had come to their table said, happily, "Congratulations again!" Everyone at the table smiled, lifted their glasses to them and repeated, "Congratulations!" All their energies had returned to the happy colors they once were and they all looked human again. They seemed to have no memory of what they had just participated in.

As they made their way inside, Ben scanned the room to see if there were anymore inside. No one on the inside of the restaurant seemed to have a clue.

They couldn't pay their bill fast enough. They barely heard the hostess congratulate them on their engagement and ask if everything was to their satisfaction. They didn't know quite what to say to that, Ben nodded and quickly handed her the money, making sure to include a nice tip.

Instead of walking to the car, as soon as they were out of site, Ben put his arms around Elizabeth and they disappeared.

In a split second, Elizabeth found herself sitting in Grandma's car with Ben beside her in the driver's seat.

"Thank you! I didn't feel like walking to the car after all that." Elizabeth's voice was shaky. *This experience was nothing like the visit from the Willows.*

"Lizzy, let's pray." Ben took her hands in his, taking note of the ring on her finger and remembering why they were there. They thanked the Lord for protecting them and prayed a prayer of protection over their ride home and over their families.

When they were through praying, Elizabeth asked, "Ben, have you ever tried to teleport in a car before?"

"No," he smiled and gave her that look. "But there's always a first!" He held tightly to her with one hand and the other firmly on the steering wheel as the car suddenly disappeared. Elizabeth opened her eyes and they were sitting in Grandma's driveway – car and all!

"Ben, that was amazing! You did it!" She was almost in tears, she was so grateful they didn't have to drive all that way home after that experience.

Ben thought about never being late for work again as the two went inside to tell Grandma about all that had happened. He texted his mother to see if she could come over. It was only just after 8:30 and she didn't have to leave for work until 10:30 or so.

"What are you two doing back so soon? Is everything all right?" Sarah asked as she greeted them at the door. She sensed something was wrong. As they walked through the doorway she saw a glimpse of what took place. It set her back a step.

Ben looked at her, "How much did you see?"

"Enough ... let me go put the coffee pot on." She gave Elizabeth a huge hug before turning for the kitchen. "Thank you, Jesus, for bringing them home safe."

Elizabeth felt peace return as she stepped into Grandma's house. "Grandma guess what Ben did? .... He teleported the car! We came straight here from the restaurant parking lot." She snapped her fingers, "Just like that! Car and all."

"What?" Sarah exclaimed, "Wow! .... That opens some new possibilities, doesn't it, Ben?"

"Right? I'll never have to worry about being late for work again." He chuckled. He was rarely ever late for anything.

"The ring!" Sarah reached for Elizabeth's hand. "Let me see!" As she turned her hand the ring sparkled from the light of the lamp in the living room. "I take it you said yes." They laughed. "It's even more beautiful on your hand! Congratulations, sweetheart! I want to officially welcome you to the family, even though you've been a part of us ever since the seventh grade. I love you, Lizzy."

She gave her another hug as she reached for Ben's hand, "Ben, congratulations to you too. It's been a long time coming, for you, hasn't it?"

"Yes," Ben said emphatically. He turned toward Elizabeth, "I mean, I know we're only 19, but Lizzy, I've wanted to marry you since the day I met you."

"And I never thought about marrying anyone else but you, Ben. I love you so much." Elizabeth glowed as she reached to kiss him.

Just then Rachel came through the door. She finally got to see the ring on Elizabeth's finger. "Lizzy, you're family now!" She hugged them both and congratulated them as tears welled up. "I'm just so proud of the two of you. You were meant to be together and it's so wonderful to get to see it all come into fruition."

Ben and Elizabeth shared everything with them about their experience at the restaurant.

"So it was right after you put the ring on her finger and kissed, the lady came up?" Rachel asked.

"Yup," Ben said.

"I think that was significant," said Sarah. "After she accepted the ring and you kissed, you were officially engaged. It may have started things in motion we don't yet know about. I say that, because it mentioned your children."

"I think so too," added Rachel.

Elizabeth got a chill. "Well then, what's our wedding day gonna be like? I thought those demon things were all locked up. They haven't been released yet, so how did they get to the restaurant?"

"I don't think those demons were the actual ones from the temple." Ben added, "I think it was a warning from the demon world trying to scare us off."

"Ben, I think you're right. They wanted to scare you both away from the temple." Rachel added, "But it's awesome how your prayers and praises created that invisible barrier!"

"It was," Ben confessed. "I was so glad to see them stop where they did. But I felt the Holy Spirit, I knew we were going to be all right."

"Oh my goodness," Elizabeth exclaimed. "I was so scared! But when I saw them stop like that, I was like, thank you God, thank you, Jesus, and just kept thanking Him." She added, "But they were so horrible looking. And the way they kept clawing at us, it was awful … and the smell …" She thought for a moment, "But the Holy Spirit, I could feel Him telling me they couldn't hurt us, and not to be afraid of them …. That He was there with us."

Sarah smiled, "The Holy Spirit will never leave you or forsake you. You heard Him because of the relationship you have with Him. You're familiar with His voice. Never forget that with Him living inside of you, they cannot possess you, though they may try and make you think they can, they cannot. Don't let fear overtake you. Perfect love casts out fear."

"And to think they were once more beautiful than any of us humans," added Rachel.

Elizabeth had forgotten about that … they were fallen angels and only turned hideous after their fall.

"They were once as beautiful and radiant as Eliel." Rachel sadly admitted.

"Wow, I never thought of it like that," Elizabeth confessed. "That's really … unbelievably stupid! Who would want to trade all of heaven for that horrible existence?"

"I'm not sure they realized that was going to happen to them until after they allowed themselves to be deceived – until after they made the choice to follow Satan," Sarah speculated.

"Man, I'd be wanting to work that liar over for tricking me into that," Ben remarked. "But instead, they hate God. That's crazy."

"Maybe it's like with us. The Bible says after you go down that path for so long, you'll be given over to a depraved mind …." Rachel added.

They were silent for awhile as they sat around the kitchen table drinking coffee and taking it all in.

Then Rachel cracked a smile, "I can't believe how the people inside the restaurant had no clue!" She started to laugh, "I mean, can you imagine, sitting in a booth next to the window with this … thing … slithering up the window two inches from your face and not even seeing it?"

They all broke out laughing.

"So, after the breeze carried the demons off, everybody just picked themselves up and went back to what they were doing?" Sarah added ... triggering another chain of laughter in the room.

Rachel was laughing so hard, she could barely speak, "...And when you left they all said congratulations and were all smiles again?" Another bout of laughter broke out.

"And Lizzy did great!" Ben added. "She was right there with me praising God and staying with it." He gave her an admiring look, "You didn't run away. You didn't crack under the pressure. You were awesome!"

"It's not because I didn't want to." A sheepish smile came over her face.

"I know ... I wanted to run away too." Ben added. "But in spite of the fear, we faced it and we won."

"And don't worry about your wedding day, Lizzy. We're gonna have that so covered in prayer they won't be able to get within miles of you two." Sarah reassured her.

"God's got this, Lizzy," Ben added. "He's faithful to His people. Just don't dwell on it, keep giving it to God and everything will work out fine."

"My wise Ben," she smiled and snuggled further into his shoulder.

## Chapter 11 - Wedding Plans

"So with everything that's happened I suppose it would be in poor taste to ask if you've set a date yet?" Rachel looked at her son.

They all began to laugh ... again.

"Not yet." Ben smiled, "But as a matter of fact, Lizzy, why don't we go to the tree house and talk about it?" He looked at his watch. "It's only 9:30, your parents don't expect you yet ... What do you say?"

Elizabeth agreed, grabbing a couple soda-pops out of the fridge for the trip. In the north she learned, when she first moved to Michigan, they call it pop. In the south, they call it soda. Her solution was to combine the two and it always stuck with her.

Ben looked at his mother and grandmother, "We'll be back later so I can take Lizzy home in the car, if that's okay."

"Of course." Sarah said, "If I'm sleeping, wake me if you want to talk."

The couple disappeared.

There were no trails leading to the tree house deep in the woods behind the house. Even though there was a small clearing just in front of it, no hunters or hikers ever bothered it or even seemed to notice it. Ben built it when he was fourteen. It had become his favorite private place to get away. The only other person he ever brought there was Elizabeth.

He originally tried using solar lights for night-time visits, but the tree cover was so thick, there wasn't enough sunlight shining in from the clearing to charge the batteries during the day. So he used regular old-fashioned battery powered lights.

Ben did a mind-sweep of the area. It was clear. It had been awhile since they were there. He took a rag from his pocket he grabbed before they left the house and with lightening speed, wiped down the two wicker chairs and the end table before Elizabeth could set the drinks down.

Ben took her in his arms and they just stood there in the center of the little treehouse. Elizabeth clung to him and put her head deep in his chest. He rocked her gently back and forth, as if swaying to music that was theirs alone. He brought his hand up from her waist and gently held her head as she rested it against him.

"You know I'd never let anything happen to you, Lizzy." He kissed the crown of her head, thinking about the events at the restaurant.

"I know … I feel safe with you. I've always felt safe with you."

"Oh, my gosh, I forgot! …Are you okay? From when I pushed you at the restaurant? You're not hurt, are you?" Ben said, now breaking their embrace to look at her. "I was worried I might have pushed you too hard and forgot to ask you at the house. Oh, Lizzy, I'm so sorry!"

"No, I'm fine." She reassured him. "It almost felt like I was surrounded by this invisible cushion. I never felt a thing." She smiled up at him.

He picked her up, legs and all – and twirled her around in his arms. He loved twirling her. Then he stopped and looked at her in the dim light from the camping lamps. "You're so beautiful," he said, "I'm the most blessed man on the planet to have you." Elizabeth always thought she was way more blessed to have him than he ever was to have her, but she didn't argue with him. She just enjoyed the moment.

Ben sang the first part of, "Give Me a Lifetime," by Anthem Lights, as he twirled her a few more times. He had a great voice and Elizabeth loved listening to him sing, especially that song!

"So … we're finally, officially engaged!" Ben stopped in mid-twirl.

That handsome, confident smile she so loved shown in the lamplight.

"Lizzy, I'd marry you tonight if I could. When do you want to do this?"

She thought for a moment, "Well, we need to think about so much … where we're going to live … college … how we're going to support ourselves … all of that …."

Ben set her down in the wicker chair. He pulled the other one up facing her and took her hands in his. It felt so nice to finally feel the engagement ring on her finger. He told her all about the talk he had with her father last year. How Grandma didn't want to live in that great big house all by herself and wanted them to live with her. That she wanted to will the house and the property to them, keeping Rachel's house, of course. Rachel didn't want the land willed to her, she insisted on her mother giving it to Ben. They talked about her going to college during the week full-time and Ben going part-time – keeping his part-time job at Selvy's, in the beginning, and seeing how all that worked out.

"Your dad *really* made it clear not to screw up your college," Ben confessed. "But after we talked about all that, he and your mom gave me their blessing and prayed with me."

"Oh my goodness, all this behind my back," she smiled, actually admiring Ben for taking charge and thinking all this through. "Well, it sounds like you've taken care of everything. Grandma really wants us to live with her? What about when we have kids?"

"She's beyond ready for that," He grinned. "She loves kids, crying and all. And the house has five bedrooms, a sitting room besides the living room and a library for heaven's sake. It's big enough, if things get too hectic, she said herself, she can go somewhere quiet or go work on her pottery in the shed. We talked about all that." There was silence for a moment. "So, what do you think? Want to live with Grandma? I mean, if you don't want to do that, we'll get an apartment or whatever you …"

## CHAPTER 11 - WEDDING PLANS

Elizabeth stopped him, "No, I *want* to live there! She's been my grandma since we moved here." Elizabeth began to cry. "I don't remember my real grandparents, she's always been there for me and made me feel like I was truly one of her own grandkids. You're mom too ... they always made me feel like family." She began to laugh a little, through her tears, "Even if they were mad at me, I always knew they still loved me. I'm just taking all this in, it's so wonderful."

"Right?" Ben chuckled.

"And I love that old house so much! Oh, Ben, it sounds like a dream come true! Is this all really happening?"

"Well," he said, "let's pinch each other. If it hurts, it's real."

"Ouch!" Ben called out as she pinched his arm.

Laughter rang out into the forest from the tree house as the two danced in the moonlight to music only they could hear.

"So what do you think of next month?" Ben didn't even want to wait *that* long. "A September wedding would be awesome!"

"So ..." Elizabeth said slowly as she sat back down in the chair ... "you know my mom has always wanted to plan a big wedding for me." She said with a little remorse, knowing the planning would, more than likely, take longer than a month.

"What? A month isn't long enough?" He asked.

"Well, I don't know. But ... she made me promise her a long time ago that I would not run out and elope when I got married and I'd wait long enough for her to plan a big wedding."

"You agreed ... didn't you?" Ben smiled, surrendering as he shook his head.

"Yes," she said. "And I need time to pick out and order my wedding dress and pick out the bridesmaids' gowns ..." Her mind began to race ....

"All right, what about October? Surely we can get married by October."

Ben looked forlorn.

"Awe," she took his handsome face with his meticulously trimmed beard in her hands and looked deep into his hazel green eyes, glowing as the dim light caught his face. "You look like a poor, lost puppy dog!" She kissed him. "October might be long enough to get everything done. If we start right away." Her mind began to race again with a mental list of all the things that would have to be done. It was growing by the second, like a long scroll opening up across the sky. She shook it off and took a breath. "What time is it? Let's go tell Grandma," she said, looking at her watch.

"It's 11:30," Ben said, "I need to get you home …. Hey," he began, "maybe we could talk to …"

"If they're up!" Elizabeth finished his sentence.

He took her in his arms and they teleported to Grandma's to get the car.

She was already in bed sleeping so they didn't wake her. They headed over to Elizabeth's house. The lights were on ….

As they exited the car, Ben's stomach did another flip like it did before he left work earlier today. *This is finally it! Her parents … the final frontier ….*

Elizabeth was so excited she felt giddy as they entered the house and saw both parents sitting in the living room.

"October?" Sam was hoping for a little longer time frame to plan everything.

"Sam, do you remember what it was like when we wanted to get married?" John smiled at her.

*Oh good, he's on our side,* Ben was a little surprised.

"Besides, Rachel and Sarah will be right there at your beck and call. They'll help with everything." John reassured her.

*Were they actually agreeing?* Elizabeth and Ben were just about floating, they were beside themselves.

"Yeah, Mom, you know they will … and I'm not working or going to school right now, so you'll have me 24/7. I'll help too." Elizabeth coaxed her mother. "We can do this!" She smiled that huge, sweet smile that always melted everyone in the room.

"How can I say no to all this?" Sam conceded.

Elizabeth squealed with joy as she engulfed her mother with a huge hug and did the same to her father. "Thank you, thank you so much!!!"

There wasn't a dry eye in the house as they sat and talked about all the plans to be made until the early morning hours.

Ben wanted the date to be the first part of October, as they all looked at a calendar, but agreed to late October. Especially after listening to the women go on about time for dress fittings, caterers and invitations.

First thing Saturday morning after he returned home, Ben told his mother about the date as she came through the door on her way home from work, just after 7:30. He saw Grandma was up. He walked over and told her all about it. Then called Pastor Matt, telling him the good news and making sure he would be free that day to marry them.

He was free, but before he agreed to marry them, however, he made two counseling dates for them. He never married anyone without counseling them first. Ben was okay with that and actually looked a little forward to it. He knew Elizabeth would be all right with that too.

He spent the rest of the morning in the woods. He wanted to properly thank God and just spend some quality time with Him. He also asked for wisdom and revelation in dealing with those demons.

Elizabeth and her mother spent most of their morning on the phone telling friends and relatives about the news. Laura agreed to be her maid of honor and Brooke her bridesmaid. They were both so excited for her and said they knew this was coming. They just didn't think it would be this soon.

Elizabeth did not want a long procession of bridesmaids. She wanted her wedding to be small and simple, just a few friends and if any relatives would make the trip from Florida to attend, that would be great, she thought. She was thinking maybe twenty-five people or so.

"Twenty-five people?" Her mother retorted when she told her. "Honey, I don't think you've thought this through. Your father and I have friends we would like to invite. What about Ben's relatives and friends? And what about the people from church?"

Elizabeth suddenly felt like a tiny dot in the schematics of what was THE WEDDING! She quickly realized this day was not just for her and Ben, it was for both families and the people they loved. She conceded – but still only wanted one bridesmaid and a maid of honor. She had other friends from school and church she could ask to be bridesmaids, but was never really close to any of them like Laura and Brooke.

# Chapter 12 - Discovery

Two weeks went by, it was Friday and Ben was at work. He had just finished changing the fuel pump in a pickup. He was tightening the final bolts when he heard James saying something in the office about the Au Sable River in the newspaper. He quickly finished up and went to see what James was going on about. After the visit from the Willows, he was anxious to see it come. Now, with the wedding, he was in no hurry.

"What's going on?" Ben asked, wiping the dirt and grease from his hands with an orange shop towel as he poked his head through the office door.

"There's a big write-up in the paper about some kids finding ruins or something at the Au Sable." James was still reading the article.

*Now it begins,* Ben thought.

"They're gonna have some people from Michigan University (U-M) come to use some underground mapping radar over the area to see what it is." They had a photo of two boys standing by what looked like stone steps they had uncovered in front of a hill in the woods next to the river, near Lumberman's Monument. It was on the front page so it was in color. "We may have our very own Machu Picchu right here." James smirked as he turned the page to finish reading the story on page two.

"Oh, look! It's you and Lizzy!" James pointed to a photo of them all dressed up on page three.

Ben stepped into the small office with two desks. The larger desk was piled with two stacks of pink and white work orders with black smudges all over them and two photo frames that held pictures of the Selvy family. The other desk had a photo of Elizabeth with Ben's mom and grandma at the river that was taken the summer before, mixed with a smaller, single pile of smudged work orders. Both desks each had a gnarly, medieval looking coffee mug sitting on them with coffee stains underneath, compliments of Grandma's handy work. They were actually quite comfortable to drink out of and were good conversation pieces with customers.

The announcement read, '*Mr. and Mrs. John Shiels are pleased to announce the engagement of their daughter, Elizabeth Shannon Shiels to Benjamin Michael Adan, son of Mrs. Rachel Adan. Elizabeth graduated this year from Elm Creek High and plans to attend college next year. Benjamin is a mechanic at Selvy's Garage in Elm Creek. He also graduated this year from Elm Creek High and plans to attend college next year while working part time.*

*The wedding will be held, Saturday, October 22, at 3:00 p.m., at Elm Creek Fellowship Church in Elm Creek. A reception will be held immediately following the ceremony at the Elm Creek Country Club'*.

"She's a knock-out! But I don't know about her choice in a fiancé." James chided.

"Yeah, yeah, yeah … I honestly don't know what she see's in me, but whatever it is … I'm sure glad she does," Ben smiled with admiration as he looked at their photo in the Elm Creek Herald. "While we're on the subject, I've been meaning to ask you, would you do me the honor of being my best man?"

"Me?" James acted surprised, but was hoping he would ask him. "Aren't I a little old to be your best man?"

"Well, yes," Ben chided. "But old men can be best men too, that is if you can make it down the isle."

"Ha, ha, ha …" James feigned offense. "I'd be honored to be your best man."

"All kidding aside, you're my best friend, James. Thank you." The two men shook on it.

"Does the article say when U-M is coming?" Ben asked, as they moved their focus back to the Au Sable story.

"Looks like next week," James pointed to the sentence where it said Professor Virginia Hittorn is expected to visit the site with a team next Thursday. The story also said the county had closed the area off to visitors and set up barriers so no one disturbs it.

They were still reading the article when they heard car tires squealing ... then a loud crash. The two men ran to the edge of the shop driveway to see. Two cars had smashed and mangled into each other at the intersection of Main and Second Street, about four blocks away from the garage. They ran to the scene as James called 911 on his cell. People started to gather around. Both drivers were unconscious. They could see the woman in the blue Ford Focus squeezed up around the air bag. Blood was gushing from her head. Ben could see the ambulance on its way but they were fifteen miles out. He disappeared around the corner and teleported to the ambulance. It felt like a little bump in the road as the ambulance drivers found themselves suddenly a quarter mile away from the scene.

"Wow, I don't know how we did it, but we're here!" The driver looked at his partner, shaking his head, making sure he was seeing correctly.

"That's weird, I don't remember the drive over here ... but I'm not looking a gift horse in the mouth, let's go." They were told this was a pretty bad accident and were calling for the jaws of life.

Ben quickly went back to the scene, James didn't even notice he was gone as everyone gathered around. He knew he could bend that door back and get the woman out, but with her injuries, he might do more harm than good. He also couldn't do it with everyone there watching, so he stood feeling helpless with everyone else as the ambulance pulled up, sirens blasting. He didn't like that sound. It brought back memories of his father's death, but he learned to cope with it through the years.

The man in the gray Toyota Corolla had regained consciousness. The firemen were now on the scene, telling him to stay put until they got his vitals. Another team went to help the woman, along with the paramedics. The police arrived and closed off the road to keep onlookers at a distance.

"We can't save everyone." Ben could hear the words of his mother echoing in his mind every time something like this happened. At least this time he was able to get the ambulance there much sooner. *Thank you, Father,* Ben said to himself, then said a prayer out loud for each of the victims as James stood in agreement, along with others that were standing around, before they left the scene.

After they got back to the garage, they heard a helicopter. They watched from the driveway as they life-flighted the woman to Saginaw.

As the two men went back to work, Ben was reminded of his first time … When he was six.

He was over at his friend, Tommy Riley's house. They were playing in the barn and had climbed up into the loft. Tommy got too close to the edge and fell. He fell face first on the barn floor. He was unconscious and his face was bleeding pretty bad.

"Why did God give us these gifts if we can't use them?" Ben remembered asking his mother and grandmother. They were in the car on their way home from the hospital. "Why do we have to keep it a secret? Why can't anybody know about it?" He was crying. "Tommy's my friend, I had to help him," Ben sobbed.

"Honey, we're not saying you shouldn't have helped Tommy. We're just saying to think about the way you do it so people don't know you're doing something they can't do," Rachel sympathized with him. "Like, instead of teleporting Tommy to the living room, you could have taken him to the front door and kicked at the door and yelled for his mom …. Does that make sense?"

"I guess, but I was so worried about him I didn't think about that, there was so much blood." Ben began to cry again, "He wouldn't wake up. I thought he was gonna die!"

His mother added, "Remember the doctor said mouth wounds always look so much worse than they normally are because they bleed so bad? He's gonna be all right."

"Awe, Ben, honey, it's okay, we understand. It's hard when there's an emergency like that to remember to help them in a way no one knows about. We're not angry with you," his grandmother tried to comfort him too. "You'll see. You'll get really good at helping people with them not knowing you're doing anything they can't do. It'll be all right, honey."

Tommy's mother said she didn't even hear them come through the door. She was so concerned about Tommy she never gave it another thought.

"And Tommy's gonna be all right, you heard the doctor, right?. He stitched his lip all up, there's no concussion and he's gonna be just fine," Rachel said.

Today, his friend, Tom, still had the one and a half inch scar where they put twelve stitches from his lower right lip to the bottom of his chin.

That evening, Sarah was over visiting Sophie. Everyone was talking about the accident in town and the discovery of the steps at the Au Sable. After all, it's not every day the small town of Elm Creek has a huge accident in the middle of town and a story published in the newspaper that discovers ancient ruins all on the same day.

Ben was with his mother at home. They had just finished eating dinner and Ben was relaxing in the living room. The local television station showed the accident on the news. They found out the man came out of it with a broken arm. Both cars were totaled. Ben's mouth dropped when he heard them say the woman was Professor Virginia Hittorn from U-M. She survived with a severe head injury, which resulted in a mild concussion and two broken ribs. She had lost a lot of blood. Doctors said if she would have had to go another five to seven minutes without help, she may not have survived. They said she was on her way to visit the site where the boys discovered the stone steps at the Au Sable before bringing the team up when the accident happened. Then it showed a photo of her on the screen.

"Hey!" Ben let out a yell. "That's the demon lady from the restaurant!" He grabbed his cell to call Elizabeth. She was with her mom shopping for a wedding dress. Then he put his phone down … *Maybe now wouldn't be a good time to tell her that.*

Rachel was in the kitchen washing the dinner dishes. She stepped into the living room with a dish towel wiping her hands. "What?"

"See that woman?" Ben pointed to the television. "That's the lady from the restaurant, the blonde demon lady!"

"Whoa! That's the professor that's going to be handling the dig?" Rachel was blown away. "We should meet for prayer when Mom gets home tonight."

Ben agreed.

The news said they were going to either postpone the U-M visit until Hittorn recovered or see if they could find someone else to head up the initial inspection.

"I found the most beautiful dress, Ben!" Elizabeth called on their way home. "I wish you could see it!"

"I can't wait to see you walk down the isle wearing it," Ben smiled, thinking how beautiful she will look.

## CHAPTER 12 - DISCOVERY

"We also found the perfect dresses with our sage, caramel and apricot colors for Laura and Brooke. I think they're going to love them."

"They're perfect!" Ben could hear Sam in the background, "classy but not too over the top."

"Mom wants to know if your mom is there." Elizabeth said.

Ben gave his mother his phone. Rachel and Sam began talking about other wedding preparations, which he knew could go on for at least another half-hour to an hour.

While they were on the phone Ben went outside to talk to God. The sun was setting, this was one of his favorite times to pray as the last rays of light danced through trees. He prayed for direction. He prayed for wisdom and revelation in the knowledge of Him. That the eyes of his understanding would be enlightened to know the hope of His calling, like in the book of Ephesians, some of his favorite scriptures he memorized and used often.

The future memory the Starling showed him was haunting him. He kept seeing Elizabeth in a dark, black place, surrounded by hundreds of demons closing in on her. She was all alone … and … she was pregnant! "Oh God! Please show me what to do! I know You didn't allow the Starling to let me see that for nothing … if I couldn't do anything about it. Please show me what to do," Ben cried out loud to God. "Should I tell her about it? Should I keep this all to myself? Please, Holy Spirit, show me what to do."

Immediately the Holy Spirit showed him his grandmother and his mom … "Share this with them."

Later that evening after Grandma got home from her visit with Sophie, the three of them met for prayer. Elizabeth decided to stay at home and help her mother with more wedding plans so it was the perfect time for Ben to share this with them, and tell Grandma about the professor.

"No wonder you never wanted to talk about it," they both said, when he told them.

They each began to pray in English but wound up praying in their prayer language and interceding. With tears and supplication they prayed into the night, asking God to intervene, to show them the way through it, the way out.

Then about 1:30 a.m. Sarah began praising God and dancing. Her tears turned into shouts of joy. Ben and Rachel felt something change, a peace came over them.

"Come on, Mom ... don't keep us in suspense ... what did God show you?" Rachel finally asked.

Ben was so grateful, even before he heard the details – that God showed one of them something – he got on his knees and began thanking God for Elizabeth and their children to come.

"How about some tea?" Sarah looked at her daughter.

"That sounds like a great idea," Rachel went into the kitchen and made three cups of chamomile tea as they composed themselves and gathered around the kitchen table to hear what God showed Sarah.

"C'mon, Grandma, what did the Lord show you?" Ben was more than anxious.

Sarah's face lit up through her tears. They were tears of joy. She finally said, "I saw Lizzy and you ..." She began to sob again, "... and your son! .... He is so beautiful!" She could barely get it out, "...you were all healthy, happy and well! Rachel, you too! We all were. And it was finally over. Everyone was fine!"

Rachel grabbed her mother more tissues.

"The Holy Spirit is amazing! He showed me a glimpse of the future, along with all the thoughts and feelings, just like I was right there in it. Like I will be right there in it! Whenever it is." She smiled, "The demons were all gone from the temple." Sarah wiped her eyes again. "I also felt a closeness and gratitude towards the Willows. I believe they will become great allies and friends."

She continued, "I don't know how all of this will play out, but we need to stay in prayer and mind God. Be watchful and diligent. This is not going to be a walk in the park. It felt like we had overcome a great battle. Let's not take anything for granted, even if it seems like a small thing, let's share it with each other and do our best to stay on top of this."

"We can't try to run away from it. That'll just make things worse." Rachel interjected. "We need to do what we know to do – and do what we committed to do with the Willows, or God will not honor that."

They all agreed.

"For God has not given us a spirit of fear, but of power, of love and a sound mind." Sarah quoted her version of 2 Timothy 1:7. She reached out and gently held Ben's face in the palm of her hand and with the other, took Rachel's hand in hers. "And love is the greatest of them all. Perfect love casts out all fear."

Their faith and their resolve grew even stronger that night.

# Chapter 13 - Lessons Learned

The next couple of weeks were pretty normal. Wedding plans forged ahead with caterers, menus, invitations, dress fittings and the like. They saw on the news and in the paper that U-M decided to postpone their visit to the Au Sable until Professor Hittorn recovered. Which Ben thought, gave he and Elizabeth more time to finally get married!

Ben told Elizabeth about the professor, but never told her about the future memory the Starling gave him. He wasn't sure how she would take it and thought if she knew, it may change the outcome. *The Holy Spirit never told me to tell her.* Telling Mom and Grandma was enough. She stopped asking about it anyway, with the wedding on her mind and he was relieved.

They hadn't been seeing as much of each other these days. She was helping her mother with wedding preparations, as promised, and going to gown fittings. Every chance she got though, she was over training with Rachel. Ben tagged along and helped too. He wanted her gifts – all their gifts – to be as sharp as they could be for the times ahead, they all did. Sarah helped too. The four of them worked together as much as they could, prayed together as much as they could and went on with life and the wedding.

Sarah and Ben always loved the praise and worship portion of church because of the beautiful auras people gave off – that sadly – no one else could see. They loved to hear the word spoken by the preacher too, edifying and building up, teaching and equipping the saints. But when the congregation got caught up in the praise and worship portion of the service, their auras were magnified. The colors were so intense, the building would literally burst at the seems with light. And when the people really got caught up in singing to the Lord and forgot about their earthly miseries and set their whole hearts on heaven, sparkles of light would come out of their mouths and float to the ceiling as they sang. It would gather there at the highest point of the ceiling until the singing was over. There were times the entire ceiling sparkled. Ben and his grandmother wished it would happen in every service, but the things of this world weigh heavy on many. Even though they try to give it to God and leave it there at His feet, they find themselves picking it right back up. More often than not, only a few people – usually the same people – would sing with sparkles on a pretty regular basis.

In times of fervent prayer, auras grow in brightness as well. Ben saw the whole church building lit up one time, in the middle of the week, with light bursting through the seams of every crack and crevice. As he entered the building and came to the sanctuary, the only person there was the pastor – praying.

" … Everything in His Word is true. Don't take it for granted or try to reason the things of God away. Don't follow the masses. They are the blind leading the blind." Pastor Matt said, Sunday morning during service. It was the day before Labor Day. He talked about the horrific events in the world, the talk of one-world-order and the horrible events in the Ukraine. He lead a prayer for the people of Ukraine as Russia bore down hard on them.

"Don't look for the approval of men. You will find it, until they turn on you. Look for God's approval in everything you do and it will go well with you because the end is near. Be strong and courageous, knowing who you are in Christ. We are sons and daughters of the Most High God." He closed with this, "Make it your business to know Him through His Word, for there you will find the answers to every problem life can throw at you. Read His Word!"

After service Ben and Elizabeth met Pastor Matt in his office for their first marriage counseling session. His desk was neat, with minimal clutter. His various credentials from Bible colleges proudly hung behind his desk on the wall. Memorabilia and family photos donned his desk and the walls of the office from former Pastor Appreciation days and gifts from members in the congregation. A mug from Grandma was among them.

The chairs were comfortable. A box of tissues was always present at the corner of his desk. He had a large bookshelf against the wall to his right filled with books. One book in particular that caught Ben's eye was Smith Wigglesworth. *Now there was an awesome man of God!* Ben reached for the book and began reading the back cover when Pastor Matt returned from an unexpected errand.

"I apologize for the delay. Let's get started." Pastor Matt saw Ben with the book. "Have you read any of his books?" He asked.

"Yes, actually, Grandma has a couple. I haven't seen this one, though." Ben finished reading the back cover. It was entitled *Smith Wigglesworth on the Holy Spirit.*

"You can borrow it if you like, just remember to bring it back when you're through," the pastor was familiar with folks that forgot to bring his books back. "I think I will, if you don't mind," Ben smiled, "Thank you."

Pastor's wife, Katie, poked her head in the doorway to the office. She was of average height and just a little plump. Just plump enough to make her more lovable, Elizabeth always thought. She had short, curly, light brown hair, and was always full of energy. "I'm going to pick up some lunch for the four of us when you're through. How does pizza sound?"

Everyone loved the idea.

"Okay, so let's get down to business. We have a lot of ground to cover and a short time to do it." Pastor Matt wasn't one to waste time. "So ... marriage, eh? You two want to get married ....?" He smiled as he opened a folder. Actually, he was beaming ... knowing their backgrounds, their commitment to God and the fact that they were both still virgins. It was a great delight to him to be able to counsel them and help them in what he believed to be the potential for one of the most successful marriages he'd seen since he and his wife married some thirty-six years ago.

They talked about everything from arguing, fighting fair, money issues, bedroom issues, bathroom issues and more ... a couple things turned both Ben and Elizabeth a little red faced, being virgins, some of these subjects were things they hadn't thought about.

"... and don't speak negative things about your spouse or dwell on negative thoughts about them, because once you do, it magnifies into this gigantic whirlwind that can overtake everything in your relationship. You begin to focus on every negative thing about them and forget the good, when it should be the other way around. Speak positive things about them to others or you will lose their trust. Once trust is lost, it's hard to get back. Try to work your problems out between each other. If that don't work, talk with a Christian counselor or pastor, don't go talking to friends and family, if you can help it, that often-times makes things worse in the long run."

He continued, "Communication is the key. Remember to respect each other and honor one another. Words spoken in anger can never be taken back, mind what you let flow out of your mouth. It's best not to speak until you're calm. And if you are a stuffer, and don't tell your spouse when something is bothering you, that is a loaded gun waiting to go off! That's when resentment builds. It's not a good place to be. I mean, there are some things you can overlook and let roll off your back, but if you find they are sticking to your back, then you need to address it. Not in anger. Think it through before you express your feelings so you don't wind up saying things you'll regret. Have respect for each other and honor one another, even in times of disagreement, fight fair. And it will go well in your marriage."

Elizabeth and Ben took it all in. They highly respected Pastor Matt's opinion and felt they were better off having sat through his counseling. They had one more session to go. That was set for next week, five weeks before the wedding.

"So, what do you think of that news about the discovery at Lumberman's Monument?" Ben asked Pastor Matt and Katie during lunch.

"I think it's really interesting," said Katie. "Can't wait to see what it is."

"Ancient temple ruins isn't something we see everyday in our area." Elizabeth chimed in.

"Well, we don't know what it is yet," Pastor Matt added while chewing his pizza. "Personally, I'm going to wait and see what they dig up before I get all worked up about it."

"What's to get worked up about?" Ben asked, as he reached for another piece of pizza with extra bacon, black olives, mushrooms, pepperoni and sausage. The pizzas from Pepperoni Sam's, which was a family owned business in Elm Creek, were the best. These toppings were his favorite.

"Well," Pastor Matt paused to swallow, "I just think it may be a hoax. But if it's real, well, I guess that would make it pretty interesting."

"Pastor Matt," Ben wanted him to open up a little more, "personally, I think if it *is* a temple, that we, as Christians, need to go back to the Bible and re-read some of the text with these things in mind. I mean, it's happening all over the world and we can't deny the evidence forever. I think our history books are all wrong. The temples they're finding in Peru and other countries certainly weren't built with stone chisels and copper tools. They're precise right down to a thousands of an inch. And we're talking granite here, not some soft rock like limestone. The technology blows the engineers' minds. Some of it we couldn't duplicate today."

"So are you saying you think the Bible is wrong?" Pastor Matt asked.

"No, not at all," Ben retorted. "I think we are the ones who are wrong. God can't lie, like men. And the Bible has never been proven wrong. I think we – mankind and the Christian community – got it wrong because in our limited minds, the way humans think – that if we can't fathom it, than it couldn't be true." Ben continued, "There are spots in the Bible that just don't make sense, if you listen to most preachers today and from the past. And … we skip over some of the parts we don't understand because we don't take God at His word sometimes, we need an explanation that we can wrap our minds around, so the Christian world says things like, well, that was a metaphor, or the writer didn't have a better way to explain it. But I think they explained a lot of those things just as they happened, no metaphors, no miss-interpretations, just as they happened." Ben stopped and felt he'd said more than enough as he took another bite of pizza, waiting to see what Pastor Matt had to say.

"Wow, that was a mouthful, Ben." Pastor Matt said. "Some of what you're saying may be true," he confessed. "But I just want to wait and see what unfolds there."

*I can see this is gonna be a work in progress,* Ben thought. But he knew Pastor Matt loved the Lord with all his heart and the Holy Spirit would reveal it to him when the time was right.

Katie changed the subject and asked them how their wedding plans were going, since it was only six weeks away. Elizabeth began to tell her about the dresses and all the preparations, which took up the rest of their lunch conversation.

"Well, if there is anything I can do to help, let me know," Katie said before they parted ways.

They stopped at Elizabeth's house after church so she could change clothes. Her parents were having dinner with some friends so they decided to hang out there for while.

"Lizzy we need to think about our honeymoon." Ben smiled, taking her into his arms.

"Oh, wow ... yeah, I haven't really thought about that." She took a moment, "To be honest, Ben, I don't care where we go. Why do we need to go on a honeymoon anyway? We can go anywhere we want, whenever we want."

"Well, for one thing we need some alone time." He held her closer.

"Okay, yes, we do!" She hadn't allowed herself to think too much about sex for fear she wouldn't want to wait until they were married.

"Another reason is just to be able to tell our grandkids where we went on our honeymoon someday, that we even had a honeymoon. I think it'll be neat." Ben smiled his huge, warm smile.

"Yeah, and for my parents' sake ...."

"Right?" Ben chuckled.

"Well, I've always wanted to visit New England, Boston actually." She invariably loved history and had always wanted to see the old covered bridges.

"There's more than a hundred covered bridges in Massachusetts and five in Boston alone! I've always wanted to visit the Freedom Trail, see the Old North Church and all the other sites – Faneuil Hall and the Old Corner Bookstore. I'd just love to soak that all in," Elizabeth said. "But what about you? Where would you like to go?"

Ben smiled and shook his head, "Lizzy," he chuckled, "It truly doesn't matter to me. I'm good with Boston."

"Yahoo!" She let out a squeal.

"But we're traveling the regular way. I don't think it'd be right to use God's gifts for that." Ben confessed. "No teleporting."

"Okay, yeah, you're right." She got the laptop out and sat on the couch.

After some digging around for hotels and airline tickets, she said, "Oh my gosh! Ben come look at this."

He sat down next to her.

"Look at this!" Lizzy was definitely upset about something. "I hate COVID! I just noticed this at the top of the page." She continued, "We can get a first class, non-stop flight and a nice hotel right in town for six nights, all for around $2,000 but I don't want any part of these quarantine restrictions!"

At the top of the airline page it read: "COVID-19 Alert:" 'Travel requirements are changing rapidly, including need for pre-travel COVID-19 testing and quarantine on arrival.'

"Do you remember all the mess that happened in 2020 when this all began with people traveling and being stranded at airports? I don't want to get anywhere near an airport!" Elizabeth emphatically stated. "You never know when they're going to lock everything down again with all these variants out there."

"Wow, you're right. I don't want to get caught in any of that either. I'm sorry." Ben gave her a hug. "The day will come and we will go to Boston, I promise."

"Wherever we go, we need to drive."

"Yup!" He said. "I'm good with that. How about somewhere in Michigan? It is a great tourist state, after all."

"We could visit the beautiful Au Sable River and stay near Lumberman's monument. Wait – we already live here." Her voice trailed off with the last few words as her enthusiasm dwindled.

"We don't have to decide right now. Let's just give it some time and think about it."

A few moments passed. She closed the lid on the laptop and they just sat watching re-runs of re-runs on TV.

"I know where we can go!" Her smile returned after a half hour or so. "What about Copper Harbor? Rachel talked about how beautiful it was up there, the winding trails and the black stones on the beaches. I always thought that would be a cool place to visit." Then her smile disappeared again. No, that won't work, by late October they'll have snow up there, or a good chance of it. We need to visit that place in the summer."

"Okay, so let's think southern Michigan. Saugatuck is beautiful. Remember? Grandma took some of her pottery down there for an art show once. We went with her."

"Oh, yeah. I loved it there. We'll have to check that out." Elizabeth had had enough searching for the day and decided to forego their plans to go anywhere else for the day. She snuggled into Ben and fell asleep minutes before her parents arrived home.


That evening after Ben was home, he was thinking of the pastor's sermon from that morning. The part about not looking for the approval of men, because you will find it, until they turn on you. It reminded him of the first time he met Eliel ….

"There ain't no God! Bunch a damn sissies! Need to cry to God every time ya get hurt? God's just a crutch! There ain't no one listening! You don't need no crutch, you can make it on your own two feet! That's what my dad says, so I know it's true."

The ten-year-old boy kept hearing those words echoing over and over in his head as he sat in his favorite tree in the woods behind his house after school that day. *Was God a crutch?* Ben had never heard any of his classmates talk like that before. He'd heard them cuss sometimes, but not an outright attack on God like that.

One of the girls scraped her knee. It was bleeding pretty bad, so her friend prayed for her to get better and for God to take the pain away. Rory laughed at them and started making fun of them for praying. He was popular and even Ben thought Rory was pretty cool … until today. He felt a little guilty, too, because he didn't stick up for God, he chose to stay out of the conversation. He didn't know what to say.

As he sat pondering all of that in the tree, suddenly, he heard a voice, booming through the trees, "God *is* real!" … then softer, like a reverberation, "God *is* real … God *is* real."

Ben sat up even straighter on the tree limb – he looked around stretching his neck to get a better look at his surroundings … nothing … just as he started to relax again … tiny sparkling lights began to twinkle in front of him. Ben blinked a few times, thinking maybe he had something in his eyes. Then the lights began to turn slowly, moving counterclockwise in a cone-shaped whirlwind, of sorts. It was beautiful.

"He is all things to them that follow Him, even to carry them in times of need. Something everyone needs at times." A voice came from the sparkling lights as they grew in number. "He's more real than the tree you're sitting in." The lights began to take the shape of a man. A huge man with armor – and wings! In mid air!

*How did he know all that?* Ben was just about to get out of there and teleport home when he realized this might be the angel Mom and Grandma always talk about – Eliel!

Ben stayed.

"God *is* real. Just like your gifts are real, young Benjamin." A fully formed, honest to goodness angel, Ben guessed was about 20 feet tall, floated before him in mid-air. As he slowly opened and closed his wings, Ben could hear the wind swoosh beneath their power, but never felt any breeze from it. He wore golden armor. He was magnificent and glorious! Light glowed from him. He was much more radiant than Shemariah or any of the other Dubheians. Ben was afraid because of his overwhelming presence. He put his head down and just froze.

The being reached out and touched his chin, tilting his face upward. "I am Eliel, sent by the Father to watch over you."

As Ben looked again into the face of the angel smiling down at him, he began to quiver. He was so big!

"Don't be afraid young one." The angel smiled at him. "I've watched over you since the day you were born, like your generations before you."

Ben finally looked at his face and just stared at him as all the stories he heard Mom and Grandma tell of Eliel came flooding in. His quivering subsided and a wide smile emerged as his young face brightened and the two just smiled at each other for a few moments. The angel's smile felt familiar to Ben. An overwhelming pride and sense of grounding washed over him.

*It's all true! .... And Rory is so wrong!*

A feeling of anger welled up towards Rory and he felt ashamed for not sticking up for God. His face flushed hot. He wanted to go back there to that moment in time and punch Rory right in the face!

As Ben was thinking of tearing Rory up, Eliel began to shrink. His wings disappeared and his clothes changed. Now he was sitting on the branch with Ben. He looked about twelve, Ben guessed, his blonde hair was now cut the same as Ben's and his clothes looked like any other kid.

Ben remembered them telling him how Eliel could change like that and he was finally seeing it for himself! He was thinking they could both go and beat up Rory together!

Eliel sensed his thoughts. "God doesn't force anyone to believe in Him." Eliel's voice was different too; he sounded like any other kid. "It's right to be angry about what Rory did. And … it's okay to defend those that are weak."

"So I should have punched him in the face!"

"Well, no …."

"So what should I have done?"

"Everything except the fighting back part."

Ben thought for a moment, "You mean I'm just supposed to stand there and let him hit me in front of everybody?" Ben wasn't liking this scenario. Not because Rory could have physically hurt him, it was the embarrassment. He didn't want to look like a sissy!

"You could easily block him. But don't hit him back in anger like that. That's not how God wants His children to be. Besides, with your strength, you could kill him if you let your emotions get out of hand, Benjamin." Eliel leaped to the ground from the twenty foot branch.

"So what's my strength for," Ben followed and hit the ground with a thud, "if I can't use it when I need it?"

"Take my hand." Eliel reached for Ben. As they joined hands, Eliel took him straight up, like lightening into the atmosphere, morphing into the huge, magnificent angel he was as they went. His great wings opened up and steered them upward further and further until they reached the upper stratosphere, then into space itself. Ben didn't feel cold and he didn't feel hot. He knew there was no air up there, yet he was breathing.

*All believers are a peculiar people set apart and hated by many in the world.* Eliel spoke to him telepathically now. *The things of God are foolishness to those who are perishing. You and your family have been given gifts beyond what most believers have. Your family has served the Lord for many generations, showing great faith. You have been set in a place most believers do not go, but remember, your gifts are not for you, they are for God's glory. They are to help your fellow man and further the kingdom of God on earth,* he said as he pointed to the huge blue-green globe slowly turning in front of them.

Ben turned and saw the earth before them, how the clouds moved with it as it slowly turned, the flat land, the mountains and the oceans. It was a beautiful sight, a wondrous sight! It took Ben's breath away for a moment as the realization of where they were took hold. He clutched Eliel's huge armband as he stood on the edge of it and watched the earth move …. Eliel had grown that large.

Then Ben heard a sound. As he listened he realized it was coming from the earth. Kind of a humming - whale sound … it was beautiful. It was peaceful. *It's alive!*

*What you hear is Earth's song. Every planet, every star, every galaxy and every universe – everything the Lord has made sings to Him. Just like the birds, the trees and every living thing on earth sings praise to the Father, so the heavens do likewise.* Eliel explained.

Ben was amazed. *Do they all sound like that?*

*Each is unique. They sing in harmony with one another.*

He let out a boisterous laugh as he took Ben back down to the tree in the woods where he found him. Shrinking back down to an 'earth-size' giant, and setting Ben down ever so gently on the branch where he found him.

"Remember, young Benjamin, your Father in heaven loves mankind. The rain falls on the just and the unjust, alike. Defend those that cannot defend themselves using wisdom. Study the scriptures. Lay hands on no man suddenly. It is His will that everyone come to the knowledge of Jesus

Christ and be among many brethren, yet He gave everyone a free will. We cannot force them." Eliel then said, "I must go now, but be mindful of the story of Samson, do not be proud and arrogant so that although your days on this earth are numbered, they will be much better than Samson's." As twinkling lights began to swirl around him, he added, "Keep yourself, young one …. And praise be to the Living God, my God and yours." Then he was gone … all was silent.

Ben didn't know how long he sat there on the tree branch soaking it all in. Some of Eliel's answers to his questions left him with more questions. Finally, instead of teleporting, he walked the entire way home, with a light heart that day from his favorite spot in the woods. He knew the story of Samson in the Bible but planned on reading it again that night.

There was much joy in the house that evening as Ben shared his great adventure with his mother and grandmother, meeting Eliel for the first time and everything that happened; how he took him up above the earth and they saw it turning; how Eliel became this huge giant angel, so big he was standing on his armband! … how the earth sang … and about Rory.

As Ben climbed in bed that night he asked, "So, Mom, can I talk to Eliel anytime I want? Can I – like, call him?"

His mother smiled, she remembered asking those same questions when she first met Eliel. "That would be nice, wouldn't it? But angels are not ours to command, they are God's." She kissed his forehead as she tucked him in bed. "When we need something, we ask God. If He sees fit, He'll send an angel, but don't look for Him to. God wants us to feel after the Holy Spirit inside of us. For it's by the power of the Holy Spirit that the Father raised Jesus from the dead that lives in you, in all who believe. He's greater than any angel, He's the third part of the Godhead and the One that gives us power."

"So He's God, right? God lives inside of us." He looked puzzled. "Then how come I can't see and talk to Him like Eliel?"

"You mean in physical form?"

"Yes."

"We will when we get to heaven; that's what the Bible says. But for now, we're all being tested. If God popped out in front of us every time we were going to do something we shouldn't or got a little confused or wanted to go somewhere we shouldn't – that would be like cheating on the test. He wants people that are sincere, people that know how to apologize and be willing to change, to repent and call on His Name. The Bible says no man can see God and live. I personally believe that's because He's so wonderful and so beautiful, we'd kill ourselves trying to get back to Him. We'd say to heck with this life," his mother smiled her warm, soft smile that could soothe even the wild beasts, if she had a mind to show it to them.

Ben listened intently and smiled back at his mother sitting on the edge of his bed.

"So we have to live by faith here. Those that believe and pass the tests of this life will join Him in everlasting life. Then we'll be with God face to face, forever in the light."

"Okay," Ben yawned. "I guess that makes sense." He rolled over on his side. "I want to pass the tests." His sleepy little voice trailed off.

*My little ten-year-old is becoming such a man.* Rachel thought as she remembered the day they brought him home from the hospital, as all mothers do, no matter how old they get.

She kissed him good night as he drifted off to sleep thinking he would read Samson tomorrow.

Ben never again failed to help anyone in need, if it was within his power to do it. His time with Rory came soon enough. Ben did exactly as Eliel instructed, he blocked his punches, looking him straight in the eye … it only happened once. Rory was a little freaked out by it and never bothered anyone about praying or God again, at least not when Ben was around.

# Chapter 14 - The Great Rock

It was Friday, Elizabeth stood in her bathroom mirror looking at herself. She was going to be a married woman soon. *Six more weeks .... Will I look different?* She tilted her head and held up her left hand in the mirror to see what her engagement ring might look like to others. *It's beautiful! I'm so proud to be marrying Ben! The sweetest, most thoughtful, handsome man in the Northern Hemisphere! My superman! .... My real life superman!* She smiled at herself in the mirror as she pulled her hair up. *I'll look even better!*

"Father, please bless our marriage and keep our children safe," she whispered out loud. "And thank you for Your gifts. Sometimes they may not be what I want them to be, but I want Your will for my life. And if that means going through a little hardship here and there, then so be it." She smiled again at her reflection, "I trust you, Father." She stared at herself … "I want to get it, Lord." With a serious look, she said, "I want to be the best I can be for you. Please bless the gifts you gave me and help me to make them as powerful as you meant them to be in my life, for Your glory."

Just then she heard Ben pulling in. He got out of work early – noon, to be exact. *Time for more training!* She bounced out of the bathroom and met Ben at the door.

"Bye, Mom, not sure when I'll be home, but I'll be at Ben's."

"Okay, honey," her mother answered from the laundry room. "Love you!"

"We love you too." They both answered as they headed out the door.

## CHAPTER 14 - THE GREAT ROCK

Rachel was already outside by the big maple. A huge rain storm went through in the early morning hours. All the foliage looked surreal, it was such a vibrant green.

"When it rains like that, you can feel the plants and trees from a much greater distance," Rachel smiled. "It's really cool. Give it a try Lizzy."

Elizabeth focused on the maple. After a few moments she said, "Oh, wow! Yes! I'm seeing, what? A ten or fifteen mile radius?" She could see everything the plants were seeing. She could focus in on any particular area she wanted. "It even seems clearer than normal."

"Yeah, it's really neat how a good fresh rain can do that to the roots."

"How long does this usually last?"

"Depends on how deep the rain soaked in and how dry it's going to get over the next few days. I've seen it last a week or so." Rachel answered." This is the first really good rain we've had in awhile."

"Yeah, because this is the first time I've experienced this." Elizabeth was enjoying the view.

"It's got to soak the ground pretty good and I think the last time was around the time you were just getting started. It only lasted a few days."

"Oh, my gosh!" Elizabeth said with a shaky voice, tears welling in her eyes.

"What is it?" Ben asked.

"The water!" She paused. "It's been here all along! Through everything! The water is as old as the earth! It's alive! And it remembers!"

Rachel and Ben both smiled and kept quiet to let her experience it.

"No more, no less." Elizabeth was overwhelmed by it, "It just keeps regenerating in the clouds over and over. Nothing is lost and God never has to add more to it."

Sarah had walked up as Elizabeth was still talking and overheard her. "In the books of Adam and Eve, Adam talks about how the water was in the garden of Eden and it flowed out from under the roots of the Tree of Life.

From there it split into the four rivers over the earth. It was the only thing on the earth that was from the garden, really. Adam said they never cared for or had any use for it when they had their bright nature. They never even really thought about it, but now it meant everything."

Elizabeth teared up again. Rachel and Sarah did too.

"When Adam and Eve realized it was the same water that flowed from the Tree of Life," Sarah added, "they threw themselves in it and tried to kill themselves, again, hoping God would let them back in the Garden. They did kill themselves, actually, and God sent His Word, which we all know is the Lord Jesus, to bring them back to life … again."

"Oh, my gosh, Grandma! That's terrible!" Elizabeth said.

After a few moments Sarah asked if they all wanted to go back into the house for a bit, she had something to show them.

As they walked back to the house Elizabeth was still taking it all in. "It's just so amazing! We're bathing in the same water that Jesus was baptized in! We're drinking the same water King David drank."

"Yeah, it's hard to wrap your mind around," Rachel added. "It's very cool."

"Scientists have known this for a long time, and it's crazy how no one talks about it. They don't teach it in school, they may mention it, but don't really explain it, so no one really gets it. But they've recently come to theorize that water has a memory," Ben remarked. "Some scientists from Germany are experimenting with it, I think."

As they entered the house, Sarah asked them all to sit at the kitchen table. One of her coffee mugs was at each of their places. They all sat down.

"Hey, there's nothing in here," Ben joked, putting the mug back on the table.

After Sarah took her seat, she said, "Watch." She looked at Rachel's mug and it began to float above the table! They all sat back in their chairs.

"Mom, are you doing that?" Rachel asked, looking at her mother, then at Ben.

"Don't look at me, it's all Grandma!" Ben exclaimed.

Sarah didn't stop there, while Rachel's mug was still in the air, one by one, she began to levitate all their coffee mugs. Then, one by one, she set them back on the table. The final one, her mug, she caused to twirl a few times before setting it down.

"Grandma, that's awesome! How long have you been working on this?" Ben asked.

"Just today. I was in the shed working on a mug on the wheel. After I cut it free, the idea just popped into my head to give it a try. So I said, okay, Lord, that would be cool! And it worked!"

"One more gift to add to our arsenal," Ben said. "Way to go Grandma!"

"Grandma, you rock!" Exclaimed Elizabeth. "I wish I could do that."

"You know what? I think you can! I think God is strengthening and multiplying our gifts because of the end times." Sarah said emphatically. "Give it a try! Rachel you too."

Elizabeth stared at the mug. "Was it hard at first? How long did it take the first time?"

"Actually it wasn't all that hard. I just had faith and accepted that I could do it and wow! It happened pretty quick." Sarah added, "But even if it doesn't work right away, keep trying."

"Oh! …. I did it!" Rachel exclaimed, "Look!" There it was, her mug, floating above the table.

"Praise the Lord!" Her mother shouted. "Lizzy, I think you've been given that gift too, just accept it, feel it. Ask the Holy Spirit to reveal it to you."

Elizabeth felt the Holy Spirit nudging her to accept it as fact and just believe it. She saw it right there before her eyes, first with Grandma, then with Rachel. *I can do this!* A few more moments and … there! Her mug was floating above the table too!

"How cool is this?" She squealed as the mug continued to obey her. She lifted it higher, then floated it over to Ben and sat it down in front of him. "Does this mean I can call and skip rocks across the water like you, Ben?"

"Probably so!" He was beyond happy for all of them. He always wished the rest of his family could do the things he could. He never liked being the only one.

Sarah talked with Ben about the fact that if God was increasing their gifts, then He was probably increasing his at the same time. "Have you tried anything new lately? Something you haven't tried before? Or maybe something you tried in the past and couldn't do?"

"No, but I'm going to now." He admitted.

"What's the heaviest thing you've ever lifted?" His grandmother asked.

"A pickup truck," he exclaimed. "But now I'm thinking of trying some boulders."

"That's a great idea because I'm wondering if size isn't the issue, if it's not all in our heads. We have to overcome our own doubts," Sarah added. They all agreed they would keep working at lifting larger things.

"What do you say we all take a trip to ... I don't know ... how about Arizona?" Ben ran his fingers through the beard on his chin, thinking .... "Let's go to the Grand Canyon."

"Wait!" Rachel interrupted. She knew once Ben made up his mind they would all be there before you could blink. "Let's remember to change our clothes and get some water."

Sarah, Elizabeth and Rachel went to the secret room upstairs and found their "traveling" clothes, Rachel grabbed the canteens, washed and filled them with fresh water. Their ensemble included big, floppy, straw hats to hide their faces from satellites, various colors of camouflage clothing –

## CHAPTER 14 - THE GREAT ROCK

Sarah chose brown today – *that color should go well against the river,* gloves and heavy work boots.

Ben wanted to see if he could scan the area he was thinking of. He had never tried to look that far away before. He closed his eyes and concentrated … yes! It was a secluded spot on the Colorado River with huge rocks scattered along the sides and in the center … and … where humans were scarce. "There's nobody in the area."

After their clothes were changed, hair tucked under their hats and canteens of water attached to their belts, they looked like special forces from Vietnam or somewhere, with those big floppy hats. They would always laugh at each other. But no one would recognize them, that's for sure.

They gathered in a circle after setting their cell phones on the table. As they were putting on their gloves, Ben reached his arms around them and said, "Remember, don't look directly up so the satellites can't pick up your face … Ready?"

In the blink of an eye the four found themselves standing on the edge of the Colorado River. The breathtaking, steep rock formations on either side of the narrow banks echoed the sounds of water as it gracefully flowed down the river. Pink granite rocks and boulders sat scattered along this stretch of the riverbed. There was a huge one about the size of Sarah's clay shed in the middle of the river. Ben had his eye on it as everyone else took in the scenery.

As he approached the magnificent, ancient rock, the life energies glowing from it were beautiful and intense – blues, yellows, reds and greens. The entire place was glowing from the energy of the high rock faces. Every river gave off its own wonderful energy. He looked back and saw his three companions wasting no time lifting some pretty hefty looking boulders. His grandmother gave him a nod; she was also admiring the different energies.

He smiled back at her as he found the closest spot to his target on the bank. He bowed his head. "Father, please open the eyes of my understanding, for Your glory."

Elizabeth saw it first, "Look!" She pointed to the boulder in the middle of the river floating in mid-air. All their rocks suddenly fell to the ground as they watched Ben move the enormous piece of granite to the river's edge and set it down next to him. The rock dwarfed Ben. It was much taller than any of them expected. They were all speechless as they walked around it. The lower half was mostly covered in mud. The wet parts glistened in the hot Arizona sun. It was magnificent!

They all touched it and felt a great sense of inexplicable peace as the sun's rays danced off the wet, diamond-like quartz and feldspar in the granite.

After a couple minutes, Ben said, "Okay, it's time to put it back." The great rock was the size of two of Grandma's sheds, one on top of the other.

"Hey, there's some carving on here, inscriptions and things!" Sarah was fascinated as she wiped off what mud she could from the lower half. "Do you know where my camera is?" She said looking at her grandson.

"Your regular camera?" He asked.

"Yes. Should be in my study on the bookshelf behind my desk."

"Got it." Ben disappeared and was back in about five seconds with camera in hand. "Right where you said it was," he held the black case out to his grandmother. She expeditiously took about twenty photographs before Ben lifted it again. Without a sound and seemingly with little to no effort, he set the enormous rock right back where he found it, in the middle of the river. The positive energy force emanating from it was not only beautiful, but powerful, almost magnetic.

"Do you feel that?" Ben looked at everyone.

Elizabeth and Rachel said they felt overwhelmed by it – a great sense of peace – as if they were being drawn to it. They weren't sure if it was their emotions or something else.

Sarah saw the magnificent beauty of its energy. "I do feel it, Ben. It feels magnetic!"

"My thoughts exactly!"

After a few more minutes of admiring their surroundings, Ben said, "Well, I think it's time to go."

The four of them spent the rest of the weekend close to the house, lifting everything they could think of while honing their speed and accuracy in moving objects. They each improved everyday.

That next Thursday, two days before the wedding shower, Elizabeth and Ben met with Pastor Matt for their last marriage counseling session. He gave more godly wisdom about marriage and children. How parents need to be on the same page when it comes to discipline and support the other, not allowing the kids to play one off the other, which is so common in today's society where one parent will give in, against the will of the other. How that, in essence, teaches the children manipulation, which is, at it's core, a form of witchcraft.

Ben didn't mention anything further about the temple at the Au Sable to Pastor Matt. He would wait for the Holy Spirit's nudging before bringing it up again.

The wedding shower was held, Saturday, September 16. It was great fun. Sam decided to have it at the church inside the fellowship hall. It could hold around seventy-five people, which was way bigger than they needed, since they only invited around thirty people. They played some fun games the guests enjoyed. Elizabeth and Ben got some wonderful gifts. With them moving in with Grandma after the wedding, their list of needs weren't as big as others, since Grandma already had everything, spices, kitchen appliances, washer, dryer, beds and all the bathroom amenities most newly weds would need. They felt so blessed. So they decided to ask for things like bed sheets, a comforter, bath towels, etc.

Laura did a great job keeping track of what each gift was and who gave it. She and Brooke volunteered to help Elizabeth with the thank you cards the following Tuesday. John grilled steaks for everyone that evening after work and Sam fixed all the trimmings. The thank you cards, fashioned after the wedding colors of apricot and caramel, were all mailed out promptly on Wednesday morning.

# Chapter 15 - The Reptilians

The last Tuesday in September, Ben's Baby Ben wind-up glowed 2:30 a.m. from his nightstand. The old alarm clock was a gift from Grandma. He loved it, it was so loud, it could wake him no matter how deep his sleep. But he couldn't sleep tonight. He felt restless. He couldn't put his finger on any one thing … *was it Elizabeth?* He didn't think so. *She did great all weekend. The shower was awesome and she was really happy with the way it turned out.* Was it the wedding? *Lizzy and her mom got that under control and are ahead of schedule.* So what was it? *Is it Mom?* She was off work with a cold. They didn't want her to come in until she tested negative for COVID. Her results wouldn't be in until tomorrow. *No, she's barely sick, it's not Mom.*

An image formed in his head of big, black helicopters, he could even hear them. Behind them he saw two larger craft hovering …. *The Reptilians!* He recognized their ships.

Throwing his covers off, Ben changed into his black clothes. He woke Mom then went to Grandma's and woke her.

"They're at the monument." Ben told them as he pulled the black ski mask over his face. I need to see what they're up to.

"We'll stay alert in case you need us," Rachel said as she put on a pot of coffee.

Ben was up river from them in the woods about 100 yards away. He had a pretty good view but couldn't hear them talking. He heard heavy machinery. As he made his way closer he realized they were digging! *They're looking for something in the temple.* He edged his way closer. There were no trucks. *How'd they get the excavator and backhoe here?* He realized they must have carried them in on two of the three helicopters parked in a clearing they had obviously created nearby. There was no clearing in that part of the woods before. *And the third one to carry away whatever it is they expect to find.*

He teleported back home. "Mom, I need you to come with me. Do you feel well enough? I'm hoping you can get a sense of what they're digging for, unless you and Grandma, together, can do it from here. But with the Reptilians there, you may need to get closer." Reptilians had the ability to block 'seeing' from the spiritual realm, to a certain extent.

"We've been concentrating on you and that temple all this time and can't see anything." Sarah said, "Rachel is probably going to have to go with you. I'll go too, if you want."

"No, Grandma, I need you here to be our anchor." Ben didn't want to put his grandmother in danger unless there was no other choice. Plus, he knew she would keep praying for them.

Just then his mother came down the stairs all dressed in black. "I'm ready, and yes, I'm fine."

Back at the Au Sable, Ben brought Rachel to the opposite side where he was before. They were silent, listening …. He signaled to her that he was taking them closer. Instead of walking, Ben teleported her closer. He brought her about 50 yards away but never let go of her in case he had to move them back or get out of there. Then he moved them to about 100 feet away, under good tree and brush cover. Rachel signaled to him that was good. Ben tried to listen through the noise of the heavy equipment while Rachel concentrated on their thoughts.

They could see about twenty men, dressed like soldiers, all in camo.

## CHAPTER 15 - THE REPTILIANS

The excavator was hard at work digging. There was a huge pile of dirt. The backhoe was pushing it into a pile as the excavator brought it out of the deep tunnel they had already dug. He saw two Reptilians working with the men, probably directing the dig because they remembered the layout of the temple. They were about eight feet tall. Ben always thought they looked like cartoons with their tails, scales and alligator-like heads. Their heads were like a cross between a gator and a gecko. He especially thought about cartoon figures tonight as the occasional light that shined on them from the headlights of the machinery only allowed small glimpses of their outlines.

But what were they looking for exactly?

"We're almost there!" Ben heard one of Reptilians remark in English. They had distinct, raspy voices.

Rachel signaled to Ben it was time to leave. They couldn't talk there and she got the information she was looking for.

At the house Rachel said, "I couldn't tell if they're a branch of the government, or some other group, but they're looking for gold and artifacts … and … the tombs of the priests. The Reptilians are helping them find the treasures in exchange for the bodies of the priests. They want to control the demon spirits embodied in them."

"Oh, man, we can't have that," Ben said. Then he disappeared. He knew exactly where the tombs of the priests were from the memory of the Starling. The diggers were only about 30 feet away. He had to stop the dig somehow.

He remembered the huge granite stone from the Colorado River. *That would do it.* He teleported to it. Even though it was pitch dark, he knew he was standing on top of it in the middle of the river. He could hear the rushing water around him as he put his hands on the great rock, "Come on, baby, I've got a job for you!" He put it smack-dab in front of the tombs. There was a rumble in the ground, a small earthquake, as the earth moved to make way for the giant rock. It positioned itself right where Ben asked it to, in front of the diggers, blocking the tombs.

The workers all stopped as the earth shook under their feet. It only lasted for about three seconds. They stood still for a moment, then continued working. Men were pulling what looked like a modified mining cart with regular tires into the newly made tunnel, led by one of the Reptilians.

*They're hoping to bring that out filled with gold and jewels, no doubt.*

Ben just wanted to make sure they couldn't get to the tombs…

It wasn't long when the excavator came out of the tunnel with no dirt. The driver exited his vehicle and sought out one of the Reptilians and what appeared to be the human in charge. He couldn't hear what they were saying, but the Reptilian got in the excavator with the driver and they re-entered the tunnel.

Ben waited ….

The Reptilians always seem to have an agenda that is self-serving. They aren't as benevolent towards humans as most of the other extra-terrestrials. They preferred to work with governments, trading technology for favors – *looking the other way, mostly, cattle mutilations, human abductions.* Ben didn't trust them. They were prone to twisting the truth just enough to make their agenda seem reasonable. *What are they gonna do with demons? Why would they want them?* Ben was getting concerned; they still hadn't come out of the tunnel. Although the Reptilians had immense strength compared to humans, he highly doubted even a team of them would be able to move that huge piece of granite.

Ben suddenly began to feel they were watching him from the ship above. He immediately teleported to the Rocky Mountains and waited a couple minutes on a cliff ledge to be sure they weren't able to follow him somehow, then he went home.

## CHAPTER 15 - THE REPTILIANS

Back at the house, they prayed in the name of Jesus for wisdom and revelation in the knowledge of the Father of glory, asking Him to open the eyes of their understanding that they might know His will in this.

While they were still praying, without a sound, the slightest twinkling of tiny, white orbs of light began to dance around each of them. Sarah noticed it first. Her face lit up with a wide smile. She kept silent and watched as the lights danced to the center of the room becoming a sphere. Rachel and Ben saw it too, now. Ollie and Cookie came in from lounging in the kitchen and were as excited as everyone else! Cookie was dancing on her hind legs, waiving her front paws in the air and Ollie was whining and panting with his tail wagging emphatically as they paced back and forth around the living room, waiting. They all watched as the ball of light stretched out and 'unzipped.' Eliel stepped through the light, with his magnificent wings and armor, glowing white and filling the house with the peace of the Lord.

"Greetings in the name of the Father of light," Eliel's deep, resounding voice echoed through the walls of the home he had visited for six generations. The house seemed to welcome him.

As he shrank down to man-size Eliel – he gave the dogs a proper greeting, knowing they would be beside themselves until they got to say hello. Then he said, "The Father has sent me to tell you the Reptilians want control over the demons to use them for the final battle."

Eliel never wasted time getting to the point. "They are in league with the anti-Christ, who is working even today, planning strategies for the end. They believe the demons from the temple will be a great asset in seducing God's holy people, turning them away from the Truth."

"Help us, Jesus," Sarah whispered her thoughts out loud.

"Benjamin, the great rock you placed in front of the tombs tonight will keep them from going any further." Eliel said.

"I'm glad to hear that," Ben admitted.

"It is inscribed with the teachings of the Messiah."

They all paused a moment to let that soak in …

"So … John 10:16! … Jesus *did* visit the Americas while He was here!" Sarah said in amazement.

"Yes. He stood on that very rock and spoke to the peoples of that area. Later they inscribed his teachings on the rock." Eliel added, "The rock is sacred. The Reptilians cannot pass over it. They have become confused and can no longer see what is beyond it."

Ben bowed his head and thanked the Lord at His awesome works to lead him to that rock. His abilities seemed so small and insignificant at that moment. He repented for having even the slightest feeling of pride in himself for making that happen. He realized it was all the working of the Holy Spirit! *The gifts truly belong to the Father. We're just using them.*

Rachel went over and kissed her son on the forehead. "I'm so proud of you!" She hugged him.

"Proud of me? The Holy Spirit is the one. He led me there!" Ben confessed.

"But you heard him," his mother smiled.

"Okay, yes, I heard Him."

"I think they saw me tonight," Ben admitted after a pause.

"Do not worry." Eliel smiled, "They were watching you, but they cannot follow you and they do not know who you are. You are clouded to them because of the Holy Spirit. Even when you speak with them face to face, they cannot see who your are."

"Thank you, again, Holy Spirit!" Ben resounded with a sigh of relief.

"Would you like to stay and have some coffee or tea with us?" Rachel asked Eliel.

He accepted the invitation.

"So what about the other E.T's? Like the Willows? They know who I am." Ben asked Eliel.

"The Willows are the guardians of all the trees and plant life, appointed by the Father. The Holy Spirit does not have to protect you from them because they are with us."

"Wow … I just wish Lizzy was here right now to be a part of this." Ben didn't want her to miss this time with Eliel. "Would it be all right, Eliel, if I went and got her? It should only take a few minutes."

"Yes, bring Elizabeth." Eliel answered.

Ben pulled out his phone to text her.

Rachel stopped him, "I've got a faster way now, Ben," she smiled as she closed her eyes. After a moment she said, "I woke her. Give her a minute; she's getting dressed." It was now around 3:30 a.m.

Elizabeth got up immediately after Rachel woke her and told her about Eliel being there. She pulled her hair up in a quick bun, brushed her teeth as fast as she could and threw on a pair of jeans and a t-shirt. She almost forgot to lock her bedroom door, she was so excited to see Eliel again. She didn't want to miss anything. Her parents were sleeping. *But you never know.* She knew that with her new-found abilities, she would be able to sense if they were trying to wake her – banging on the door – she could have Ben bring her back before they got too flustered.

While they waited for Elizabeth, Sarah interjected, "Eliel, our gifts are really increasing. We three girls can levitate objects now and communicate telepathically. It's awesome!"

"Yes, the Lord has increased all of your gifts for the times ahead. Ben, you will be able to communicate with them more easily as well, practice it." Eliel said.

"Awesome! I will," answered Ben.

"There are other gifts you all share that will present themselves when you need them," Eliel added. "Listen to the Holy Spirit. He will guide you."

Although they each wanted to ask him what they were, they knew by his choice of words, they would discover them when it was time.

"Lizzy's ready, Ben," Rachel said.

He disappeared and was back in less than a minute.

"What took you so long?" Rachel smiled.

"I had to kiss her!" Ben beamed.

"Eliel! It's so nice to see you!" Elizabeth said as Eliel stood and gave her a hug.

"And it's nice to see you, Elizabeth. Congratulations to you both on your engagement." Eliel took her left hand purposefully to look at her ring. "It's beautiful." He looked at them both with a more serious look, putting Ben's hand on top of hers. As he held their hands in his, he added, "May the blessings and favor of the Father continue to be upon you and protect you wherever you go. As He did the night this ring was given." He looked down at the ring again, then released their hands and embraced them both.

Just then, Rachel came in holding the large, ornate silver tray with a matching tea set that had been in the family for generations. Eliel remembered it well. She set the tray on the coffee table. As they each made their coffee or tea, they filled Elizabeth in on what happened at the Au Sable.

"No wonder I felt so much peace when I touched that rock," Elizabeth remarked. The others nodded remembering they felt the same way.

"So I was going to go over there and take a look after the sun comes up, would you like to come with me?" Ben looked at Eliel.

"I cannot interfere anymore than what the Father allows. But … perhaps." Eliel reached for the tea tray to make himself another cup of coffee.

"Sarah, do you remember what your grandfather told you about this silver set?" Eliel looked over at her, stirring his coffee.

"Yes!" She smiled, realizing Eliel apparently did too. "I do remember. He said it was a gift from a pastor. He and his wife gave it to my 6th great-grandparents on their wedding day, in 17… something … and it has never tarnished!"

"To Samuel and Rebekah Brought in 1741!" Eliel smiled. "Ten generations before you, Ben."

"Wow, yeah," Ben was thinking, "they would be my 8th great-grandparents wouldn't they?"

"You were there weren't you, Eliel?" Rachel beamed as her eyes welled up with tears.

Eliel just smiled as he looked over the workmanship. *I am glad to see you still use it. It was meant to be used, not set on a shelf somewhere.*

Realizing that same tea set would be her responsibility some day, Elizabeth became a little emotional. *I've used and washed that tea set so many times!* They never told her the history of it. She was overwhelmed. Yes, it was just a tea/coffee set, but it had been in the family for ten generations!

"The gifts of God that you possess have followed the line of Noah since ancient times." Eliel explained. "Appearing in some generations and not in others. Samuel and Rebekah were the first in your line to receive gifts once again, after more than a millennia of darkness, following the great persecution after the Savior returned to heaven. When the word of God was taken from you and knowledge was shut up."

"Yeah, the dark ages," Ben added. "They were in darkness all right. All the Christians were martyred – the only light in the world. They became so ignorant and full of themselves, they even thought the world was flat and they'd fall off the edge if they went too far. They had no prior knowledge of the planets and the stars because it was all taken. They basically started from scratch again."

"Right?" Rachel interjected. "They all knew in Jesus' time and before, about the planets and the stars. They understood how the planets were round and revolved around the sun and all that. It only took a couple generations for mankind to lose all that after the books were burned. And we still pretend that no one had this knowledge prior to modern times, although it's in the books of Enoch and all over cave drawings and ancient temples," she shook her head.

Eliel looked at Sarah. "It was during the time of the Great Awakening. Samuel and Rebekah had great faith, like children, never doubting the Father's word and eager to learn and experience more. Always thinking of others and willing to sacrifice whatever was needed to see His will done, even before they married."

"Eliel, thank you for sharing all that! I ... " Sarah stopped and looked around the room at her family, "all of us ... have always wondered when the gifts began and the story behind it."

"You are welcome, Sarah," Eliel smiled. "The Father heard you."

They all sat around talking in the living room for awhile about the past.

Then Eliel looked over at Ben, "Benjamin, it is almost dawn ... I will go with you."

With all the family history being discussed, Ben almost forgot about the temple at the Au Sable. "All right!" He gave a 'booyah' with his fist as he got up from the couch, "I'll go get ready."

"Remember you need to take me home first, Ben," Elizabeth called to him from the bottom of the stairs.

"Oh, yeah, that wouldn't be good," he chuckled.

The morning sun was just peaking through the trees. The birds were already awake and singing. The late September morning breeze was a little chilly. The air smelled so crisp and clean at the river. It felt peaceful, in spite of what took place just a few hours ago.

Everything was covered up with fresh dirt. Even their footprints and the tracks from the heavy equipment were gone. But anyone could tell there was some kind of digging going on, if they knew the area. Three large piles of trees were lying on the ground where they created the clearing for the helicopters. But with no one allowed on the site right now, who would even ask? *Clever* ....

"Will they be back?" Ben asked Eliel.

"The mercenaries found what they were looking for. They will not be back." Eliel answered. "They were hired as independent contractors by an obscure branch of the government. If I told you their name it would do you no good. They would seek you out for even knowing it ...." He continued, "The Reptilians will come back when Professor Hittorn gets close to the tombs."

"Okay, so ... will she be working with them?"

"No, she will have no knowledge of them."

Ben asked if he should put the stone back in the river. Eliel said no, its presence will be of great significance as things unfold.

Ben said his goodbyes to Eliel at Elizabeth's and his favorite spot on the river, which was only a couple hundred yards from where the digging took place. He thanked Eliel for coming and for sharing that family history with them. It meant so much to them all.

Everyone was tired after being up all night. Rachel was still there, sleeping in the recliner in the living room, tucked in with a blanket from her old room. She wanted to be there in case Ben needed her again. Sarah went back to bed and Elizabeth was safely home.

Ben yawned and stretched as he longed for his own bed just then. Instead, he reached for the left over coffee his mother had made a few hours ago when this all began. It was a little warmer than he expected and decided that would suffice as he poured it into one of his favorite travel mugs he kept at Grandma's, after changing his clothes.

He woke his mother in the recliner and filled her in on what happened at the river before he left for work.

# Chapter 16 – Commiseration

It was the first Saturday in October. Ben took his truck to pick up Elizabeth for more training. On their way back, they saw three Hereford cows, one in the middle of the road and two standing in the shallow ditch. They had apparently gotten out of their pasture somewhere nearby. Ben stopped and they both exited the truck. The white-faced cows stopped eating grass long enough to look up at them. One let Elizabeth get close. She began to tell Ben where they were from when he interrupted her.

"I already know, I heard you! I heard you talking to the cow!" Ben walked closer to her in amazement. "A couple miles down that side-road, right?" He pointed in the direction of the farm.

He couldn't take his eyes off her. At that moment when his mind connected with hers, her beauty glowed, not just the gorgeous redhead on the outside and the wonderful aura surrounding her. She glowed from deep within. She was so beautiful, he was overwhelmed. He felt her love for him and she felt his love for her in a way that was so deep, to their very souls.

He was filled with passion. He took her in his arms. Their emotions welled up inside them. Suddenly the cows were of little significance. They kissed as never before, with such voracious hunger their bodies ached for one another. After a few moments, Ben pulled away just enough to look deep into her eyes with tears welling up,

"Oh, Lizzy, I ... I ..." The pain in his face was evident. He never finished the sentence. He used every ounce of strength he had to resist what his body was aching for. They both just held each other and wept as they stood alongside the roadway.

In those few moments, they both realized how easy it would be to forget their commitments to each other and to God, and just let their passion take over. They were glad they stopped before that happened, each knowing the other was worth the wait.

After a few moments, Elizabeth said, "Let's take them back."

"The cows? You mean you can have them follow us? …. In the truck?"

"Yes, I think so." The other two cows had also come close to them now. They got back in the truck, turned around and slowly headed down the side-road and the cows followed them. It was as if they were tied to the truck.

As they crept down the road, Elizabeth smiled over at Ben, admiring his strength. Not his physical strength, which was awesome, but his inner strength. She reached over from the far side of the truck and touched his arm. Not wanting to sit too close at the moment for fear neither of them could resist another onslaught of passion.

"I love you so, so much, Benjamin Adan … three more weeks … just three more weeks." She smiled her huge, warm smile, "We're worth the wait. We got this."

"We *are* worth the wait," he beamed, obviously having regained control of himself by that time. "And … I want God's blessing and favor over our lives, even in this. I don't want to mess that up."

"Me either," Elizabeth said, "me either."

They rode the rest of the way in silence.

"Their farm should be up here on the right," Elizabeth said after they went about a mile and a half.

Ben knew the place. "I think this is that young couple's farm."

"Do you know them?"

## CHAPTER 16 - COMMISERATION

"No, I know *of* them. Grandma had mentioned them a few years ago when they first moved in. I don't come this way very often, but when I have, I've seen the guy out working and kids playing in the yard."

"Uh ... how are we going to explain these cows following us?" Elizabeth looked around realizing it probably was a little odd.

"Hmm ..." Ben looked around, "Maybe I should borrow some feed from Sophie." He stopped the truck just out of sight of the house and looked to see if Sophie, or anyone was in her barn at the moment. No one was there. "Be right back," he said to Elizabeth as he put the truck in park and vanished. Elizabeth sat there hoping no one would go by just then and ask if everything was all right. Just as she was considering sliding into the driver's seat, Ben re-appeared with sweet feed spilling over the large metal scoop he had borrowed as well.

"Here we go!" Ben put the truck in gear after handing the sweet feed to Elizabeth. As they approached the driveway it looked as if no one was there. The cows followed all the way in. Elizabeth went around the back of the truck and fed the cows from the feed scoop while Ben knocked on the front door. No one answered. He scanned the house, the barn and the entire property. No one was there. Their closest neighbors were a half mile further down the road. The other cows were gone as well. Ben remembered them having at least fifty head of Herefords the last time he drove by their place.

"I think they're out looking for the rest of their cows," Elizabeth said as she led the three they had found to the gate.

Ben scanned the fences and found the weak spot along the road just past the house. He also saw some other weak areas. "Lizzy, I'm going to see if I can fix some of this for them."

"Can I come with you?" She didn't want to stay there alone in the driveway.

"Sure, let's go," Ben took her hand in his and they disappeared.

The fence posts were wood. One was broken off, lying flat on the ground and the two on either side of it were leaning and ready to go as well. The fence was also lying on the ground still attached to the posts. It was really loose from the cows pushing against it. It had been stretched almost to the point of breaking. There was a creek bed along this side of the property. The ground was lower here and the dirt was wet and loose from the recent rains. Cow tracks were all over the place. It was clear this is where they got out.

Ben caused the earth to rise about twelve inches in that area and left the fence alone.

"Ben, that looks great, but isn't the owner going to wonder how the terrain suddenly changed like that?" Elizabeth asked.

"Yeah, probably, but hey, the creek may have gotten lower in this spot, who knows?" Ben smiled.

Just as they got back to the truck they heard some whoops and hollers towards the neighboring farm and saw cattle coming up the road with the sound of a four wheeler and a pickup truck pulling up the rear.

Elizabeth and Ben stood in the roadway just on the other side of their driveway to make sure the cattle didn't pass the farm and continue down the road.

They were all white-eyed, bellowing and nervous. Elizabeth spoke peace to them as they approached. Ben opened the gate and when they got there, they all just walked right in. Not one of them tried to dash in a different direction and run off as critters of the bovine persuasion most often do in times of stress.

"Good cows!" Elizabeth said out loud as the last one entered through the gate.

"Thanks for your help," said the tall, dark haired, lanky man in his late twenties or early thirties. He had a cloudy light gray aura, which would be expected after his morning ordeal.

As he got off the four wheeler, he said, "I'm Gary Wenther," shaking Ben's hand and then Elizabeth's as Ben made their introductions.

He pointed to the old black chevy pickup pulling in with a young woman and three kids inside. "That's my wife, Julie, and our kids."

The two older boys came running over after jumping out of the truck, anxious to meet the new people. Julie walked with a limp as she came to greet them while holding the hand of their youngest so he didn't run off. Ben saw her aura was a dark, cloudy gray. He could tell she was full of worry that went way beyond the cows getting out.

"My wife, Julie," Gary said, putting his arm around the pretty, dark haired woman, "This is Caleb, our youngest. The oldest here is Chris and our middle young'un is Abe." He said pointing to each of them.

The two older boys stood still, facing forward, with proud smiles, allowing the visitors to inspect them while his father introduced them. Then Chris said, "I'm the oldest, I'm eight! Abe is six and Caleb is three," pointing to each of his brothers.

All children, unless they were seriously abused, had beautiful rainbow auras, which all three possessed brightly. Ben could tell they thoroughly enjoyed the morning's events.

Elizabeth took to them immediately. "Yes, Chris, and as the oldest, I'll bet you're a big help to your mom helping her watch over your younger brothers."

"Uh-huh!" Chris smiled shaking his head up and down.

"What adorable boys you have! You must be so proud!" She said looking at Julie.

"Thank you, we are," Julie smiled, giving a quick glance towards the house. "Would you like to come in for some tea? I have some made."

Elizabeth could tell she wasn't ready for company and hoping they would decline the offer. "Oh, we'd love to, but maybe some other time, we have to get back." Elizabeth answered.

"Okay, yes," Julie gave a smile of what Elizabeth surmised as relief, "definitely, next time!"

Ben told Gary about the three cows they found. "I just live down Brought Lane over there," he said, pointing in the direction of his house about three miles away. "Want some help fixing that fence?"

"Oh, no … thanks … I appreciate the offer, but I can manage." Gary wasn't used to anyone offering to help.

"Are you sure? I'll round up some fence posts and be right back. Between the two of us, we can knock that out in an hour or so before the cows decide to make another great escape."

"Well …" Gary's face brightened, "to be honest, I'm fresh out of fence posts at the moment. I'll replace yours next time I get to town, if that's all right."

"You bet," Ben replied.

Gary smiled and shook his hand again.

"But I don't want to take advantage …."

Ben stopped him, "No! Not at all … I'm glad to do it! It's the weekend, man, I'm not working today. Besides, neighbors are supposed to help each other. I'll be back in just a bit." He and Elizabeth jumped into the truck and off they went. He remembered to take the feed scoop back to Sophie before he left again.

Ben couldn't find any fence posts at his place, so he went in to town and bought half a dozen at the local hardware and feed. As soon as he was out of sight from any traffic, he teleported to cut his time down. He didn't want to tell Gary he bought them just for him. He wasn't going to lie, but also wasn't going to offer that information.

## CHAPTER 16 - COMMISERATION

After he was back at Gary's, as the two men got out of the truck and approached the low spot where the cows got out, Gary stopped and just stood there scratching his chin, looking up and down the fence line in that spot.

"Is something wrong?" Ben asked.

"Well," Gary began, still looking around, "I could swear the ground was lower in this spot. A lot lower. It's the craziest thing … but it's a good thing!"

Ben didn't comment, allowing Gary to draw his own conclusions, he just walked to the back of the pickup and started pulling the fence posts out.

As they worked on the fence, they shared a little about their lives.

Gary told Ben they had moved there from Wisconsin four years ago. He worked as a truck driver for a local company where he was home most nights. Ben told Gary about working at Selvy's Garage and, of course, the wedding.

Gary then shared that his wife had recently become disabled. "After she had Caleb, our youngest, she started having problems, stumbling, falling. She was diagnosed with muscular dystrophy. The doctors say she could die young, or wind up in a wheel chair. It's really unpredictable. They also say it could go into remission and she could live a full, happy life. No one knows for sure."

"That's really sad," Ben said. "I'm sorry. Do you mind if I ask … are you a believer?"

Gary looked at him, not quite knowing what he was talking about....

"Do you believe in God?"

Gary looked a little uncomfortable. Ben could tell he wasn't used to talking about God. Gary looked down, focused on a fence staple and pounded it in as he squinted his left eye to shield it from the smoke rising out of the cigarette dangling from his mouth. Then he said, without looking up, "Yeah, I believe there's a God. We went to church a few times before we moved here, but ...." He shrugged his shoulders, then was silent.

Ben felt such compassion for him and his situation. *Holy Spirit, please don't let me blow this. I don't want to say too much, but I want to say what You want him to hear right now.*

"The last staple," Ben handed it to Gary as he stepped back to survey their work, "looks like it'll hold for a while."

Gary gave a smile of relief as he pounded it in – glad it was the last staple and glad Ben wasn't going to push the 'God thing' on him just then.

They had only used three of the fence posts, Ben put the other three in Gary's barn before he left.

"Oh, hey, don't you need those?" Gary asked.

"No, you may need them worse than me. We don't have any cows." Ben said as they both chuckled. "I use them once in a while for Grandma's fence around her garden and some for the root cellar. It's all good for now."

There was an old root cellar on the Brought property, in the actual sense of the word. It was in the side of the hill by the woods, generations old. Ben had used some fenceposts to help reinforce it on the inside. He had put new cement blocks around the doorway and hung a new door on it. He hollowed out the inside even more and made some fresh shelving for the underground storage area. They made good use of it, especially these past couple years with supplies being threatened and most of America's goods now being imported and sometimes sitting at docks, waiting to be unloaded.

Sarah grew an extra-large garden this year. Even with all the wedding plans going on, Rachel and Elizabeth made time to help her can more vegetables than ever before, this fall. They even canned beef and pork this year. It never froze in the root cellar and it never got above about forty degrees. The doorway to the cellar was in the side of the hill, but it went underground about 13 feet with a second door at the bottom of the cellar.

"Here's my cell number." Ben said as he handed Gary a piece of paper before he climbed in the truck to leave. "I meant that about neighbors helping neighbors."

"Thanks." Gary took the paper and pulled out his cell, texting the number on the paper. "Now you got my cell too, that goes both ways."

Ben started the truck and paused a moment, "We go to Elm Creek Community Church with Pastor Matt Birc, if you're looking for a good church. Pastor Matt loves the Lord and he's not boring." Ben smiled as he pulled away, hoping Gary would accept the invitation.

After Ben got back, Elizabeth told him she sensed Julie was full of fear, desperate for a way out. Fear of not being the wife and mother she always wanted to be, fear of dying with the kids still so young. "And they don't have any family here, they're alone in this. I'm thinking they left Wisconsin to get away from their families, on both sides."

"Man, that's a rough situation," Ben shook his head. "When Gary told me about her MD, I asked him if he believed in God. He got real uncomfortable so I changed the subject. I gave him my number and invited him to church before I left, though. We need to pray for them. I believe God wants to heal her."

"Yes, He certainly can. He can restore everything the cankerworm has stolen from them." Then using her brassy church voice, added, "Just like the Bible says, praise God!"

"Amen, my sista!" Ben shouted, giving her a high five as they headed out to the clay shed to see what Mom and Grandma were up to.

Instead of just lifting large things, Sarah and Rachel decided to see how precise they could become with their new-found talents. They were attempting to paint glaze on some coffee mugs. When Ben and Elizabeth entered the shed they saw what looked like a scene from a cartoon. Two paintbrushes were floating in the air, dipping themselves into the glaze and painting the coffee mugs!

"Oh, that's cool, you guys!" Ben exclaimed.

"Right?" They answered, still concentrating.

"How creative is that?" Elizabeth exclaimed.

"Lizzy, I think you and Ben should try this," said Sarah.

Elizabeth eyed a mug on the shelf. She called it over. "How's this one?" She asked Grandma.

"Oh, yeah, any of them are fine, chose any mug you like too, Ben."

Just then his phone rang. "Hey, Tom, what's up?"

"What day did you say we're supposed to meet at the tux shop?" Ben had asked Tom Riley to be his groomsman.

"This Tuesday, I think, give me a sec, I'll check." Ben thumbed through his phone. "Yup, this Tuesday at 5:00 p.m. They're open 'till seven, so should be time to get everything done."

"Okay, I should be there no later than five," Tom said.

"Yeah, they wanted us to come in September so we gotta make this happen," Ben chuckled. "You want to ride with us? James and I should be leaving the shop early to clean up, then heading out about 4:00. We can run by and pick you up."

"Well, ... okay, let's ride together." He agreed. It's about a forty minute ride to O'Connors, in East Tawas and they thought it would be good to have the extra time to catch up.

## CHAPTER 16 - COMMISERATION

Tom would be turning twenty soon. He now manages his parents' farm with his father getting up in years. The hundred plus year old barn, where he fell out of the loft when he was a kid, still stands and is used everyday. Tom and his father had re-painted it the custom red and white barn colors a few years ago. "Oh, the stories that old barn could tell," he would say. They raise mostly Angus and Hereford beef cattle, grow corn for silage to fill their eighty-five foot silo and put up hay every year. They also attend the same church as Ben and his family.

After the phone conversation, Ben said, "Okay, let's get on with this fantastical finessing!" He called a brush over and dipped it in the blue glaze. Instead of painting a mug, the brush touched the end of Elizabeth's nose, then continued to Grandma's nose. By that time, Rachel saw what was happening, she was able to fend off the one aimed at her, momentarily. Needless to say the shed grew loud with laughter and piercing protests as a glaze war broke out. No one made it out unglazed!

# Chapter 17 - Commitment

That evening, after Grandma had her shower to get the glaze off and Rachel went home to take her shower, Ben was waiting for Elizabeth to finish showering in the upstairs bathroom. He was next. Up to this point, through the years, he had been able to control his thoughts about sex pretty well. But today, after touching her mind, her very soul, when he read her thoughts – while he waited for her to finish – he was reminded that when they are married they could take showers together. He'd thought of these things before but not like today. He could hardly stand it. He could hear the water falling on her body as he stood by the bathroom door. He went into the next room and began to pace the floor in what was going to be their bedroom in just three weeks. Then he looked at the bed and felt he would come undone! He had to get out of there! He went outside, and in one great leap, he went about three quarters of a mile to his favorite tree in the woods behind the house. He continued to leap straight up into the clouds a few times trying to release his energy. He finally jumped up to his favorite limb.

"Oh, God! Please help me," he said out loud. "Holy Spirit, I can hardly stand it! My whole body aches! I want her so bad! I want to be with her! I want to consume her! Please, help me control myself!"

As he paced back and forth along the wide limb he was standing on, the words of Pastor Matt came ringing in his mind. "… don't allow yourself to be alone with her if you're feeling vulnerable!" The voice in his head repeated three times, "… don't allow yourself to be alone with her if you're feeling vulnerable, if you're feeling vulnerable! … don't allow yourself …"

*"Have enough respect for her and for yourself – and the Lord – Have enough respect for her and for yourself – and the Lord – to stop before you get to that point ... BEFORE ... you get to that point. It's not impossible, people do it everyday and God wouldn't have required it if it was impossible."*

Ben finally sat down on the limb. He knew what he had to do. *I'm gonna have to tell Mom and Grandma ... oh, man ... but they'll make sure we're not alone together ... they'll help us ....*

He knew Elizabeth was having some of the same thoughts. She looked at him differently tonight, her body gestures were different. They were like magnets being drawn to each other. They avoided reading each other's thoughts again ... *thank God*, Ben thought, as he leaped from the limb and walked slowly back to the house, giving himself enough time to let this all soak in. He was determined not to let this get the best of him. He was going to keep his commitment and do this right before God! *Only three more weeks, three more weeks.*

Ben focused his thoughts on the new couple, Gary and Julie Wenther, remembering their situation. He hoped to see them in church. *Maybe even this Sunday. Call them, Father. Your word says no one can come to You unless You call them. Call them Lord!*

When he got back to the house, everyone was in the living room. Elizabeth was sharing with them what had happened today with the cows and the Wenthers, while Ben showered.

Rachel and Sarah both sensed that the sexual attraction between Ben and Elizabeth was ... intensified.

After Elizabeth finished telling them about Julie's MD, their adorable children and all that happened, while Ben finished up in the shower, Rachel said to Elizabeth, "So ... you and Ben ... are you two doing all right?"

Elizabeth glanced up to the second floor, in the direction of the bathroom where Ben was.

She knew what she was talking about. She was a little embarrassed, but could always talk to them about anything. They had had all sorts of honest conversations in the past about life, sex included.

After a moment, while nervously picking some fuzz off the arm of her sweater she said, "We read each other's minds today." She looked up at them as tears welled up in her eyes, then looking to the floor she confessed, "This is hard!" She began to cry openly. "I wish we could just get married right now. I love him so much!" Then she said, looking up at them, "We barely …." She stopped. She heard Ben coming down the stairs. She began wiping her tears. Sarah and Rachel, by then, were sitting with her on the couch.

Ben knew what they were talking about and actually was relieved. He was struggling with how to approach the subject. He sat in the chair farthest away from them. Putting his left ankle on his right knee, with his left thumb and index finger holding his face up with his elbow on the arm of the chair, he began to wiggle his left foot, as he often did when he was working something out.

They all sat in silence a few moments. Then Ben and Elizabeth both tried to speak at the same time. Elizabeth stopped, waiting to hear what Ben had to say.

"Lizzy, I love you so much." He paused. "But until we're married – I can't be alone with you anymore. I don't trust myself right now." He turned his head and looked away from their gaze. "I think that for the next few days – maybe until the wedding – you shouldn't come over unless I'm working, unless I'm not here. He got up and opened the front door, "Mom," he stopped, facing the outside, "would you please take Lizzy home?" Not looking at any of them he stepped outside and shut the door behind him. No one knew where he went.

Elizabeth began to cry. No one talked for a long while. Finally she got up, gathered her things and stood before Rachel. As Rachel got her car keys and her purse, Sarah embraced Elizabeth. Elizabeth just stood there feeling numb, as Sarah held her, Rachel joined them.

Before they departed Sarah said, "This too shall pass, honey. This too shall pass."

Elizabeth gave a slight nod as her and Rachel walked out the door.

The next few days were so painful for both of them. It was like someone had died.

"Lizzy, aren't you going to church this morning? Are you feeling okay?" Her mother looked at her daughter sitting at the kitchen table that next morning, still in her pajamas, looking peaked and all worn out. "Are you sick?" She felt her cheeks and forehead with the back of her hand for any sign of a fever. Elizabeth's bouncing, happy personality was suddenly … gone!

"Elizabeth! What happened honey?" Her mother pressed after finding no signs of fever. It was glaringly obvious something happened.

Elizabeth looked at her mother and told her that she and Ben had decided to stop seeing each other for a while. Sam immediately got the wrong impression. "What did he do? Are you calling off the wedding?"

Before she could answer, her father, who was getting ready for church, overheard them and came from the other room, "What's going on? Did he hurt you?"

Elizabeth stood up shaking her head, "No, no, nothing like that." Her eyes were swollen from crying all night. She was all cried out and just felt numb at that point. "We just decided that …" She hesitated on how to word this … "for the sake of our … celibacy … we're going to stay away from each other for a while ... maybe until the wedding."

Samantha and John just looked at each other not knowing what to say at first.

Then her father asked, "Was this a mutual thing?" He searched his daughter's face, wanting to make sure Ben hadn't tried to force himself on her.

"Yes, ... it was actually his idea." Elizabeth didn't look at either of her parents. She turned and went in the living room and flopped on the couch, wrapping her seafoam green housecoat around her.

"So, you both are really okay, you're just taking a break from each other? That's not a bad thing." John straightened his tie. "Years ago it was common for the betrothed not to see each other for a while before the wedding," her father added. "You'll be okay, honey."

"John, I think you'd better go to church without me this morning, give us some mother-daughter time." Sam whispered.

"Okay, will do, honey." He whispered back. In a louder voice he said, "I love you both," as he kissed Sam goodbye, then left for church.

"Wow, honey, I don't know quite what to say about all this, other than I commend you both," her mother said, once they were alone. "I know this is going to be hard, but it's not the end of the world, this is a good thing. This is a God thing!" She went and made Elizabeth a cup of coffee. They spent the day watching movies, mostly old comedies, and eating junk food and ice cream together. Sam missed those days of spending time with her daughter. And Elizabeth was reminded how much she enjoyed her mother's company.

After church, her father spent the rest of his day making himself scarce by puttering in the garage and completing some odd jobs around the house. Only coming in to get a refill on the junk food.

## CHAPTER 17 - COMMITMENT

Monday, at work, James couldn't help but notice Ben's countenance.

"Ben, you look like you lost your best friend!" James commented as Ben drug himself around the shop.

Ben gave him a sarcastic grin, shook his head and didn't comment.

James stopped what he was doing and walked over to where Ben was working under the hood of a Ford sedan. "Hey, what's up, man? Is everything okay?"

Ben took a deep breath, let it out and stood up. "Yes, ... I did. I lost my best friend ... temporarily."

"Hey man, ... I'm right here! I'm your best friend!" James smiled, trying to lighten his mood.

Ben managed a smile, but it left as quickly as it came. "Lizzy and I are staying away from each other for a while. Maybe 'till the wedding."

James was silent for a moment, "Oh ... you mean ... oh! The sex thing?"

Ben just looked at him.

"Wow, dude! You're really serious about this aren't you?"

"I made a commitment and I aim to keep it." Ben said firmly as he stuck his head back down under the hood of the car.

"I'm proud to know you Benjamin Adan!" James' mustache grew as wide as his smile. "You're one of a kind."

"Not really, there's other Christians not having sex until their wedding night. The statistics say more now than in the past." Ben added.

"Really? That's pretty incredible, actually. Especially with the world the way it is, getting worse everyday. That's really cool. Praise God!" James didn't say things like that very often. "Praise the Lord!" He said it again as he walked back to what he was doing.

Rachel and Sarah decided not to contact Elizabeth, Monday. If they hadn't heard from her by Tuesday afternoon, Rachel thought she would give her a call. This was hard on them too. Elizabeth was already a family member to them. They hated to see either of them suffer. Even if it was for their good, it was still hard. They missed her too.

Tuesday, after waking around 2:00 p.m., Rachel called Elizabeth.

"Hey Lizzy, how are you?"

"I'm okay. How's Ben?"

"He's okay too … moping, probably same as you … but he's fine." Rachel said. "I was thinking, you know the guys are going to O'Connors tonight to get fitted for their tuxes. I thought maybe you might want to come over. Mom's got those mugs fired we painted the other night. They look pretty cool. I could come pick you up if you want to come over."

"Well, I can drive Mom's car, but yeah, I'd like that. Call me after Ben leaves, okay?" Her voice brightened a bit at the end. Being able to be with them made staying away from Ben seem a little easier.

James and Ben pulled into Tom's driveway with James' dark blue, Toyota pickup, right around 4:10 p.m.

"Hey, the farm looks great!" Ben remarked as Tom approached the truck. It was always a happy farm. Ben could see its aura.

On the way to the tux shop, the three men made small talk about family and work, James and Tom mostly. James commented on how beautiful the bridesmaid's dresses were. "Natalie's dress is gorgeous! Downright beautiful!"

Ben and Elizabeth had asked James' daughter to be their flower girl.

"That Glass Shoe, or whatever, in West Branch, has been around forever." James added.

"It's The Glass Slipper." Ben chuckled, correcting him.

"Oh, yeah." He laughed. "Shiela got her wedding dress from there when we got married. Pretty nice place."

Ben smirked, "Man, I think Grandma got *her* wedding dress from there!" Everyone laughed. It was true, Grandma *did* get her wedding dress from there. "They rent tuxes too, but I like O'Connors." Ben added. "They've been around forever too."

"Yup, my parents shopped at O'Conners when they were our age. I just got some jeans from there a couple months ago. A little pricey, but made well. They should last me awhile." Tom offered.

As James turned from River Road onto Monument Road, he noticed the trees and said, "The colors are intense this year. Might last into November."

"I know, right?" Tom added. "The weather's been pretty warm, they might."

The rich orange, red, yellow and mahogany colors almost glowed to the naked eye as the sun began to make its way down for the day on the heavily wooded area near Lumberman's Monument.

Ben could only wish they saw what he was seeing. The aura from the fall forest was breathtaking.

"Have you been on the river lately? It's beautiful," Tom exclaimed.

"No, not lately. Been too busy getting ready for the wedding and all." Ben said without much enthusiasm.

"Hey, what's with you tonight, Ben? You're usually the life of the party. You down about something?" Tom asked.

"No, I'm good. It's just that Lizzy and I decided not to see much of each other for a while ... maybe until the wedding."

"What? How come? You two sick of each other already?"

"No, just the opposite." Ben replied.

James let out a boisterous laugh. He couldn't contain that one!

"What's so funny?" Tom asked.

Then Ben began to laugh. They all began to laugh. It was contagious!

Finally Tom said, "I don't even know what I'm laughing about! But it's funny enough just watching you two!"

Then Ben fessed up and told him he and Lizzy didn't want to have sex until their wedding night. It was getting more difficult to honor that, so he/

they decided not to see each other for awhile…

"Man, I honestly don't know that I could do that, Ben." Tom confessed. "That's … amazing!"

"Well, I made a promise to God, to Lizzy and myself a long time ago about that – and I don't want to mess it up." Ben admitted.

"I respect that. I can respect that, Ben." Tom added.

"Yeah, I was pretty blown away when he told me," James said. "He said there's more young Christians today that are staying celibate 'till their wedding night. That shocked me too. More power to 'em!"

"Wow, that's incredible." Tom said.

"So, Tom … we're standing up for an honest to goodness man that's doing this the honest to goodness right way! I'm personally proud to be a part of it." James declared as Tom seconded the statement with – "Here, here! Me too!"

They made it to O'Connors around 4:50 p.m.

"Lizzy's going to like this!" Ben exclaimed as he showed James and Tom the tux he chose. Remember, our wedding colors are apricot, caramel and sage, so chose accordingly, gentlemen!"

"So what does that mean, you want me to walk down the isle in an apricot tuxedo?" James ribbed.

"No, black tuxes, just make your tie – or something – apricot, sage or caramel…" Ben laughed, "We are country rednecks to the core!"

"And proud of it!" Tom declared.

Denise was a great help. Without her, they would have been lost. After they picked everything out, she measured them and told them their tuxes should arrive the week of the wedding. She would call as soon as they came.

They were about half-way home when Ben got a text from Grandma.

"Lizzy is here, do you want her to stay to say hello? Or would you rather not see her tonight?"

Ben replied, "I would LOVE to see her, just don't leave us alone. Does she want to see me?"

Grandma replied, "Don't know yet, will let you know."

After another mile or so his phone dinged again.

"Yes!"

Ben had left his truck at James' house, so after they dropped Tom off and reached James' place, Ben said his goodbyes to James and couldn't wait to get his truck out of sight. He teleported almost to his driveway, then drove the rest of the way in.

Elizabeth was waiting for him in the doorway and walked outside as he pulled in. Her heart was racing, you would have thought they hadn't seen each other in months! It was only three days.

Ben jumped out of the truck and ran to her, stopping just before he reached her. She stopped too. They just stood there about six feet away, looking at each other. Then Ben reached for her and she took his hands in hers.

"How are you?" She asked.

"Miserable!"

"Me too!" She smiled up at him.

"So, what are you guys doing?"

"Grandma fired the mugs we painted the other night. They turned out nice. Want to come see?" She asked.

"Okay, yeah." He thought that would be a nice distraction.

Mom and Grandma were good chaperones. They stayed at the door until they headed toward the house. The aroma of Grandma's pot roast filled the air as they got closer to the door.

The mugs were on the table.

"They're colorful, I'll say that." Ben said looking them over remembering the fun they had.

"Yeah? Well if we would have fired ourselves that night, I'll bet we would have had more color than these mugs!" Rachel laughed.

"Are you hungry? Dinner's ready." Grandma said as she pulled the pot roast out of the oven.

Ben looked at Elizabeth, "Would you like to stay for dinner?"

"Uh … well … yes!" She beamed, "I'd like that."

Ben told the ladies how the mens' tux expedition went. "Lizzy, you're going to love my tux!" He exclaimed. "Can't wait for you to see it!"

"You two are going to be the most handsome couple on your wedding day!" Rachel exclaimed. "Like the beautiful people on the cover of a magazine. Wait 'till you see Lizzy in her wedding dress."

"Yes, Laura, Brooke and Natalie's dresses are gorgeous too." Sarah added. "The whole wedding party is going to look like a magazine cover."

Mom and Grandma's comments became distant as Ben and Elizabeth admired each other from across the table. The grace of God had touched them. He enabled them to see, to grab hold of the wholesome joy being together was going to bring. How they were each – truly – worth the wait and how it was so much more than that. He strengthened them as they honored Him. They glowed. Even Rachel saw their aura tonight. How beautiful it was!

"Praise the Lord," Sarah whispered under her breath.

"Amen," Rachel whispered back, as they realized what was taking place.

Ben wasn't afraid of her anymore, he was respecting her. And she, likewise, was respecting him. They saw clearly how right, right was.

# Chapter 18 – Animals In Heaven?

Later that week, excitement grew as the wedding day approached. Rachel contacted Pastor Matt and set up the wedding rehearsal for the day before the wedding, at 3:00 p.m. She had the rehearsal dinner reservations set for 5:30 p.m. at the steakhouse in East Tawas, figuring that would give them an hour and a half for the rehearsal at the church and allow for the forty minute drive to the restaurant.

Ben and Elizabeth had decided to test the waters and start seeing each other again, as long as they weren't alone together, and it seemed to be working great. So they all continued training together.


"I never knew how beautiful everything could be. Now I know why you and Ben always felt a little sorry for me that I couldn't see life energies." Rachel told her mother one morning, later that week, over a cup of coffee after work.

"I'm so glad you can see them now! And they're not only beautiful, they're a protection as well. You can see how people are feeling." Sarah answered.

"Yeah, … I *know* …." She was silent for a while, fiddling with her coffee mug. "I keep thinking of little Ben when Mike was killed." Rachel's voice was shaky. "I just wish I could have stopped it! I wish I would have sensed what Benny was talking about sooner. Poor kid. Poor Mike! I still struggle with that, Mom. And now that I can see auras, it's all come back, rearing its ugly head." She tearily confessed.

"Oh, honey, you did all you knew to do! Ben's fine! God's grace has covered him in that and allowed him to heal. You should let His grace cover and heal you. Forgive yourself for whatever it is you feel you need forgiveness for, from that day. There's nothing more you could have done, honey! I'm sure God isn't holding you responsible for anything. You're beating yourself up and letting the enemy goad you into it every time he reminds you about it." Her mother added, "God's not the one reminding you of that day. You need to take authority over that and take those thoughts captive, in Jesus' Name!"

"You're right." Rachel grabbed her third tissue. "I *have* been letting the enemy do that to me, haven't I?"

"Sounds like it to me."

"I rebuke that in Jesus' Name and, yes, I take those thoughts captive, into the obedience of Christ."

"Yup, 2 Corinthians 10:5, quote the word, baby! That's where the power is."

"I love you, Mom," Rachel snuffled as Sarah wrapped her arms around her daughter and spoke comfort and peace over her.

"I love you too, honey. My sweet Rachel, my sweet baby girl."

Cookie never liked it when anyone was sad. She whined and danced on her two hind legs, waving her front paws in the air as she wagged her plumey, white tail. Rachel picked her up and snuggled her in her lap. She knew Cookie was just trying to make her feel better.

"Yes, baby, I'm fine. Yes, you're making me feel better." Rachel stroked Cookie's somewhat curly, white and brown, fluffy hair. "It's so nice she doesn't shed like Ollie, but I don't think I could handle all the clipping."

"Ha! Me too!" Sarah laughed. "I'm not very good at it. She needs to be clipped right now. But I like that she doesn't shed all over the furniture."

"Yeah, they both have their little pros and cons, don't they?" Rachel gave Cookie more loves.

"If God made a maintenance-free dog, I'd be getting one of them!" Sarah laughed. "But they're such great company. They're worth it. Not to mention what a good watch dog she is."

"Yeah, she barks at *everything!*"

"She does, not much gets past her."

One evening, Sarah was sitting on the couch with Cookie. She stroked the soft coat of her constant and loyal companion. She had had other dogs and cats through the years, but Cookie was special. Sarah knew the day would come, in the next few years, where she would pass away and leave her. She would miss her so much. She wanted to remember every hair on her smart and wonderful friend, her eyes and the way she looked at Sarah. It was reminiscent of something that happened 48 years ago.

She was 15, riding her horse, Star, bareback, as she almost always did. She was stroking her golden mane as she rode her walking down the familiar trail, thinking the same thoughts she had been thinking about Cookie – with tears running down her face and dripping into her mane. She didn't want to forget one moment with the beautiful, majestic friend God had given her, realizing that inevitably the day would come when she would pass away. Sarah would be left alone without her lifelong friend. The sadness overwhelmed her. Star was her best friend and companion. She was a chestnut with four blonde socks and a blonde mane and tail. She had a white star in the middle of her forehead and was as gentle as the day is long.

She had been her best friend since about the age of two. Sarah rode her almost everyday after she was around seven. Growing up together, as Star was the same age as Sarah, they had the greatest adventures out in the woods on the trails behind Sarah's house. Imagining all sorts of things and playing them out. What an imagination she had in those days! Although Sarah's gift of communicating with animals was just coming into fruition at that point in her young age, Star was always a willing companion to each new adventure, seemingly able to sense her thoughts as they played together and worked out the scenarios from Sarah's imagination.

Sarah believed she would see Star again in heaven. The book of Enoch talks about the animals in heaven … the Lord will ask them how they were treated by their masters. Yes, if the book of Enoch is true, we will also be judged on how we treat our livestock and our pets.

Colton Burpo, now in his twenties, visited heaven when he was four years old. In the real-life book and movie, *Heaven is For Real,* Colton also talks about the animals in heaven. Sarah found comfort in that. Even though her family had been given gifts far beyond what most people have, they were not given the answers to everything. Just like everyone else, faith was still required for a great many things. Besides, how could Jesus come back riding a white horse if there are no animals in heaven?

"You spoil that dog so," Rachel would scold her mother.

"Yes," she would say with a wide smile, "I spoil her for all the dogs in the world who aren't loved and taken care of by their humans." Sarah would look at her daughter, "As if you don't spoil Ollie." And they would laugh at each other's little oddities.

# Chapter 19

# For I Know The Plans I Have For You

Wednesday morning Sarah's phone rang, it was Sam.

"...so I've gotten a lot of the RSVP's back. Looks like most everyone we invited is coming. I'm excited about that! My sister, Shelly, and my niece, Adrian, are coming from Florida. Ron and the kids are coming too. They're going to stay in East Tawas and make a little vacation out of it. They love it there. Every time they bring Adrian's family they want to stay over there instead of here at the house. They love Lake Huron, reminds them of the ocean." Sam continued with the names, "John's cousin from Wisconsin is coming with his family. Some of your relatives from Bay City RSVP'd and one from Ann Arbor." Sam said as she rifled through the envelopes.

"Oh, that's great!" Exclaimed Sarah. "Which ones from our side are coming?"

"Well, let's see," she paused trying to find the envelopes, "Beverly and Ken Adan from Ann Arbor, Dorothy and Roger Imswirth from Linwood, Kurt and Melissa Imswirth from Bay City, and a Saginaw address, Shelly and James Adan." Sam paused, "I think there's more. They came last week and I've got them in the drawer."

"That's wonderful. So, are you all squared away with the caterer for the head count?" Sarah asked.

"Well, if I'm not, with only a week and a half to go, I doubt they'll let me change anything," Sam laughed. "I told them anywhere from 200 to 250 people, so I think we're covered."

"Okay, so what else do you need Rachel and I to do?"

"Well, for now, nothing. The flower shop will be delivering the flowers to the church the day before, probably during rehearsal. Cindy, from the country club, is going to oversee setting up the tables and chairs along with the decorations for the wedding table and the other centerpieces. She has been a godsend. So – I think we're good for now." Sam let out a sigh of relief. "But I reserve the right to ask for your help if something else comes up," she chuckled.

"You bet," said Sarah, "On one hand I can't believe it's here already and on the other hand it seems like it took forever."

"Lord knows I feel the same way. Glad it's almost over and sad at the same time to be losing our baby girl … but not really. Things aren't going to be that much different than the way they are now, and I'm glad of that." Sam shared, "We love Ben so much. They were made for each other."

"I believe that too, they were made for each other. And I'm so excited to have them move in here with me! You know how I feel about Lizzy. I'm really looking forward to that," Sarah added. "And if I need a little privacy or whatever, I can go to the den or the shed or wherever. There's plenty of space here."

"You can come visit me!" Sam demanded.

"I will!"

It was Friday morning, Rachel just pulled in from work. Sarah walked over and met her as she was getting out of the car.

"How was work?"

"Oh, it was all right." Rachel looked tired. "How was your night? Is everything okay?" Her mother normally didn't meet her at the car like that.

"Yeah, everything's all right. I just want to make plans to go over and

## CHAPTER 19 - FOR I KNOW THE PLANS I HAVE FOR YOU

anoint the country club."

They had been praying everyday for continued protection over Ben and Elizabeth ever since the night they were engaged. Praying over their wedding, the rehearsal dinner and their honeymoon, asking God to give His angels charge over them and protect them from any demonic forces that may try to come against their marriage.

For their honeymoon, Ben and Elizabeth had decided to go to Saugatuck for a few days then drive up to Traverse City and spend a couple days there. They found out, however, that you have to be 21 years old or you can't check in at most of the B & B's and hotels they were looking at. They found a hotel that would let 18 year olds check in, in Holland, but they really wanted to go to a bed and breakfast. They also realized they wouldn't have been able to go to Boston either, not until they're 21 at least.

Elizabeth's dad said he would see if he couldn't pull a few strings and find them a place but they said no. "If we can't do this on our own, the right way, we'd rather wait."

So Rachel wound up renting a secluded cabin for four nights on the shores of Lake Huron in Tawas City for them.

"At least we can tell our grandchildren we went on a honeymoon, of sorts." They conceded.

As the two women headed for the house, Rachel added, "Not only should we anoint the club, but I think we should anoint the church too."

"I agree. I actually was going to bring that up," Sarah smiled. *Great minds ....*

"Okay, so ... when do you think we should do it?" Rachel reached to make a pot of coffee out of habit. "Wait, Mom do you want me to make some fresh coffee? I really don't want to drink any this morning, I've got to get some sleep today, but I'll make some for you if you want."

"No, I've got a fresh pot at home, I'm good."

"Oh – this is still hot from Ben." Rachel felt the side of the coffee pot. He had left for work just minutes before Rachel got home.

"No thanks, honey, I'm good, really."

They sat down at the kitchen table. "I thought about having Ben take us to the club at night. But it makes me feel like I'm doing something wrong, sneaking in like that."

Rachel laughed, "Oh, Mom! ... well, we could call them and ask them to let us in after they close."

"That's another idea. And if we went at night, without permission, they may have alarms." Sarah shook her head. "We'd have to wear our black clothes. We'd have to depend on Ben to get us out of there if something happened." She added, "I just don't have a peace about any of that. So I was thinking we should just go while they're open, tell them we just want to look around and discretely pray and anoint as we go."

"Yeah, that would work." Rachel smiled at her mother. She was the most practical and open person she knew. And ... she was usually right in the end. *Gotta love her.*

They had decided to visit the next day, Saturday, a week before the wedding. It was a piece of cake, really. They went for lunch and told the server they wanted to look around a little after they finished their meal. They anointed the four corners of the building on the outside, the doorways and all. Everyone was so busy doing their own thing, they hardly noticed them. They also visited the church and anointed it likewise, covering everything in prayer.

That Sunday, about fifteen minutes before church was to start, Elizabeth looked over and saw Gary and Julie Wenther, along with their kids, sitting on one of the back rows in the sanctuary. She found Ben and they went over to greet them.

"We have room where we're sitting, why don't you come sit with us?" Ben asked, after they all said hello.

"I can help you with the boys too." Elizabeth said. "Do you want to meet the kids' Sunday school teachers? We can meet them right now, there's time."

Julie agreed. The two older boys followed as they walked out of the sanctuary while Julie held the hand of the youngest. Elizabeth could tell she was self-conscious about her limp.

"The kids usually stay in the sanctuary during worship, then before Pastor starts preaching, he will dismiss the kids for Sunday school. But you don't have to put them there. They can stay with you if you're more comfortable with that."

"Oh, no, that's fine. I don't mind putting them in Sunday school class, as long as they're good." They both laughed, knowing how that sometimes goes.

Elizabeth introduced Julie and the boys to their teachers. Ages four to eight were in the same class.

Chris and Abe would be in the same classroom, but Caleb, who was three, would go into the younger kids' room. The older boys began playing immediately so they left them for a few minutes to see how Caleb would do in the other classroom. There was a boy and a girl about the same age already playing when they entered. Caleb went straight for the toy shelf and pulled out a big dump truck and began playing.

"I'm not sure how well this will go over, them being separated," Julie said. "Especially for their first time."

"We can always bring Caleb back in the service with us and if the other boys want to stay, or whatever, either way is fine. Parents do it all the time." Elizabeth offered. "I'm just so glad you guys came! We love it here and hope you will too."

Just then Katie, the pastor's wife, walked into the classroom. Elizabeth introduced them. Katie's bubbly personality could make anyone and everyone feel at home. She embraced them with enthusiasm and made sure they were comfortable.

Music erupted from the sanctuary as the worship team began with "Graves into Gardens," so they took Caleb and gathered Chris and Abe from the other classroom and headed back.

"Wow, looks like a lot more people when they're all standing and clapping." Julie looked around as they walked through the sanctuary doors.

"Yeah, we're a happy bunch!" Elizabeth said as they found Ben and Gary over where the Adan's were sitting on the right side, in the fourth row. There were around a hundred people in attendance that morning, which, for their small town, was a good turn-out.

Elizabeth and Ben weren't sure if the Wenthers had ever been to a pentecostal church service before, but they seemed to be enjoying it and the boys were remarkably well behaved.

When the praise and worship was over, Elizabeth went with Julie to take the boys to their classrooms. Chris and Abe had no problem going into their classroom and Caleb went straight for the same dump truck and began playing. Julie and Elizabeth exited the classroom without incident and went back to the service.

There were a number of new people there that morning, so Pastor Matt chose to speak about the love of God and how to know Him better.

"There is an empty spot inside every human being. Mankind has tried to fill that void with all kinds of things since the beginning of time. Nothing can fill that hole in your heart, that empty spot that keeps you searching for completeness - happiness - wholeness, not wealth, not alcohol, not drugs, not sex and not another human being." He chuckled, "I mean, I love my wife." He looked out into the congregation where Katie was sitting. She already knew what he was going to say and was nodding her head in agreement, smiling. "Katie, you know I love you. You know you're the crème de la crème to me. You are the love of my life and have always been the love of my life." He looked at the congregation, "She truly is the best wife and mother I could have ever asked for. She is my best friend and I would give my life to protect her. But even with all of that … she can't fill that empty spot in my heart, in my soul … 'cause only God can do that. That spot was created specifically for God and God alone."

"And even though I may think I'm all that and a bag of chips – I can't fill that empty spot in her heart either. Katie knows that only too well!" Everyone was chuckling. "We are always going to let each other down in some way or fashion because WE'RE HUMAN! We're not perfect."

"God is the only one that can fill that empty space. Nothing else fits. Oh, you can pull and squeeze and push to try and make something else fit, but it won't satisfy for long. You'll soon find yourself wanting something different because nothing else, except God, can complete you." Pastor Matt walked back and forth on the platform as he often did when he preached.

"Have you ever noticed how unhappy – people that don't know the Lord – are? They'll have times of laughter and moments of happiness, yes, 'till the next day when the hangover kicks in, or they have a big bruise on their face from the brawl at the party the night before or a beating from their spouse. Some love the drama, they live for the drama and their emotions are constantly moving up and down, up and down. All that drama makes me seasick! Like a ship being tossed to and fro by the waves! Their happiness depends on the moment. They're having a good day until something happens to give them an excuse to be depressed or mean or ugly to those around them. They're happy 'till their best friend sleeps with their wife, 'till they find their having thoughts of suicide because they have no hope for their future. No answers for their lives. And the pain goes on and on."

"So how do we get out of that? How do we break free from that way of thinking? That way of life?" He looked around the congregation. "Jesus said in Matthew - 'Come to Me, all *you* who labor and are heavy laden, and I will give you rest. Take My yoke upon you and learn from Me, for I am gentle and lowly in heart, and you will find rest for your souls. For My yoke *is* easy and My burden is light.'"

Pastor Matt then added, "So only the Prince of Peace can change our lifestyle, our hearts and our minds, through the cross. When we realize what Jesus, the Christ, did for us on that cross, taking all of our sin, our wrongs upon Himself, who had no sin, and gave his physical body over to be beaten and tortured and to finally die on the cross – just to save us! Before we even knew Him! While we were still wallowing in the darkness and in our sins He did this for us – He didn't wait until we cleaned ourselves up because we couldn't! And this was for past, present and future!"

"The real kicker is, He didn't stay dead! He rose from the dead three days after they killed Him! Death couldn't hold Him because he never sinned! He made it, folks! He made it out of this life spotless!" He added, "And Buddha is still in the grave, Muhammad is still in the grave and so on …. He's the only one that rose from the dead!"

"That's why we have to ask the Lord Jesus to forgive us for our sins. He's the only one worthy! And if you, Mister or Misses Perfection, think you've never done anything that needs to be forgiven of, the Bible says your own self-righteousness has become your sin. Romans 3:23 says - 'For all have sinned and come short of the glory of God.' The Apostle Paul also talks about that if you confess with your mouth the Lord Jesus and believe in your heart that God has raised Him from the dead, you will be saved. Read Romans 10:9-13."

Just before the close of Pastor Matt's sermon, Susan, one of Caleb's teachers, brought him to his mother with tears in his eyes.

"I'm sorry," Susan whispered, "He played for quite a while, but then he wanted Mommy."

"Awe," Julie reached for him as Gary picked him up and set him in Mommy's lap. "Thank you," she said as Susan turned to head back toward the classroom.

Susan nodded and gave her a wide smile, "You're welcome, he's adorable!" She whispered back.

At the close of his sermon, Pastor Matt encouraged them to read the Bible. "If you want to know what God expects of you and you want to know who God is and what He is all about, read His Word! Ask questions when something doesn't quite make sense. It's a huge book filled with every kind of sin and every kind of good there is. It's the best book I've ever read! But that's just it, it's not just a book, His Word is alive, sharper than any two-edged sword able to split even bone and marrow and prove a man."

"So, where's God?" He held up his Bible, "He's in His Word! Read it! It'll change your life! Start in Ephesians. Ask questions! If you don't know anyone that has the answers, call me! Leave a message if I don't answer, I WILL call you back. You're not alone in this. Find a church member you feel comfortable with, talk about God in your conversations. Ask questions."

Julie and Gary's aura was brighter than the day they first met them. And it got brighter as Pastor Matt preached.

## CHAPTER 19 - FOR I KNOW THE PLANS I HAVE FOR YOU

After service, Sarah invited the Wenthers to come have Sunday dinner with them. "I've already got a huge pork roast in the oven and it'll only take about an hour or so to get the trimmings ready. There's plenty of food for everyone."

"Oh, and Grandma can cook, let me tell ya!" Ben added. "You won't be disappointed, unless you don't like pork."

"No, we like pork, it sounds great. But, Julie, do you feel up to it?" Gary looked at his wife with genuine concern. He could tell she was getting tired.

"Yeah, I feel up to it. Why not? Let's do it." Julie smiled.

After they got to the house, Elizabeth encouraged Julie to sit in the recliner and rest. "Would you mind if I took the boys outside to show them around?" Ben and Gary were already outside in the barn.

"Are you sure you want to?" Julie asked, "They can be a handful."

"You bet I do. I need the practice!" She smiled as she ushered the boys outside and left Julie with Rachel and Sarah as they worked on the dinner preparations.

"It's hard to believe that next Sunday, Ben and Lizzy will be on their honeymoon!" Rachel said to Julie as they watched Elizabeth outside with the boys through the huge, wavy picture window of drawn cylinder glass from the early 20th century. It had four-inch multi-colored stained glass squares all around it and each square was set in its own little wooden frame.

"They sure seem to be made for each other," Julie added as she watched. "Where are they going for their honeymoon?"

"Well, they wanted to go to Boston, but with the COVID pandemic they didn't want to get caught in any sudden lockdowns at an airport or hotel. Then their age became a factor, because they're not 21, so they decided to just rent a nearby cabin for a few days." Rachel told her.

"Oh, wow ... yeah, I don't think I'd want to take any long trips right now either."

"Ben told Lizzy he'd take her when they turned 21 and things get back to normal, whenever that's going to be."

"Right?" Julie answered sarcastically, "What's normal? I don't even know what that is anymore."

"I feel the same way. I believe we're living in the end times."

"Gary and I were just talking about that. That's one of the reasons we wanted to start coming to church."

"That's awesome, you're on the right track. The Rapture could actually happen at anytime now. I don't think there's any prophecy yet to be fulfilled before His coming. But no one knows the day or the hour. Jesus said to just keep watch for the signs of the times and use discernment .... Just keep on keepin' on!"

They were silent for a moment, then Rachel said, "Julie, I want you to know that if you have any questions about the Bible or God, you're welcome to call or stop by anytime. There's almost always someone here. And no question is silly, stupid or dumb! Don't let the enemy steal that away from you." Rachel said firmly. "He's a liar and a thief. He wants to confuse and distract people to keep them from learning the truth. Don't let him do that to you."

"Thanks, I appreciate that." Julie smiled. Her aura became brighter. "Okay, so I have a question now, if you don't mind."

"Not at all! You go, girl! If we don't know the answers, we know how to find them, so ask away." Rachel was always excited to share about God.

Julie looked down into her lap, "How do you know ... when you're saved?" Then she looked up at Rachel, hoping for an answer she could wrap her mind around.

"Well, first of all, you'll have a peace about it. Another way to put it is the Holy Spirit will bear witness with your spirit that you're saved,"

Rachel explained. "But first, let me ask you – now, I'm not looking for you to answer. These are rhetorical, just pose these questions to yourself: Do you believe God exists? When you asked God to forgive you for your sins, did you mean it? And what I mean by that is did you commit to trying your very best to stop doing them? Not that you'll never make a mistake again, but the important thing is you ask God to forgive you, no matter how many times you fall, pick yourself back up and keep trying, keep asking for forgiveness each time. It's what the church world and the Bible calls repentance. To apply yourself to getting to know God better, to read His Word."

"Yes!" Julie answered without hesitation. Tears welled up in her eyes.

"Do you believe that God loved the world so much He gave His only begotten son that whoever believes in Him will have eternal life?"

"Yes!"

"Do you believe that Jesus died on the cross and three days later, rose from the dead because He lead a sinless life and death couldn't hold Him?"

"Yes!"

"Do you believe Jesus has the power to forgive sins because of His sacrifice?"

"Yes!" Julie reached for a tissue as tears streamed down her face.

"Okay, then! Sounds like you're saved to me!" Rachel gave her a huge smile and a hug. "It's a walk where no one can ever say they've made it, that they've reached the pinnacle of their salvation and can't learn anymore. We're always growing and learning because if God showed us everything that was wrong with us all at once, we'd probably wind up in a fetal position on our bed and never leave." She laughed.

God's patient with us. He's never too busy and never too far away. He can answer you, literally, in a heart beat."

"This is all so very, very cool!" Julie smiled with a far-away look, taking in all of Rachel's words. Her aura was beautiful.

"Do you have a Bible? 'Cause I'd be happy to give you one of ours, if you need one."

"Thanks, but we do have a Bible. What book was that Pastor Matt said to read?"

"It was the book of Ephesians. That book tells you who you are in Christ and so much more. It's in the New Testament, so it's towards the back. Have you read the Bible much?"

"Actually, not really. I mean … a little … but it was hard to understand, so …."

"Oh, do you have the one with the thee's and the thou's in it? That one can be hard to understand."

"Yeah, it had all the Old English. It's really confusing in some places."

Rachel went to the bookshelf and found a New International Version. She flipped to Ephesians and put a marker there for her. "Take this NIV, it should be easier to understand. It's got a few highlighted areas and some notes, I hope you don't mind. But keep your other Bible too, it'll help with some of the translations later as you study more."

"Oh, I couldn't take your Bible."

"We have more, see." Rachel said, pointing to another two dozen or so Bibles her mother had collected over the years.

"Wow," Julie exclaimed, looking at the shelf. "That's a lot of Bibles!"

Rachel laughed, "We like to have different versions for reference and that. But really, today, I look up a lot of things on my phone. There's some great Bible websites where you can look up a gazillion different versions. And there are free Bible apps you can download. I love listening to the audio Bible. The one I've got now has a man with an English accent." She laughed.

"When I read the Bible, I try to remember to pray every time and ask God to help me understand it; and that I would rightly divide it, so I don't become a kook."

They both laughed.

"I'd like to pray with you, if you don't mind. Would that be all right?" Rachel asked.

"Of course, yes." Julie was a little nervous. No one had ever prayed for her before. She didn't know quite what to expect, but she was surely willing.

Rachel took Julie's hand and said, "Father God, we come before You at this very moment and thank You for bringing Julie, Gary and their children into our lives. We thank You that Julie gave her life to You today. Your Word says that the angels in heaven rejoice when one person turns to Christ and receives salvation, and we thank You for that, Father. Now I pray and ask Your blessing over her and Gary and the boys. Protect them, Lord, and encourage them. Help them to feel Your presence, feel Your love for them in their lives at home and wherever they are, that they would feel Your peace as they apply themselves to You and Your Word. For Your Word says You know the plans You have for them, plans to prosper them and not to harm them, plans to give them hope and a future. So in Jesus' Name we ask, believing, and thank You for it … Amen."

Julie reached for more tissues with shaky hands and without looking up. Her eyes had become a fountain of tears. As she sniffled and wiped her face, she said, "That was the most beautiful … those were the most beautiful things … anyone has ever said to me. Thank you."

She stood and hugged Rachel. And Rachel comforted her as a sister.

Sarah stayed busy in the kitchen. She was praying for Julie and the family under her breath the entire time. She got the potatoes and side dishes ready for dinner and set the table, trying not to be too noisy. She certainly didn't want to be a distraction to the beautiful thing that was taking place in the living room.

## CHAPTER 19 - FOR I KNOW THE PLANS I HAVE FOR YOU

Elizabeth had taken the boys up on the hill to the raspberry bushes.

"Ouch!" Chris shook his finger and quickly put it in his mouth. A little blood was coming out of the end.

"Be careful of the thorns," Elizabeth picked a few ripe berries for the boys. The other two waited patiently for what Elizabeth was going to give them so they wouldn't suffer the same fate as their older brother.

"Here you go," she held out her cupped hands full of berries as they began to devour them.

"That's the best I ever tasted!" Abe exclaimed as he reached for more.

"I want more, please!" Caleb declared, as his older brothers seemed to be eating them faster than he could grab them.

"Okay, I'll pick some more. And Caleb's first this time." Elizabeth smiled as she quickly filled her hands again.

"These bushes were planted by Miss Sarah's Grandmother almost a hundred years ago." She told the boys, knowing they wouldn't grasp the significance, but wanted to say it nonetheless.

"Wow!" Chris exclaimed, "That was way back in the olden days! Did they take that long to get ripe?"

Elizabeth laughed, "No, they get more berries every year."

Suddenly, she heard something in the woods, something big. Then she smelled it. It was a bear. As the realization of looming danger filled her senses, all of a sudden her thoughts were on the boys. In an instant, all three of them flew to her side and stuck like glue. She didn't even realize what she had done until afterwords. She held tight to the three boys as she communicated with the bear.

Ben was still in the barn with Gary showing him some of the old horse harnesses his great granddad used to plow the fields with. Then he saw the bear and felt Elizabeth's apprehension at the raspberry bushes. Just a second, Gary, I'll be right back. He walked out of the barn as calmly as

## CHAPTER 19 - FOR I KNOW THE PLANS I HAVE FOR YOU

he could, as if to take a whizz around the corner. As soon as he was out of sight, he shot to the hill, which was about 75 yards away. He walked up behind them as they were facing the woods.

The bear had come to eat raspberries! Elizabeth told him they were just leaving and he could eat all the berries he wanted. He let out an audible grunt as he impatiently waited for them to leave. After all, bears weren't used to waiting for anything.

Ben heard the entire thing and gave a sigh of relief as the boys and Elizabeth turned to face him.

"Hi guys," Ben said to the boys. They looked a little disoriented, but weren't crying. It was like they just got a big hug from Elizabeth all of a sudden, and that was that. They apparently didn't really feel or notice their bodies pull towards her as she called them to her.

"What do you say we all go to the house and see if Grandma's got dinner ready?" Ben added, thinking it best if they go indoors to let the bear alone. Even though Elizabeth could talk to him, it didn't mean they were all going to play nice together. They were going to give him his space.

Ben poked his head in the barn and told Gary he thought dinner was ready while keeping his mind's eye on the bear. The bear stayed around the raspberry bushes for about 15 minutes or so, skillfully pulling berries from the branches with his mouth, without hurting the bush, then went his merry way, back into the woods.

The boys never saw the bear and didn't know why Elizabeth chose to hug them all of a sudden like that, but grown ups do funny things sometimes. They just took it in stride.

Once they found the right combination of books to make a booster seat for Caleb, they all enjoyed the meal and had good conversation. They talked more about God and life, in general. Ben and Elizabeth invited them to their wedding. Rachel and Julie exchanged cell numbers and Rachel made a mental note that even with the wedding coming up, she would make it a point to reach out to her sometime that week if Julie hadn't called her.

# Chapter 20 - Rose Petals And God Bubbles

On Monday, Sarah and Rachel went to East Tawas and had lunch at the steakhouse. Afterward, they prayed and discreetly anointed the building to cover the rehearsal dinner. It was another piece of cake, like the country club. No one really paid them any mind.

Tuesday, Ben left work early to pick up the tuxes before they closed. The alterations on Elizabeth's dress, along with Laura, Brooke and Natalie's dresses, were all finished the week prior. They now hung in their respective closets, waiting for the big day.

For Elizabeth and Ben, the week drug by. They had decided not to see each other on Thursday. Sam had made an appointment for her and Elizabeth, that day, to each get a massage and facial, their nails done and pedicures in West Branch.

Elizabeth didn't want anyone else but her mother to fix her hair the day of the wedding. She was really good at it and could have easily been a hair stylist.

The day actually went pretty fast. She made a group video chat to Laura and Brooke that evening and before she knew it, it was nine o'clock.

Elizabeth's Aunt Shelly, her mother's sister, along with her cousin, Adrian, her husband, Ron and their two kids were arriving from Florida, Friday afternoon. They were renting a car from the airport in Detroit and driving up that evening. They had adjacent rooms reserved at Tawas Bay Resort. Even though it was cold and they couldn't go swimming, they

## CHAPTER 20 - ROSE PETALS & GOD BUBBLES

loved being on the lake.

John's relatives from Wisconsin were also arriving on Friday, and would be staying at McDuffy's Inn, in Elm Creek. They decided to make a vacation out of it as well, since this would be the kids' first time in Michigan. They left on Tuesday morning and were driving over, going up through the Upper Peninsula and taking the Mackinac Bridge down. They were staying over in St. Ignace on Thursday, to visit Castle Rock, along with Paul Bunyan and Babe, the blue ox. Friday morning they were all looking forward to driving across the five mile long Mackinac Bridge, the longest suspension bridge in the western hemisphere.

Friday was finally here! Rehearsal day! Ben woke up early. His mother was still sleeping. She had taken Thursday night and the rest of the week off work. Ben was so full of energy, he could hardly keep his feet on the floor as he made coffee and sat down at the kitchen table to read the Bible and pray and to thank God for his life and his bride to be. He could hear a cardinal whistling happily outside as the first rays of sunshine broke through the trees. He felt like he was in a fairy-tale, but it was so much better than a fairy-tale – *because this is real!*

He read the scripture in I Corinthians that talks about how no eye has seen, no ear has heard, neither entered into the heart of man, the things God has prepared for them that love him. But by His Spirit, God reveals them to us who have the Spirit of God inside us. That we might know the things that are freely given to us by God.

"Freely given! That we might *know* them! ... It's never-ending." Ben said out loud as he smiled, looking out the kitchen window. His eyes twinkled as he tried to grasp the infinite wonders God has in store for His people. The coffee pot gurgled its last few drops, filling the house with its aroma. Ben heard his mother stirring.

Her first words were, "Oh, how great – coffee!"

## CHAPTER 20 - ROSE PETALS & GOD BUBBLES

Sam and John were at the church by 2:30 p.m. to meet the florist. Elizabeth decided to wear her hair down today, since it would be up tomorrow. She wore a solid purple dress with a multi-colored shawl of green and purple for the rehearsal and dinner.

The rest of the entourage, including Pastor Matt and Katie, were all there by around 2:50 p.m. and rehearsal began promptly at 3 o'clock.

The fragrance of fresh flowers filled the sanctuary. It was decorated so beautifully for the happy occasion with their wedding colors of apricot, caramel and sage green.

Natalie was so cute. She was all smiles pretending to throw rose petals from a basket as she walked down the isle, becoming keenly aware of how much fun being a flower girl was going to be. When they were going over their vows, James searched through his pockets as if he lost the ring, cutting up as usual.

Everyone was excited for the joyous day ahead. Sarah and Rachel shed happy tears as they watched the years of prayers for Ben coming into fruition. That he would find a good and godly wife that loved him. Sam and John, likewise, shed happy tears seeing their prayers for their daughter coming to pass as well. That God would give her a husband that loved her more than himself and love God more than he loved her. It was all coming together and their joy was full.

When rehearsal was over, they were all about to leave for the forty minute drive to dinner when Rachel felt the Holy Spirit nudge her to anoint the vehicles. She heard screeching tires in her head but couldn't see any details. She quickly went to her purse and grabbed the anointing oil and went outside before the others and anointed each vehicle, praying for safe traveling mercies and pleading the blood of Jesus over them. "The enemy

## CHAPTER 20 - ROSE PETALS & GOD BUBBLES

will not rob us of this joy today! In Jesus Name!" She declared as she headed back inside the church.

As everyone gathered outside to leave, Rachel, not caring if it seemed a little awkward to some – stopped them and said a prayer of safety and protection over them as they each traveled to the restaurant.

"Why don't you ride with us?" John said to Rachel, Sarah, Ben and Elizabeth. "There's enough room for all of us."

Everyone piled in to the new, red Ford Explorer. John had recently traded in the sedan and wanted them to check out their new ride.

"This is four-wheel drive isn't it?" Ben asked as he and Elizabeth seated themselves in the very back. "Nice!" He added, looking around.

"Yup, and it has heated leather seats with all the other amenities," John said proudly. "No more getting stuck in the drive-way in the winter."

Sam nodded in agreement, "Right?" She smiled.

Pastor and Katie drove their own car. Tom rode with James, Shiela and Natalie while Laura and Brooke rode together in Brooke's car. Shiela made arrangements with her mother to watch their other two kids. So it became a four-car caravan, all headed to Tawas.

"So, Tom! You and Brooke make a pretty nice looking couple. Any sparks there?" James probed.

"Oh, well, I'm not sure, but I'm willing to try and find out!" Tom replied with a smile.

Shiela laughed, "James, you're such a trouble maker!"

"Trouble? How is that making trouble? I'm just stating the obvious!" James retorted with a sly grin.

Shiela added, "Okay, maybe not trouble, this time! But an instigator!"

"Hey, love makes the world go 'round, don't ya know! I'm just trying to do my part!"

Everyone laughed.

Sarah, Ben and Elizabeth all heard Rachel's thoughts, so they were fine-tuned and keeping an inconspicuous, sharp eye on the road. Pastor Matt and Katie were behind them. It was almost impossible to see James and Brooke's vehicles, but Ben could see them.

Elizabeth imagined a huge God bubble of faith around them all as the minutes to the restaurant ticked down.

"Y'all are awful quiet back there." John exclaimed, looking at them in the rear-view mirror. His southern accent was more pronounced when he was in a good mood.

"I'm just taking in the scenery," Ben said, looking at Elizabeth. "I'm still pinching myself making sure this is all real. She's going to be my wife tomorrow!" He smiled his wide smile as he kissed her.

Elizabeth beamed and kissed him back.

"Oh, now you two are gonna have plenty of time to do all that after the ceremony!" John grinned.

Sarah remarked how adorable Natalie was, almost dancing down the isle as she pretended to toss the rose petals. "She's got a lot of her dad in her."

"Yeah, but just the good parts, God willing," Ben chuckled.

They were just coming up to the turn on to US 23. The two lanes of traffic on each side were fairly heavy. The light turned green and John turned left. Ben, Elizabeth, Grandma and Mom all turned around to see the others make the turn. As Pastor Matt made the turn, a car heading southbound on US 23 came speeding through the light. The four of them immediately focused their thoughts and grabbed the car. The driver hit the break pedal. They all heard screeching tires. The car came to a stop, inches away from Pastor's car. It seemed to bounce back slightly as if it hit something, but it wasn't the car. The two vehicles sat there, stopped in the middle of the intersection for a couple seconds before the driver heading south sped off. Pastor Matt reluctantly made his way through the turn, wondering if they shouldn't report it, but they didn't get the license plate number, so he continued on to the restaurant.

*So was that it?* Rachel heard her son, silently, from the back seat.

*I hope so, but let's not let our guard down,* she answered, without words.

Elizabeth and Grandma both heard them and agreed.

"What the hell was that?" John yelled. "That guy must be drinking or on drugs or something! Did anyone get his license plate number? I'll turn him in. He shouldn't be driving in that condition. The light was red for how long before he came barreling through?"

No one commented on John's railings. They just let him get it off his chest.

By that time James made it through the light but Brooke and Laura got stuck waiting for the next one. Since there were no trees or bushes, Elizabeth trained her mind on the grass at the corner on M 55 and looked through its eyes. They made it through okay. Elizabeth gave an audible sigh of relief. That was the first time she ever tried seeing through grass. *Pretty cool.*

Rachel gave her a nod, smiling in agreement.

They finally saw the sign for the steakhouse. All four vehicles made it.

"Are you both all right?" John asked Pastor Matt and Katie as they exited the car.

"Yes, we're okay …. Man," Pastor Matt scratched the back of his head, "That was a close one! Thank God for His protection!"

"Yes, thank God," Sam added as she went to Katie's side.

"I'm okay," Katie reassured her as the others pulled in.

As the Selvy's and Tom approached, Tom said, "Boy, it's a good thing you prayed over us at the church, Rachel. Did you see how that car kind of bounced back just before it got to their car? Man, that was something!"

Elizabeth knew it was what she saw beforehand and decided to say it, "Well ... our God is a great, big God! He can do whatever He wants! I believe there was a huge God bubble of faith surrounding Pastor's car and that's what made it bounce back!"

"Right?" Katie agreed. "Amen! Thank you, Jesus!"

The meal was fabulous. Some ordered Walleye, others ordered Lake Perch or steak. It didn't matter, all the food there was great. Shiela gave Natalie her phone to play games, to keep her occupied. The evening was filled with good conversation and some complimentary toasts to Elizabeth and Ben.

Ben, Elizabeth, Rachel and Sarah kept their mind's eye on all of them until everyone made it home safely that night.

"So how do you feel now, after they're all home?" Ben asked his mother as they sat in the living room at Grandma's.

"I feel a peace. I believe that one incident was it, praise God nothing serious happened." Rachel admitted.

"The entire day and the dinner was all great. It was blessed. God watches over His people," Sarah added as she yawned, thinking about the wedding tomorrow. "I'm so excited for tomorrow! I may be tired, but hope I can actually sleep." She smiled proudly, looking at Ben.

They prayed together before parting to turn in for the night.

Ben had a hard time falling asleep and so did Elizabeth.

"I love you, Lizzy!" Ben told her, as he did every night since their minds touched. "I can't wait for tomorrow!"

"I love you too, Ben. I don't know if I can sleep, but I'll try." She answered.

In keeping with their plans not to have children right away, Elizabeth had decided to use birth control pills instead of some of the other options her doctor told her about. She studied the pros and cons of each and thought that pills would be the safest with the least side effects. At the advice of her doctor, she began taking them a week ago.

As she laid there in her bed, she realized this would be the last night she would sleep in her room and in this bed. It made her a little sad.

Ben was thinking about that too. This would be his last night in his bed and in his room. They would each be moving to a new place, even though it was right next door at Grandma's. They had slept over at her house on many occasions, at different times, of course, but neither of them had slept in their great grandparent's room before. The largest bedroom in the 5,000 square foot house. The room they were going to call theirs. It would be new to them both. It was on the second floor and on the other end of the house from Grandma's room, which was on the first floor.

## Chapter 21 – The Wedding

As the first rays of sunshine danced through her bedroom window, Elizabeth yawned and stretched in her bed. She smiled. *So this is what my wedding day feels like!* She laid there thinking about the itinerary as adrenaline began to course through her veins. She gave thanks to God, praying for protection and blessing over the entire day, then jumped out of bed and headed for the shower.

Sam and John were sitting in the little breakfast nook having coffee as Elizabeth came down the stairs.

"Here she comes! Our beautiful bride to be!" They said almost in unison.

Elizabeth smiled at her parents, "It's finally here!" She reached in the cupboard for her favorite mug from Grandma, made herself a cup of coffee and sat down with her parents to watch the bird bath through the kitchen window at the nook. It was now void of water this time of year but the birds that hadn't flown south for the winter, mainly Cardinals, still visited it.

"Let's just enjoy these few minutes of peace before the hustle and bustle." Her mother smiled at her daughter, sipping her coffee.

"Lizzy, I want you to know how proud your mother and I are of you." Her dad said. "We have a peace about your marriage to Ben, even though you're both young. I don't believe you could've chosen a better man. He's honest, hard working and he loves the Lord."

"And he loves you!" Her mother smiled proudly.

The rest of the morning was filled with makeup and hair – hair, hair, hair,

## CHAPTER 21 - THE WEDDING

phone calls from the caterer and the cake lady, then more hair. Her mother adorned her head with a beautiful crystal studded tiara as the final touches commenced. Sam convinced her they would be able to get her dress on at the church without messing up her hair or makeup. So Elizabeth decided to be comfortable until then and threw on a pair of jeans and a t-shirt.

The vintage style lace wedding gown was an off the shoulder design with long sheer, lace sleeves. Her matching veil was beautiful.

Rachel had made prior arrangements with the cabin owners to pick up the keys for Ben and Elizabeth's honeymoon stay before the ceremony. Loading a beautiful arrangement of apricot colored roses with caramel and sage green accents into her car, along with a fruit basket and some assorted chocolates, she drove to Tawas. She arranged them on the glass-top pine log table in the cozy, little cabin with a card Grandma had stuck seven, crisp one hundred dollar bills in for spending money. The envelope read, 'Mister & Misses Benjamin Adan.' She prayed and anointed the entire cabin inside and out and made it back in plenty of time to get ready for the wedding.

Once Elizabeth's hair was finished, her mother slowly spun her around in the chair, "da-da-da-da," she sang the first four notes of the wedding song – as she faced her young beauty toward the mirror.

"What a knock-out! Ben's going to be mesmerized!" Her mother exclaimed.

She was absolutely beautiful. Like a princess from a fairy tale. Her shiny red hair was loosely woven and pulled to the crown of her head. Sam embellished a few braids by weaving in some shimmery, tiny jeweled threads, then wove the braids back in to the rest of her hair. The tiara was small and more unassuming. It was perfect.

Elizabeth snapped a few pre-wedding shots of her and her mother.

"Just remember not to share those with anybody yet." Her mother said making her way to finish getting dressed. It just feels like bad luck or something, even though I don't believe in all that." She chuckled as she left the room.

Elizabeth just laughed, "Right?" Today, she didn't want to think about anything except Ben and the wedding. Not the demons, not the temple, not the negative side of ANYTHING! It was like the Lord had her wrapped in one of those God bubbles, like Pastor's car yesterday. She could feel His blessing and favor on her and all around her. That invisible force that says, "Rest under the shadow of My wings and enjoy! I've got this!"

It was two o'clock and guests were starting to arrive at the church. Grandma let Ben take her freshly waxed car and she rode with Rachel.

Laura and Brook cracked the door to the sanctuary every few minutes to see who was there.

"Remember, Lizzy, you CANNOT leave this room. No one is to see the bride before it's time." Her mother reminded her as she exited the room.

*Thank God there's a bathroom in here!* She wasn't going to put her dress on until about twenty minutes before the wedding. Even though it was removable, the train was long and if she had to use the restroom after putting on the dress, well, let's just say there may be a delay. It took longer to re-attach the train than it did to put on the dress. She didn't mind not being able to go out and greet guests. She could see them arrive through the eyes of the huge weeping-willow tree in front of the church.

Natalie paraded in to say hello to her as Sam was leaving. She looked like an adorable miniature version of the Maid and Matron of honor, in the floor-length, rusty-apricot gown with caramel and sage-green embellishments in her hair.

"Hi," Natalie said, all smiles, with her hands cupped inside each other, nervously pivoting her body back and forth.

"Hi there!" Elizabeth reached out her hands from the chair she was sitting in. "Where's my hug?"

Natalie trotted over and embraced her. She loved Lizzy. She was her favorite babysitter. She always made her feel special.

"Thank you for being my flower girl."

"You're welcome." Natalie smiled nervously.

"Hey, last night you were really looking forward to today. Are you a little nervous with all the people out there?"

"I think so." She pivoted back and forth.

"Well, you just remember how beautiful you are … look in the mirror." Elizabeth made sure Natalie could see her whole body in the full-length mirror. Her aura became much brighter as Elizabeth spoke peace over her, out loud, in Jesus' Name.

"And think how proud your mom and dad are of you. If the people make you nervous, just pretend there's no one there, like last night, and all you see is Ben, Tom and your daddy waiting for you at the other end."

"Okay," She looked at Elizabeth, "I think I'll be fine now," she decided – and scampered off.

Sam met Natalie at the door again, with Rachel and Sarah behind her.

"You are so, so beautiful! Wow!" Rachel and Sarah both commented on how awesome her makeup looked and her hair! "Absolutely gorgeous!"

"Sam, you have really out-done yourself!" Sarah commented.

"We just wanted to say how proud we are of you, and how much we love you!" Rachel said to Elizabeth.

"And how excited we are to have you as an official family member!" Sarah added as they each gave her a little hug, being careful not to smudge any makeup or mess up any hair.

After they left and the two were alone once again, Sam looked at her daughter, "Well, honey," tears welled up in her eyes, "it's time to get that beautiful wedding gown on you." She smiled.

## CHAPTER 21 - THE WEDDING

Just as Sam was doing up Elizabeth's dress, Laura and Brooke came through the door to wait for the procession to begin.

"Lizzy, who is that guy sitting next to Ben's grandmother?" Laura was smitten with the handsome, tall man in the black suit with long, blonde hair. "You got to come see." She led Elizabeth to the door. "I love his hair!" Eliel's thick hair was pulled back with small braids mixed in his pony tail.

Elizabeth smiled, "He's an old friend of the family. His name is Eliel." She didn't know he was coming until she saw him walking up the entrance through the willow. She thought it was incredibly sweet that he would honor them like that.

"El … iel?"

"Yeah, El-eee-el. His name means 'angel sent from heaven.'"

"He sure looks like an angel, and did you say, *old* friend?" Laura asked. He didn't look a day older than 28 or so.

"Well, yes … his family and Grandma's family go way back.

"I want to meet this guy. Can you introduce us after the ceremony?" She took a step back and thought a moment, "He isn't married, is he?"

Elizabeth laughed, "No."

"Is he gay?"

"No." She laughed again. *This oughta be fun … . !*

Just then Elizabeth's father knocked on the door and gave them the five minute warning. Shiela brought Natalie in to wait, making sure she had the basket of rose petals and the bride and bridesmaids had their bridal bouquets. She was friends with the florist and wanted to ensure the flowers were all perfect.

Ben was nervous, but more anxious than anything. He was wanting the ceremony to begin. James and Tom were fidgety as well. James was cutting up, which put them all more at ease.

## CHAPTER 21 - THE WEDDING

*Finally,* Ben thought as he heard the music change (even though they were exactly on time). He saw Brooke coming down the isle, with Laura and Natalie waiting in the wings. When it was her turn, looking around at the faces in the assembly, Natalie hesitated. Just as everyone thought she was going to need some help, she remembered what Lizzy told her. She looked straight down at her daddy at the other end of the isle, which now seemed much longer than she remembered. Taking the petals out of the basket, she began to toss them as she gracefully made her way to the front of the church and proudly took her place next to Brooke.

The music changed and the familiar "Here Comes The Bride" began. They liked being traditional.

Everyone stood and faced the back of the church. At that moment, before he could see her coming out, Ben saw her aura glowing through the doorway. It was so beautiful. When she stepped out and he saw her in her wedding gown, for the first time in his life – his knees got weak! They told him that might happen, but Ben never thought it would happen to him, he laughed at the thought. Nonetheless, his knees were wobbly! He began to weep – and sob! He was able to gain control over the sobbing about the time her father took her in his hands to accompany her down the isle, but the tears continued to flow. As they got closer, Ben saw her father's face was all wet too. He quickly glanced around the room and surmised there wasn't a dry eye in the house! Even Eliel's eyes were wet.

As the two came together to say their vows, their auras were so bright, mingling together and electrified, it was overwhelming. Sarah found herself leaning on Rachel and Eliel.

Once Ben had placed the wedding ring on Elizabeth's finger and Elizabeth placed Ben's ring on his finger, which was a thick, solid band of 14k gold, they lit the unity candle and chose "I Will Be Here," by Steven

Curtis Chapman, for their song. The entire ceremony was beautiful. It was like a dream to Ben and Elizabeth, as if they were watching it unfold as spectators while inside their own bodies.

Once the ceremony was complete, Pastor Matt said, "I now pronounce you man and wife! Benjamin, you may kiss your bride!"

As he took her in his arms, it felt like they were kissing for the first time.

Then Pastor Matt said with his boisterous, preacher voice, "Ladies and gentleman, I would like to introduce to you, for the first time ever, hailing all the way from Elm Creek, Michigan, Mister and Misses Benjamin Adan!"

Everyone clapped, hooted and cheered as they walked down the isle together for the first time as husband and wife.

Their parents, Sarah and the entire wedding party stood in the receiving line. Being in the front row, Eliel was among some of the first to greet them. Elizabeth revealed to him, while greeting others, about Laura wanting to meet him as he approached.

He chuckled out loud, giving her a nod. *Okay, I got this.* He answered and smiled. He was about six people back in the line.

*Grandma?* Elizabeth imparted her thoughts to Sarah, *Did Eliel visit you on your wedding day?*

She answered back, *Yes! And he came to Rachel's wedding as well.* She smiled, glancing her way.

"Laura, here he comes!" Brook nudged her and whispered as Eliel was two people from them.

Everyone seemed to take note of him. Not only because of his good looks, but he seemed to radiate goodness, which is naturally attractive to everyone, even if they don't realize what it is.

"Hello, I'm Eliel." He reached out his hand, "You must be Brooke."

Brooke smiled nervously, holding out a limp hand, *he knows my name!?*

"And you must be Laura." Eliel took her hand in his. "It's nice to meet you. Elizabeth has chosen well in her two best friends." He smiled at them both as they tried not to look overwhelmed.

"Thank you," was all Laura said. She didn't know what else to say. She was overcome by a feeling of goodness. When he shook her hand, it didn't feel like she thought it would. She felt as if she shook the hand of her brother or a close family member. The sexual attraction was gone!

James and Tom were intrigued by Eliel as well, when he shook their hands, they seemed to admire something in him. A sense of honor and integrity. *Who is this guy?* They each thought to themselves.

Eliel introduced himself to Sam and John, after greeting the Adans. When he shook their hands, the Lord imparted an even greater peace to them, a knowing – this marriage was ordained of God and God is in it. Sam had a confidence she'd never felt before – a sense of security, of protection over her and their family with a greater hope for things to come.

After everyone had come through the receiving line and greeted them, the wedding party and relatives made their way back inside the sanctuary for photos. They had hired a local photographer that had great recommendations. Sam noticed how well he covered the ceremony, snapping shots of everything as it happened. *Live shots are always so much better ... if they turn out.* She chuckled to herself, having imprinted every moment indelibly to memory.

When it came time to leave for the reception, one of the church members pulled Grandma's car up for Ben and Elizabeth.

"Whoa!" They both laughed. In big, white letters, the words "Just Married!" were written on the hood, the sides and the back window. Streamers with cans were attached to the rear-end. James and Tom pulled up behind to follow them through town for the traditional horn-honking to let everyone know, Ben and Elizabeth were just married!

"Oh, no, guys – C'mon!" Ben said.

"Oh, YES!" James said, "We are doing this!"

Ben and Elizabeth looked at Grandma to make sure she was onboard with this. She gave them a nod, smiling. She knew all about it way in advance. She was even part of the conspiracy. She made the streamers for the car last week.

"Okay, let's do it!" Elizabeth said as they headed for the car. "Wait," she stopped, "can I take this train off first?" She asked looking at her mother. They quickly went into the other room and detached the train.

The dinner at the reception was wonderful. They hired a Christian disc-jockey to play some of their favorite songs. For their traditional first dance, they chose the song from the ceremony, "I Will Be Here," followed by "Give Me a Lifetime," the song Ben loved to sing to her, along with other Christian artists like Matthew West, David Crowder, Lauren Daigle, Newsboys, Third Day, TobyMac, Phil Wickham, etc.

The wedding cake was beautiful! With a retro flare, it had a lighted fountain underneath four pillared tiers of white cake with white buttercream frosting and opulent piping all around. Graceful and elegant sprays of apricot and caramel roses with sage-green leaves and baby's breath adorned the edible work of art. For the topper, the bride had red hair and the groom had brown hair and a beard, similar to Ben's. Sam was determined to find a bride with red hair and a groom with a beard! She searched until she found the one she wanted and finally ordered it online to give to Norma, the lady from church that made the most beautiful and delicious wedding cakes on the planet.

Apparently Eliel's presence caught the attention of some of the other guests as well. A few people came to them and asked about him at the reception. Was he a relative? Where was he from? Who was he? …. That sort of thing. They would answer vaguely, with things like, I'm not sure where he is now. He travels a lot. His family and Sarah's family go way back.

Sarah told Ben and Elizabeth he always attended the ceremonies, but never came to the receptions.

When it came time to open their gifts, they were overwhelmed by the generosity of their friends and relatives. Rachel gave them an all-paid trip to Boston that was good for the next three years. It gave them plenty of time to turn twenty-one and to hopefully, avoid any complications from the pandemic.

They were ecstatic! Especially Elizabeth. She made no secret how disappointed she was about not being able to go there for their honeymoon!

"Thank you, Mom," Ben hugged his mother.

Elizabeth gave her an enormous hug, thanking her for such a wonderful gift!

Sarah gave them a card. When they opened it, there was the deed to her house inside, along with a check for $2,000.

"Grandma, NO!" Elizabeth was afraid to touch it.

"Now I know what I'm doing. I know you'll let me live there until I go on to be with the Lord someday and I wanted you to have that security. So accept it and be happy!" Sarah hugged them both. They were overwhelmed.

"I love that house so much! I promise I will always treat it with love and care for it like it was a family member!" Sobbed Elizabeth. "It *is* a family member!"

Ben was choked up, "You could've waited for a few years, Grandma ... wow! You know we'll take good care of it." He said, giving her a huge hug as well.

After the gifts and cards were all opened, and Laura and Brooke had recorded everything, they realized there was nothing from Elizabeth's parents.

Her father looked at them and said, "Well, it's just that ... your gift wouldn't fit on the table." He smiled, "Come with me." They followed John and Sam to the door of the country club. When John opened it, they saw a brand spanking new, black Ford Explorer with 4 wheel drive, parked at the door. It had a huge white bow on the hood! This thing had leather seats and all the amenities! Just like the new vehicle they bought for themselves, only a different color.

*No wonder they wanted us to ride to the rehearsal dinner with them and John talked so much about all the features!* Ben thought. "This is too much! Wow!" He exclaimed.

Elizabeth was crying again. "Dad, Mom, thank you!" She hugged them both. "Ben's right, this is too much!"

"Well, we don't want you getting stuck in the snow either!" Her father smiled as Sam handed them the keys. "It's all paid for, totally yours." John added, proudly, as he opened the driver side door for Ben. Then he went around to the passenger side to open the door for Elizabeth. He reached for the glove box and pulled out an envelope. Inside was the free and clear title that was in both Benjamin and Elizabeth Adan's names. "All you have to do is register this with the state, and you're good to go. Your insurance is paid for, for the next three years."

"Oh, man! You didn't have to do that! I don't know what to say! Thank you so much!" Ben said as he held the steering wheel and looked around at all the frills the vehicle had to offer. "Praise God!" He declared.

"Yes! Praise God!" Elizabeth echoed.

## Chapter 22 – Finally Alone!

When it came time for the happy couple to leave the reception and make their way to the honeymoon cabin, Elizabeth asked Ben, "Should we take Grandma's car or our new car?"

They decided to take the new car since it had a temporary plate for the next three weeks and was insured.

Rachel, Sarah, Sam and John took care of the gifts. Sam and John had employed some people from the country club to help with the clean-up.

As Ben and Elizabeth got on the road with their suitcases packed and loaded, they realized this was the first time they were alone – since forever! Since they had made the decision to not be alone with each other three weeks ago.

Ben turned down a side road and pulled over, putting the four-way lights on. Once he put the vehicle in park, he just sat there and looked at his beautiful bride, still in her wedding gown, just without the train. Her makeup and hair were still pristine. Somehow her makeup made it through all the tears. *She is so, so gorgeous!* She looked at him, smiling. They allowed their minds to touch again. It filled their hearts, their souls – and their bodies! It was like they picked up right where they left off the day they found the cows on the side of the road. They were on fire! They lunged at each other with such emotion and passion. This time they didn't have to stop! …. Except for the car that was coming their way from the opposite direction. They decided to compose themselves and wait until they got to the cabin.

## CHAPTER 22 - FINALLY ALONE!

Mom's directions and the Google app were good. They arrived with no wrong turns. It was a quaint, little cabin that sat about 300 feet off the road down a winding driveway lined with maple and white birch trees – totally romantic and private. The nearest neighbor was about 300 feet away and there was a privacy fence between them.

As they pulled up and shut the vehicle off, Elizabeth reached for the door handle and Ben stopped her.

"I want the honor of doing that," and in the blink of an eye, he was standing outside her door, opening it for her. He wouldn't let her feet touch the ground.

With the keys in his hand, Ben swept Elizabeth up in his arms and slowly carried her to the cabin door. They savored every moment, every step, every breath.

The next morning Ben awoke to the sound of a rooster crowing. He turned to see the girl he had loved since the seventh grade lying next to him in the bed. The woman that had given herself to him completely last night. It was even more wonderful than either of them had imagined!

The beautiful being he would spend the rest of his life waking up to, thriving with, having children with, growing old with, was right there next to him and would be for the rest of their lives.

As he watched her sleep, he reached over and caressed her cheek with the back of his hand. *I will take care of her for the rest of my life and love her as I love my own body.* He thanked God for Elizabeth, and was reminded of the scripture, "He that finds a wife finds a good thing, and receives favor from the Lord."

He wanted to make her breakfast so decided to look around the cabin, especially since neither of them had left the bed, only to use the bathroom, once they entered through the door last night.

## CHAPTER 22 - FINALLY ALONE!

He saw the flowers and the card sitting on the table and reached for the box of chocolates as Elizabeth stirred. He opened the box, brought them to the bed and jumped back in.

She cracked her eyelids just enough to see. "Good morning!" She smiled from her pillow, "What are you doing?"

"Good morning my beautiful wife! I found some chocolates." He said as he reached to give her the first one.

"Oh, how sweet!" She sat up in bed.

They both chuckled at the pun.

Their next three days and nights were spent pretty much the same as their first. They only left the cabin for food and walks on the beach. They loved sitting on the covered back porch in the comfortable rocking chairs, watching the water. This was much better than a hotel room or a bed and breakfast somewhere, even that portion of the beach where the cabin sat was private and all their own.

While they were gone, Sarah and Rachel put their gifts in a spare room and a banner up across the front porch they ordered in town. It read, "Welcome Home Mrs. Elizabeth & Mr. Benjamin Adan!"

To give the newly weds more alone time, they made up Rachel's spare room and Sarah gathered what she needed to stay with her daughter for the next couple weeks or so. They put some of the flowers from the wedding in Ben & Lizzy's new bedroom and the rest throughout the kitchen and living room.

"Lizzy can throw out what she doesn't want," Rachel chuckled, as she looked around, thinking it was a bit much.

It was Wednesday afternoon when they pulled in the yard.

"That new black SUV will take some getting used to," Sarah beamed as they walked out of Rachel's front door to greet them.

"Right? Totally awesome!" Rachel answered.

Once they saw the banner, the flowers, flowers and more flowers, unpacked and were getting settled, Rachel called and asked if they wanted to have dinner with them. They invited Elizabeth's parents over too.

"I mean, we don't want to intrude, but …" Rachel snickered over the phone.

"Of course," they laughed, Ben had his phone on speaker.

"Living on love is great, but food is good too." Rachel teased.

"I don't know, I *like* livin' on LOVE!" Ben said with his raspy voice. "We may lock ourselves away and never come out!"

Elizabeth hit him on the arm.

"Just throw some food by the front door and run!" Ben laughed.

"We'll be there!" Elizabeth shouted over Ben's clowning.

Elizabeth looked at herself in the mirror as she was getting ready for dinner. *I do look better married!* There was a grounding, a deep commitment, deeper than she imagined. It changed her somehow. There was a connection to Ben that engulfed her very soul, her core. It was so beautiful. She thanked God for Ben and thanked Him for watching over them and blessing their marriage and their children to come. She had a glow about her that wasn't there before.

They never expected Grandma to move in with Mom like that. Although, that time was sheer bliss for the newly married couple. Ben didn't have to go back to work until the second week in their alone-time together.

They brought the rest of Elizabeth's things over from her parent's house and visited with them awhile, and Mom and Grandma, but other than that, they pretty much just enjoyed being with each other, spending time in the

## CHAPTER 22 - FINALLY ALONE!

woods together and in the tree house.

One morning, Ben took her to their favorite spot on the river, without the truck. They looked over the area where the digging took place. Nothing was disturbed, everything looked the same. Leaves had fallen over the ground and covered most of the bare spots. They realized no one would even know, except them, what had taken place there just a month ago.

"There isn't too much time left before the ground freezes. I wonder if they're going to wait until spring to start the digging." Ben said looking around.

"That would be all right with me." Elizabeth smiled, hanging on to Ben's arm as they walked through the beautiful forest of yellow, red and orange leaves. The area the boys initially uncovered was untouched by the diggers, so everything looked the same as the photograph in the paper, except for a few more leaves on the ground. Soon the ground would be totally covered with leaves, then the snow would come.

A few days later, Ben, Elizabeth and Sarah were at Rachel's going through the pictures from the wedding and found some photos of little Chris Wenther dancing with Natalie Selvy. They were so cute! Since they had ordered the photos in triplicate, Rachel called Julie to see if she and Gary wanted some.

While Rachel was on the phone with Julie, Sarah said, "Oh, wow, look at these!" She showed them two photos of Ben and Elizabeth during their first dance at the reception. There was a white light glowing above their heads in one of the photos. In the other, the light was glowing from their chests. It was beautiful. Like rays of sunshine rising in the morning, shooting out between their bodies as they danced.

"If only the photos could have picked up what *we* saw, eh Mom?" Rachel said after hanging up the phone with Julie.

"Oh, yeah!" Sarah agreed. "You two were glowing like the aurora borealis! It was awesome!"

"Kind of like right now." Rachel commented as she and her mother looked at the two love birds at the other end of the table ... they were radiant.

The next morning, around 10 a.m., Julie came over with the kids to pick up the photos Rachel had called her about.

"They're so cute!" Julie exclaimed as she looked at her son dancing with the beautiful flower girl.

Chris smiled sheepishly as he looked at the photos of himself dancing with Natalie, then went back to playing with his brothers in the living room.

Rachel showed her the rest of the photos as the boys played with the toys their mother had brought for them.

When Julie came to the photos of Ben and Elizabeth dancing with the light shining above them and between their torsos, she exclaimed, "Wow! What's that?"

"Right?" Rachel said, "Isn't that something?"

"Yeah, it's like their love for each other is glowing! These are awesome photos. No matter how it happened, these are great!" Julie exclaimed.

"We think so too," remarked Rachel.

Julie visited with Rachel until her second cup of coffee was gone and the kids began to get restless. She had been reading the Bible and asked Rachel about Ephesians 6 and the armor of God. Rachel explained about wrestling not against flesh and blood, but against principalities and powers in high places, basically the demon world. How for that reason we are to put on the whole armor of God to withstand the demonic forces. How we have been given authority over them in the name of Jesus and can command them to be silent and to leave. If we believe and don't doubt.

"That's a little scary, I've got goose bumps!" Julie looked a little overwhelmed. "I have a lot to learn."

"It sounds scary, but really, we all grew up with them in our heads without realizing it."

"Now you're really scaring me!" Julie rubbed the new goose bumps appearing on her arms.

"Think about this that Pastor says all the time, 'If Satan could kill us, we'd already be dead!' God has put boundaries on him. It's not as bad as you're imagining except for in extreme cases, Julie, really. They are familiar. That's why you'll hear pastors or others talk about "familiar spirits." That's the negative forces, the demonic forces around us trying to influence us. You know, like when you feel the urge to trash the lady wearing the bad dress, and talk about how ridiculous she looks, or lose your patience with the people at the grocery store, for example, or the urge to tell a lie. Those are negative forces, demons, that want to influence us. And, of course, that goes from the smaller examples up to the more extreme, but for most of us, it's the small things they trip us up on. They come as 'the good guys' trying to trick us."

"Okay, kind of like the good angel on one shoulder and the bad angel on the other you see in cartoons." Julie remarked.

"Yeah, it's kind of like that, for the most part." Rachel continued, "Studying the scriptures is a lifelong thing. None of us have reached the top. We all struggle with our own fears and problems. Sometimes we overcome and we win, other times we fall. The main thing is we pick ourselves back up and continue, never giving up."

"God's grace covers you. It's not by works, so no one can boast, it's by grace we are saved, because of His mercy and love toward us, because of what Jesus did on the cross. The Holy Spirit will reveal things to you as you apply yourself. He's real. Don't ever think for a moment He's not right there with you, because He is. And remember, He who is in us – is greater than he who is in the world. When you pray according to His will, expect an answer in faith, believing that God heard you and wants to answer your prayers. God *loves* it when you believe Him!"

Rachel told her about some Christian ministers and teachers on television and the internet that teach all of the Bible truths. Teaching about how healing and deliverance are still active today and about being filled with the Holy Spirit and speaking in tongues.

"Maybe we should think about having a Bible study once a week or so, even once a month, either over here or at your house. Is that something you and Gary might be interested in?"

"Do you mean with you guys?" Julie brightened.

"Yes, Mom would be all for that! Ben and Lizzy would too, I know they would. It's a great way for all of us to be able to learn more."

"I'll talk with Gary about that, I think he'd be onboard with it. I'll let you know." Julie said as Caleb, her youngest, tugged at her arm. He wanted to go outside and play by the raspberry bushes, remembering what fun they had with Elizabeth the day they came for dinner, and how tasty the raspberries were.

"Honey, we'll visit the raspberry bushes some other time, it's time to go home now," Julie said as she and the kids gathered up the toys they had brought. "See you Sunday," she said as they headed out the door.

Rachel had not forgotten to bring them into remembrance before the Lord each day, and would continue to pray for the beautiful family God had brought them, they all prayed for them, daily.

## CHAPTER 22 - FINALLY ALONE!

It was almost dusk, Ben and Elizabeth were sitting at the kitchen table writing thank you cards, using the notes from Laura and Brooke, being sure to write a personalized note for each card when Ben suddenly straightened in his chair, smiled and said, "The Dubheians are coming to visit!"

Elizabeth dropped her pen and looked into the living room, expecting them to show up like the Willows.

Ben laughed. "No, they usually knock at the front door."

As she turned toward the front door, there was a knock. Her heart began beating so hard in her chest, her face went flush.

Ben took her hands from across the table, "That's just Mom and Grandma."

"Oh!" She let out a nervous laugh. She had wanted to meet the Dubheians since the first day Ben told her about them. They had never visited while she was there and was really looking forward to this day.

"C'mon in!" Ben shouted.

Sarah and Rachel were alerted to their coming and were excited as well. They were also looking forward to the day Elizabeth got to meet them.

"So do they just appear at the door?" Elizabeth asked.

"No, they still park out in the apple orchard." Sarah smiled, motioning for Elizabeth to come stand by the big picture window in the living room to watch for them.

After about five minutes, which seemed like an hour to Elizabeth, Rachel looked up in the sky and pointed to a light moving towards the farm, growing larger as it approached. As it got closer the light faded and a shiny, black, cigar-shaped vessel appeared. It was approximately forty feet in length with a blue strip of light that traveled lengthwise along each side in sort of a curly-cue fashion. It landed without a sound at the edge of the apple orchard.

"Wow!" Was all Elizabeth said. A wide smile came over her face as she took it all in.

A door opened, much like the door of a plane, and three very tall, luminous beings, each between eight and nine feet tall, with blonde hair and dressed in white, shiny clothes stepped out. By the time Ben opened the front door, they had all shrunk to approximately six and a half-feet tall.

"Greetings in the Name of the Father and our Lord Jesus, the Christ!" Shemariah said as they entered.

Elizabeth was taken with their appearance. They looked exactly like humans, only they were much better looking than we were. Their hair was a lighter blonde than Eliel's. She thought of them as the version of mankind without all the flaws. The goodness in them actually caused their faces to glow. Their blue eyes were so full of love. Their countenance gave a peace that was similar, but not as intense as Eliel's. To her they seemed like beings that may be one step down from Eliel.

As she was introduced and shook each of their hands, Elizabeth was overcome with a sense of joy and well being from the energy flowing from them, again – much like Eliel.

"It's nice to finally meet you, Lizzy," Shemariah said, as he shook her hand.

"I'm honored to meet you! I've heard so much about you all." She smiled sheepishly, looking down, not knowing what else to say. She almost felt like she was in the presence of royalty of some sort.

"Come, sit," Sarah motioned toward the living room after the greetings.

"Would you all like your usual?" Rachel called from the kitchen.

"Yes, please," Uri and Noam answered.

"I'd like some tea this time, if you don't mind," Shemariah said.

"Sure thing, coming up," Rachel answered.

Elizabeth got up to help Rachel.

Ben touched her arm, "Sit with me, Lizzy, Mom's fine." He smiled a wide, proud smile at her.

"Oh, okay." She said nervously and sat back down next to Ben on the loveseat.

"We came to congratulate you on your marriage and welcome Lizzy into the family." Shemariah said.

They asked how their gifts were coming along. Ben told them about Elizabeth's emerging gifts and what Eliel had told her. Sarah proudly told them about how Elizabeth found the neighbor's horse, Tilly, along with all the other abilities they were working on.

Uri encouraged them to keep going and to try new things, because their gifts were alive, just as they are alive. The thought of that opened new doors to them.

They talked about the Willow's visit and the temple at the Au Sable. Shemariah told them they were not able to interfere with the battle coming out of that, but reassured them the Willows were more than able to see it through.

"So you have a history with the Willows?" Rachel asked.

"Yes, we all were created at the same time and have had fellowship one with another since the beginning," Shemariah answered.

"How cool is that?" She smiled, "That's just so awesome to imagine."

Ben asked them about some of the Reptilians being Watchers and if this temple held the evil spirits from their offspring.

Shemariah confirmed their suspicions.

Then Noam stood to his feet, "We would like to pray a prayer of blessing and protection over you," he said, looking at Ben and Elizabeth.

Ben and Elizabeth stood. Everyone stood around them in a circle, laying hands on them. As Noam began to pray in the Name of Jesus, a light shown above Ben and Elizabeth. They prayed for blessing upon their marriage and strength for them in the difficult days to come, asking the Father to grant them protection, wisdom and revelation during the dark days. Sarah and Rachel were now included in the prayer, as they asked the Father to give them His peace, His favor and His grace to carry out His will with exceeding excellence. That they would be as bright lights, drawing many from the darkness of this world.

After the prayer was through, they noticed the light above their heads had trickled down and engulfed all four of them. They were glowing like the Dubheians!

"Don't be afraid, the glow will fade by morning," Uri offered, smiling.

They stayed until their tea was gone, which was their usual drink of choice, all except Shemariah, he normally drank coffee. Before they left, they gave them each a wafer to eat. It was a light-brown square, that looked like a cracker.

"This will strengthen your bodies," Shemariah told them.

They each put the wafer in their mouth and began to chew, it tasted like honey. As they chewed, the wafers grew larger in their mouths. It was as if they had taken a big bite of food! They didn't mind, they were delicious!

The Dubheians each gave everyone a warm hug before they exited through the door.

"Never forget you are children of the most-high God. You have been given authority over the enemy, in the Name of Jesus, so don't be afraid of them." Noam added before they left.

They watched from the living room as Noam and Uri entered the craft. Before Shemariah entered, he turned and looked at Sarah through the huge picture window, telling her the protection over the farm from human or alien radar and listening ears was still intact. Even satellites, anyone suspicious of them would just wind up passing over the farm, as it had been for generations. Although the Brought family always tried to avoid doing

## CHAPTER 22 - FINALLY ALONE!

too much that would raise anyone's curiosity outside of the house.

They watched the craft as it began to hover a few feet off the ground. The blue stream of light lit up and whoosh! It silently shot straight up into the sky so fast if they would have blinked, they would have missed it.

Once they were gone, Elizabeth had more questions about the Dubheians than ever before.

"Do all of them have that glow like Shemariah, Noam and Uri?"

"Unfortunately, no." Ben answered. "God gave everyone free choice just like us. Some of them have lost their glow completely."

"Yes," Sarah added, "So if you ever meet one that doesn't have that glow, be on your guard."

"Well, can't they just create a glow to fool you?"

"Yes, but it's like the difference between real barbecue and liquid smoke, you'll know the difference now that you've met the good ones. They can't fake that peace," Ben added.

"Okay, yeah, I almost felt like I was in the presence of royalty of some sort."

"Funny you should say that," Rachel smiled.

"Why, what do you mean?"

"Shemariah is the ruler of his people. Noam and Uri are his closest guards and advisors."

"Oh my goodness!" Elizabeth felt nervous again. "Why would the ruler want to come here? Doesn't he have more important things to do on his home planet?"

Then Sarah added, "Well, if your life-span is only a few decades long, like ours is, then yes, but what if you are eternal? And a messenger of God as well?"

They gave her a minute to let that soak in.

"And remember, Jesus said whoever is greatest among us must be the servant. It's the same for Shemariah, he's never given the impression he's above getting involved with the 'lower' species and helping with his own hands."

"And let's face it," Ben laughed, "even with all of man's arrogance and pride, thinking we know everything and are above everything – we *are* the lower species."

"Right?" Everyone got a chuckle out of that.

"Many of them have a glow, but few of them are as illuminated as the three of them." Rachel offered. "And that doesn't mean the ones with a weaker glow are bad, we just need to read them the same way we read people."

"To the other extreme, just like humans, some of them are working with the Reptilians and other ET's that are not obeying God," Ben said.

"So were some of the Dubheians also part of the fallen Watchers?" Elizabeth asked. "Because they look a lot like some of the people I saw in the memory Ben showed me that built the temple."

"Yes, sadly," Sarah said. "But they originally built the temple before man was even created, remember. Later, three of them became Watchers, and like the Grigori, the Dubheians mourn for them even to this day. We humans are used to losing our loved ones because we are mortal, it's still painful, but we've grown accustomed to it. When you're eternal and have never lost a single person, that's huge! Unlike the Grigorians, they never stopped serving God with gladness. They knew where the blame belonged from the start. And the Grigorians came around as well, so…" She added, "And they're not dead, they're locked up and will be brought before the Lord the day of their judgement, just like humans."

# Chapter 23 – The Dig

It was the first Tuesday in November; Ben was starting his first day of work as a married man. Grandma was still at Mom's for another week. So they had another week alone together, but now with Ben working, it gave Elizabeth a chance to get used to the house on her own before Grandma would move back in.

"I don't want to go back to work, Lizzy. I just want to stay here with you." Ben moaned as he held her close under the covers after shutting the piercing alarm off on the Baby Ben.

"Right? I'm going to miss you. But I'll be okay." Elizabeth snuggled deeper into his arms and pulled the covers closer. "What's nice is Grandma and Rachel are just next door."

"Yeah. If we were living someplace else, like in an apartment or in a city somewhere, I'd be worried about you being left all alone."

"But God is good!" She kissed his cheek. "You know, I think Grandma should move back in. She doesn't have to wait another week."

"Oh, let Grandma do it her way. She's got her reasons and she's wiser than both of us. I'm sure there's something she wants us to learn from this, so I'm okay with it."

"All right." She conceded. "Well, how about I have everyone over for dinner one of these nights this week? My parents too."

"That's a great idea. They'd love that." He gave her a tender kiss then went to take a shower and get ready for work.

Elizabeth had sausage, eggs and toast ready for him when he got out of the shower.

"Man, you start treat'n me like this and I'm keep'n you!" Ben grabbed her as she buttered his toast.

"You're keeping me weather you like it or not!" She chided.

"I love you so much!" Ben picked her up and twirled her in the middle of the kitchen as she giggled, trying to put the knife back on the counter. "I'd keep you even if you were the worst cook in the world!" Then he carried her back upstairs.

Ben didn't mind chomping down his cold breakfast as he rushed out the door. It was the best breakfast he'd ever had before work!

As he pulled into Selvy's, feeling like the happiest, most blessed man on the planet, he glanced at the newspaper stand in front of the garage. Through the scratched and yellowing plexiglass, he saw Professor Virginia Hittorn's picture on the front page, along with headlines that read, "Inspection and dig at Au Sable to begin tomorrow."

"Now there's a sight!" James ribbed, as Ben came through the door of the office reading the newspaper. "Don't you look like an old married man!"

According to the article, Prof. Hittorn was all healed up and ready to come with her team, tomorrow. They were bringing their ground-mapping radar. If they found anything, the team was ready to begin digging the next day. They wanted to move quickly, Hittorn was quoted as saying, since they only had a month or so before the ground began to freeze.

The next day, at the break of dawn, two TV crews, one from Alpena and the other from Bay City/Saginaw, along with four newspaper reporters, flocked to Lumberman's monument to film as Prof. Hittorn arrived with her team. A black suburban with three U-M vehicles following behind it pulled in not long afterward. A U-M helicopter loaded with more advanced ground-mapping radar landed in the vacant part of the parking lot. They would do sweeps from the air, mapping the ground, while the teams on the ground would map more specific areas.

The university welcomed the publicity, although Professor Hittorn did not share their enthusiasm. She forced herself to accommodate them and allowed them to tag along. Some curious local residents had also showed up, but she didn't allow them to join the expedition.

Rachel, Sarah and Elizabeth watched the live coverage on television at Rachel's house. Ben kept up as much as he could, watching from work on the little TV hanging from the wall in the office. But he could look and 'see' them anytime. They had short spurts of live coverage, breaking into the regularly scheduled programs as it all unfolded throughout the day.

Around 10 a.m., they broke in again with live coverage of the professor talking, "We expected this structure to be remnants of the Ottawa Indian tribes, also called Odawa, but they didn't have a written language, that we know of." She paused, "We're finding symbols etched in the stones that bare a striking resemblance to the petroglyphs found in the highlands of Peru." The cameraman zoomed in on more freshly uncovered stones. "I don't believe this is the work of the Ottawa or other indigenous tribes from recent history. This site may be much older," the professor said. "As we continue to uncover this, we're finding that some of the markings are relief sculptures, indicating a highly advanced technology." There were spirals, zigzags and other symbols etched into basalt and granite stones along the walkway they were uncovering. "We'll have more information after further analysis," she added before the network went back to their program.

A while later, Ben decided to 'look in' on the dig. He overheard Hittorn talking with a colleague off camera. They were talking about the ancient gods and the Watchers.

"They're all extraterrestrials, if you ask me. They're technology's way beyond ours, even in today's standards." The younger man said to her.

"Yes, but the university doesn't want to hear that, so as always, we'll need to come up with another explanation." Hittorn sighed as they walked up the hill. "I'm expecting them to chastise me because I mentioned a highly advanced technology on the air."

*Wow, even they know!* Ben was sitting at his desk, finishing up some paperwork from the last vehicle he'd worked on. *"As ALWAYS, we'll need to come up with another explanation???" What else have they dug up over the years?*

As he sat there thinking about what she said, James walked in the office with paperwork in his hands.

"All finished! – Man! I don't think these people ever changed their oil. No wonder the head gasket blew!" James said as he sat down at his desk. "The car's only four years old! I just wish people would realize vehicles need more than gas to run."

"Did you tell them about the oil?"

"Yes!"

James and Ben were always trying to give people advice about taking better care of their vehicles.

"But you know how it is, some people just don't get it, man." Then James shook his head, chuckling, "I mean it's a profit for us, but it could've been avoided, so it's whatever."

As the two men sat behind their desks filing out paperwork and talking about their day, the station broke in with more news from the dig. The announcer said something about radar results. They watched as the professor came into view. The younger man Ben saw and overheard talking with the professor earlier was standing beside her.

"I'm happy to announce they have finished the aerial mapping of the site. These initial results from our team in the helicopter have just come in." They showed images of the radar on the screen. "It seems we have a very large complex here, according to these findings, there is a huge structure there in front of us," she said pointing to the hill, "and dozens of smaller structures with roads and pathways. It looks to be about one square mile." The screen zoomed out to show the boundaries. It went under the river just like Eliel mentioned.

"Apparently, the riverbed was further north than it is today, as you can see, the structures go under the river." Hittorn added. "We will begin the actual digging tomorrow. We want to uncover as much as we can before the ground freezes. We'll spend the winter months analyzing what we find, then resume digging in the spring." She added, "We are very excited about this ancient structure and look forward to discovering more about our past."

The news announcer came back to inform viewers the site is off-limits to any visitors at this time and would be strictly enforced.


The next day at sunrise, news crews and the Oscoda Township Supervisor, along with some of the Iosco County Commissioners were at the parking lot at Lumberman's Monument waiting for Hittorn and her crew for photo opportunities.

Reporters were already live, talking to officials about how proud they were that a discovery of this magnitude would be found in their little neck of the woods as the U-M team pulled up with an entourage that included three 18-wheelers hauling the heavy machinery for their dig.


"Well, Ben, you already know what they're going to find." Elizabeth said, as they sipped freshly brewed coffee in bed that morning, watching things unfold on the television in their bedroom. "I wish I could see it."

"I wish I could show it to you." Then Ben lit up, "Maybe I can!"

"What do you mean?"

"Well, if I can talk to you telepathically, why can't I share a memory with you?" He said, as he sat up straighter in bed.

He concentrated on the memories from the Starling, then opened up his mind to Elizabeth.

She began to see images of shiny, tall, blonde people in elaborate clothing, like you might see on television of people from ancient times; elaborate headdresses, gold armbands and ornate gold necklaces with jewels. She saw images of massive stones levitating, the construction was nothing like she had ever seen. Effortlessly, it seemed, the stones floated into place, as the one she presumed to be the leader, directed everything. She saw flying discs in the sky. The top of the tallest pyramid was flat, it was the landing place for the largest craft. It was huge, she guessed the craft to be the size of at least two football fields. It overshadowed much of the complex when it landed. The tops of eight other structures were flat as well. They were landing places for smaller craft. She saw the layout of the complex. It was magnificent. All in all, there were about thirty structures there.

Then, it seemed after some time had passed, she saw figures of feathered dragons with bird-like beaks and wings, but teeth like an alligator, being carved with light out of stone. She had seen similar figures on television from other digs around the world. The dragons were erected at the entrance of the main pyramid. A knife with a jeweled handle made of gold came into view. It was being lifted into the air by someone with darker skin and black hair, more like an American Indian, with markings all over his face and arms, in an elaborate headdress. He plunged it into someone! Blood spurted all over him. His eyes rolled into the back of his head. He had a feverish, wicked smile as he licked the blood that spattered on his lips. She saw so much blood! People were being sacrificed! So many people! So much deception! So much evil!

Elizabeth's breath was racing as if she'd just ran a mile. "That's enough. I've seen enough!" She opened her eyes.

Ben stopped.

"I'm sorry, honey," Ben held her in his arms. "My sweet Lizzy, I'm sorry."

"That was like something out of a horror film I'd never go see!" She said as she composed herself. "I could feel the evil, it was so real!"

"That's because it *was* real." Ben continued to hold her. "I thank God for Jesus everyday, more than ever after the Starling showed me that. In the Bible where Jesus was talking about His death, He said, 'Now is the judgment of this world; now shall the prince of this world be cast out.' That's a really profound statement! And if you look at the history, much of the witchcraft, demon possessions and magic came to an end after Jesus' resurrection. It wasn't as commonplace. The power of it was gone, and only those of mankind that chose to hang on to it, which I believe was their choice, continued in it, but the source of the power was gone. It was put under the feet of Jesus. No longer free to roam the earth."

He continued, "So Jesus not only took the keys of death and hell from Satan, he took his power when He was crucified, and rose from the dead. And now, it's the power of the Holy Spirit that's holding the evil at bay. When He's taken up, when the rapture comes, evil will run rampant again with the anti-christ, before the Lord returns. And just like the Bible says, it's getting worse everyday, building up to that point because more people are seeking it. They've lost their sense of right and wrong."

Elizabeth held her husband for a moment, then she sat straight up in the bed, "They don't know what they're digging up! They don't know what they're doing! Ben, we should stop it!" She climbed out of bed and paced the bedroom floor, rubbing her shoulders and arms as if she were cold. "We need to tell Grandma and your mom about this!"

"Honey, Lizzy, calm down," Ben tried to comfort her. "This isn't a surprise to God. They're doing this all over the world. They've been digging this stuff up for years now." He waited, then added, "It's just that it's so close to home now."

"You got that right." She continued to rub her arms as she stopped and pulled back the curtains of the second story bedroom window, looking out at the garden below, trying to focus on something normal.

Ben went and stood by her side, "Remember, the Holy Spirit is all over this." He paused, "And remember the Willows? Remember the cocoon? We have the power to bind the demon spirits. We don't need to be afraid of them."

After a few more moments, Elizabeth asked, "Would you mind if I shared what I saw with Grandma and your mom?"

"Not at all, you go right ahead."

Ben glanced at the clock. He had to leave in a half hour for work. "Maybe I should stay home from work today."

"Oh, no, Ben, I'm going to spend the day with Grandma! I'll be fine!" She said with determination. "As a matter of fact, I'm calling her right now and ask if she'll come over before you even leave for work!" She was determined not to let this get the best of her as she picked up her phone.

Elizabeth already had the television in the living room on to watch for any new updates at the dig when Sarah walked through the door.

"Would you like some eggs and ham for breakfast?" Elizabeth asked as she stood at the stove and cracked open two eggs into a cast iron skillet for Ben. He was just getting out of the shower.

"Awe, thanks, Lizzy, but it's too early for me." She took a seat at the kitchen table. "I will have some coffee, though."

"I so appreciate you coming over like this. I'm sorry to ask you, but I just don't want to be alone right now." Elizabeth said as she got Grandma's coffee.

"Oh, honey, I'm glad to do it. Now tell me what's troubling you."

"Well, this morning, we were watching the news, live at the monument, and I told Ben I wished I could see the temple. So he showed it to me."

"Wow, that must have been awesome!"

"It was. It's really magnificent! But then I saw the sacrifices and the evil." Elizabeth shuddered, as she set Grandma's coffee down in front of her. "It was so real. It threw me. It really threw me for a loop."

Sarah took Elizabeth's hand and motioned her to sit down beside her. Immediately she wondered if Elizabeth saw the memory of the future the Starling showed Ben, although it didn't seem so.

"I would just LOVE it if you'd spend the day with me, Grandma." She laid her head against her shoulder for a moment. "And if you have anything to do, can I just go with you? I'll help any way I can."

Sarah laughed, "Okay, but I really didn't have anything planned except to go to church tonight, so I'm looking forward to spending the day with you."

Elizabeth returned to her eggs. "You know, Grandma, I wish you wouldn't wait for this Saturday to move back in." She put Ben's breakfast on the table. "Why don't we move you back in today? You've been gone long enough from this house."

"Yeah," Ben added as he sat down to eat. "I could have your things over here in, what, ten minutes, tops? And that's just because you'd have to tell me what to take!" He laughed.

"Oh, no," Sarah chuckled. "I appreciate that I'm loved, and looking forward to moving back home, but I'm not moving back in until Saturday.

I believe God gave me that time-frame, so I'm keeping it." She smiled, "Besides, it's only three more days."

Shortly after Ben left for work, the news broke in showing the unloading of the equipment and Professor Hittorn introducing another professor that had joined the team, Professor Jim Moules from the university. He had a clean-shaven face and looked to be around the same age as Hittorn, a tall, stout-looking man with dark hair that was beginning to gray around the edges.

They talked about clearing a path to get the machinery to the dig site. "The ground seems stable enough and it won't take but a couple hours to clear it. If we have to we can bring in some gravel to strengthen any weak spots we may encounter. But we're confident we'll have the equipment at the dig site shortly," Hittorn stated.

"Grandma, how could I have faced those demons at the restaurant, in person, namely Professor Hittorn there, she pointed to the television, without as much fear as I had when I saw the things Ben showed me this morning?"

"It could be because you didn't have time to think about it beforehand."

"That may be, but the level of evil I felt with the memory was more intense than the evil I felt at the restaurant." Elizabeth confessed.

"Hmmm ... we need to pray about that." Sarah bowed her head, Elizabeth followed suit. They bound the spirit of fear and asked for protection over their minds. They asked the Lord to reveal the situation to them.

After the prayer was over, Sarah reminded her of that night at the restaurant. She asked if she remembered how she thought those demons were from the temple and Ben said no, that he felt they were other demons, not from the temple, simply trying to scare them both off.

"Assuming Ben was correct – now, put that together with what the Willows said. They said these demons bound at the temple were particularly evil and cunning and it was mandated that they not be allowed to roam free."

Elizabeth's face, first wide-eyed, changed to a face of resolve. "You're right, they're worse than Hittorn and those demons we saw! And ... we *are* going to stop them! Not the dig, but the demons themselves! Yes! We are, in Jesus' Mighty Name!"

"Yes, that's my girl!" Sarah said, "And we need to keep our focus and not get distracted by anything, even what we might see, hear or feel," Sarah added. "The Willows will come when it's time, because God has sent them to help us."

It was early afternoon by the time the U-M team got the heavy equipment to the dig site. They didn't waste any time unearthing the fifty foot pathway to the hill. The path went deeper and deeper into the ground as they went. They were at about twelve feet below ground level by the time they reached the hill.

The next two days, as they used the heavy equipment to dig in front of the hill, the teams on the ground began to dig up the hill, mostly by hand with shovels, pickaxes and brushes. They worked until just before dusk Friday and Saturday, uncovering some of the stairway at the foot of the hill, which was twenty-five feet wide. They also uncovered the feet of what was presumed to be two huge statues that sat on either side of the stairway. Professor Hittorn and Professor Moules described them as guardians. Of course, they didn't know what the statues were at this point, but Ben and Elizabeth knew.

The hill was so steep, almost straight up on that side. They commented that Monday, they would have to work from bucket trucks that could lift them higher as they went. They let everyone know from this point on, the digging would become mostly hands-on and proceed at a much slower pace.

## Chapter 24 – My Yoke Is Easy

Elizabeth and Ben woke early Saturday morning. They were both excited to have Grandma moving back in with them today. Elizabeth went through the house with a fine-tooth comb, making sure everything was spotless, just the way Grandma had left it. Rachel had decided after work, she would stay up and help with the move and nap later, since it was the weekend. Sarah hardly had to lift a finger other than to point to something as her family accommodated her every need and did all the lifting and bending.

"You're spoiling me, and making me feel guilty!" She retorted as Elizabeth took a basket of clothes from her arms.

"You'll just have to get over that, Grandma!" Elizabeth smiled as she bounced out of the room, carrying the basket.

Even though the Dubheians had a protection in place, they didn't want to push the envelope and just call everything over to the other house. It only took them twenty minutes to do it the regular way anyhow. After all, it was the occasion of it that was exciting.

"Well Grandma, now you'll have to put everything away, so you're not getting off scot-free here," Ben added as they brought the last of her things to the farmhouse.

Elizabeth and Rachel made a nice brunch for everyone and invited Elizabeth's parents over. They just enjoyed each other's company and catching up with Sam and John the rest of the day.

That following Sunday no one was late for church. Everyone moved their clocks back one hour as daylight saving time ended. People always enjoyed the extra hour but no one looked forward to it getting dark before 6 p.m.

Rachel had invited the Wenthers over for dinner after church.

The worship was powerful. God showed up and people were touched and moved in their spirit. A couple of the older gentlemen even got out of their seats and danced in the isles for a bit. Pastor Matt preached a salvation message.

He compared the Christian life to the atheist's, "… So if I'm wrong and the atheist is right, what have I really lost? I lived a good life and I simply cease to exist. I haven't lost anything by serving the Lord in this life. But if I'm right, what has the atheist lost? … Wow!"

"Many think that just living a good life is going to get them to heaven, but I'm here to tell you that couldn't be further from the truth!" He continued, "The Bible says plainly, it's not by works we are saved so that no one can boast, but by grace through faith, believing in the Son of God and humbling ourselves, believing in One who is greater, our Creator, our Father. So our pride is also addressed in this. Do we want to admit there's a right and a wrong way to do things? Do we want to admit that we've done wrong and need forgiveness? Or is our pride going to get in the way? Are we going to let pride keep us from paradise? From heaven? Where there'll be no more sickness? Where God's going to wipe away every tear from our eyes? Where we'll live in peace forever with the Lord? I know I'm not! I'm going to fall at His feet and say, 'Lord Jesus, please forgive me! I repent! I'll turn around, I'll change! I'll spend the rest of my life changing for You!'"

He continued, "God gave us all a free will, and He'll defend your right to choose all the way to the gates of hell. He won't make you come to Him. But Jesus invites all who are weary and heavy laden to come to Him. He said for His burden is easy and His yoke is light."

"And please don't make the mistake of thinking you have to clean yourself up in order to come to Him. That couldn't be further from the truth. Fact is, we can't. We cannot do it on our own. He accepts you just the way you are, warts and all! He loved you before you even *knew* who He was. Just give your life to Him and He'll help you along the way."

Ben glanced over at Gary, they were sitting in the same row. His face was all red and he was wiping his eyes. Julie was elated, her aura was brighter than they had ever seen it. But she sat there quietly, pretending not to notice, letting her husband experience all the Lord had for him.

Before Pastor even gave an altar call, Gary stood up and walked to the front. He knelt down in front of the whole congregation and gave his life to Christ right then and there.

Four more people went up and gave their lives to Christ. It was beautiful. The Spirit of the Lord was so strong, everyone could feel it. Elizabeth didn't think there was a dry eye in the house as she glanced around.

Ben and Grandma looked up at the ceiling. It was sparkling. The entire ceiling was covered. Elizabeth and Rachel saw them looking up. They looked up too and finally saw it! It was as if the ceiling was covered in tiny jewels. They finally got to see the wonderful, miraculous, physical essence of love, adoration and worship before it disappeared through the ceiling and went up to heaven.

"The Bible says the angels in heaven rejoice over one sinner that repents. So they're surely rejoicing today over our people here!" Pastor Matt exclaimed, before he led the entire congregation in the sinner's prayer. Then he went down and prayed for each of them individually as the worship team went back to the platform and played, "When The Glory's In The Room," by Brandon Lake.

After service, the Adans weren't sure if the Wenthers still wanted to come over for dinner, but to their joy, they did.

After everyone got to Rachel's house, Ben asked Gary if he would help him bring the folding table and chairs from Grandma's to set up in the living room at Rachel's for the kids to eat at. He was hoping Gary might want to talk about God as well.

As they were on their way, Gary said, "Hey, Ben, would you mind if I had a quick cigarette? I don't smoke in the car with the kids and I haven't had one since before church."

"Oh, yeah, let's go over here," Ben said, leading him to the other side of Grandma's house. It would always be Grandma's house to him and Elizabeth.

"I hope the women don't mind," Gary said, lighting the cigarette.

Ben laughed, "As long as you pick up your butts and don't smoke in the barn or in the house, they're cool."

Gary chuckled, "I don't even smoke in *our* house!" He looked around the farm. "I really do want to change, and I know there's a LOT I have to work on." He blew out smoke, trying not to let it go towards Ben.

"Oh, yeah, but see," Ben looked up at the clouds in the sky, "the enemy will come with a whip, telling you you're not doing it fast enough, or good enough, or tell you, you don't deserve to be saved. God's mad at you because you're not trying hard enough." He took his eyes off the clouds and looked straight at Gary, "Truth is, he's a liar. He'll try to distract you with those things and get your eyes off what's really important."

"What's that?"

"You really want to know?"

"Yes! I really want to know!"

"Well, we hear it so much, and mostly just take it for granted, but it couldn't be more true."

"What is it?" Gary said impatiently.

"It's reading His Word." Ben said, "It's not just reading it, but studying it and doing our best to do what it says, applying it to our everyday life. And I can tell you right now that you smoking cigarettes is not one of the 'so called' vices that'll send you to hell." Ben smiled as Gary looked at him in amazement.

"What?" Gary's aura immediately became brighter.

"I'll show you the scriptures when we get back in the house. It's really amazing the rules and regulations man laid on us, in the name of religion, that God never intended."

"I've heard Pastor Matt talk about God not being religious, but I really don't understand how all that works," Gary added.

"It can be confusing at first, but it's really not as complicated as it looks."

While they were outside, everyone else was in the house. Julie was so excited that Gary had went to the altar, she was in tears.

"I'm just so proud of him! My husband got saved today!" She exclaimed. "I just wanted to say that out loud." She confessed. "I'm pretty sure those Bible studies we talked about are going to be okay with Gary now, for sure." She beamed.

"You bet!" Rachel added, "Mom, before they leave today, we should get the calendar out and all sit down and see what nights would be best. We could do once a week, every other week or even once a month."

"I'm all for that," Sarah answered.

"Me too!" Exclaimed Elizabeth. "Ben will be too, I'm sure."

Once the table and chairs were all set up, Ben got his Bible out. He sat with Gary at the kitchen table as Sarah and Rachel made all the fixings for tacos. Elizabeth and Julie played with the kids in the living room. Of course they loved playing with Cookie and Ollie too. Especially Ollie, Cookie wasn't as kid oriented, being so small, she was afraid they would step on her. So after a few minutes of near misses, Cookie decided to make herself scarce and climb into Rachel's bed.

"Oh, wait a minute, I'll be right back," Gary went to the car and brought back his Bible. "I might as well start learning how to find my way around in this thing." He said as he sat down across from Ben.

Before they began, Ben closed his eyes, bowed his head and said, "Father!" With enthusiasm, as if God was right there in the room (which He was), "Please open up the scriptures to us and take the veil off our faces so Your truth will be plainly seen."

He took Gary to the Gospels of Matthew and Mark where Jesus talked about clean and unclean. How nothing that enters the body from the outside of a man can make him unclean because it goes through the body and out. But what comes out of our mouth comes from the heart and out of the heart come murder, adultery, lying, etc. That is what makes a man unclean.

Then he took Gary to the book of Colossians and showed him the scriptures that talk about taste not, handle not, touch not. How these are rules made up by men and they all perish with the using and promote false humility.

They went to Romans chapter 14 and read about the weak and the strong and how Paul instructed the Romans not to flaunt what they allowed if it was going to offend someone else. Because to him who believes something is a sin, to them, it is sin; to be careful not to get into arguments about it. The strong shouldn't judge the weak and the weak shouldn't judge the strong. We all have to answer to God for what we do.

"So basically, you need to search your own heart before God to see if you believe it's a sin to smoke, to drink or eat anything others may think is a sin. If you think it's a sin, it is sin to you," Ben said. "And if you don't feel condemned by it, the Bible says you'll be happy for it, giving thanks to God for everything."

Julie had come to the table overhearing the conversation and listened too. Gary sat there shaking his head. He was so relieved because that's all he could think about was what a bad person he was for smoking.

"Now the Bible talks a lot about drinking wine and strong drink," Ben added. "Jesus even drank wine and it was actually His first public miracle. He created wine at a wedding feast. But drinking in excess, getting drunk–is shameful, which I translate as sin, unless your sick or dying or something." He continued, "I personally also think of drugs in this category because they change you. It, basically, makes you drunk with whatever drug you take. But cigarettes don't alter your thinking, so you make up your own mind about that." He added, "Tobacco was widely used throughout the centuries. I believe it was such a trivial thing they never even mentioned it in the Bible. But again, that's just me, you need to decide for yourself about these things."

"Have you ever smoked?" Gary asked Ben.

"Me? No, I've never smoked," Ben answered. "Not because I thought I'd go to hell over it, but because I was never around it. I didn't even know anyone that smoked growing up, so, I just never developed a taste for it." Then he added, "Besides, Mom and Grandma would've beat the tar out me!"

They all laughed.

"You got that right!" Rachel called out from the living room. "I just believe smoking is bad for our health and it stinks." She added, "It's so addictive that if you can avoid it from the start, you're better off. But I'm not going to condemn anyone for it or think they're a bad person because of it."

"Personally, I agree with Rachel, but also I believe there are some foods that are worse for us than smoking," Sarah added, "with all the additives in food nowadays, causing dementia, cancer and all sorts of other sicknesses and our FDA just keeps approving everything. So who are we to judge?"

"But what if I don't want Gary to smoke?" Julie asked.

"Well, to be honest, if you have trouble with Gary's smoking, because you're his wife, and shouldn't let anything come between you, he should probably try to quit so it doesn't cause strife, to keep peace in the marriage." Sarah answered. "At the very least, not smoke in front of you and you both should agree not to talk about it. Paul says it like this, 'Everything is permissible but not everything is beneficial.'"

Julie smiled and looked over at Gary. "I'm just messing with you, honey. Whatever you decide is all right with me, just not in the house." She kissed his cheek.

"What does Pastor Matt think about it?" Gary asked.

Sarah answered, "Pastor Matt thinks smoking is a disgusting habit, but would never tell someone they're going to hell because of it."

They all began to laugh again.

"The reason I want you to know all of this upfront, is because so many people think once they stop smoking and stop drinking, for instance, they're all good with God. While, honestly, they haven't even scratched the surface." Ben continued, "Without realizing what they've done, they've become self righteous. They think they've done it all and don't have to do anything else to follow the Lord, when that couldn't be further from the truth. Satan's master plan is to get us off track, thinking these outwardly things matter to God more than moral character. What's in your heart is what matters to God. Do we talk about our brother or sister and pick apart everything that's wrong with them? Fault finding is a demon spirit and it can rob us of God's blessings quicker than anything. God wants us to surrender the thoughts and intents of our heart to Him. How much do we really care about others? Do we get angry all of the time and always make an excuse for it, mainly blaming others? Do we have self control and 'own it' when we do something we shouldn't or is it always someone else's fault? Do we show respect and honor for the things of God and others? Do we actually read His Word so we know what He expects of us? The Word is what will really change a person."

"Dang, Ben, you should be a preacher!" Gary was taken with the fact that such a young man had all this "God stuff" in him.

Once the meal was ready, everyone had their fill of tacos, chips and salsa and enjoyed the rest of the afternoon watching football on television.

Cookie even reappeared when dinner was served. She and Ollie never missed an opportunity for leftovers!

In the 4th quarter, during a commercial break, the news came on telling everyone to be sure to watch the evening news as they would have more interesting information about the ancient ruins discovered at Lumberman's Monument.

"What do you make of all that, Ben?" Gary asked.

"You mean the temple?"

"Yeah, I think that's pretty amazing for our area."

"Oh, yeah, we all do. As a matter of fact, we're watching that pretty close," Ben answered. "Our favorite fishing hole is just a few hundred yards from where they first made the discovery."

"You like to fish? We do too," Gary said. "Although we never go. We haven't been fishing since we were in Wisconsin!" Gary said, realizing the stress they'd been under with Julie's sickness and work, just trying to survive.

"They've got it all shut down and no one can visit that area at the moment, but we'll all have to go sometime."

"It'd be so much fun to take the kids fishing!" Elizabeth beamed.

"Yeah, for the first ten minutes or so!" Julie laughed, "But it would be a good time."

"There's some spots further downstream we could go to. Or we could go somewhere else, it doesn't have to be the Au Sable." Ben added.

They all agreed they would make the commitment to go fishing together soon.

Before the Wenthers left, they made a Bible study night for that next Thursday. Their first meeting would be at Grandma's and everyone was looking forward to it.

Pastor Matt baptized them the following Sunday.

## Chapter 25 - Voices

Monday, the digging resumed. The U-M team had two bucket trucks brought in that lifted two workers in each bucket to dig out the statues, working from the top down, while others worked to uncover the steep stairway that lead to the top of the hill.

Word had spread of the amazing discovery. It was beginning to make national and international headlines. Hotels were busy accommodating news reporters from across the nation, other archeologists, ancient astronaut theorists and curious visitors from out-of-town wanting to get a first-hand look. Although visitors were not allowed on the site at this point, they came anyhow. They began to gather each morning at Lumberman's Monument, which, by the end of the week, had become a household name to many across the nation.

By Wednesday, they had managed to remove the top dirt about three quarters of the way to the top of the stairs and uncovered most of the statues to reveal two fifteen-foot tall feathered, bird-like dragons with scales and two legs positioned on their bodies like where a bird's legs would sit. They were skillfully carved, depicting wings with plumage around their heads and below their gapping bird-like beaks with huge teeth. Their barbed tails were wrapped around their bodies. Their eyes, although plain-looking, seemed to follow anyone that looked at them. Some of the workers made comments how they felt as if they were being watched and had the creeps, a foreboding, but that information was not made public.

## CHAPTER 25 - VOICES

The results of the radiocarbon dating also came in on Wednesday. They estimated the site was built anywhere from 600 to 100 BC, which could mean it was built around 2,600 years ago, but Ben and Elizabeth knew the site was much older than that; it was pre-flood. Professor Hittorn said they believed it was built around the same time as Teotihuacan in Mexico. She also said the layout of the complex was similar to Teotihuacan.

Late that evening, around midnight, Ben and Elizabeth were sleeping in bed.

Elizabeth woke to the sounds of children crying. "Ben!" She shook him. "Do you hear that? I hear children crying!" She jumped out of bed and ran to the window. As she peered through the curtains down on the grounds below, she realized it wasn't coming from anywhere near the house.

As Ben gathered his senses, he said, "They're coming from the temple!"

"Are they real or from the past?" She searched her senses.

Ben did a mind-sweep of the temple area, "They're real." Ben exclaimed as he jumped out of bed and went to the secret room to change his clothes.

Dressed in black from head to toe, including a ski mask to cover his identity, Ben kissed his wife, then disappeared, while Elizabeth stayed behind and prayed, interceding for them.

As he stood in front of the temple, it was completely silent in the darkness. There were no sounds of crickets chirping or animals rustling. The cold night air filled his lungs as his every exhale gave him away. He turned his flashlight on and looked around. There were three bicycles parked near the stairway. He could hear three distinct voices. Then he saw them in his mind's eye. They were at the priests' burial chambers standing right in front of the tomb with the seal that guarded the demon spirits! *How in the*

**234** CHAPTER 25 - VOICES

*world did they get there?* "Jesus, help us." He immediately went to them.

"Help us!" Three boys that looked to be between eight and twelve years old, stood crying, "Somebody help us!" They clawed at what looked to be a stone door that was shut.

Ben waited a moment in the darkness to watch them before he revealed himself.

"Maybe there's another way out!" One of the boys said as he began to look around with his flashlight.

"What are you boys doing here?" Ben disguised his voice so they wouldn't recognize it if they ever talked to him afterward.

The boys looked in his direction, shining their flashlights toward him. When they saw his black outline they all screamed again and started running down another corridor.

"Wait!" Ben appeared in front of them. "I'm here to help you!" He grabbed all three of them in his arms and held them fast as they struggled to get free. "I'm not going to hurt you! Calm down!" He held them in place until they finally stopped struggling. "I'm going to get you out of here, but first tell me how you got all the way down here?"

They were silent.

"I've got all night, so if you don't want to talk, we can just stay down here." Ben said.

There was silence for about three seconds, then they all started talking at once.

"There was this voice!"

"It called us by name!" The rest was garbled as they all tried to give their version at the same time.

"Slow down! One at a time! You," Ben pointed to the tallest, "tell me what happened."

"We wanted to see the temple for ourselves. Our parents don't know we're here. Tommy and Jimmy were spending the night at my house."

"Okay, then what?" Ben asked. They were finally getting somewhere.

"We have a clubhouse not far from here. It's actually a treehouse. We all left the house on our bikes after my parents went to sleep." The boy said. "We went to the treehouse and got our flashlights."

"Okay, so how long have you been here at the temple?"

"I don't know, maybe an hour?" He answered.

"So what happened after you got here?" Ben asked.

"We parked our bikes and started looking around." He stopped and looked at the other two boys.

"Yeah, then what?" Ben asked.

"I was shining my flashlight on one of the dragons and it spoke to me!" The smallest boy, Tommy, added. "It knew my name."

"Then it called me and Andy. We both heard it at the same time!" Exclaimed Jimmy.

"What did it say to you?"

"It said, 'I have something amazing to show you.' And a stone moved underneath him, between his feet, and there was an opening."

"It said, 'Come through the opening and I'll show you.'" Tommy added.

"So we went in and ... got lost." Andy sobbed. "We couldn't find our way back. Then we got to this opening and saw all these statues and stuff. While we were looking around, a stone moved and closed off the way we came. Now we can't get out!"

"Are you going to help us get out?" Tommy asked Ben with a shaky voice.

"Yes, I am!" Exclaimed Ben. "Did the voice say anything else?"

They looked at each other.

"Yes," added Tommy. "It told us the only way out was to smash that thing off the rock."

"What thing?"

## CHAPTER 25 - VOICES

The boys led Ben back down the corridor to the opening where he first found them. They pointed and shined their flashlights on an ornately carved four by eight foot granite rectangle that stood about three feet tall. They pointed to the disc in the center of it. It was a gold disc, with a relief carving, the three priests lay together in the one tomb beneath it. It bore the images of the dragons with symbols around it. The boys didn't know it was a seal, or that the disc was associated with a tomb for that matter. They just thought it was a big, fancy stone with a picture carved in it.

"It told us to smash that off there and we would be free." Andy told Ben.

"Did you try to smash it?" Ben asked

"No, we just went back to the doorway that closed and tried to get it open when you came." Jimmy said.

"Was that it? Or did it say anything else?"

"That was it," they answered.

"Okay, so do you want to know what that is?"

Tommy said no, but the other two boys hesitantly shook their heads yes.

"Well, let me just say I'm glad you didn't mess with that. It's evil." He could see they were already scared enough without him telling them anymore details. "Now, before I get you out of here, I want you to promise me you'll never, and I mean NEVER, come back here again like this. Can you promise me that?"

They all agreed whole-heartedly. "We promise!"

Ben put his arms around them and in the blink of an eye they were standing in front of the temple where their bikes were waiting. They were already in shock, so as they were trying to figure out how they made it to their bikes so fast, Ben immediately said, "Show me the opening you went through." Not giving them too much time to process what just happened.

The boys didn't want to go any closer to the statues. They pointed to the one on their right. But when Ben went to take a closer look, they followed him.

"Can you point to where the opening is?"

"It's not there anymore. It was right there between his feet." Andy pointed.

Ben shined his flashlight on the area but couldn't see anything that indicated an opening. He believed the boys, nonetheless. He saw where their tracks led beneath its feet and disappeared. He caused the sand to cover their tracks.

As Ben led them back to their bikes he said, "Andy, did you say everyone was spending the night at your house?"

"Yes."

"Okay, what's your address?"

He told Ben.

Then Ben said, "Now I want you all to get on your bikes and huddle close to each other." After they were together, he said, "Now, Andy, Jimmy, Tommy, I want you all to think of Andy's house and his driveway." Ben stood beside them and told them to close their eyes and say, "Thank you, Lord Jesus, for sending this man to help us." He put his arms around them as they repeated the words. They all disappeared from the temple and reappeared in Andy's driveway before they could open their eyes. Ben was gone too.

The boys could hardly believe it! They were back at Andy's house, safe! They looked around for the man dressed in black and realized he was gone.

"I think he was an angel," Tommy said as they quietly made their way down the driveway so as not to wake Andy's parents.

The boys agreed they would never do that again!


That next morning, after Rachel got home from work, Ben and Elizabeth told her and Grandma what happened.

"So do you think it was a demon spirit that spoke to the boys or could it have been the Reptilians?" Elizabeth asked.

"I don't believe it was the Reptilians. They would've just went in themselves. But demons can't do anything here on earth without a host. They need to convince a human to do it for them, so I believe it was the demons," Ben answered.

Sarah and Rachel both agreed with Ben.

"The Holy Spirit must be shrouding the location of the priests so the Reptilians can't see it." Sarah added, "Or they would've already taken what they wanted."

"Yes," Ben added, "and Eliel said they'd return when the professor got close."

"So where is it?" Rachel asked, "Are they far from it?"

"It's deep in the center of the complex. Unless they find a hidden door or something, like the boys did, it'll take them awhile. At least 'till summer, I'd guess." Ben answered.

"Do you think the boys will be okay?" Elizabeth asked.

"Well, they're alive!" He answered. "I'm sure they'll be fine. They'll never forget it, that's for sure." Then he added, "Pray for them, Lizzy, that they'll heal up okay and have no lasting scars."

They all agreed to pray for the boys.

Then Sarah said, "Lizzy, the next time something like this happens, please come and wake me. I'm just one floor below you and we need to stick together when it comes to these kinds of things, no matter how trivial it may seem."

"I'm sorry, Grandma. The thought crossed my mind, but I figured Ben would be back before I knew it, to be honest."

"You could have also texted me or shared your thoughts with me at work." Rachel added, "Please don't ever think you're bothering me or that there's

ANYTHING going on at work that's more important than you guys!" She continued, "I mean, I probably wouldn't have dropped everything and left over this situation, but we could have been communicating, just in case."

"You're right. From now on, no matter what, I'll make sure you both know. We'll make it a rule!" Elizabeth said decidedly, "and vise-versa, that goes both ways."

They all agreed, pointing out that division or separation can be an open door for the enemy.

Since it was Thursday, Ben had the day off from work, so they all decided to study the scriptures, namely Isaiah, and practice their skills the rest of the day and get ready for the Bible study that evening with the Wenthers.

Rachel was chosen to speak. After praying about what would be best to talk about, she planned to continue a study in the book of Ephesians, then to just spend the rest of the evening answering any questions they might have.

Elizabeth helped with the kids so Julie and Gary could focus. They were learning so much, you could see a change in their countenance. Their faces were brighter, they seemed to be more at peace. It was obvious they had been studying the Bible on their own and growing in the Lord.

Digging at the temple continued through Saturday, with no more incidents. By this time they reached the seventy-five foot summit, cleared the top and were working their way down the north side of the pyramid. News crews were all over it. It only protruded about 60 feet from the surrounding area because the base of it was twelve feet underground. They used drones to show the area and film from the top. It became obvious the drones were not allowed to get close enough to make out the many carvings on the walls, but it was quite a sight, nonetheless. Many residents from the area were glued to the news each day to watch the ancient ruins come to life. Everyone was talking about it.

"It's hard to believe that hill I used to climb as a boy had a temple under it!" One of the residents remarked as a local station interviewed visitors in the parking lot at Lumberman's Monument one morning.

"I just think it's a wonderful and integral part of our history. We're looking forward to hearing what U-M has to say about who these people were and what their culture was." Said one woman who was there with other family members.

"I can't wait until they have tours! We want to go inside!" Said one boy, standing with his family.

"We want to see the dragons!" His sister added with such excitement.

Elizabeth cringed as she watched the innocent children, and grown-ups too, for that matter. *They have no idea what they're unleashing.* She remembered what Ben said, "The Holy Spirit's all over this. God's got this. The Willows will come to help us when it's time." That made her feel better about the situation.

# Chapter 26 – Reptilian Watchers

The digging continued earnestly for seven more days, until just before Thanksgiving. They managed to initially uncover most of the pyramid, but still needed to go over it with brushes and fine tools for the more delicate work. The structure, according to the radar results, was the largest of the two pyramids at the site, with around twenty smaller structures throughout the temple complex.

Professor Hittorn announced they would resume on the Monday following Thanksgiving and continue through the first week of December or so, until the ground froze.

They showed a clip of some artifacts that were found while digging around the edge of the hill. They mostly consisted of clay pots and broken pottery shards.

"We'll send these off for further analysis," Hittorn said. "We're hoping they'll give us more clues as to who the inhabitants were."

"You know Grandma, I may have heard this before from ancient alien theorists or somewhere, but it seems like the older the site, the larger the stones and little or no hieroglyphs, no writing of any kind on some of the oldest ones, like Puma Punku, the site with the huge 'H' blocks." Ben remarked as they watched the news about the dig. "And you know, that actually would line up. I'm thinking some of these discoveries, like the Au Sable temple, are not only pre-flood, but pre-man, before Adam and Eve."

"Back then everyone knew there was only one God, right? No matter what planet they came from." He said, "And take into account the scriptures that talk about how Satan's great trade and wealth made him proud, before he fell. It could have been here on earth all this took place and the reason God banished him to earth. So places like Puma Punku may be from that era of time before Satan's fall. No one worshipped other gods then, his was the first sin. So these structures could have simply been housing for them, or whatever their needs were, and would explain why there are no writings on them. What do you think of that?"

"It certainly could be," Sarah answered. "The idea for man to worship other gods, it seems to me – when you look at all this, only came after the Watchers descended on Mount Hermon and lied to the people, telling them they were their gods. Satan tried to get man to worship him before that but I don't think that worked out too well. They already knew God, although they were disobedient."

She continued, "And after Cain killed Abel, he went to live in the land of Nod, with the 'others.' He was rebelling against God, but there's no mention that he actually worshipped another god, because I don't believe that idea had yet been manifested, taking into account that the Watchers came down during the days of Jared, who hadn't been born yet, when Cain killed Abel."

"The legend says Puma Punku wasn't built by the Incas." She continued, "The Incan ruler, at that time, told early explorers it was already there. They said it was built by the gods in one night." She added, "And you're right, there's no writing found anywhere at that site and it's thought to be one of the oldest found, although there's no way to date it."

"And look at the Tiwanaku temple in Bolivia that's only half a mile from Puma Punku. The god they worshipped there, Viracocha, according to legend, was a Watcher and created a race of giants on the earth, just like the other Watchers did on all the other continents. Another interesting thing that lines up with the Adam and Eve books is that the locals say Viracocha always wore a mask and said if the people saw his face they would run away." She added, "In the books of Adam and Eve, God made the 'Satans' show Adam their true form and they were hideous. They became that way after they rebelled against God. So that all makes sense too."

"Yeah, so, I'm thinking Tiwanaku may have been built either right before the flood, and some of it survived, or right after the flood, in honor of their Watcher god, Viracocha," Ben added, "wanting him to come back. Because he was gone after God locked them all up, just before the flood. And Puma Punku might not only be pre-flood, but pre-man and before Satan fell."

Elizabeth thought about all that and asked, "So, are you guys saying the only reason there's writing on temples is for worship?"

"Pretty much," Sarah answered. "Also for their history and way of life, but that was secondary."

"So I wonder what they're calling this dragon god at the temple here?" Elizabeth asked.

"I don't know. The Starling never told me its name," said Ben, "but he was certainly blood-thirsty, just like the rest."

"He could be related to the Reptilians!" Sarah exclaimed out loud as she put two-and-two together. "That may be why they're wanting to control the demons trapped in the tomb."

"Yeah!" Ben's mouth dropped, "That tomb may hold some of the demon spirits that came out of the Reptilian giants! That Watcher may have been Reptilian! It would explain the dragons. And the giants he created were his children!" Ben stood up as if to go somewhere, but he paced the living-room floor. "The next time I see Eliel, I'm going to ask him."

Elizabeth's wheels were also turning, "And I remember the Willows telling us those demons were particularly cunning and evil. At the same time, I remember you, Ben, telling me the Reptilians are pretty cunning too, how they always seem to have a secret agenda." She thought more, "Wait a minute, I thought the Watchers were the Grigori!"

Sarah laughed, "Lizzy, I love the way your mind works! Yes, at least two of them were Grigori, but there were 200 Watchers that fell in total, so I'm assuming they were from a number of different planets with multiple races. One of the races could have easily been the Reptilians."

Sarah continued, "Actually, there's a German-Bolivian scholar named Arthur Posnansky who studied the ruins of Tiwanaku for nearly 50 years. He estimated, because of the alignment to the stars, that it could be more than 15,000 years old. But mainstream scholars laughed at him for his astonishing estimations."

"Well, that would definitely be pre-flood and pre-man." Ben said as he sat back on the couch next to Elizabeth. "It's really anyone's guess. That radiocarbon dating could be so far off, there's so many variables that can affect that outcome. And Posnansky's estimations, who knows?" Ben stroked the beard on his chin, "Grandma, could I ask Eliel about all this stuff? I mean, would it be like cheating if asked him to tell me?"

"Ah, well, I can tell you one thing, if you ask Eliel something he isn't supposed to divulge, believe me, he'll let you know." Sarah laughed. "Not in a bad way, you don't have to be afraid to ask him. He'll just flat out tell you."

"Okay, because I'm thinking the less writing or no writing, the older the structure, but that may not be accurate either. And I've never prayed about it, so."

He thought some more, "Then there's also the possibility that places like Puma Punku were pre-fall, before Satan fell. Then after his fall, and before man, Satan and the third of the angels that fell with him, may have constructed some of these places with writing to promote their own selves, pointing these structures to their own home planets, because they were all stuck on earth." He paused, realizing how confusing that was. "That is, if some structures with writing were built before man."

"Anything's possible, Ben." Sarah chuckled, "This isn't something I've ever approached God about either. But maybe it's time."

There was a knock at the door. Sarah knew it was Rachel, not because of her gift, but because she always knocked three times before she opened the door. Even when she was little, if she would knock at someone's door, it was either seven times or if she knew them and they were expecting her, she would knock three times. Sarah wasn't even sure Rachel was aware of it, but she loved the little mannerisms of her daughter.

"Hey, what's everyone up to?" Rachel sat down at the other end of the couch. Her hair was still wet as she had just gotten out of the shower. It was morning-time for her, working the night shift.

They filled her in on their current discussion about the temples. She said that was something she'd never really thought about either.

Rachel pulled out her phone to make a list, "I want to try and finalize everything for Thanksgiving dinner, because I'm going to do my last shopping excursion tomorrow morning after I get out of work, since it's the eve of Thanksgiving eve." She smiled. "So if we need anything I can get it then, if there's anything left on the shelves."

"Right?" Sarah shook her head.

"Let's go over the menu one more time and I'll look through the cupboards to see what we have," Elizabeth volunteered. She was excited, this was her and Ben's first Thanksgiving married. Sarah had gladly agreed to let her make the turkey this year and Rachel volunteered to help with the trimmings. Although everyone insisted that Grandma still make her mouth-watering apple pie and Lizzy's mom bring her famous yams with pecans and marshmallows. They would always joke about not needing a turkey, with all the trimmings and desserts to eat.

Not much had really changed with them being married, concerning the holidays. Elizabeth and her parents had been spending Thanksgiving and Christmas with the Adan/Brought family since Ben and Elizabeth were in middle school, except for the few times the Shiels went to Florida to visit Sam's sister. They would trade off year to year as to who's house they were going to have it at, but they almost always spent the holidays together. The Lord had blessed them as they each truly valued the other's friendship and loved one another as family right from the start.

This year would be different as they invited the Wenthers for Thanksgiving as well. Everyone was looking forward to it, especially Elizabeth. She absolutely adored Chris, Abe and Caleb, and loved helping Julie look after them. John, Ben and Gary were looking forward to watching football. The women liked football too, so it was another family tradition they all enjoyed together.

Work on the pyramid continued after Thanksgiving through the first week of December. On their last day, hundreds of people gathered in the parking lot at Lumberman's Monument to show their support, along with news crews from across the nation. Professor Virginia Hittorn and Professor Jim Moules were becoming quite the celebrities with all the news coverage. They promised to be back in the spring.

"As soon as the ground thaws, we'll be back to continue our work. We're hoping it will be no later than the first week in April, but we'll see. It all depends on the weather," said Professor Moules.

Professor Hittorn wished everyone happy holidays and let viewers know they would be working in the lab through the winter, analyzing their discoveries and planning the best ways to proceed when they resumed in the spring.

Christmas came and went without any temple or demonic incidents.

Bible studies continued with the Wenthers. They were growing in leaps and bounds. Gary and Julie both received the baptism of the Holy Spirit at Grandma's house the week before Christmas, during a Bible study that turned into a Holy Ghost revival! The entire household spoke in tongues as the Holy Spirit gave them utterance. It was a beautiful time of healing and restoration for Julie and Gary. Christmas meant more to the Wenthers this year than ever before as the peace and joy of the Lord entered their lives in a much deeper way.

Ben put a snow plow on the front of his truck and made some extra money plowing driveways while the cold winter months drug by. But Ben and Elizabeth didn't mind, they enjoyed snuggling under the covers together at night – and – just like the teenagers they were – sledding on the snow-covered hills in the woods behind the house during the day, when they had time.

Elizabeth especially enjoyed taking Julie and her boys out sledding behind the house. Grandma Sarah loved sharing memories with the boys of how she used to ride her horse bareback, she didn't like saddles back then. In the winter she would ride around the farm and pull her friend behind her in a saucer with a rope made of binder-twine that was tied to Sarah's waist.

"Boy, when that saucer hit something, I knew it!" She chuckled, "One time, I went flying right off her back-end when the saucer hit a tree root. It just stopped right there! Star kept going, that rope tightened around my waist and I flew straight off her back!" Her eyes twinkled as she remembered it like yesterday. "My friend and I were fine – knocked the wind out of me and I had a couple bruises, but it must have been a sight!" She laughed. "I was about your age, Chris, and my friend was a year younger than me."

"You rode a horse all by yourself when you were as old as me?" Chris's eyes grew big, never having been around horses.

"Oh, yeah, we did all kinds of stuff back then." Sarah stopped. She realized telling them about how her parents began to teach her to drive the family car as soon as she could reach the pedals and see over the steering-wheel – and driving the tractor at that age, might get her in trouble with Julie, so she changed the subject. *The times sure are-a-changin'.* She felt bad for the kids of today. They weren't allowed to have any responsibility, therefore, they didn't know how to be accountable. It always amazed her that many sixteen-year-olds today could barely handle the responsibility of driving a car and follow the rules, let alone eight-year-olds.

## Chapter 27 – Hostages

It was a warm, sunny Saturday morning, toward the end of March. Ben woke early and went downstairs to pray and read his Bible as he often did. As he made a pot of coffee, he realized he was restless, but wasn't sure why. He read about the time after Armageddon, in Isaiah, 11:6-9:

"The wolf also shall dwell with the lamb, and the leopard shall lie down with the kid; and the calf and the young lion and the fatling together; and a little child shall lead them. And the cow and the bear shall feed; their young ones shall lie down together; and the lion shall eat straw like the ox. And the sucking child shall play on the hole of the asp, and the weaned child shall put his hand on the adder's den. They shall not hurt nor destroy in all My holy mountain; for the earth shall be full of the knowledge of the Lord, as the waters cover the sea."

Ben smiled to himself, picturing what that will be like, seeing the bear and the lion eating grass like the ox, with children playing and romping with them, even the snakes no longer threatening. *Filled with the knowledge of the Lord! Even the bugs won't bite anymore! I'm looking forward to that day!*

He watched a couple of Cardinals playing in the bare tree branches through the kitchen window, one of the few species of birds that stay through winter. As he thought about all that he'd read, Elizabeth came downstairs and he shared it with her as she made herself a cup of coffee.

Then he said, "I think we all should pay a visit to the temple today," as he finished the last of the coffee in his cup. "What do you think of that?"

"I'm game," she said as she sat down beside him at the kitchen table, stirring her coffee.

"Cool, I'll see if Mom and Grandma are up for it," he said as he went to the coffee pot and made himself a second cup. "Mom should be home from work any minute."

They heard Sarah stirring in her room, which was just off the kitchen.

"Oh, good! Grandma, you awake?" Ben called.

"Yup! I'm up!" She called back. "And yes, I'm game too!" She overheard them talking.

Elizabeth made a fresh pot of coffee for Grandma as she poured the fourth and last cup from the pot. She knew Grandma loved fresh coffee. A twelve-cup pot would only yield four of Grandma's mugs, which everyone used. They weren't only cool looking, they were comfortable to drink out of, having the lips fluted with the overall shape being sort of a bottom-heavy hour-glass, which helped the coffee stay in the mug instead of spilling at the slightest weave.

Elizabeth loved living with Grandma. It just felt right. She loved her company so much, they both did. Instead of an inconvenience, she was a blessing. If they needed time alone, there were tons of places they could go and it was never a problem.

Just then Rachel knocked on the kitchen door before she walked in, "Yup, I'm game too!" She smiled at Elizabeth as she closed the door behind her. She had told her while she was driving home from work about Ben wanting to visit the temple today. "Oh, that coffee smells good," she exclaimed, as the pot gurgled out the last few drops of water into the grounds.

The four of them sat around the kitchen table planning their visit to the temple. They decided to go as soon as they could muster themselves together.

"Well, if there's still snow on the ground there, I think we should wear white," Sarah said.

"Let me look," Ben closed his eyes and concentrated on the complex. Yup, all snow, white it is!"

"Mom, I think you should bring your camera today so you can take pictures of the writing on the walls and anything else of interest," Rachel added.

"Good idea," Sarah answered.

Once they were all ready, dressed in white from head to toe, they huddled around Ben. He checked the area one more time to make sure there was no one around and off they went.

He took them to the front where the kids had their bikes parked before. The snow-covered ground was pristine, just a few animal tracks here and there, but no humans had been there. The two bird-like dragons, now completely uncovered, stood staring at them. Ben checked the area where the boys said the door opened between the feet of the one on the right – nothing there. They were all on their guard for physical and spiritual presences. The mid-morning sun was bright. An early warm spring breeze moved through the bare tree branches in the forest around them. The sound of birds happily singing was the only sound they heard.

Ben motioned for them all to come close. He pointed up as he put his arms around them and took them to the top of the pyramid. The snow was beginning to melt there as the sun hit the top of it directly. The stones, with the earth and grass no longer protecting them from the elements, were a little slippery.

"Wow!" Elizabeth said it first. They all echoed her as their eyes took in the frozen, pristine white landscape below, which was breathtaking against the naked trees. You could see much farther than in summer. The Au Sable was so beautiful as it wound through the bare forest, making its way to

## CHAPTER 27 - HOSTAGES

Lake Huron. The ice was already beginning to break up where the water moved the fastest, depicted by the darker spots along its carved path. The entire river would soon be free of ice once again along with the landscape.

Sarah looked down and found there were carvings even on the stone she was standing on, although much of it was still covered by ice and snow. The warm weather caused the snow to harden but she managed to scrape off a good portion of it and found a carving of the dragons with some form of writing around them. She got her camera out and began taking photos. She also got photos of the landscape.

Then Ben took them back down along the east wall where Sarah could take more photos.

Rachel and Elizabeth talked with the trees. Rachel remembered in years past this was such a happy forest. Today, however, it was filled with a foreboding, a dread of the things to come. Yes, even the forests have the ability to discern the coming season, and theirs was wrought with the evil that would soon come upon it.

All of a sudden, Sarah stopped taking photos and looked over at where Ben was standing. He was about 4 yards away from her. A beam of light appeared out of a cloud-less sky next to him. She couldn't see a craft, the light just seemed to fade as it went higher and higher into the bright blue sky. They both sensed it was the Willows. Ben backed away a few feet and waited. Rachel and Elizabeth felt their presence as well, and came and stood next to Sarah.

As the swath of light grew wider, the outline of three beings emerged. They saw it was the same three that had visited them before, Byron, Trazier and Ombeye.

*Greetings Brought family.* Byron said to them, telepathically.

*Greetings,* Ben replied in the same manner.

*We have come to tell you the Reptilians are planning to breach the federation agreement. Their greed is feeding their impatient nature. They intend to abduct Professor Hittorn and Professor Moules, with another, Michael Broward. They need three people for the spirits to indwell. They cannot open the tomb themselves, they need the humans to do it for them,* Byron said. *They plan to take them tonight, before the ground thaws, before they can dig anymore.*

Ben thought for a minute and looked at Grandma.

*Whatever it takes, Ben,* she said, also without speaking.

Ben remembered the three boys who were lured to the tomb, *three*.

*Okay, so what can we do?* Ben asked Byron. His thoughts went to abducting them himself and taking them somewhere, but would the Reptilians know?

*No, they would not know where you have taken them. The Holy Spirit clouds you, the Reptilians cannot see what you do,* Byron read his thoughts. *But there is ... a problem. One of them is in communication with them, a Satan worshiper.*

*Professor Virginia Hittorn!* Elizabeth spoke up, telepathically as well.

"No," Byron answered out loud this time, with his leaf-rustling willow voice, "Professor Moules."

They were surprised.

"So, is Professor Hittorn innocent in all this?" Ben asked. They all spoke out loud now.

"Yes, she and her team have no knowledge of the satanic forces in their lives," Byron answered.

"They must have a lot of missing time!" Rachel added.

"Right?" Elizabeth said sorrowfully.

"What can we do about Professor Moules, then?" Ben asked.

Byron answered, "They need three. If Professor Moules is the only one they can find, they cannot open the tomb."

"Gottcha!" Ben answered with a smile. "So how long do I need to hide them?"

"You will only need them to be gone for the night." He answered. "We have a diversion planned for them shortly after they find them missing."

"Okay, but how long will that last? I mean, what's to prevent them from coming the next night, or the night after that, or choosing someone else?" Ben asked.

"The Reptilians want to use these three in particular because they are in charge of the dig and would not raise suspicion." Then Byron made a gesture that looked like a smile, "And our diversion will last as long as it takes the humans to uncover the tomb on their own."

Ombeye and Trazier also smiled.

Then everyone smiled, even the tiny leaves on the vines of the Willow's heads and garments that cascaded from their shoulders all sparkled and moved.

"All right then!" Ben felt more at ease with the task at hand, not feeling the need to know about the details of the diversion. He knew it was above his 'pay grade,' his knowledge. "We can do this!" He had an isolated cave in the Grand Canyon in mind, where the only way in or out was him.

"That is a good choice," Byron commented as he read Ben's thoughts again.

As Ben thought about it, he realized keeping them separate would be better. They would just think it was a bad dream. If he put them together, they might realize it wasn't just a dream. There was a second cave not far from the first that would also work well for Michael.

"Take them by eleven o'clock." Byron said, as the beam of light reappeared.

"Wait!" Ben shouted, realizing how fast they disappeared the last time. "Can you tell us anything more about the time frame when they will discover the tomb? And should we just wait until that happens?"

"We will be back; you will know." Byron said as the three of them each bowed their heads, saying goodbye, and disappeared into the light.

Later, after they were back at the house, Ben began to watch Professor Hittorn. He hated watching people like that, it was disgusting to him, but this was for a good cause. He guessed Michael Broward might be the one she was with the day he overheard them talking about ET's. It didn't take him long to find him. Even though it was Saturday, they were all at the university working on perfecting a testing procedure that might give them more accurate results on radiocarbon dating. Hittorn was all in a rush to get it done before Monday for some reason. After watching him for awhile, he found this Michael was Michael Broward.

He visited the caves to make sure there was nothing in there that could hurt them during their stay. Among other creatures, there were some snakes and spiders, so he went back to the house and brought Elizabeth to the caves. They prayed a prayer of protection over them. She spoke to the snakes and all the creatures in the caves asking them to leave, telling them it was only for the one night, and they did as she asked.

"I want you to have these ready for them before they get there," He didn't notice Sarah was standing next to him until she spoke, he was so engrossed in his thoughts, back at the house. She was holding two blankets and two flashlights. "I'll have some lawn chairs, water and toilet paper ready for them when it's time as well." She set them in the laundry room. "And anything else you think they might need."

"Okay, thanks, Grandma." Ben replied, "Michael is a smoker, so I better make sure he has plenty of those." He chuckled.

It was going on 9 p.m. Ben took the items Grandma had put in the laundry room and placed them in the caves.

## CHAPTER 27 - HOSTAGES

He had watched Virginia and Michael as they went home that evening, making a mental note of where they put their coats. Although the caves were warmer than outside, they were still a chili 45 degrees or so.

It was now 10:15 p.m. Ben didn't want to wait any longer. "Close enough." He said as he kissed his wife and disappeared, dressed in black from head to toe.
Elizabeth, Sarah and Rachel were all praying and watching too. Their sight was limited, but they could sense what Ben was thinking and feeling.

Ben looked and saw that Virginia was already tucked away in bed. He appeared at her closet and grabbed her coat and found her shoes. He disappeared and took them to the cave. He looked around, checking one more time that everything was in its place for her and said another quick prayer. Then taking a deep breath and letting it out – he disappeared out of the cave and reappeared in her room.
He stood at the side of her bed. Her night light cast a black, shadowy 6'3" figure towering over her. She opened her eyes just in time to see him reaching down to scoop her up in his arms. She opened her mouth to let out a scream as they disappeared. Her screams may not have been heard at her house, but they were sure bouncing around in the darkness of the cave! She flailed about wildly. Ben didn't speak to her. He just put her down and disappeared. With an afterthought, he went back – found the flashlight and turned it on for her before disappearing again. *Learn as I go,* he thought to himself.

Before going to get Michael, he visited his cave and turned the flashlight on for him. He looked again to see where Michael was at. He was taking a shower! *Oh, man...* Ben thought as he looked at his watch. It was 10:30 p.m. *Well, he should be done before eleven.* He waited.

Finally, at 10:50 p.m., Michael was out of the shower and dressed for bed. He was just leaving the bathroom when Ben appeared behind him. Michael turned and saw him. He tried to run, but Ben was right there. Micheal stopped, turned and drew back his fist. Ben let him punch him square in the face, his nose to be exact. *I owed him that one.* Ben shrugged it off and grabbed his arms. They disappeared. Once they were in the cave, Michael struggled to get free. Ben released him and realized he had forgotten to get his coat and shoes. He went and got them, along with three packs of cigarettes, finding them in the cupboard where he kept them. *I don't know how much he'll need, but even if he chain-smokes, this should be enough.* Ben took them to the cave. Michael had grabbed the flash light and was looking around. He didn't even see Ben set his things in the lawn chair.

After Ben got back to the house he watched them to make sure they were okay. He saw Michael feeling around in his pockets, realizing he only had his pajamas on.

"Shit! What's the sense of having cigarettes with no lighter!" Michael yelled at the darkness.

"Ha!" Ben laughed as he went back to Michael's house, found his lighter, and set it on the lawn chair for him in the cave. It took him another ten minutes to find it, but he was sure glad when he did.

Virginia was crying, sitting in her lawn chair wrapped in the blanket Sarah had provided. Ben felt for her. He remembered what the Willows had said, that she had no knowledge of the satanic forces in her life. He began to pray for her as Elizabeth, Rachel and Sarah joined in. They prayed that she would be delivered from the evil that came upon her, for her salvation, that God would call her and reveal His truth to her. They also prayed for Michael. Ben continued to keep an eye on them. None of the Brought family slept that night.

Just before sunrise, Ben changed into his black attire once again to take his hostages home. They had both fallen asleep. Elizabeth, Rachel and Sarah concentrated on them to cause their sleep to be deeper. Ben appeared behind each of them, placed his hand on their shoulder and took them to their beds, both unaware of his presence. Touching their coats, still on their bodies, they gently dissolved right where they lay, and re-appeared in his hand. Ben smiled, remembering the day they discovered they could do that, not long ago. He placed them back where they belonged. He also took their other things, put them in their respective places and cleaned their shoes with lightening speed. Michael had smoked two-and-a-half packs of cigarettes. So Ben, for the first time in his life, bought three packs of cigarettes, making sure they were the same brand, to replace them. He also took care to put the lighter back where he found it, in keeping with the dream scenario. Then he brought the blankets, lawn chairs and other items home – it was done. His mission was complete.

Ben arrived home just before the sun appeared over the horizon. "What a night!" He said, as he collapsed on the bed where Elizabeth was already waiting. Church would have to wait until next week.

They woke about 3 p.m. Ben watched Professor Hittorn and Michael to see what they would say about the previous night. But they didn't say anything. To Ben's relief, they each, apparently, thought it was a bad dream and never mentioned it to anyone.

On Monday, Ben overheard a conversation between Professor Hittorn and Professor Moules while they were working at the university.

"I tried calling you, Saturday, just after eleven and there was no answer." Jim said to Virginia. Apparently, he had come up with some sort of excuse to be calling her at that late hour.

"Oh, I was asleep, dead to the world," she exclaimed. And no more was said.

Jim wondered if she might be having an affair or something, because he knew she wasn't home. The Reptilians visited each of their houses and found them both gone. They asked if he knew where they might be, but he had no idea. He suspected they might be having an affair with each other. It wasn't uncommon for a younger man to be drawn to an older woman, especially a woman of high position like Professor Hittorn. He wondered if they were at a motel together, but didn't press the issue.

## Chapter 28 – Removing The Seal

A few more weeks went by without incident and spring was doing its magnificent work. The snow was gone, some wildflowers and ferns were beginning to peak through the earth and yes, the ground was thawed. Spring rains had made the road to the site soft and caused a delay in moving the heavy equipment, but that didn't prevent the university team from going in the first Monday of April, with much fanfare.

News crews and committed fans gathered once again at Lumberman's Monument to cheer them on and find out what their next steps would be. Some of the fans were holding hand-made posters saying "Go U-M!" with a colorful painting of the dragons on either side. A news team found the source of the posters. An artist had set up a little store in the back of his van in the parking lot. Using acrylic paints, which dry fast, he painted them as customers watched, and sold them for $20 each. There was quite a line that had formed. The news team caught it on camera. Officials quickly shut him down, saying it went against their ordinances as people boo'd. They caught that on camera too.

Professors Hittorn and Moules said their next steps were to keep dusting and uncovering everything the team could until the heavy equipment arrived.

"Our radar shows there are tunnels beneath the ground. There's much more under the temple grounds to discover, so that's where our focus will be, once the heavy equipment is back," Professor Hittorn said. "We'll work above ground, uncovering more artifacts until they get here. There's plenty to do."

"Wow, they're going to go for the tomb first." Elizabeth exclaimed, as they watched the news. Although the tomb was not directly beneath the temple, it wasn't far, just north-east of it.

"When they start following those tunnels, it'll only be a matter of time before they reach the tomb." Ben admitted. "Could be days."

That evening, as they often did, they all decided to gather for prayer to seek the Lord's wisdom and discernment for the times ahead. They asked the Lord what gifts they needed to work on and just gave everything to Him, laying it at His feet, especially Elizabeth. They all prayed hard for Elizabeth. The Holy Spirit had never asked them to tell her what Ben saw concerning her in this battle.

Ben thought about the memory from the Starling almost constantly now. Some days were more difficult than others, but he kept giving it to God, saying each time, I trust you, Jesus. I know this will all work out for good and we'll all be okay. Ben realized he couldn't let that cloud his judgement. So even though he thought about it everyday, he also thought about the victory Grandma saw and chose to focus on that. Ben found favor with God, and God gave him special grace, helping him to keep things in their proper perspective.

Ben prayed out loud while everyone stood in agreement, "We are Your's, Lord, we surrender our will to you! We surrender the thoughts and intents of our hearts to You, Father, because we trust You. Your will be done. Teach us, oh, Lord. Use us and direct us for Your glory, in Jesus' mighty Name."

It was another two weeks and the later part of April before the ground dried up enough to support the heavy equipment at the site. Sometimes Ben and his family just wished it would all hurry up and get over with.

They felt ready, but Sarah cautioned them, "This may not unfold the way we think it will, it rarely does, so be on your guard, but don't be afraid. We are warriors! We are more than conquerors through Christ! We will protect the people and those involved – and each other. We will be victorious in the end! This I know! I've seen it! Praise the Lord!"

Another week went by, one of the excavators got stuck while digging around the tunnels on the north side of the pyramid. The water table was still high because of the melted snow and rain, but the operator managed to unearth a good portion of it before he got stuck. Just before the end of the day, workers uncovered a small entrance there, which was actually very close to the tomb. Since it was so late in the day, they decided to stop there and explore the opening further in the morning.

That night, a member of the U-M team who had been planning to sneak in and find some of the artifacts and treasure for himself, decided tonight would be the perfect opportunity! *Who would know, if they haven't discovered it yet? How would they know it's missing?* Roger Hershe said to himself as he snuck in after dark with a flashlight and pick-axe. Knowing the complex well, he parked his car as close to the site as he could, alongside the road, and walked through the woods to get there. It was a pretty straight shot from where he parked, cutting through the woods. It was actually closer than Lumberman's parking lot. His plan was to open the entrance and go into the tunnels they had uncovered earlier that day.

As he walked to the entrance of the pyramid, he felt an eerie feeling, like someone was watching him. He shrugged it off as nonsense. The dragons didn't speak to him like they did the three boys. The demons needed three people, not one. He made his way over to the north side and climbed down in the hole dug out by the excavator, that revealed the opening.

It was a small opening, only big enough for a child to get through. The stones in that area of the tunnel were smaller and easier to manage. He positioned his flashlight in the dirt just right so he could see without having to hold it and dug more dirt from around the opening. Then he began to beat at the rocks with his pick-axe. The sound was pretty loud, but since there were no houses in this area, he wasn't too concerned about it. The stones began to fall one by one and soon he had an opening large enough for him to crawl through.

His heart raced as he gathered his flashlight and pick-axe and crawled inside. Once he got in, he found he could stand. The air smelled dank, like a cellar, only more intense. He shined his light around and found the ceilings were about eight feet tall and curved at the top. He reached in his pocket and pulled out his compass. It was reading correctly, north was just a little to his left as he faced away from the pyramid. He shined his light towards it, but decided to go to the north east, away from it. As he walked he noticed writing along the ancient wall, leading in a straight line about seven feet up. He couldn't begin to interpret it, nor did he care to. This was his first year studying archeology and really had little interest in those things anyway. He was in it for the artifacts he could get to sell on the black market.

He walked about seventy-five feet more and saw an opening up ahead. A wide smile came over his face, his heart was beating almost out of his chest and he began to sweat, even though a cold chill came over him. He pressed on even faster.

As he got closer and his light shined into the opening, he saw something reflecting. *Gold!* He thought as he entered the opening and shined his light around. He saw two seven foot golden statues of the dragons standing on either side of an ornately carved stone rectangle. There was other pottery and shiny things but he was interested in the rectangle. Something was shining from its center. He stepped closer to it and saw where the boys had wiped some of the dust off the lid of the tomb. He wiped more dust off the gold disc with the dragons and writing around it.

"This is a seal of some sort," he said out loud, running his fingers around it. "It'll be worth millions!" He smiled a feverish, wide smile, as he took hold of his pick-axe and began to gently work around its edges. It was starting to give! He felt a little breeze and wondered where that could be coming from, but shrugged it off. He began to feel sick to his stomach but kept working to break the seal free. The breeze grew stronger. He stopped and looked around – *nothing*, he shrugged it off again. Then he heard a crack and felt it come free from the center beneath it. It was his! He picked up the heavy fifteen-inch golden disc and held it to his chest. He barely noticed the breeze intensifying. He was drunk with the thought of riches. The breeze became a mighty wind, so he could hardly stand against it.

Suddenly he looked and saw a fiery red light shooting from the hole where he'd taken the seal. It lit the entire tomb area, then shot out and lit up every tunnel all at once. He heard voices, thousands of voices. Something was touching him.

"They're touching me!" He twisted and turned, then tried to run. Just before he entered the doorway he came from, his body went prostrate in mid-air, about four feet off the floor. "No-no-no-no … Noooo!" He shrieked, then let out a blood-curdling scream just before his body began to convulse. After a few seconds he hit the floor with a thud, still clutching the seal to his chest. The wind suddenly stopped like a vacuum. All was quiet and the red light disappeared, as if nothing had happened. His flashlight was lying on the floor, shining on one of the dragons.

Sarah suddenly woke. The Holy Spirit quickened her, she knew the demons had been released. She immediately jumped out of bed and reached out to the others, her mind touching theirs. Within seconds, they were all at her bedroom doorway.

"Lord Jesus," she said as she grabbed her housecoat and put it around her, "show us what to do." As they all made their way to the kitchen.

"I can feel the forest," Rachel said.

"I can too," Elizabeth added.

"They're taking the brunt of it right now." Rachel said sadly.

"They're possessing the animals there too, anything they can find," Elizabeth cringed for them.

They began to pray. They prayed for protection over the forest, the river and the animals. That the evil would not cause them lasting harm. Then they began to pray for the people, for they knew it was only a matter of time.

"They seem to be staying in the forest, almost like there's an invisible perimeter they can't pass," Ben said as he watched, he could sense where they were.

"Praise God!" Elizabeth exclaimed, with a sigh of relief.

"I have been preparing for this for a long, long time," a voice said from the other end of the room. They turned with a start and saw an old man sitting there at their kitchen table, drinking cold coffee that was still in the pot from the day before, in one of Grandma's mugs! Like he'd been there the entire time! Suddenly an overwhelming sense of peace filled the room. It reminded them of when Eliel would visit.

"Grandma, Mom," Ben said, "I'd like to introduce you to the Starling." He smiled and bent to shake his leathery hand.

The Starling was dressed the same as he was at the river. He took off his brown fedora and set it on the table as he stood to hug him, "Blessings to you, and to your family," He turned to face them all, "In the name of our Father and the Lord Jesus Christ, greetings."

Elizabeth also shook his hand, "I saw you the day you visited Ben and Eliel at the river, but we never actually met, I'm Lizzy."

"Yes, Elizabeth, I do remember you." He looked at her and Ben, "You two are married now," he smiled approvingly and added, "Well done!"

"Sarah, Rachel, (no one told him their names) I'm happy to finally meet you both in person as well." He shook their hands.

They all sat down around the kitchen table. Elizabeth had made a fresh pot of hot coffee. Rachel asked him if he would like a re-fill.

"Yes, I would. That's good coffee." He smiled.

"This'll be even better, it's fresh!" Rachel remarked, as she re-filled his mug.

"So tell us, do you have a perimeter set up around the area to keep the demons in?" Ben wanted to get right down to business.

"Yes, it will protect the people living around the area. But whoever enters the perimeter will be subject to them, unless they have the Holy Spirit. The spirits won't be able to actually possess anyone unless they can convince them to allow it. They cannot enter their bodies by force now." The Starling answered.

"Okay, what exactly do you mean when you say, 'now'?" Sarah asked.

"Remember the three boys? If they would have broken the seal," The Starling answered, "they would have been overtaken – possessed. Professor Hittorn and the other two – they would have been possessed if the Reptilians had been successful." He looked at Ben. "Breaking the seal gives them permission to possess the soul of whoever breaks it and whoever is there when it is broken. But they need three souls to accomplish it, to take the place of the three priests." He stopped for a moment, then added, "Tonight, there was only one that broke the seal."

There was silence for a moment.

"What happened to him?" Elizabeth asked.

"He is dead." He paused. "They took their wrath out upon him for breaking the seal alone." He lowered his head for a moment. "But his breaking the seal has afforded us an opportunity to hold them. It has dealt the enemy another great blow." He looked at the four of them, "Now, they cannot leave without a soul. They are stuck there until they can find an unwitting human. Then, only those that entered the soul can leave. There are too many for them all to possess one soul, they still need three. Until there are three souls, they cannot all leave."

"Okay, so where are the Willows? If we can get there with that cocoon, we can trap them all before sunrise!" Ben said, looking around into the air, waiting for them to appear at any moment.

"They are not coming tonight." The Starling said, "They will return in the morning."

"Okay, so, Professor Moules will be the first, he's already in league with them! Should Ben go and hide him for awhile?" Elizabeth asked.

"No, we cannot interfere with the natural order of things. When Ben interfered with the professor and the other, Michael, it was to stop the Reptilians from going against the laws of the Great Counsel. There are no laws being broken by Professor Moules' presence at the site tomorrow."

Sarah couldn't help but think of the Watchers' story from the books of Enoch, and what Ben told her about him. She was wondering if he had ever been able to go home yet. To see God, face to face again; see his kin. She remembered how Enoch had pleaded with the Grigori and how they sang a sorrowful song to God. She almost broke out into tears.

He looked at her, knowing her thoughts, and said, "When Michael,

Uriel and the others set me free, just before the great flood, I returned to the Father. Yes!" He smiled. "He allowed me to return home for a time too, then to come back to earth, to see this to the end." His countenance brightened, "I can see His throne room even now." He looked up with great admiration as he stood and spread his arms wide. His appearance began to glow white, brighter and brighter. They saw such wonderment, such joy, such love on his face. The light shining from him became so bright, they had to look away. They couldn't see his true form, as the light filled the entire house. Although his true Grigorian form was so enormous, the house would not hold him.

"Thousands upon ten thousands of His angels, my kin among them, are there ministering and doing His work." His voice was no longer the voice of an old man, but what sounded like a mighty wind. "And everything will be accomplished according to the will of the Father of Light. For His Word cannot be undone, nor can it return void. It will accomplish what He purposed." As he finished speaking, his appearance faded back into the form of the old man.

Everyone was undone! They just witnessed someone looking at the very throne room, looking into the very presence of God right before their eyes! There wasn't a dry eye in the house. They worshipped God, longing to see what he saw. They all spoke in tongues and gave thanks to the Lord, knowing one day they too would see it. The presence of the Holy Spirit was so great, they could barely stand. Then they worshipped even more ... it was beautiful.

After forty-five minutes or so, as they began to compose themselves, Ben asked the Starling, "So is there nothing I can do to keep Professor Moules away from the demons?"

"The demons, by their very presence there, are breaking the laws. So, once the professor, or anyone else has interaction with them, you can interfere."

"You mean I have to wait until they have a conversation with someone?" Ben said.

"Yes."

"Well that's just ... gonna be difficult." Ben shook his head.

"Remember the Willows will be there to help you. They will instruct you." Said the Starling. "They will be here at dawn," which was only an hour away.

"Will you be there too?" Rachel asked.

"I will be there, but you will not see me, for the most part." He smiled at her.

"Can you interfere?" Elizabeth spoke up.

"Yes, to a point." He answered, "But do not concern yourselves with my part in this. The Willows will explain more. I must leave you now, but remember who you are! You are children of The Most High God and have been given authority over the powers of darkness in the Name of the One who bought you with His sinless blood!" The Starling faded away right where he sat, as he did the first day Ben and Elizabeth met him at the river.

It was nearly dawn, Sarah, Rachel, Elizabeth and Ben were all changed into camouflage from head to toe, awaiting the Willows' arrival.

There were five this time, along with Byron, Trazier and Ombeye, were Kish and Tayhl. Kish was enormous and powerful looking, where Tayhl was small and stealthy. Trazier carried the cocoon, as before. They all had what looked like a cyclone spear that glowed green in their right hands.

"Your clothing must be changed," Byron told them with his leaf-rustling voice. "You will need to blend in with the other workers. Do not worry, they will not remember you."

## CHAPTER 28 - REMOVING THE SEAL

After they quickly changed into jeans, t-shirts and a light jacket with a ball cap on their heads, which was what most of the workers were wearing, they re-assembled in the living room with the Willows.

"Okay, so what's the plan?" Ben asked.

Byron spread his hands out before them as he did when showing them his home planet. This time he showed them the temple complex and the workers. The demons looked like a dark mist weaving in and out around them, looking for weak vessels.

"Demons cannot read the minds and hearts of the people. They have to wait until they hear them say something or see them do something that might lead to an opening for them." Byron explained. "They already know Professor Moules. He will be their first target."

"The Starling said we have to wait until the demons speak to them." Ben said.

"Yes," Byron said, "We will all be able to hear them. Once they speak, one of you need to be at the side of the human and bind the demons in the Name of Jesus through the power of the Holy Spirit. Then once they are bound, we will be able to capture them in the cocoon."

"Okay, question," Ben interrupted, "Can I transport them somewhere else once the demons speak to them?"

"Yes, but you cannot leave the perimeter with them. You must stay within the boundaries the Starling has set up, so that may not be productive."

"So it would only be a matter of time before the other demons found them."

"Yes."

"And how many demons are there?" Rachel asked.

"Three hundred thousand." Byron answered.

"Wow! So a hundred thousand can possess one person!" Elizabeth reasoned.

"Yes. But they are in legions of ten thousand." Byron explained. "So when you bind the one speaking, you are binding not only him, but ten thousand to one hundred thousand, depending on how many legions they choose at the time."

"So we need to do this ... up to thirty times?." Ben surmised.

"Yes, in theory." Byron answered. "Once they know what we are up to, they may break their legions down into five thousand, or even less. We will have to play this by ear, as you humans say."

"So you'll know how many are in the cocoon?" Ben asked.

"Yes, we will know."

"Okay, so Professor Moules – he's going to be the biggest challenge. Is there anywhere I can take him, any prayer of protection I can pray over him, where he is no longer able to contact the demons or for them to speak to him, once first contact is made and the first bunch are in the cocoon?" Ben asked.

"No." Byron answered.

"This is going to be a busy day!" Ben exclaimed.

"A few busy days, in your time." Byron answered.

"So if Professor Moules, or anyone else becomes possessed, we can still bind them and drive them out, right?"

"Yes, but that will not be as easy, especially if they are welcome." Byron answered. "God has given us all a free will."

"Okay," Ben said, thinking out loud, "is there any way to keep them at the complex then? Instead of letting them run free in society, until we can drive the demons out of them." He was trying to think of every angle.

"Yes," If anyone becomes possessed by them, we can keep them at the temple complex. There is a secret chamber."

"Okay, now we're getting somewhere!" Ben smiled.

"The Starling has created a hedge around it. The rest of the demons will not be able to free them, nor will they be able to enter the chamber."

## CHAPTER 28 - REMOVING THE SEAL

Once they were through talking, they all joined by holding hands. Trazier tucked the spear between his arm and shoulder as he reached for Rachel's hand, she was next in the circle. He was holding the cocoon with his other hand, so Kish put his huge hand on his shoulder.

As Rachel put her hand in Trazier's, she expected it to be a woody feel, but it was very soft and human-like. She felt his energy, it was like the Amazon rainforests might feel all combined. It was powerful. She wondered if she felt it so strongly because her gifts were centered around the earth and growing things, as his were. They exchanged smiles. He felt her energy as well. Ombeye held Sarah's hand; she had the same experience.

"Let's kick some demon butt in the Name of Jesus!" Ben yelled just before they all disappeared.

# Chapter 29 – Cat And Mouse

It was a beautiful sunny morning as they arrived at the site. But there was no breeze, there were no sounds, no birds chirping, no squirrels rustling about – nothing. Everything was eerily still. The U-M team hadn't arrived yet. Ben looked and found they were about five minutes away. But they still had to make their way through the news crews and fans, so they had at least twenty minutes before they would arrive at the dig site. The perimeter set up by the Starling began just after Lumberman's Monument and just beyond the road, so news crews, passers by and visitors were safe.

Rachel and Elizabeth tried communicating with the forest. It seemed dead. There was no response. They split up and walked a little ways through the forest, trying to find any response – nothing. So they met back up with Ben and Grandma and the rest of the team.

The Willows took them to the secret chamber, it was a large cave deep underground, away from the tunnels and near the edge of the perimeter on the other side of the river, to the north, with no outlets.

Once they were back in the forest, the Willows disappeared to the naked eye, but they could sense their presence and hear each other's thoughts.

*I think we should split up.* Ben said, all telepathically now, *Grandma, you and Mom stay together, Lizzy, you're with me.* He looked at his grandmother and mother, *We're going to the gate. They won't waste any time with Moules, once they can reach him. You and Mom stay here out of site, until you can blend in with the other workers.*

## CHAPTER 29 - CAT & MOUSE

Normally Professor Hittorn and Moules rode together, along with Michael Broward. But today, Professor Moules brought his own vehicle. Ben and Elizabeth found some brush for cover near the gate. They waited and listened.

*Now as soon as they speak to Moules, I'm going to get in his car with him and bind the demons. You stay here and I'll come right back for you.*

She nodded. None of them had been able to teleport like Ben, but it wasn't from lack of trying. She agreed to stay put until he came for her.

They heard a vehicle coming. It was Professor Moules. He was traveling at a pretty good clip in spite of the rough trail. He was anxious to meet the darkness he knew was waiting for him. The moment he entered through the gate, which was where the perimeter began, they were on him. Ben and Elizabeth saw the dark cloud envelope his vehicle. They heard the demons speak.

"We have been waiting for you." A multitude of voices said to Moules.

That was all it took for Ben, he disappeared and entered through the black mist, and appeared in the passenger side. It was so black inside the vehicle he didn't know how the professor could see the roadway before him.

"In the Name of Jesus, I bind the powers of darkness!" Ben shouted into the black mist. Trazier apparently was able to change his size, because he immediately appeared in the back seat with the cocoon, and actually fit in the 4x4 suburban! The screams and screeching reminded Ben of the experience he and Lizzy had at the restaurant the night he proposed.

"Who are you?" A voice came from the darkness.

Trazier said to Ben, *Don't answer them.*

Light shot out from the cocoon with all the colors of the rainbow. You could hear the sound like a rushing wind that whistled, as the demons were sucked into it. Then suddenly, the cocoon made a zipper sound as it bounced a little in Trazier's hands and the light disappeared.

Professor Moules slammed on the brakes, but Ben and Trazier disappeared just before Ben's face hit the windshield. The professor never saw them through the black mist. His vehicle swerved to the right and he wound up stuck in a low spot on the side of the make-shift trail.

Ben, Elizabeth and Trazier watched from behind the brush as he got out of the vehicle, cursing.

They waited for the demons to return, but there was nothing.

Then they heard Byron, *They are re-grouping for their next move. Be on your guard.*

They were thinking the rest of the team should be coming any second but Professor Moules had bi-passed the morning ritual with the news crews and fans in order to meet the demons before anyone else arrived. Ben looked and saw the rest of the team was still at the parking lot.

Elizabeth felt something watching them from behind. She turned and saw a bear standing on his hind legs about fifteen feet away. She tried speaking to him, but to no avail. His growls became more threatening, then he lunged at them.

She stopped him in mid air and held him there, and said, "In the Name of Jesus I command you demons of darkness to come out of this bear!"

As soon as she said that, Trazier held out the cocoon, the colors of the rainbow shot out of it.

They heard the familiar screams and screeching, the whistling wind, then the zipper. The bear was free. Elizabeth prayed a prayer of protection over the bear, and it went on its way, peacefully.

They looked back at Professor Moules, the demons had taken him while they were pre-occupied with the bear. He was starring right at them from about fifty feet away, yes, the demons knew and now he knew – where they were. With a wicked smile he walked quickly toward them.

Ben stepped out from the brush to meet him.

The professor hit Ben with such force, he flew fifty feet through the air. He kept his pace, walking toward Elizabeth. But Ben, only slightly inconvenienced, immediately appeared in front of him once more and they both disappeared.

Only seconds passed and Ben was back at Elizabeth's side.

*He's in the chamber.* Ben said as he looked Elizabeth over. *Are you okay?*

*Yes,* she answered, waiting for the onslaught of the rest of the team to arrive.

He said to her, *If they send anymore animals, can you hold and suspend them while I concentrate on the humans?*

*Yes, I should be able to do that.*

*Be right back,* Ben said.

They heard vehicles approaching.

Ben went to Rachel and Sarah, telling them everything that happened in a moment. Telepathy was so much faster than the spoken word. He brought them to help Elizabeth in case they bombarded her with possessed animals, as the vehicles made their way through the perimeter. *We'll all just follow them as they make their way to the site,* Ben said as they braced themselves for the battle.

Professor Hittorn and Michael were first in the procession. There were three other vehicles with five people in each. He focused his thoughts on all of them, but paid special attention to the professor's vehicle. They passed by them – nothing.

"Michael look! It's Jim's suburban!" They stopped in the road, the others behind them stopped as well. Virginia and Michael exited their vehicle, calling for the professor. Some of the others did too.

"Jim," they called. "Professor Moules." But there was no response.

"He must have walked to the temple," she finally concluded. So everyone re-entered their vehicles and proceeded to the complex. His vehicle looked fine, other than being stuck in the mud, no flat tires or anything amiss that they could see.

*They're planning another strategy,* Ben said to the others. He transported them to a closer spot. They were almost there – still nothing. As they reached the complex and exited their transports, the U-M team began calling for Professor Moules again.

Ben told the others, *If they speak to one of the other workers besides Michael or the professor, take care of it, but also keep your eyes on those two, they are the demons' main focus.*

Then he spoke to Byron, *We could use a couple more cocoons, if you've got them.*

"Hey, come look at this!" One of the team pointed as he stood over the area where Roger Hershe had dug out the opening to the underground tunnel. "Maybe the professor's in here!"

Three team members climbed into the opening with flashlights. Virginia and Michael were right behind them. They saw a Reese's candy wrapper about fifteen feet from the entrance lying on the floor in the tunnel, heading away from the pyramid, so they went that way.

The Reptilians were waiting for them in the chamber of the tomb ahead. Since they no longer could get to Professor Moules, they had intended to use Virginia and Michael to house the rest of the demons for them to control.

Ben sensed their presence. Just as he was going to leap there himself, Byron stopped him.

*Don't be concerned with the Reptilians, we will take care of them.*
*Okay, I'm cool with that!* He exclaimed and stayed put.

"Jim?" Professor Hittorn called, "Are you in here?"

It was silent.

As their flashlights came upon the opening to the chamber of the tomb, their light reflected the gold from the dragon statue closest to the opening. They saw a body lying on the floor. The Reptilians were gone, the Willows took care of them as they said they would.

"Oh, my god! Jim!" Virginia picked up her pace.

One of the other workers reached the body first, "It's not Professor Moules. It's Roger Hershe!"

"What the ... hell?" One of the other team said. "I thought that looked like his car parked alongside the road on the way here!"

"Roger Hershe? He's that new guy, isn't he?" Virginia exclaimed as she rushed to the body.

"Yes, he's a new intern. Well, he was." They told her.

They saw Roger's flashlight lying on the floor, amazingly still shining, however dimly, on the dragon farthest from the opening.

She reached down and almost touched the golden seal he still clutched to his chest, but thought it best not to. His eyes were still open and his face was hideously contorted. He looked as if he'd died from fright. It was a gruesome sight. She had to look away.

"Someone call the police." She said sadly.

"There's no service down here," one of them said as he kept hitting redial on his phone.

They shined their flashlights around the chamber. They saw the dragon statues, the other furnishings and the tomb. The lid was still in tact. There was a burn mark in the center where light had shot out of the hole in the lid. But there was no sign of Professor Moules.

"Don't touch anything." Virginia exclaimed. "Let's all just leave this as it is and get back above ground and call the authorities." All those treasures and artifacts didn't mean very much at this point.

Ben and the others overheard everything that was said as they kept watch over them, while at the same time – listening to the team above ground for any demonic activity. There was nothing so far.

As Hittorn and the others headed back down the tunnel toward the opening, she said to Michael, "This is going to delay everything. They're going to shut us down until this is all taken care of." She shook her head in disgust. "And where's Jim? I wonder if he had anything to do with this?"

"Stranger things have happened. The investigators will find out." Michael assured her. "They'll get to the bottom of this. It shouldn't take too long, but we really don't have a choice."

They were lagging behind the others as they talked. Suddenly, the black mist came on both of them. It engulfed them.

They heard a voice out of the blackness, "We can help you with all this. You don't have to wait. Let us show you."

Ben was already there. They didn't even have time to answer before he bound the demons. This time it was Tayhl with a cocoon.

At the same time there were three others above ground the demons approached. Sarah, Rachel and Elizabeth were on them immediately. They couldn't teleport, but they learned how to move with lightening speed.

Kish was there with a cocoon for Sarah, Trazier had one for Rachel and Ombeye had one for Elizabeth.

While the cocoons were doing their work, the demons approached another worker. Sarah left Kish and went to the other person and bound the demons. This time Byron came with a cocoon.

Surprisingly, none of the intended victims remembered anything.

Immediately after, they all met in the woods where they couldn't be seen.

*How many did we get in all?* Ben asked.

They didn't speak out loud.

*Counting the demons that initially tried to enter Professor Moules, 135,000.* Byron answered. *We caught 100,000 the first time with the professor.*

*That's good news. Sounds like they've split into legions of 5,000 now though.* Ben said.

*Yes.*

*Can you tell how many actually entered Professor Moules while we were pre-occupied with the bear?* Ben asked.

*Yes, he has all he can hold, 100,000.* Byron answered.

*Okay, so we're down to 65,000?* Rachel asked.

*Yes, we caught 10,000 in the bear,* Byron said, *but these that remain will be more difficult. Do not underestimate them.*

It wasn't long before Iosco County Sheriff Matt Brodge arrived with his deputies, along with the coroner. Professor Hittorn and Michael Broward took them to Roger Hershe's body while the rest of the team were told to wait to be questioned. Ben, Elizabeth, Sarah and Rachel stayed out of site and watched. There were no more demonic incidents.

"So you have no idea the whereabouts of Professor Moules?" Sheriff Brodge asked Professor Hittorn as she sat alone in the back seat of the patrol car, with the Sheriff and another deputy in the front.

"I have no idea," she answered. "The three of us, Professor Moules, Michael Broward and myself, normally ride together, but today, Jim said he was driving his own car because he wanted to leave early. That's all I know."

"And what is your relationship with Moules? Were you ... romantically involved?"

"No," she answered. "We worked together, that's all."

"Was he married?"

"No, not to my knowledge." She stated, "but he never really opened up about his family life. I never really knew too much about him, personally."

When the sheriff got to Michael Broward, he asked many of the same questions, "I have to ask ... were you, at any time, romantically involved with Professor Moules?"

"No!" Michael responded, "I'm not ... of that persuasion. And to my knowledge, neither is Professor Moules."

"Did he have a wife or girlfriend you were aware of?"

"No," Michael responded, "not that I know of, but he did like to visit strip clubs," Michael offered. "He mentioned it a time or two."

"Which ones? Exactly?" The sheriff asked.

"I don't know, he never mentioned names." Michael answered.

When Sheriff Brodge was through questioning everyone, he reserved the right to question all of them further at a later time. "I'm going to ask, actually insist, you not to leave town tonight," He said to them corporately. "There should be enough hotels and motels in the area to accommodate everyone for one night. Our office will contact you tomorrow if we have any further questions. If not, since you are all from the Ann Arbor area, you will be free to return to your homes, but none of you are to leave the state until I say so." He added, "You must make yourselves available for further questioning."

They all agreed.

Once the coroner had the body removed, they sent everyone away and taped off the entire entrance.

As the U-M team was leaving, news crews met them at the entrance. Someone already leaked the information. But Sheriff Brodge warned them not to speak about the incidents, so they told news crews they had no comment, barely slowing down for them as they passed through the gate. Roger Hershe's car was being towed to the impound as they drove past it, about a half mile from Lumberman's Monument. The police left Professor Moule's vehicle where it was, since he could not be deemed officially missing for at least twenty-four to seventy-two hours.

The Brought family, along with the Willows, stayed to watch over the sheriff and his deputies until they were through. It was almost dark as the last patrol car left the scene, making sure the gate was taped off. The demons, apparently, were not interested in law enforcement.

After the family was safely home, they sat down with the Willows to discuss their next move … and what to do with Professor Moules.

They were glad to see the Willows had all shrunk in size to fit at the kitchen table so they could have a comfortable discussion.

"So, do you drink coffee?" Rachel asked. "We are avid coffee drinkers."

"No, but I will try it," Answered Byron.

She was elated, because she didn't know what else they could offer them.

"Anyone else want to try some coffee?"

"I have always wanted to try a Coke," Ombeye spoke up.

"Okay, yes! We have Coke." Rachel reached in the fridge, "Would anyone else like to try a Coke?"

Kish and Tayhl wanted to try a Coke and Trazier wanted coffee.

"Okay, two coffees and three Cokes coming up!" Rachel said as Elizabeth gave her a hand.

The kitchen table could seat eight, so Elizabeth sat on Ben's lap.

"So first of all, what are we going to do with Professor Moules?" Ben asked.

"We should probably take him some food." Sarah offered.

"Although he does not require food in his state, it would be good for him to remember it." Byron stated.

"So he's that far gone?" Elizabeth cringed.

"Should we take him a blanket and a lawn chair?" Rachel asked. "Maybe a flashlight?"

"He does not require the necessities the human body requires right now. They would use these things as weapons against you." Byron continued, "His soul is … sleeping. He is barely aware of what is going on around him."

Ben said, "I'm assuming if we go and drive the demons out of him right now, he'll just return to them."

"Yes, it would not be productive. Driving these spirits out, once they possess a human, will be more difficult." Byron looked at the four of them, "You must fast and pray, when it is time. You will know."

They recalled the scripture in the Bible where the disciples couldn't drive out an unclean spirit and Jesus told them they needed more faith, basically, and that this sort required fasting and prayer.

"Well, I've been wanting to take off a few pounds," Sarah chuckled.

"Right? Me too," Elizabeth and Rachel both said at the same time, trying to make light of the situation.

"Lizzy cast them out of that bear easy enough, so … it's harder with humans?" Ben asked.

"Yes," Byron answered.

Ombeye looked down into his Coke. As the dark mixture fizzled in the glass, the leaves and tiny vines from his head and shoulders all moved forward to look too. He took a sip. He held it in his mouth for a moment, then swallowed, while everyone watched.

"Ahh…!" He smiled, and took another sip. The "hair" from his head and shoulders shimmered and bounced around a bit. They seemed to like it too!

Kish and Tayhl both followed with similar reactions.

Byron and Trazier had already finished their coffee, heat apparently wasn't an issue because it was still piping hot when they drank it down!

Rachel made a fresh pot and refilled their mugs.

"I drink my coffee with sugar and cream sometimes, would you like to try it?" Sarah offered.

Byron and Trazier agreed, so Sarah put two teaspoons of raw, organic sugar in each cup, which was the only sugar they ever had in the house, along with a generous shot of non-homogenized cream they got from a local dairy.

They both smiled, after gulping that down. Clearly, they liked their coffee better with cream and sugar.

"So how are we going to capture the rest of those demons?" Ben asked. "Is there any way to bind them before they talk to a human?"

Byron shook his head, no. "We will have to wait."

Ben kept watch over Professor Moules. He took him some bottled water along with a couple lunch-meat sandwiches and some chips in a paper sack. He set them down in the cave and disappeared before he even knew he was there. The demons had gathered around where the secret chamber was, but they could not enter. Ben could see the black mists moving about. Even the animals that were possessed gathered around that area, but none of them could enter where Professor Moules was being held, thanks to the Starling.

The next day, even though the U-M team was not allowed to comment to news media, they managed to get a statement from Sheriff Brodge.

"All we know, at this point, is we have a dead body, Roger Hershe, and Professor Jim Moules is missing," He said. "We're asking anyone that may know the whereabouts of Professor Moules or has any information on Roger Hershe, to please contact our office." It aired on the morning news along with each of their photos.

It was late in the afternoon. Since the sheriff had no more leads, he had no further questions for Hittorn and her team and let them all go home.

Locally, word spread quickly that the place was cursed. One of the U-M team had apparently stopped off at a local pub to play some pool before going to his hotel that night and in the course of conversation, told some of the locals what happened. They believe it was one of the team that found Hershe's body, because residents were talking about the look on his face and how he was still clutching the golden seal to his chest when they found him.

That Sunday after church they met Pastor Matt and Katie, the Wenthers and Elizabeth's parents for lunch at the RC Cafe, their favorite local place to eat. Finding a place to seat thirteen people was no problem for the staff, they were used to large tables on Sunday and one was just leaving.

While they were waiting for the table to be cleared, they could hear people talking about the temple.

"That place is cursed, I don't want anything else to do with it." One woman remarked, sitting at a table with five other people.

"Yeah, well, we're probably going to find that professor and the dead guy were in cahoots and the professor got greedy." Another at her table remarked.

"Okay, if that's true, why would he leave that solid gold disc behind with the dead guy?" Another spoke up.

"What do you think of all that talk about curses, Pastor?" Gary, looked at Pastor Matt, knowing they had all overheard the conversation.

Pastor Matt hesitated for a moment, then said, "Well," he glanced at Ben, remembering the conversation they had after one of their marriage counseling sessions about the temple, "the Bible talks about witchcraft and sorcery, all that stuff. We shouldn't underestimate the powers of darkness. We should pray and cast out our enemy. We've been given that authority in the Name of Jesus. But I wouldn't go looking for it, that's for sure."

"Personally, I don't know that I believe in curses and all that mumbo jumbo," John added.

"Oh, I don't know, honey, like Pastor says, we shouldn't underestimate this stuff. I'm just praying for protection over my family, in Jesus' Name!" Sam chimed in.

Sarah added, "If your heart's right before God and you're not dabbling in that sort of thing, a born again believer cannot be cursed. It'll bounce back to the one doing the cursing."

Just then the hostess came to seat them at their table. As they made their way across the restaurant, they heard other people talking about "Awake not Woke."

"I wish he was our governor," the man said, as the hostess seated them next to the couple talking.

"Maybe we should move to Florida," the woman answered her partner.

"So how are you feeling, Julie?" Rachel asked, once they were seated.

They had all agreed to take a break from the Bible studies for awhile, with spring planting, cows calving and all, Gary and Julie were pretty busy.

"I'm doing very well, actually!" She exclaimed. "Better everyday!"

"That's fantastic!" Rachel said, "I'm expecting your symptoms to wither away and never come back!" She added.

"I am too!" Julie answered enthusiastically. Then quietly, so only Rachel could hear, she added, "I've been quoting the promises about healing out loud! And it's working!"

"She's been doing a lot better." Gary added, then looked at his wife, "You haven't had any falls or accidents in ... a long time ... at least a couple months!"

"Nope!" She smiled from ear to ear. "The doctor calls it remission, I call it healed!"

They all enjoyed catching up with one another. Sam and Katie asked Sarah if she'd made any new pottery lately. Which she hadn't, she'd been too busy with demons and ET's. She thought how nice it would be if they could just tell everybody, then almost laughed out loud at the thought of it.

Elizabeth made sure she sat next to the Wenther boys. "What do you mean you don't like your chicken strips, did you try them?" She said to Abe as the five-year-old fussed over his meal. "I love chicken strips!"

"Yeah, me too!" said Chris.

Even little Caleb agreed, "Yeah, I WOVE chicken stwips!" He said as he took another bite.

Abe must have felt out-numbered, he decided to try them and wound up finishing the entire plate.

"Lizzy, you're so good with them." Julie smiled, watching her dote over her children. "You're going to be the best mom, someday soon."

"Oh, I hope so." Elizabeth answered. "I can't wait!" Then glanced over at her father, remembering that he made it very clear he wanted her to finish college and having a family might delay that. Although he wasn't even paying attention to their conversation, he was talking with Pastor Matt and the rest of the men.

Pastor Matt, John and Ben were talking to Gary about buying one of his steers and splitting it between them.

"Our freezer's getting down there, isn't it Katie?" Matt asked his wife.

"What?" She was talking with Sam and Sarah. "Oh, yes, actually. Are you guys talking about getting some beef? We'll make room!"

"Sam do we have room in our freezer for a third of a beef?" John asked.

"Oh man, that would be nice wouldn't it? Let me check when we get home. There's probably some freezer-burnt things I can toss out to make room," she laughed.

"We're good, between us and Mom, we can always make room for beef in the freezer," Ben smiled.

"All right then, why don't you all stop over tomorrow after work and you can take your pick," Gary said.

"I think I'll let Pastor and Ben make that decision, I wouldn't know what I was looking for," John chuckled. "I don't know the first thing about farming or raising cattle. I grew up in the suburbs and am content being a suburbian," he happily stated.

Everyone smiled. Elizabeth especially, she loved her daddy. She loved his blunt honesty and openness.

Ben and Pastor agreed to meet Gary around 6:30 that next evening to pick out a steer.

# Chapter 30 – Dome Of Darkness

After they got home from the restaurant, Ben checked in on the professor and took him more food and water, although he wasn't eating or drinking anything. The remains of his previous meals lay torn and scattered in pieces throughout the cavern. His physical appearance was degrading. He looked more like the walking dead instead of the professor.

The next few days were quiet, except for the news media hounding the sheriff. He still had no leads on the death of Roger Hershe and no one had come forward concerning Professor Moules' whereabouts. It was as if he had no relatives or friends in the entire world.

It was Thursday night around midnight when Elizabeth had a dream, well … she thought it was a dream. She woke startled and sat up in bed. She saw and heard who she thought were Chris and Abe Wenther wandering through the forest at the Au Sable alone, crying.
"Help!"
"Help us!"

*What a horrible dream,* she thought. *That can't be real, they have no way of getting there!* Then she heard them while she was awake.

"Where's my mom? I want my mommy!" She heard little Abe's voice distinctly. She thought it sounded like Abe, anyway.

"No! Leave us alone!" She heard what sounded like Chris's voice. "I want my Mom! ... I want my Dad!"

"Ben!" She shook him, "Ben, wake up!" She threw her covers off and jumped out of bed, "Something's wrong!"

"What is it?" Ben said yawning, trying to crack his eyes open.

"I can hear the Wenther boys crying out! At least I think it's the Wenther boys. They're in the forest at the Au Sable!" She went to the window and pulled the curtains back to get a clearer picture from the maple, but there was no response. She could see everything up to the perimeter, but nothing beyond it.

"What? Lizzy, honey, that can't be real. How would they get there?"

"I don't know! At first I thought it was just a dream, but I can hear them still! While I'm awake!" Her voice was shaky. She loved those boys as if they were her own flesh and blood.

"I'll tell you what, I'll scan their rooms and see if they're in bed." He was silent for a few moments.

There they were, safe and sound, sleeping away in their beds. Ben also checked on Julie and Gary. Everyone was safe and sound in their beds.

"No foul play, Lizzy. The whole family is safe and sound in their beds."

"Well what am I hearing? Am I hearing their dreams?" She brushed her arms and shoulders as she paced the bedroom. "No, something's wrong, Ben, I can feel it. Maybe it's not the Wenther boys, what if it's some other kids?" *Kids again,* she thought, *it seems like I'm always hearing the kids.*

"I'll scan the woods." He was silent again.

"I'm waking Grandma and Rachel this time," she said as she closed her eyes, focused on them and woke them from their sleep. "I'm going downstairs and putting on a pot of coffee." She shared everything with them in a moment's time. They all knew everything by the time they gathered around the kitchen table.

When Ben scanned the Huron Forest at the Au Sable, he saw a thick darkness enveloping everything within the perimeter the Starling had set up. Then he heard them. Two small kids were crying out, but he couldn't find them!

"Please help us!" A little voice cried out. He heard sobbing from a smaller voice and imagined they were both about the same ages as Chris and Abe. *Where are they? Why can't I see them?*

Ben came downstairs. For the first time in a very long time, he felt a little helpless. He didn't like that feeling and he certainly didn't like the thought of not being able to find the children.

"I can't see them!" He looked at his family, "I heard them, but I couldn't find them."

"Maybe the reason you couldn't find them is because they're not real. It may be a trick from the spirits to lure us into a trap of some sort." Sarah stated.

"That might be, but there's a thick, black mist over everything within the perimeter, I can't see through it."

They began to pray, "Holy Spirit, please show us Your truth in this. Give us clarity of mind. Are there children out there, Lord?"

After a time of prayer, they all felt the cries were real. There *were* children out there! They all could hear them now.

Elizabeth's whole body ached. She wanted to just go and rip the demons apart and find those kids! *How dare they use kids!* She was in physical anguish. As she looked up, trying with everything inside her to see them, she disappeared!

"LIZZY!" They all yelled.

Immediately Sarah and Rachel grabbed hold of Ben and off they went into the forest.

"Lizzy!, Lizzy! Where are you?"

"What a time to find out you can teleport!" Rachel exclaimed, as they searched through the black mist that covered everything in the woods.

Elizabeth found herself in a dark place. Ben was right, the black mist was so dark, she couldn't even tell where she was for a moment. Then she heard them.

"Somebody help us!" They were on her left, she turned and went in the direction of the voices. She couldn't even see the trees until they were three feet in front of her. She ran into a couple of them, then slowed her pace.

"Leave us alone! Stop! ... I want my Mommy!" The kids cried out.

She was getting closer. Their sobs were more audible.

As she approached, she saw a red glow. It was coming from the trunk of a huge tree. She recognized it was the mighty oak she spoke with on numerous occasions. The trunk of it was at least three-and-a-half feet across. It wasn't talking to her this night. It was in anguish too.

"Here you are, Elizabeth!" She heard voices coming from a hole the demons had created in the tree. It reminded her of the voices from the restaurant, the night Ben proposed, only more foreboding.

She stood still. "God, help me!" She whispered.

"What do you seek?" The voices echoed each other.

She didn't answer them. She walked closer to the tree. The trunk was split open with a huge, gapping hole. It was a much larger space on the inside than on the outside. She peered into it and saw yellow and red light that appeared as flames inside of it. As she concentrated, she saw a huge, red demon, about 12 feet tall, whose face resembled a wolf, with no hair, standing upright, on two feet. He had two, ten-inch horns that curled up with spines along the edges of them. It had a hideous, evil face with huge teeth. He was holding two small boys that resembled Chris and Abe by the hair of their head in each of his huge, clawed hands. Even his claws were red. His hands were so big, he only used two fingers to hold each of their little heads.

"Is this what you're looking for?" The demon laughed a nightmarish laugh at Elizabeth as he raised each of the children off the ground by their hair. The boys let out blood curdling screams, as some of the hair let loose from their scalp.

Elizabeth was furious! She stepped into the hole of the tree. She didn't notice it close behind her.

Ben, Rachel and Sarah searched the entire area, calling out after Elizabeth, but could not find her. Ben was beside himself. He looked in on Professor Moules, she wasn't there either.

"In the Name of Jesus, I command you to put them down and leave this place!" Elizabeth said firmly.

"Hahaha!" The echoing laughs persisted as the demon allowed the children's feet to touch the ground once again. "These children are mine!" Then, in the voice he apparently used to lure them, he said, "They agreed to come with me." His voice sounded like a woman's voice, tender and kind.

The echoing laughs began again.

"No!" The children screamed and cried out as the demon lifted them off the ground again by the hair of their head.

"Stop!" Elizabeth screamed. "Let them go!"

He looked at her with his piercing yellow-red eyes. A twisted smile came over his wolf-like face, "And who will take their place?" His smile grew wider and more evil as he waited for her reply.

Elizabeth looked around, nothing but red and yellow flames in the hole of the tree. She remembered Proverbs 3, "Don't be afraid of sudden fear, or the onslaught of the wicked when it comes, for God will be your confidence and He will keep your foot from being caught."

Then she bowed her head and said, "Lord, Jesus, I commit my soul and my spirit to You, and You only. Please watch over me and save us from this evil."

She lifted her head and said, with resolve, "Take me instead!"

Immediately, the boys disappeared and were home, safe in their beds. Thankfully, they would not remember anything about what happened to them. The last thing they would remember is walking along the road near the temple. They would not remember sneaking in.

The demon grabbed Elizabeth by her hair, letting the shiny, red strands fall between his huge, clawed fingers. He smelled it and lingered for a moment, then lifted his head and said, "Ahhh!"

Then he flung her by her hair, through the spirit realm, to the top of a great rock. She heard something crack as she landed. Searing pain came from her right leg and her head where her hair was torn from her scalp. More demons appeared. They held her down as they wrapped her in chains and taunted her, laughing and growling in her face. She screamed out in pain as one of them twisted her right leg. He laughed as he chained it down. She passed out ... then went into a deep sleep.

"My God in heaven, please, please!" Ben pleaded, "Please show me where my wife is!"

## CHAPTER 30 - DOME OF DARKNESS

Immediately he heard the Holy Spirit, *She has offered herself in place of the boys, your time of sorrow has come. Take courage, I will be with you.*

Ben flung himself to the ground and wept.

He thought about wasting every inch of this temple and turning it to dust with his bare hands. He thought about bringing Professor Hittorn and her crew all together and annihilating them all at once. He thought about going to Professor Moules and ripping him apart, piece by piece. Or even letting the professor rip him apart. At least it would end his pain.

Then he thought about Jesus and the Father's Word. He thought about Eliel and the Starling. He remembered the victory Grandma had seen in the spirit.

He slowly pulled himself from the ground.

Eliel and the Starling were standing next to him, along with Sarah and Rachel. They all stood there together, in silence. The black mist disappeared from the forest, it accomplished what it set out to do. Rachel and Sarah were wiping their tears. Then Eliel wrapped his arms around them … and took them home without Elizabeth.

Rachel didn't even make coffee or tea. They all just sat in the living room in silence.

After some time, Ben finally asked, "So what do we do now?" Looking at Eliel and the Starling, then at Grandma and Mom, tears welled up again in his eyes.

Then he bolstered himself and sat straight in his chair as he looked at each of them. "We're going to beat this! That's what we're going to do! And Lizzy's going to be all right! We're going to find her and we're going to save her! In Jesus' Name!" His voice strengthened with every word. "Now where do we go from here?"

The faintest smile came over Eliel's face. He was glad to see Ben come around so quickly.

The Starling spoke first, "Professor Hittorn and four of her crew have been overcome by their familiar demons. They are leading them through the gates now. They will be possessed by the temple demons the next time you encounter them."

"I'll just go and put them all with Professor Moules, I'm sure he could use some company," Ben said.

"This time, it will be best to let this unfold," Eliel finally spoke.

"Okay, but for how long?" Ben felt the anxiety coming back.

"Daylight," Eliel smiled.

It just so happened, that they had fasted all that prior day, along with Elizabeth. So they continued in the fast, eating and drinking nothing, save water, and prayed – and prayed some more. Eliel and the Starling stayed with them, never leaving their side.

While they were praying, Sarah got a revelation about the rapture. When they were through praying, she shared it.

"… When the first rapture does come, many believe the whole world will see and realize the Bible was right, Jesus is real and people will repent. But the Bible says He'll come like a thief in the night, one taken, the other left. And what if that stands true even for the dead? What if their graves are not opened and the Lord just takes them and the ground remains undisturbed?"

"Either way, even if the graves do open up, and they actually see us meeting in the air, I saw a great cover-up by the world." Sarah said, "There have already been discussions among the decision-makers, secret meetings about what to say when and if the rapture takes place. What to say about mass car accidents, and the like, throughout the world, all taking place at once. Maybe a disease or atmospheric pressure from a magnetic field that only affected a certain portion of mankind or whatever. They have alternative scenarios already in place and ready to be sent out to the news media on what to say and how to address it, should it come. I believe they already have an excuse in case graves are opened up, people disappearing right before their eyes, everything. They've discussed it all and have insidiously made their plans to belittle and disgrace anyone that says otherwise. Many will give credit to extra-terrestrials. Although we all are extra-terrestrials, they'll cling to any excuse instead of God."

She continued, "We've seen how the news media's been able to cover up so many things simply by not reporting it. They apparently believe that if they don't talk about it, it didn't happen. And in essence, it's true! They can make it go away for most of the population! They'll create another scenario for it, no matter how ridiculous, and people will buy into it! They'll belittle the rapture idea. Some may mention it as an alternative, but, of course, those that believe that are fools, heretics, trouble-makers and haters, laughing them to scorn."

"Wow, Grandma, I can see that happening," Ben said. "If we look back, they've already done that. They've been practicing that for thousands of years. Look how the Jews paid the soldiers to lie about seeing the angel roll the stone away from Jesus' tomb, and instead say His disciples came in the night while they slept and took him."

"Yes." Sarah continued, "Today, they're getting even more bold and brazen about it. Now evil is good and good is evil, and many believe them! Anyone that says otherwise is ridiculed and made out to be a fool, a conspiracy theorist or whatever label they want to put on it."

"The Lord also showed me that after the rapture, there'll be many pastors, church-goers and religious people that are left. Some of the pastors and other people will turn and repent when they realize they were missing the mark, and will become leaders in the movement for Christ, during that time. But many pastors and religious figures will be embarrassed they missed the rapture and will go along with the narrative the news media puts out in order to make themselves, and whatever portion of their congregation still left, feel good about themselves. They'll choose to believe the lies. Because they were never true believers, loving their man-made religion more than God. They'll be easily persuaded to go along with whatever the news media is saying."

"And that makes me sick inside," Rachel commented.

"I think we should warn our family, our friends and anyone who will listen that the rapture may not be this great thing where everyone will see the graves opening and those that are alive caught up in the air to meet them. Those of us that are a part of it will see it, but the rest of the world may not. It may be more of a private thing and more easily covered up, like a thief in the night."

"Mom, I believe you're right. Just like this battle we're fighting right now is connected to the end times," Rachel added. "The spiritual and physical powers and principalities are in their final stages of setting themselves in place for the take-over and to usher in the Anti-Christ." She continued, "They can't wait until we're raptured and the Holy Spirit is taken up from this world. That's when they'll have free reign, nothing to hold them back."

"Well, we're not going to let them have this group of demons!" Ben declared.

Eliel and the Starling agreed. It was not their place to divulge future events of their own accord, so they were silent and did not comment about the end times, but left it all to the Holy Spirit.

It was an hour before dawn when the Willows arrived. The five of them were each holding a cocoon this time, along with their glowing cyclone spears.

Byron looked at the Brought's all dressed in camo from head to toe. He smiled and shook his head, "You will need black today."
They didn't question him now, they just went and changed.

Eliel and the Starling seemed to know each of the Willows well by their familiar greetings. Rachel tried to imagine how many thousands of years they might have known each other. She couldn't help but wonder what this current battle meant to them. No doubt they had all seen many. It was life and death to Rachel and her family, but to them ... was it just another battle?

After their clothes were changed and they had all reassembled, Eliel looked at Rachel, knowing her thoughts earlier, and said, "Do not worry, young ones." He smiled at her, then at Sarah and Ben. "Every battle is life and death to us as well. Although life and death, as you understand it, are different from true life and death. No one ceases to exist after they leave this world, because the Father has created us all eternal. True life is to be with the Father and in His Light is life for He *is* Light, and no one can take the Light from you, if it was given to you by the Father. But death is to be in darkness, not discerning and not seeking the Light of the Father, and in death, in darkness, is weeping, much sorrow and gnashing of teeth. We are defenders of the Light as you too are defenders of the Light. And what does The Word say? If God be for us, who can stand against us?"

At those words the Willows shouted, "Hey!" and struck the floor with their spears in unison. Everyone was ready for the battle.

Ben closed his eyes and tried to see the temple grounds. "I can't see it. The black mist is back."

Eliel spread his arms around them, stretched out his wings and took them to the site.

*No wonder we needed to wear black,* Sarah thought, as they arrived and looked around. It was as if it were still night. The black mist covered everything in the perimeter, like a dome of darkness.

*Concentrate,* Eliel said everything telepathically now. *Try to see through the darkness.*

Ben, Sarah and Rachel all concentrated, but still could see nothing.

*Close your eyes,* Eliel said.

Amazingly, they closed their eyes and concentrated again – and could see everything!

*Now open your eyes.* Eliel said.

They opened their eyes and were able to see everything! It was as if it were twilight, just before the sun sets.

The demons had been busy! The entire area just north of the pyramid and almost to the river was uncovered, which included the tomb area.

Ben saw Professor Moules entering one of the exposed tunnels.

*In their human bodies, Professor Hittorn and the others were able to free him from the chamber,* the Starling explained. *He is their leader.*

*Do you see Elizabeth?* Ben was searching. *Why can't I feel her?*

*She is clouded in darkness, we must look with our eyes,* the Starling answered.

He and Eliel were invisible now, along with the Willows. Ben, Sarah and Rachel were seemingly alone on the battlefield.

As they approached the tomb area, they heard chanting inside. The tunnels and the tomb area were left intact. The earth was removed so everything was exposed around them. Everything stood as above-ground structures now, instead of underground tunnels and chambers.

The chanting grew louder and faster. They entered the same tunnel Roger Hershe used, only now it was above ground. As they approached the opening to the tomb they saw Professor Virginia Hittorn, Michael Broward and another on their knees with their faces to the ground in front of the dragon statue closest to the opening, chanting.

As they got closer they could see Professor Jim Moules along with two others bowed and chanting in front of the other dragon statue.

The chanting was at a feverish pace now. They seemed oblivious to their presence as they diligently searched for Elizabeth. *Lizzy, where are you? Can you hear us?* They cried out in their spirits over and over, but she did not answer.

All of a sudden they heard something big, it was growling, they heard something crack. Then there was an explosion that sent everyone flying in all directions. After Ben, Sarah and Rachel regained their senses and came together, they saw two huge dragons circling in the air above the temple complex.

Apparently the statues were a miniature version because these dragons were about forty-five feet long! They were magnificent, fierce creatures. Their wing-span was wider than their body was long. They were bronze-colored with two horns and huge beaks with long, sharp teeth protruding from their great jaws, just like their statues.

Moules and the rest of the team were scattered throughout the complex. As they picked themselves up, they headed for the Brought family. The dragons zeroed in on them as well and came circling.

Sarah felt something wrapping around her body, covering her. She looked down and saw golden armor gleaming from her! She looked over at her daughter and her grandson. They were glorious! Christ's breastplate of righteousness was so ornately carved! It was alive! Their helmets of salvation gleamed through the darkness! A sword appeared in their right hand and a shield appeared in their left. They were seemingly weightless! They were alive! The belt of truth girded them with such peace, they were astonished! They all looked at each other in amazement!

"Praise the Lord!" They all shouted at the same time, raising their swords.

Professor Moules was leading the pack and about seventy-five feet from them. He jumped and flew through the air toward Ben. Ben leaped to meet him in the air. As they collided, Professor Moules, who didn't look much like the professor anymore, his flesh was all bruised and rotted looking, flew back about a hundred feet and landed on the ground, skidding and rolling through the complex.

When they collided, Ben only flew back a few feet, then landed upright on the ground. He immediately continued toward the professor.

At the same time, Professor Hittorn, Michael and the other three rushed toward Sarah and Rachel while the dragons circled above. When they were approximately forty-five feet away, all at once, they leaped through the air toward them. Rachel and Sarah caught them and held them in mid air.

*How about over by those trees?* Sarah said to her daughter.

*Sounds good!* Rachel answered as they thrust them to the far side of the complex at the edge of the forest.

Rachel saw out of the corner of her right eye, about twenty more demon possessed people coming their way! "Where did *they* come from?"

Sarah looked and saw them as well and said, "That must be the rest of her team! Didn't Lizzy and Ben tell us there were a lot of people at the restaurant that were possessed the night he proposed? The demons in the animals – and whatever else they possessed, must have come out of them to enter the humans."

They looked over the complex. The explosion that took place when the dragons were released left everything exposed and in rubble. Sarah saw the great rock about thirty feet from the tomb area. She saw Elizabeth laying prostrate, and chained, just like the vision from the Holy Spirit.

"It's Lizzy!" She shouted. They rushed toward her but the dragons swooped down and stood on either side of her.

They were not deterred. They tried to pick them up and move them, but their powers had no affect on them. As they came within twenty-five feet of the dragon on their left, it breathed fire at them. They held up their shields and tried closing in, but the other dragon came, and between them both, they held Sarah and Rachel at bay as the people rushed in on them.

Then Sarah looked at her daughter, *It's been a long time since I've ridden a horse, but with the Lord's help we'll ride these dragons today!*

Rachel nodded as they both leaped through the air, positioning their shields to protect them from the fire. They each landed on the backs of the dragons. The dragons took flight and wielded, trying to pluck them from their backs, but they slid further up on their necks.

Rachel wrapped her legs tightly around the neck of her dragon and with both hands, drew up her sword. "Taste the Word of the Lord!" She yelled, and with everything in her, she thrust a mighty blow and the blade of the sword sliced off the dragon's head as if it were butter!

As its body quivered and began to convulse, Rachel jumped off. Its head tumbled to the ground and reeled in the dirt. The other dragon whirled upside down through the air, screeching. Sarah fell off and landed on the ground. The dragon flew away, retreating out of sight.

Ben and Professor Moules were still exchanging blows. The professor regained his composure by the time Ben reached him. The professor flew at Ben and grabbed him. As they moved through the air he slammed Ben against a partially fallen stone wall, causing the rest of it to fall on him.

"Your child nor your worthless female will live past this day!" The many voices inside Professor Moules spewed out a wicked laugh. "They are *our* sacrifices!"

Ben opened his eyes through the stone and rubble that fell on him. He saw the professor standing over him with a huge rock, as he spewed his words. Ben rolled away just in time as he slammed it down, narrowly missing his head.

Ben rushed him. He slammed into him with such force they dug a trench almost to the river. Then Ben picked him up with his left hand and drew back with his right. He hit him so hard he heard his skull crack as he flew through the air about two hundred feet. Ben was immediately behind him.

As the professor got up, he turned and faced him. He had a hole in his face! Ben just stood there watching him in amazement as he cocked his head back and forth a couple times and the hole filled back in!

Ben drew back to hit him again when the professor heard the dragon screeching as the other dragon lost his head. He looked up, which gave Ben the opportunity.

"In the name of Jesus I command you unclean spirits to leave him and never return!"

Immediately, Byron appeared with a cocoon.

The professor began to wreathe and convulse.

"The end is upon us." He twisted. "You will never win! The Father is weak! You humans are such easy prey. So easily persuaded! One world order is already here, because you rush to please us!"

Ben repeated his words.

The professor convulsed even more, howling this time.

"We have the rulers of every nation in the palm our hand! There's nothing you can do now! It's already begun!"

Ben repeated his words a third time, "In the name of Jesus I command you filth to leave him and never return!"

The cocoon began to whistle. All the colors of the rainbow lit up the darkness as Professor Moules dropped to the ground. The demons had killed him long before his body was ever delivered from them. But as he lie on the ground, his countenance reappeared. His skin and face returned to normal. His lifeless body at least looked like the professor once more.

The body of the headless dragon hit the ground with a huge quake. The demons fell back as they watched their god wreathing in the dust. They screeched horrifically at the sight of it. Blood spurted everywhere as its headless body stumbled around, trying to walk, flapping its wings and convulsing in the dirt. Finally the dust and blood mingled and clogged where its lopped-off head was, leaving a red, mud-caked nub as its body quivered on the ground.

Suddenly the other dragon reappeared roaring and screeching as it bore down on them spewing fire everywhere, consuming the trees and everything in its path. It headed straight for Elizabeth as she lay unconscious, chained to the rock.

Ben used his shield and leaped into the air. The dragon bore down on him with everything he had, but the living shield preserved him, growing and shrinking to protect Ben from the blaze. He jumped on the dragon's back and they disappeared. He took the dragon deep underground and left it there in a cave with no outlets, then Ben reappeared at the battle.

As he approached Elizabeth, he thought he would come undone! She was lying unconscious with heavy chains wrapped around her seemingly lifeless body. They had tied the chains down with heavy spikes they drove into the sides of the rock. Lines of dried blood came from her hairline down upon her forehead and the sides of her face. Her ears were completely drenched in dried blood that had dripped down from her bleeding scalp.

"Lizzy!" Ben screamed. "Elizabeth!" He was in anguish. "Please come back to me!" He tried to touch her mind with his.

She moaned and began to stir a little.

Sarah and Rachel kept watch at Ben's back as the demons began to regroup.

"Lizzy!" He called her name again.

Then Ben heard a great rumbling sound and the earth began to quake.

The dragon was returning with a vengeance. Ben could feel him coming up through the ground.

As it shot through the earth in the midst of them, it scattered everyone again. It flew into the air and circled, screeching and spewing fire out of its mouth as it approached them.

Ben reached for his belt. As his hand touched the buckle it began to glow. He leaped into the air as he pulled the belt from around his waist with his right hand, holding the shield in his left. The entire belt was glowing now. It grew in length as he pulled.

When he reached the dragon, he shouted, "In the name of Jesus, I bind you with this belt of truth and it will hold you fast!" And he wound it around the beast, around and around, binding its wings. It hit the ground with a thunderous quake, landing next to the dragon that was beheaded, in the middle of the battlefield. Then he took one end of the belt and wrapped its huge jaws tight. As it struggled to be free, Ben tucked its tale between its legs with the other end.

The dragon was shrieking and howling so loud, even the demons covered their ears and wailed. He banged his great head up and down on the ground, his body wreathed, trying to break the belt. But the belt of truth held the great dragon in his place.

"Kill her! Hurry! Kill her NOW!"

Sarah heard Professor Hittorn screaming from the other end of the complex as Ben bound the dragon. Everyone was scattered throughout the grounds. Sarah sprang up from where she was thrown, leaping through the air about 300 feet and landing on the great stone. She placed her feet on either side of Elizabeth's waist as the demons rushed toward them. Her mousy-gray hair turned white as snow beneath her helmet and her eyes began to glow with a piercing white light.

With everything in her, she screamed, "NnnOoo!!!" And thrust out her hands toward them.

In one fell swoop they all fell back, as if a great wind had knocked them all down.

But Professor Hittorn had positioned herself behind them. She leaped, grabbing Sarah as she flew through the air with the same jeweled knife in her hand the Starling showed Ben in the memory he showed Elizabeth, knocking Sarah off the stone. They landed on the ground together, tangled and rolling. The knife flew from her hands as their bodies twisted.

By that time, Ben and Rachel were at their matriarch's side.

They separated them and Ben held Professor Hittorn in place. He realized she wasn't as powerful as Professor Moules. She wasn't filled with the full measure of demons.

Then he said, "In the Name of Jesus, you unclean spirits COME OUT OF HER!"

Immediately, Ombeye appeared with a cocoon.

"COME OUT OF HER AND NEVER RETURN!" Ben said with great authority.

She went limp as the cocoon began to whistle and the rainbow lit up the darkness. Her bruised and battered flesh returned to normal before their eyes. Professor Virginia Hittorn was finally free.

Ben looked at his mother and grandmother, "I'll be right back!" He disappeared with the professor and took her home. He put her in her bed and said a prayer for salvation and protection over her. He immediately reappeared at the battle.

The demons had recovered from Sarah's blow and were drawing closer to Elizabeth as Ben, Sarah and Rachel braced for the battle.

All of a sudden there was a sound, or lack thereof – like a vacuum where time and space ceased. A bright, white light shot forth from the great rock, engulfing Elizabeth as she lay bound in chains. Suddenly, in an instant, the light reached out and like a rushing wind, sucked everything and everyone left into it as it shot up into the heavens. The demons, the bound dragon, the dead dragon and the people that were possessed – all were gone, even the vehicles the team had rode in that were parked at the gate were gone. It was silent.

Ben, Rachel and Sarah held their breath while they waited for the light to disappear from the rock. Ben could barely stand it.

Their armor faded from their bodies as the light from the rock slowly disappeared. They saw a form emerge. Ben's heart felt as if it would leap from his chest!

It was Elizabeth! In the flesh! Her chains were gone! She was free, sitting up and in her right mind! The black mist had disappeared as the late afternoon sun shone bright again. Her broken leg was completely healed! Even the blood was gone from her head and face. She watched as a few leaves still danced in the air on their way back to the ground in the aftermath.

They all rushed to her side as Ben took her in his arms and wept. They were all crying and thanking God. Then Ben took the great rock and put it back in its place, on the Colorado River.

Each of them laid their hands on it, giving thanks to God, remembering Jesus, Himself, stood upon it, preaching to the Indians.

"Praise the Lord," Sarah said softly, as Ben and the rock disappeared. He reappeared in seconds.

After they were all together again, Eliel appeared behind them. He wrapped his arms gently around all four of them, stretched out his great wings and softly carried them home.

"Well done! Well done, Brought family." He said as he set them all in the middle of Sarah's living room. "You are safe now. And you are whole again, glory to our God and Savior." Then he disappeared.

They were exhausted. They slept right there in the living room together, not wanting to be apart. Ben and Elizabeth slept in the loveseat, which was a double recliner; Grandma slept in the chair, which was a recliner; and Rachel slept on the huge sofa. So they were all very comfortable, but most importantly, they were all together.

Saturday, about mid-morning, Sheriff Brodge appeared on the news. He announced Professor James Moules was found dead at the temple complex, after what looked like a huge explosion that demolished almost everything except the pyramid.

"We believe he was part of a conspiracy, along with Roger Hershe and unknown others, to steal treasure and artifacts. Apparently something went wrong. It looks like there may have been multiple explosions, killing Professor Moules in the process. We're searching the area and have a forensic team there now, going through the rubble."

"They were explosions all right." Rachel exclaimed, as she shut the television off with the remote and leaned back on the couch, snuggling with Ollie.

"There sure was," Sarah chuckled, stroking Cookie, who was nestled on her lap in the recliner.
"Oh, by the way, Mom, I think your new hair looks good on you."
"Yeah?" Sarah touched her hair in various places with the palm of her hand. "I was looking at it in the mirror this morning, I think I'm going to like white."

Elizabeth and Ben were upstairs in their room.
"So what should we name him?" Ben caressed her belly.
"I don't know, what if he's a she?" She smiled.
"That too, it doesn't matter to me, boy or girl, its ours."
They beamed with inexpressible joy as they thought about bringing their first child into the world!
Then Ben said, "Like the morning dew that drips from the leaves of the trees to the ground, Father, may this day be filled with Your goodness and blessing. As honey drips from the comb, may Your goodness drip down from heaven fresh and new to us this day, in Jesus' Name. Amen."

It was mid-afternoon when the Willows appeared in their living room.
Everyone was gathered. They sensed their coming. The dogs were excited to see them too, they had become great friends.
The Willows had condensed in size so as to keep the roof on the house.
"Greetings in the Name of the Lord!" Byron exclaimed as the bright

light they rode down on faded away. Trazier held a tiny, glowing tree inside an ornately carved, blue-green vessel. It reminded Sarah of a Bonsai tree, only this tree was ... alive, like the Willows! Its leaves shimmered a peach, white and red color as they moved, along with its branches. It looked like a tiny sugar maple with proportionately-sized leaves, instead of the large leaves we normally see on the sugar maple Bonsai that man has cultivated. Its trunk was full of character, interestingly bent back and forth, giving the impression it was a very old tree.

Immediately Rachel, Sarah and Elizabeth felt its presence. It was a warm, sprightly energy that was powerfully positive. Ben felt it too.

"What a magnificent little tree!" Rachel said.

As Trazier looked down at the little friend in his hands, he said, "It is a gift." He looked at Rachel with his Willow smile that creased the bark on his face to accommodate his mouth widening.

"Hello!" Rachel said as Trazier handed it to her. The little tree shimmered. Everyone had gathered around her to look at the tree.

"How old is it?" Elizabeth asked. "Does it talk?"
"She is only three." Byron said. "She will speak when she is ready."
"Oh, you're just a baby!" Elizabeth thought of the baby in her womb.
"Yes, she is young. But she bears the fruit of the spirit and has many gifts," Ombeye spoke up.

"Wow, the trunk looks so much older than just three years." Ben noticed. The Willows chuckled, then Kish said, "She is three millennia."

That took a moment to process, then they all laughed.

"So that's young? Three millennia is young to you?" Sarah was fascinated at the thought of being able to keep the tree! They all were fascinated by it.

"Her name is Oka," Trazier said.

"Is she bound to the pot or can she walk like you?" Rachel asked.

"She is not bound, but prefers the pot for comfort." Tayhl offered. He held out his hand and Oka leaped into it. He put her on his shoulder and she shimmered a beautiful peach color with bits of red and white. Tayhl's coat and hair shimmered back at her.

"So she is a gift to *us?* Does she *want* to stay with us?" Sarah asked.

"Yes," Byron answered, "she chose you, and will watch over you — and your children," he looked at Elizabeth. "She will be of great help as the end times draw near, for the battles will intensify."

They were quiet for a moment as that reality soaked in. They knew there would be more, they just hadn't put it into words. They knew the end times were upon them and there was no turning back.

On a lighter note, Sarah asked, "What does Oka like to eat? Does she require any special care?"

Before they could answer, Rachel added. "Her energy is so positive, it's almost intoxicating!"

"She is from a planet called Jupinwe, near our star system." Byron explained. "It is much like your planet. She does not require any special care from you. She will take care of herself. Your earth sustains her. Oka is a healer. You can feel her energy because you are connected to her, and she to you, all of you."

Cookie and Ollie seemed to like Oka too. They sniffed her and wagged their tails. Cookie stood up on her hind legs and waved her front feet at her. Oka responded by waving her branches back at her. It was a great start to a beautiful friendship.

"Would anyone care for a coke or some coffee?" Sarah asked from the kitchen.

The three that drank coke last time wanted to try coffee and the two that drank coffee last time wanted to try coke.

Ben suddenly turned and looked out of the picture window facing the apple orchard, "The Dubheians are here!" Everyone gathered in the living room to watch them land.

"By the way," Ben asked the Willows, "Your spears – what are they for? I never saw you use them."

Byron smiled, looking down at his spear, twisting it in his branch-like hands as it glowed green. "They are for the Reptilians."

**Look for the sequel,**
*The Brought Family Secrets: Defenders Of The Light –* **The Reptilians***,* coming soon.

Visit tamistevenson.com to find out more, digital downloads available.

DISCARDED

Made in the USA
Middletown, DE
05 September 2022